# THE RARE OR UNREAD STORIES OF GRANT ALLEN

Edited by Peter Morton

# VULPINE
## PRESS

Published by Vulpine Press in the United Kingdom in 2019

ISBN 978-1-83919-258-6

Cover by Claire Wood

www.vulpine-press.com

# CONTENTS

# Introduction

## 1.

Grant Allen (Charles Grant Blairfindie Allen, 1848-1899) did not start writing fiction by personal inclination. Although he had taken a degree in Classics at Oxford, he knew his gift was for expository writing on scientific matters, both technical and popular; and, more generally, he thought of himself as a superior kind of journalist who could produce miscellaneous articles on topics of the hour, on travel, on aspects of language—on anything, in fact. His first two books were titled *Physiological Aesthetics* and *The Colour-sense*. Of the first, he wrote sardonically that the title alone was enough for most people; and of the second, that he had spent eighteen months on the research, accumulated several thousand references and earned the 'very fair pay' of £30.

Clearly this would not do. Writing scientific tomes might make him a reputation, but it could never make money, and Allen badly needed money. Although he came from a rich Canadian family, which bore a French aristocratic title through his mother's line, every penny he ever had came from his own labours. During his early years of struggle, he had a young wife and son to maintain, and his health—some sort of lung disease—made a semi-invalid of him for long periods and did not augur well for a long life. By the time he was thirty he had been a schoolmaster in Brighton and then a staff journalist in London, but his physique was not up to the pressure and long hours. He had also taught at a new tertiary-level college in Jamaica for three years, until it collapsed through no fault of his own and Allen had to return to England and unemployment. Penury beckoned, teaching did not appeal, and he slipped almost by default into freelance authorship: a trade which was, in his own words, 'recruited almost entirely, I believe, from the actual or potential failures of other callings'.

He worked incredibly hard. In his short life, starting in 1877 just short of his thirtieth birthday, he wrote seventy-seven books on an immense variety of topics, publishing an average of three and a half books in each one of the twenty-two years of his career. He also produced many millions of words of journalism which vanished with the day.

Of his total output of books, forty-five were novels (counting his three-decker novels as a single work), story-collections, and poetry. If Allen was critical of authorship as a paying profession at all—and he certainly was—he was especially scathing about fiction. He liked to tell people that he had stumbled into it by accident (which was true) and had persevered with it because it paid the best. 'I suppose no man ever took by choice to the pursuit of fiction', he wrote disparagingly, adding that he himself had '*declined*' into it, 'as many men drop into drink, or opium-eating, or other bad practices, not of native perversity, but by pure force of circumstances'.

Small wonder that even his admirers took him at his word. Charged with delivering the eulogy on the sensitive occasion of Allen's funeral, a close friend judged it all unworthy of comment:

> Of his fiction I know nothing, nor need I speak. He himself
> treated it as a bye-play, and I well remember that he often
> told me gaily that I should not trouble myself with his task-
> work of that kind.

Some of his hearers may have found that unnecessarily blunt, perhaps; but all of them must have heard Allen say the same thing himself at one time or another.

In truth, though, his self-deprecation was something of a protective pose. He really had an ambivalent attitude towards the kind of work which eventually made him a prosperous man. He confessed that he grew so involved in his sensational novel *For Maimie's Sake: A Tale of Love and Dynamite* that he had been unable to sleep while writing the second half, being so caught up in the actions of 'my marionettes'. Again, he took pride in his skill when his action-packed thriller *What's Bred in the Bone* came first in a field of 20,000 entrants to win a £1,000 literary prize. And, of course, when he wanted to publicise his boldest feminist ideals for a mass audience it was to the novel that he turned, with *The Woman Who Did.*

In any case it was inevitable that such a versatile and ambitious professional author as Grant Allen should have tried his hand at fiction sooner or later. 'The price it fetches is far in excess of that which is given for prose writing of any other kind, and is magnificent ... other literary labour cuts a sorry figure is comparison', said the critic Wilfred Meynell, in a beginner's guide to authordom. 'A writer cannot live by contributing to magazines, except in the way of fiction', was the novelist Walter Besant's flat judgment. The print media's demand for light, bright, short fiction was insatiable, and the supply rose to meet the demand throughout Allen's career. The production, first of short stories, then of novels and novellas, started to underpin his career quite early on and in effect subsidized his numerous other activities which he valued far more. But that did not stop him resenting it or saying that he did.

As it happens he stumbled into the short story pretty much by accident. Tasked with writing an article on spiritualism, he cast it as a narrative, 'Our Scientific Observations on a Ghost'. As a story it's not much: a ghost appears to a pair of medical students, and they apply a range of scientific tests, with inconclusive results. But the editor of the *Belgravia* magazine liked it and Allen produced more in short order, under the pseudonym 'J. Arbuthnot Wilson' to keep them separate from his 'serious' work.

Then it came about that in January 1883 the novelist James Payn took over the editorship of the upmarket *Cornhill* magazine from Leslie Stephen, tasked with the job of reversing its apparently terminal slide into extinction. Payn is forgotten now, but he was a popular author in his day and a shrewd analyst of the literary marketplace. He boasted that his goal was to make every issue of the *Cornhill* readable by anyone from cover to cover. One of his innovations was to cut the cover price in half. Another was to commission much more shorter, lighter fiction: the only fiction previously countenanced by the *Cornhill* had been serializations of novels by such prominent authors as Wilkie Collins, Eliot, Gaskell and Hardy. Allen had been contributing factual articles on the evolution of feathers and the like, stylishly written and packed with information. They were no longer required under the new regime, and Payn wrote to tell him so. However, Payn's eye had been caught by 'Wilson's' work in the competitor *Belgravia*, and he wrote via the editor to invite more. Allen liked to tell how Payn's two letters arrived in the same post. Naturally, he buckled down to the new task and produced some of his most thoroughly developed stories like *The Backslider* for the *Cornhill*. Payn insisted that they should all appear anonymously.

Relations between author and editor were not always harmonious, though Allen brushed off most difficulties with a quip and a shrug. Magazine readers of the short story in the 1880s and '90s, when Allen was producing most of his, had little taste for provocative material. The largest demand was for an amusing, sentimental or melodramatic tale that would slip down easily, preferably leaving an acceptable moral behind it. Far more readers were women than men, more of them belonged to the lower middle class than to any other, and few wanted to have their prejudices tested. Allen did better than some— than Henry James or Joseph Conrad, say—because of his readiness to compromise. The key issue was the fact that magazine editors were even more stringent than book publishers or even the proprietors of circulating libraries. There were some rare exceptions, but normally a short story had to be inoffensive in both theme and expression. Sometimes contracts contained a clause explicitly requiring that nothing was to be included which could not be read out in a family circle, but usually the requirements were unspoken and assumed. Allen took a small revenge by teasing these editors when he could. He once wrote to Clement Shorter, editor of the *Sketch*:

> Herewith I enclose two out of five short stories as per your
> esteemed order. These stories are warranted to be free from
> any opinions whatsoever—political, religious, social, philo-
> sophical or literary. They would not raise a blush on the
> cheek of a babe unborn or shock the susceptibilities of a
> Cardinal Archbishop.

No doubt this sort of thing relieved his feelings, but did not alter the fact that editors had the whip hand. One of his stories, *The Sixth Commandment*, which deals sympathetically with adultery and murder, went the rounds of the entire London press and was universally rejected. At another time he challenged an editor:

> I enclose for your consideration a short story entitled 'A
> Study from the Life'. The Editor of the *Speaker* was afraid
> to publish it. Will you be, I wonder?

The fact that it has vanished without trace gives a mute reply. So there were tensions, never resolved, expressed most tellingly in his cry from the heart, *The Pot-boiler*, included in the present selection.

## 2.

In making my choice of a round dozen of Grant Allen's short stories, I have followed two principles:

First, I wanted to indicate the range of genres in which he worked: black comedies of manners; tales of interestingly unhinged or criminal characters; dramatisations of issues of the day, especially those stemming from the controversy over Darwinism; detective fiction and science fiction. It's fair to say that Allen was more interested in ideas than people, and—as in his non-fiction essays—he was at his best when popularising and enlivening some apparently abstract notion: time travel, eugenics, Christian fundamentalism, supernatural apparitions and so forth. Examples of all of these are included.

Second, I was mindful of the fact that Allen himself had gathered some of his favourite stories into six collections, and that most of these are easily available now in digital formats. This is particularly true of his two series of linked stories featuring female detective heroines, *Miss Cayley's Adventures* and *Hilda Wade*, which because of their significance for the history of popular literature have attracted much feminist criticism. Therefore I have selected, largely but not exclusively, a group of the lesser-known ones. There is plenty of choice since Allen wrote upwards of two hundred short stories. New ones are still being identified from time to time, so it is probable that more are mouldering in the smudgy columns of newspapers and short-lived magazines. Included here is a lively story that was printed only once, another that was refused by every publication in London, and others that were never reprinted after Allen's death. All of them, each in its own fashion, have something striking and witty to say about the hopes and anxieties, the customs and habits, of late Victorian British society.

A word on how I have edited these stories. For each one I have provided an informative headnote to set it into context. Allen was extremely well read in the Bible and the ancient classics, as well as the standard texts of English literature. He was fluent in Latin, Greek, French and Italian and in the manner of the day he does not always give translations; so I have included some notes on allusions and other matters which may puzzle some modern readers.

To establish a copy-text for each story I have gone back to the last version that Allen might have seen, or where necessary to the original publication. Victorian typesetting could be erratic and defective at times, especially when done in haste for newspapers, and I have silently corrected obvious errors and adjusted the paragraphing. Allen's punctuation was rather idiosyncratic, but I have made no changes except to remove any ambiguity.

Peter Morton
Adelaide 2018

# LUCRETIA

This slight but amusing story-anecdote was the fourth story Allen wrote for the *Belgravia* magazine, near the beginning of his career. It appeared in its Christmas Annual of 1879. The story was written on the Riviera. Though still a young man, Allen had suffered a complete collapse in his health (he had a 'lung' complaint) and his friends, fearing he would die if he stayed in England, raised the money to send him abroad for the entire winter, from October to May 1879-80. Although he did not know Allen personally, Charles Darwin knew his work and he was one of these benefactors.

*Lucretia* has some semi-autobiographical elements. The story is set in Canada, at Christmas 1867. Allen was almost twenty at that date, and had gone up to Oxford in the autumn after spending the summer with his parents in Kingston, Ontario, which is perhaps when some version of the events of the story happened. Certainly, the interesting background detail of deep-winter life in Quebec is authentic. Before the next year was out, Allen had married the tubercular daughter of a Leicestershire labourer, probably without the knowledge of his upper-class parents in Canada. Perhaps from this stems the narrator's alarm about the social status of Lucretia ('the domestic manager and assistant cook of a small country inn!') and what his mother in London will think of her.

*Lucretia* only works because the narrator, unlike Allen who was born and raised in Canada, is young, naïf, not too bright and entirely out of his depth in an unfamiliar setting. In addition, he is a stuffy, snobbish and rather mercenary young Englishman. Thus the absurd misunderstandings that can arise in such a case are made fairly credible. It is a good skit on English social prejudices.

I WILL acknowledge that I was certainly a very young man in the year
'67; indeed, I was only just turned of twenty, and was inordinately
proud of a slight downy fringe on my upper lip, which I was pleased
to speak of as my moustache. Still, I was a sturdy young fellow enough,
in spite of my consumptive tendencies, and not given to groundless
fears in a general way; but I must allow that I was decidedly frightened
by my adventure in the Richmond Hotel on the Christmas Eve of that
aforesaid year of grace. It may be a foolish reminiscence, yet I dare say
you won't mind listening to it.

When I say the Richmond Hotel, you must not understand me
to speak of the Star and Garter[1] in the town of that ilk situated in the
county of Surrey, England. The Richmond[2] where I passed my uncomfortable Christmas Eve stands on the banks of the pretty St Francis
River in Lower Canada. I had gone out to the colony in the autumn
of that year, to look after a small property of my mother's near Ka-
mouraska; and I originally intended to spend the winter in Quebec.
But as November and December wore away, and the snow grew deeper
and deeper upon the plains of Abraham, I became gradually aware that
a Canadian winter was not the best adapted tonic in the world for a
hearty young man with a slight hereditary predisposition to consumption. I had seen enough of Arctic life in Quebec during those two initial months to give me a good idea of its pleasures and its drawbacks.
I had steered by taboggan down the ice-cone at the Falls of Montmorenci[3]; I had driven a sleigh, *tête-à-tête* with a French Canadian
belle, to a surprise picnic in a house at Sainte Anne; I had skated, snow-
shoed, and curled to my heart's content; and I had caught my death
of cold on the frozen St Lawrence, not to mention such minor misfor-
tunes as getting my nose, ears, and feet frost-bitten during a driving
party up the banks of the Chaudière. So a few days before Christmas,
I determined to strike south. I would go for a tour through Virginia

and the Carolinas, to escape the cold weather, waiting for the return of the summer sun to catch a glimpse of Niagara and the great lakes.

For this purpose I must first go to Montreal; and, that being the case, what could be more convenient than to spend Christmas Day itself with the rector at Richmond, to whom I had letters of introduction, his wife being in fact a first cousin of my mother's? Richmond lies half-way on the Grand Trunk line between Quebec and Montreal, and it would be more pleasant, by breaking my journey there, to eat my turkey and plum-pudding in a friend's family than in that somewhat cheerless hotel, the Dominion Hall. So off I started from the Point Levy station, at four o'clock on the twenty-fourth of December, hoping to arrive at my journey's end about one o'clock on Christmas morning.

Now, those were the days, just after the great American civil war, when gold was almost unknown either in the States or Canada, and everybody used greasy dollar notes of uncertain and purely local value[4]. Hence I was compelled to take the money for expenses on my projected tour in the only form of specie which was available, that of solid silver. A hundred and fifty pounds in silver dollars amounts to a larger bulk and a heavier weight than you would suppose; and I thought it safer to carry the sum in my own hands, loosely bundled into a large leather reticule; *Hinc illae lacrimae*[5]:—that was the real cause of my night's adventure and of the present story.

When I got into the long open American railway carriage, with its comfortable stove and warm foot-bricks, I found only one seat vacant, and that was a red velvet sofa, opposite to another occupied by a girl of singular beauty. I can remember to this day exactly how she was dressed. I dare say my lady readers will think it horribly old-fashioned at the present time, but it was the very latest and most enchanting style in the year '67. On her head was a coquettish little cheese-plate bonnet, bound round with one of those warm, soft, fleecy woollen veils or head-wraps which Canadian girls know as Nubias.[6] Her dress was a short winter walking costume of the period, trimmed with fur, and vandyked[7] at the bottom so as to show a glimpse of the quilted down petticoat underneath. Her little high-heeled boots, displayed by the short costume, were buttoned far above the ankle, and bound with fur to match the dress; while a tiny tassel at the side added just a suspicion of Parisian coquetry. Her cloak was lined with sable, or what seemed so to my undiscriminating eyes; and her rug was a splendid piece of wolverine skins. As to her eyes, her lips, her figure, I had rather not attempt them. I can manage clothes, but not goddesses. Altogether, quite a dream of Canadian beauty, not devoid of that indefinable grace which goes only with the French blood.

I was not bold in '67, and I would have preferred to take any other seat rather than face this divine apparition; but there was no help for it, since all the others were filled: so I sat down a little sheepishly, I dare say. Almost before we were well out of the station we had got into a conversation, and it was she who began it.

'You are an Englishman, I think?' she said, looking at me with a frank and pleasant smile.

'Yes,' I answered, colouring, though why I should have been ashamed of my nationality for that solitary moment of my life I cannot imagine,—unless, perhaps, because she was a Canadian; 'but how on earth did you discover it?'

'You would have been more warmly wrapped up if you had lived long in Canada,' she replied. 'In spite of our stoves and hot bricks, you'll find yourself very cold before you get to your journey's end.'

'Yes,' I said; 'I suppose it's rather chilly late at night in these big cars.'

'Dreadfully; oh, quite terribly. You ought to have a rug, you really ought. Won't you let me lend you one? I have another under the seat here.'

'But you brought that for yourself,' I interposed. 'You will want it by-and-by, when it gets a little colder.'

'Oh no, I shan't. This is warm enough for me; it's wolverine[8]. You have a mother?'

What an extraordinary question, I thought, and what an unusually friendly girl! Was she really quite as simple-minded as she seemed, or could she be the 'designing woman' of the novels? Yes, I admitted to her cautiously that I possessed a maternal parent, who was at that moment safely drinking her tea in a terrace at South Kensington.

'*I* have none,' she said, with an emphasis on the personal pronoun, and a sort of appealing look in her big eyes. 'But you should take care of yourself, for her sake. You really *must* take my rug. *Hundreds*, oh, *thousands* of young Englishmen come out here and kill themselves their first winter by imprudence.'

Thus adjured, I accepted the rug with many thanks and apologies, and wrapped myself warmly up in the corner with a splendid view of my *vis-à-vis*[9].

Exactly at that moment, the ticket collector came round upon his official tour. Now, on American and Canadian railways, you do not take your ticket beforehand, but pay your fare to the collector, who walks up and down through the open cars from end to end, between every station. I lifted up my bag of silver, which lay on the seat beside me, and imprudently opened it to take out a few dollars full in sight of my enchanting neighbour. I saw her look with unaffected curiosity at the heap of coin within, and I was proud at being able to give such an unequivocal proof of my high respectability—for what better guarantee of all the noblest moral qualities can any man produce all the world over than a bag of dollars?

'What a lot of money!' she said, as the collector passed on. 'What can you want with it all in coin?'

'I'm going on a tour in the Southern States,' I confided in reply, 'and I thought it better to take specie.' (I was very proud ten or twelve years ago of that word *specie*.)

'And I suppose those are your initials on the reticule? What a pretty monogram! Your mother gave you that for a birthday present.'

'You must be a conjurer or a clairvoyant,' I said, smiling. 'So she did;' and I added that the initials represented my humble patronymic and baptismal designations.

'My name's Lucretia,' said my neighbour artlessly, as a child might have said it, without a word as to surname or qualifying circum-stances; and from that moment she became to me simply Lucretia. I think of her as Lucretia to the present day. As she spoke, she pointed to the word engraved in tiny letters on her pretty silver locket.

I suppose she thought my confidence required a little more con-fidence in return, for after a slight pause she repeated once more, 'My name's Lucretia, and I live at Richmond.'

'Richmond!' I cried. 'Why, that's just where I'm going. Do you know the rector?'

'Mr Pritchard? Oh yes, intimately. He's our greatest friend. Are you going to stop with him?'

'For a day or two at least, on my way to Montreal. Mrs Pritchard is my mother's cousin.'

'How delightful! Then we may consider ourselves acquaintances. But you don't mean to knock them up tonight? They'll all be in bed long before one o'clock.'

'No, I haven't even written to tell them I was coming,' I answered. 'They gave me a general invitation, and said I might drop in whenever I pleased.'

'Then you must stop at the hotel tonight. I'm going there myself. My people keep the hotel.'

Was it possible! I was thunderstruck. I had pictured Lucretia to myself as at least a countess of the *ancien régime*[10], a few of whom still linger on in Montreal and elsewhere. Her locket, her rugs, her eyes, her chiselled features, all of them seemed to me redolent of the old French *noblesse*. And here it turned out that this living angel was only the daughter of an inn-keeper! But in that primitive and pleasant Canadian society such things, I thought, can easily be. No doubt she is the petted child of the house, the one heiress of the old man's savings; and after spending a winter holiday among the gaieties of Quebec, she is now returning to pass the Christmas season with her own family. I will not conceal the fact that I had already fallen over head and ears in love with Lucretia at first sight, and that frank avowal made me love her all the more. Besides, these Canadian hotel-keepers are often very rich; and was not her manner perfect, and was she not an intimate friend of the rector and his wife? All these things showed at least that she was accustomed to refined society. I caught myself already speculating as to what my mother would think of such a match.

In five minutes it was all arranged about the hotel, and I had got into the midst of a swimming conversation with Lucretia. She told me about herself and her past; how she had been educated at a convent in Montreal, and loved the nuns, oh *so* dearly, though she was a

Protestant herself, and only French on her mother's side. (This, I thought, was well, as a safeguard against parental prejudice.)

She told me all the gossip of Richmond, and whom I should meet at the rector's, and what a dull little town it was. But Quebec was delightful, and Montreal—oh, if she could only live in Montreal, it would be perfect bliss. And so I thought myself, if only Lucretia would live there with me; but I prudently refrained from saying so, as I thought it rather premature. Or perhaps I blushed and stammered too much to get the words out. 'Had she ever been in Europe?' No, never, but she would so like it. 'Ah, it would be delightful to spend a month or two in Paris,' I suggested, with internal pictures of a honeymoon floating through my brain. 'Yes, that would be most enjoyable,' she answered. Altogether, Lucretia and I kept chatting uninterruptedly the whole way to Richmond, and the other passengers must have voted us most unconscionable bores; for they evidently could not sleep by reason of our incessant talking. We did not sleep, nor wish to sleep. And I am bound to say that a more frankly enchanting or seemingly guileless girl than Lucretia I have ever met from that day to this.

At last we reached Richmond Depôt (as the Canadians call the stations), very cold and tired externally, but lively enough as regards the internal fires. We got out, and looked after our luggage. A sleepy porter promised to bring it next morning to the hotel. There were no sleighs in waiting—Richmond is too much of a country station for that—so I took my reticule in my hand, threw Lucretia's rug across her shoulders, and proceeded to walk with her to the hotel.

Now, the 'Depôt' is in a suburb known as Melbourne, while Richmond itself lies on the other side of the river St Francis, here crossed by a long covered bridge, a sort of rough wooden counterpart of the famous one at Lucerne. As we passed out into the cold night, it was snowing heavily, and the frost was very bitter. Lucretia took my arm without a word of prelude, as naturally as if she were my sister, and guided me through the snow-covered path to the bridge. When we got under the shelter of the wooden covering, we had to pass through the long dark gallery, as black as night, heading only for the dim square of moonlight at the other end. But Lucretia walked and chatted on as unconcernedly as if she had always been in the habit of traversing that lonely tunnel-like bridge with a total stranger every evening of her life. I confess I was surprised. I fancied a prim English girl in a similar situation, and I began to wonder whether all this art-lessness was really as genuine as it looked.

At the opposite end of the bridge we emerged upon a street of wooden frame houses. In one of them only was there a light. 'That's the hotel!' said Lucretia, nodding towards it, and again I suffered a thrill of disappointment. I had pictured to myself a great solid building like the St Lawrence Hall at Montreal, forgetting that Richmond was a mere country village; and here I found a bit of a frame cottage as the whole domain of Lucretia's supposed father. It was too awful!

We reached the door and entered. Fresh surprises were in store for me. The passage led into a bar, where half-a-dozen French Canadians were sitting with bottles and glasses, playing some game of cards. One rather rough-looking young man jumped up in astonishment as we entered, and exclaimed, 'Why, Lucretia, we didn't expect you for another hour. I meant to take the sleigh for you.' I could have knocked him down for calling her by her Christian name, but the conviction flashed upon me that this was Lucretia's brother. He glanced up at the big Yankee clock on the mantelpiece, which pointed to a quarter past twelve, then pulled out his watch and whistled. 'Stopped three quarters of an hour ago, by Jingo,' was his comment. 'Why, I forgot to wind it up. Upon my word, Lucretia, I'm awfully sorry. But who is the gentleman?'

'A friend of the Pritchards, Tom dear, who wants a bed here to-night. I couldn't imagine why the sleigh didn't come for me. It's so unlike you not to remember it.' And she gave him a look to melt adamant.

Tom was profuse in his apologies, and made it quite clear that his intentions at least had been most excellent; besides, he kissed Lucretia with so much brotherly tenderness that I relented of my desire to knock him down. Then brother and sister retired for a while, apparently to see after my bedroom, and I was left alone in the bar.

I cannot say I liked the look of it. The men were drinking whiskey and playing *écarté*— two bad things, I thought in my twenty-year-old propriety. My dear mother hated gambling, which hatred she had instilled into my youthful mind, and this was evidently a backwoods gambling-house. Moreover, I carried a bag of silver coin, quite large enough to make it well worthwhile to rob me. The appearances were clearly against Lucretia's home; but surely Lucretia herself was a guarantee for anything.

Presently Tom returned, and told me my room was ready. I followed him up the stairs with a beating heart and a heavy reticule. At the top of the landing Lucretia stood smiling, my candle in her hand, and showed me into the room. Tom and she looked around to see that all was comfortable, and then they both shook hands with me, which certainly seemed a curious thing for an inn-keeper and his sister. As soon as they were gone, I began to look about me and consider the situation. The room had two doors, but the key was gone from both. I opened one towards the passage, but found no key outside; the other, which probably communicated with a neighbouring bedroom, was locked from the opposite side. Moreover, there had once been a common bolt on this second door, but it had been removed. I looked close at the screw-holes, and was sure they were quite fresh. Could the bolt have been taken off while I was waiting in the bar? All at once it flashed upon my mind that I had been imprudently confiding in my disclosures to Lucretia. I had told her that I carried a hundred and fifty pounds in coin, an easy thing to rob and a difficult thing to identify. She had heard that nobody was aware of my presence in Richmond, except herself and her brother. I had not written to tell the Pritchards I was coming, and she knew that I had not told any one of my whereabouts, because I did not decide where I should go until I talked with her about the matter. No one in Canada would miss me. If these people chose to murder me for my money (and inn-keepers often murder their guests, I thought), nobody would think of inquiring or know where to inquire for me. Weeks would elapse before my mother wrote from England to ask my whereabouts, and by that time all traces might well be lost. I left Quebec only telling the people at my hotel that I was going to Montreal. Then I thought of Lucretia's eagerness to get into conversation, her observation about my money, her suggestion that I should come to the Richmond Hotel. And how could she, a small inn-keeper's daughter, afford to get all those fine furs and lockets by fair means? Did she really know the Pritchards, or was it likely, considering her position? All these things came across me in a moment. What a fool I had been ever to think of trusting such a girl!

I got up and walked about the room. It was evidently Lucretia's own bedroom; 'part of the decoy,' said I to myself sapiently. But could so beautiful a girl really hurt one? A piece of music was lying on the dressing table. I took it up and looked at it casually. Gracious heavens! It was a song from 'Lucrezia Borgia'[11]! Her very name betrayed her! She too was a Lucretia. I walked over to the mantelpiece. A little ivory miniature hung above the centre: I gave it a glance as I passed. Incredible! It was the Beatrice Cenci![12] Talk of beautiful women! Why, they poison one, they stab one, they burn one alive, with a smile on their

19

lips. Lucretia must have a taste for murderesses. Evidently she is a connoisseur.

At least, thought I, I shall sell my life dearly. I could not go to bed; but I pulled the bedstead over against one of the doors—the locked one—and I laid the mattress down in front of the other. Then I lay down on the mattress, my money-bag under my head, and put the poker conveniently by my side. If they came to rob and murder me, they should at least have a broken head to account for next day. But I soon got tired of this defensive attitude, and reflected that, if I must lie awake all night, I might as well have something to read. So I went over to the little book-case and took down the first book which came to hand. It bore on the outside the title 'Oeuvres de Victor Hugo. Tome 1er. Théâtre.' 'This, at any rate,' said I to myself, 'will be light and interesting.' I returned to my mattress, opened the volume, and began to read *Le Roi s'amuse*[13].

I had never before dipped into that terrible drama, and I devoured it with a horrid avidity. I read how Triboulet bribed the gipsy to murder the king; how the gipsy's sister beguiled him into the hut; how the plot was matured; and how the sack containing the corpse was delivered over to Triboulet. It was an awful play to read on such a night and in such a place, with the wind howling round the corners and the snow gathering deeply upon the window-panes. I was in a considerable state of fright when I began it: I was in an agony of terror before I had got half-way through. Now and then I heard footsteps on the stairs: again I could distinguish two voices, one a woman's, whispering outside the door; a little later, the other door was very slightly opened and then pushed back again stealthily by a man's hand. Still I read on. At last, just as I reached the point where Triboulet is about to throw the corpse into the river, my candle, a mere end, began to sputter in its socket, and after a few ineffectual flickers suddenly went out, leaving me in the dark till morning.

I lay down once more, trembling but wearied out. A few minutes later the voices came again. The further door was opened a second time, and I saw dimly a pair of eyes (not, I felt sure, Lucretia's) peering in the gloom, and reflecting the light from the snow on the window. A man's voice said huskily in an undertone, 'It's all right now;' and then there was a silence. I knew they were coming to murder me. I clutched the poker firmly, stood on guard over the dollars, and waited the assault. The moment that intervened seemed like a lifetime.

A minute. Five minutes. A quarter of an hour. They are evidently trying to take me off my guard. Perhaps they saw the poker; in any case, they must have felt the bedstead against the door. That would show them that I expected them. I held my watch to my ear and counted the seconds, then the minutes, then the hours. When the candle went out it was three o'clock. I counted up till about half-past five.

After that I must have fallen asleep from very weariness. My head glided back upon the reticule, and I dozed uneasily until morning. Every now and then I started in my sleep, but the murderers hung back. When I awoke it was eight o'clock, and the dollars were still safe under my head. I rose wearily, washed myself, and arranged the tumbled clothes in which I had slept, for my portmanteau had not yet arrived from the Depôt. Next, I put back the bed and mattress, and then I took the dollars and went downstairs to the bar, hardly knowing whether to laugh at my last night's terror, or to congratulate myself on my lucky escape from a den of robbers. At the foot of the stairs, whom should I come across but Lucretia herself!

In a moment the doubt was gone. She was enchanting. Quite a different style of dress, but equally lovely and suitable. A long figured gown of some fine woollen material, giving very nearly the effect of a plain neat print, and made quite simply to fit her perfect little figure. A plain linen collar, and a quiet silver brooch. Hair tied in a single broad knot above the head, instead of yesterday's chignon and cheese-plate. Altogether, a model winter morning costume for a cold climate. And as she advanced frankly, holding out her hand with a smile, I could have cut my own throat with a pocket-knife as a merited punishment for daring to distrust her. Such is human nature at the ripe age of twenty!

'We were so afraid you didn't sleep, Tom and I,' she said with a little tone of anxiety; 'we saw a light in your room till so very late, and Tom opened the door a wee bit once or twice to see if you were sleeping; but he said you seemed to have pulled the mattress on the floor. I do hope you weren't ill.'

What on earth could I answer? Dare I tell this angel how I had suspected her? Impossible!

'Well,' I stammered out, colouring up to my eyes, 'I was rather over-tired, and couldn't get to rest, so I put the candle on a chair, took a book, and lay on the floor so as to have a light to read by. But I slept very well after the candle went out, thank you.'

'There were none but French books in the room, though,' she said quickly: 'perhaps you read French?'

'I read *Le Roi s'amuse*, or part of it,' said I.

'Oh, what a dreadful play to read on Christmas Eve!' cried Lucretia, with a little deprecating gesture. 'But you must come and have your breakfast.'

I followed her into the dining-room, a pretty little bright-looking room behind the bar. Frightened as I was during the night, I could not fail to notice how tastefully the bedroom was furnished; but this little *salle-à-manger* was far prettier. The paper, the carpet, the furniture, were all models of what cheap and simple cottage decorations ought to be. They breathed of Lucretia. The Montreal nuns had evidently taught her what 'art at home' meant. The table was laid, and the white table-cloth, with its bright silver and sprays of evergreen in the vase, looked delightfully appetising. I began to think I might manage a breakfast after all.

'How pretty all your things are!' I said to Lucretia.

'Do you think so?' she answered. 'I chose them, and I laid the table.'

I looked surprised; but in a moment more I was fairly overwhelmed when Lucretia left the room for a minute, and then returned carrying a tray covered with dishes. These she rapidly and dexterously placed upon the table, and then asked me to take my seat.

'But,' said I, hesitating, 'am I to understand ... You don't mean to say ... Are you ... going ... to wait upon me?'

Lucretia's face was one smile of innocent amusement from her white little forehead to her chiselled little chin. 'Why, yes,' she answered, laughing, 'of course I am. I always wait upon our guests when I'm at home. And I cooked these salmon cutlets, which I'm sure you'll find nice if you only try them while they're hot.' With which recommendation she uncovered all the dishes, and displayed a breakfast that might have tempted St Anthony[14]. Not being St Anthony, I can do Lucretia's breakfast the justice to say that I ate it with unfeigned heartiness.

So my princess was, after all, the domestic manager and assistant cook of a small country inn! Not a countess not even a murderess (which is at least romantic), but only a prosaic housekeeper! Yet she was a princess for all that. Did she not read Victor Hugo, and play 'Lucrezia Borgia,' and spread her own refinement over the village tavern? In no other country could you find such a strange mixture of culture and simplicity; but it was new, it was interesting, and it was piquant. Lucretia in her morning dress officiously insisting upon offering me the buckwheat pancakes with her own white hands was Lucretia still, and I fell deeper in love than ever.

After breakfast came a serious difficulty. I must go to the Pritchards, but before I went, I must pay. Yet, how was I to ask for my bill? I couldn't demand it of Lucretia. So I sat a while ruminating, and at last I said, 'I wonder how people do when they want to leave this house.'

'Why,' said Lucretia, promptly, 'they order the sleigh.'

'Yes,' I answered sheepishly, 'no doubt. But how do they manage about paying?'

Lucretia smiled. She was so absolutely transparent, and so accustomed to her simple way of doing business, that I suppose she did not comprehend my difficulty. 'They ask me, of course, and I tell them what they owe. You owe us half-a-dollar.'

Half-a-dollar—two shillings sterling—for a night of romance and terror, a bed and bedroom, a regal breakfast, and-Lucretia to wait upon one! It was *too* ridiculous. And these were the good simple Canadian villagers whom I had suspected of wishing to rob and murder me! I never felt so ashamed of my own stupidity in the whole course of my life.

I must pay it somehow, I supposed, but I could not bear to hand over two shilling pieces into Lucretia's outstretched palm. It was desecration, it was sheer sacrilege. But Lucretia took the half-dollar with the utmost calmness, and went out to order the sleigh.

I drove to the rector's, after saying good-bye to Lucretia, with a clear determination that before I left Richmond she should have consented to become my wife. Of course there were social differences, but those would be forgotten in South Kensington, and nobody need ever know what Lucretia had been in Canada. Besides, she was fit to shine in the society of duchesses—a society into which I cannot honestly pretend that I habitually penetrate.

The rector and his wife gave me a hearty welcome, and I found Mrs Pritchard a good motherly sort of body—just the right woman for helping on a romantic love-match. So, in the course of the morning, as we walked back from church, I managed to mention to her casually that a very nice young woman had come down in the train with me from Quebec.

'You don't mean Lucretia?' cried good Mrs Pritchard.

'Lucretia,' I answered in a cold sort of way, 'I think that was her name. In fact, I remember she told me so.'

'Oh yes, everybody calls her Lucretia—indeed, she's hardly got any other name. She's the dearest creature in the world, as simple as a child, yet the most engaging and kind-hearted girl yon ever met.

She was brought up by some nuns at Montreal, and being a very clever girl, with a great deal of taste, she was their favourite pupil, and has turned out a most cultivated person.'

'Does she paint?' I asked, thinking of the Beatrice.

'Oh, beautifully. Her ivory miniatures always take prizes at the Toronto Exhibition. And she plays and sings charmingly.'

'Are they well off?'

'Very, for Canadians. Lucretia has money of her own, and they have a good farm besides the hotel.'

'She said she knew you very well,' I ventured to suggest.

'Oh yes; in fact, she's coming here this evening. We have an early dinner—you know our simple Canadian habits—and a few friends will drop in to high tea after evening service. She and Tom will be among them—you met him, of course?'

'I had the pleasure of making Tom's acquaintance at one o'clock this morning,' I answered. 'But, excuse my asking it, isn't it a little odd for you to mix with people in their position?'

The rector smiled and put in his word. 'This is a democratic country,' he said; 'a mere farmer community, after all. We have little society in Richmond, and are very glad to know such pleasant intelligent people as Tom and Lucretia.'

'But then, the *convenances*,' I urged, secretly desiring to have my own position strengthened. 'When I got to the hotel last night, or rather this morning, there were a lot of rough-looking hulking fellows drinking whiskey and playing cards.'

'Ah, I dare say. Old Picard, and young Le Patourel from Melbourne, and the Post Office people sitting over a quiet game of *écarté* while they waited for the last train. The English mail was in last night. As for the whiskey, that's the custom of the country. We Canadians do nothing without whiskey. A single glass of Morton's proof[15] does nobody any harm.'

And these were my robbers and gamblers? A party of peaceable farmers and sleepy Post officials, sitting up with a sober glass of toddy and beguiling the time with *écarté* for love, in expectation of Her Majesty's mails. I shall never again go to bed with a poker by my side as long as I live.

About seven o'clock our friends came in. Lucretia was once more charming; this time in a long evening dress, a peach-coloured silk with square-cut bodice, and a little lace cap on her black hair. I dare say I saw almost the full extent of her wardrobe in those three changes; but the impression she produced upon me was still that of boundless wealth. However, as she had money of her own, I no longer wondered at the richness of her toilette, and I reflected that a comfortable little settlement[16] might help to outweigh any possible prejudice on my mother's part.

Lucretia was the soul of the evening. She talked, she flirted innocently with every man in the room (myself included), she played divinely, and she sang that very song from 'Lucrezia Borgia' in a rich contralto voice. As she rose at last from the piano, I could contain myself no longer. I must find some opportunity of proposing to her there and then. I edged my way to the little group where she was standing, flushed with the compliments on her song, talking to our hostess near the piano. As I approached from behind, I could hear that they were speaking about me, and I caught a few words distinctly. I paused to listen. It was very wrong, but twenty is an impulsive age.

'Oh, a very nice young man indeed,' Lucretia was saying; 'and we had a most enjoyable journey down. He talked so simply, and seemed such an innocent boy, so I took quite a fancy to him.' (My heart beat about two hundred pulsations to the minute.) 'such a clever, intelligent talker too, full of wide English views and interests, so different from our narrow provincial Canadian lads.' (Oh, Lucretia, I feel sure of you now. Love at first sight on both sides, evidently!) 'And then he spoke to me so nicely about his mother. I was quite grieved to think he should be travelling alone on Christmas Eve, and so pleased when I heard he was to spend his Christmas with you, dear. I thought what I should have felt if—'

I listened with all my ears. What could Lucretia be going to say?

'If one of my own dear boys was grown up, and passing his Christmas alone in a strange land.'

I reeled. The room swam before me. It was too awful. So all that Lucretia had ever felt was a mere motherly interest in me as a solitary English boy away from his domestic turkey on the twenty-fifth of December! Terrible, hideous, blighting fact! Lucretia was married! The rector's refreshments in the adjoining dining-room only went to the length of sponge-cake and weak claret-cup. I managed to get away from the piano without fainting, and swallowed about a quart of the intoxicating beverage by tumblerfuls. When I had recovered sufficiently from the shock to trust my tongue, I ventured back into the drawing-room. It struck me then that I had never yet heard Lucretia's surname. When she and her brother arrived in the early part of the evening, Mrs Pritchard had simply introduced them to me by saying, 'I think you know Tom and Lucretia already.' Colonial manners are so unceremonious.

I joined the fatal group once more. 'Do you know,' I said, addressing Lucretia with as little tremor in my voice as I could easily manage, 'it's very curious, but I have never heard your surname yet.'

'Dear me,' cried Lucretia, 'I quite forgot. Our name is Arundel.'

'And which is Mr Arundel?' I continued. 'I should like to make his acquaintance.'

'Why,' answered Lucretia with a puzzled expression of face, 'you've met him already. Here he is!' And she took a neighbouring young man in unimpeachable evening dress gently by the arm. He turned round. It required a moment's consideration to recognize in that tall and gentlemanly young fellow with the plain gold studs and turndown collar my rough acquaintance of last night, Tom himself!

I saw it in a flash. What a fool I had been! I might have known they were husband and wife. Nothing but a pure piece of infatuated preconception could ever have made me take them for brother and sister. But I had so fully determined in my own mind to win Lucretia for myself that the notion of any other fellow having already secured the prize had never struck me.

It was all the fault of that incomprehensible Canadian society, with its foolish removal of the natural barriers between classes. My mother was quite right. I should henceforth be a high-and-dry conservative in all matters matrimonial, return home in the spring with heart completely healed, and after passing correctly through a London season, marry the daughter of a general or a Warwickshire squire, with the full consent of all the high contracting parties, at St George's, Hanover Square[17]. With this noble and moral resolution firmly planted in my bosom, I made my excuses to the rector and his good little wife, and left Richmond for ever the very next morning, without even seeing Lucretia once again.

But, somehow, I have never quite forgotten that journey from Quebec on Christmas Eve; and though I have passed through several London seasons since that date, and undergone increasingly active sieges from mammas and daughters, as my briefs on the Oxford Circuit grow more and more numerous, I still remain a bachelor, with solitary chambers in St James's. I sometimes fancy it might have been otherwise if I could only once have met a second paragon exactly like Lucretia.

---

[1] **Star and Garter.** Then a magnificent and expensive hotel above the Thames at Richmond, a favourite of Dickens and foreign royalty.

[2] **Richmond.** A small town (then a village) about halfway between Quebec and Montreal.

[3] **ice-cone ... Falls of Montmorenci.** An impressive waterfall, higher than Niagara, which freezes into great piles of ice in the winter, allowing sledding, *etc.*

[4] **greasy dollar notes of uncertain and purely local value.** Banks had lent their bullion, especially gold, to finance the Civil War, and US paper currency was in a chaotic state.

[5] *Hinc illae lacrimae.* Hence those tears: once a well-used Latin tag.

[6] **Nubias.** A light scarf, named after an African head-dress.

[7] **vandyked.** With a pointed or scalloped fringe.

[8] **wolverine.** An extremely dense, oily fur popular with Arctic dwellers.

[9] *vis-à-vis.* An uncommon use here as a noun, meaning the person opposite.

[10] **a countess of the *ancien régime*.** Grant Allen's own mother was from a Canadian family with a French aristocratic title.

[11] **a song from 'Lucrezia Borgia'.** An opera by Donizetti (1833). In it Lucrezia poisons six people, including her son.

[12] **Beatrice Cenci.** A murderess and heroine (executed 1599) who helped to kill her abusive father. Her story was romanticised in the 19th century thanks in part to a famous portrait by Reni and a verse drama by Shelley.

[13] *Le Roi s'amuse.* A highly melodramatic play set in 16th century France, later the basis for Verdi's opera *Rigoletto*.

[14] **might have tempted St Anthony.** A Christian monk and ascetic who lived as a hermit in the desert and overcame a host of supernatural temptations: a lively subject for many artists.

[15] **Morton's proof.** A brand of whiskey distilled at Kingston, Allen's home town.

[16] **a comfortable little settlement.** In fact, married Quebecois women had no property rights in 1867, so Lucretia's property would have become her new husband's on marriage: legally he would have needed no 'settlement'.

[17] **St George's, Hanover Square.** Then and for long after the most fashionable place in London for a wedding.

# PAUSODYNE: A GREAT CHEMICAL DISCOVERY

It's not surprising that Grant Allen, with his formidable self-taught knowledge of the sciences—especially botany and Darwinian biology—should try his hand at a science fiction story (not that the term then existed). *Pausodyne* was written early in his career for the *Belgravia* (the Christmas Annual of 1881), the magazine which had published all his short stories up to that date. It is an unsophisticated effort compared to the ingenious time travel stories that were to come, but then Allen was charting a new course. In fact, its only predecessor, apart from the legend of the Seven Sleepers, is Washington Irving's fantasy *Rip Van Winkle* of 1819. An adaptation of the idea—sleeping one's way, not from the past to the present, but from the present to the future—was used again in Edward Bellamy's *Looking Backward* (1888) whose hero, having been hypnotised for insomnia in an underground chamber, is forgotten until he wakes up in the utopian Boston of the year 2000.

A remarkable innovation of Allen's is to give Spottiswood's century-long state of suspended animation a pseudo-scientific gloss. A few years later this is exactly the strategy which H.G. Wells explained was his own invention:

> It occurred to me that instead of the usual interview with
> the devil or a magician, an ingenious use of scientific patter
> might with advantage be substituted.

Such 'patter' is exactly what Allen offers, with his references to the work of the great chemists of the 18th century and some knowing hints on the preparation of Pausodyne. When he wrote his story, however, none of Wells' best SF stories yet existed. They belong to the middle and later 1890s. It is evident that Wells knew some of Allen's work before his own career got under way, because there is a passing mention of him in *The Time Machine* (1895). Wells himself used the suspended animation idea in *When The Sleeper Wakes* in 1898, but in this case offered no 'patter' to explain it: his hero simply falls into a cataleptic trance from exhaustion.

WALKING ALONG the Strand one evening last year towards Pall Mall, I was accosted near Charing Cross Station by a strange-looking, middle-aged man in a poor suit of clothes, who surprised and startled me by asking if I could tell him from what inn the coach usually started for York.

'Dear me!' I said, a little puzzled. 'I didn't know there was a coach to York. Indeed, I'm almost certain there isn't one.'

The man looked puzzled and surprised in turn. 'No coach to York?' he muttered to himself, half inarticulately. 'No coach to York? How things have changed! I wonder whether nobody ever goes to York nowadays!'

'Pardon me,' I said, anxious to discover what could be his meaning; 'many people go to York every day, but of course they go by rail.'

'Ah, yes,' he answered softly, 'I see. Yes, of course, they go by rail. They go by rail, no doubt. How very stupid of me!' And he turned on his heel as if to get away from me as quickly as possible.

I can't exactly say why, but I felt instinctively that this curious stranger was trying to conceal from me his ignorance of what a railway really was. I was quite certain from the way in which he spoke that he had not the slightest conception what I meant, and that he was doing his best to hide his confusion by pretending to understand me. Here was indeed a strange mystery. In the latter end of this nineteenth century, in the metropolis of industrial England, within a stone's-throw of Charing Cross terminus, I had met an adult Englishman who apparently did not know of the existence of railways. My curiosity was too much piqued to let the matter rest there. I must find out what he meant by it. I walked after him hastily, as he tried to disappear among the crowd, and laid my hand upon his shoulder, to his evident chagrin.

'Excuse me,' I said, drawing him aside down the corner of Craven Street; 'you did not understand what I meant when I said people went to York by rail?'

He looked in my face steadily, and then, instead of replying to my remark, he said slowly, 'Your name is Spottiswood, I believe?'

Again I gave a start of surprise. 'It is,' I answered; 'but I never remember to have seen you before.'

'No,' he replied dreamily; 'no, we have never met till now, no doubt; but I knew your father, I'm sure; or perhaps it may have been your grandfather.'

'Not my grandfather, certainly,' said I, 'for he was killed at Waterloo.'

'At Waterloo! Indeed! How long since, pray?'

I could not refrain from laughing outright. 'Why, of course,' I answered, 'in 1815. There has been nothing particular to kill off any large number of Englishmen at Waterloo since the year of the battle, I suppose.'

'True,' he muttered, 'quite true; so I should have fancied.' But I saw again from the cloud of doubt and bewilderment which came over his intelligent face that the name of Waterloo conveyed no idea whatsoever to his mind.

Never in my life had I felt so utterly confused and astonished. In spite of his poor dress, I could easily see from the clear-cut face and the refined accent of my strange acquaintance that he was an educated gentleman—a man accustomed to mix in cultivated society. Yet he clearly knew nothing whatsoever about railways, and was ignorant of the most salient facts in English history. Had I suddenly come across some Caspar Hauser[1], immured for years in a private prison, and just let loose upon the world by his gaolers? or was my mysterious stranger one of the Seven Sleepers of Ephesus[2], turned out unexpectedly in modern costume on the streets of London? I don't suppose there exists on earth a man more utterly free than I am from any tinge of superstition, any lingering touch of a love for the miraculous; but I confess for a moment I felt half inclined to suppose that the man before me must have drunk the elixir of life, or must have dropped suddenly upon earth from some distant planet.

The impulse to fathom this mystery was irresistible. I drew my arm through his. 'If you knew my father,' I said, 'you will not object to come into my chambers and take a glass of wine with me.'

'Thank you,' he answered half suspiciously; 'thank you very much. I think you look like a man who can be trusted, and I will go with you.'

We walked along the Embankment to Adelphi Terrace, where I took him up to my rooms, and seated him in my easy-chair near the window. As he sat down, one of the trains on the Metropolitan line whirred past the Terrace, snorting steam and whistling shrilly, after the fashion of Metropolitan engines generally. My mysterious stranger jumped back in alarm, and seemed to be afraid of some immediate catastrophe. There was absolutely no possibility of doubting it. The man had obviously never seen a locomotive before.

'Evidently,' I said, 'you do not know London. I suppose you are a colonist from some remote district, perhaps an Australian from the interior[3] somewhere, just landed at the Tower?'

'No, not an Austrian'—I noted his misapprehension—'but a Londoner born and bred.'

'How is it, then, that you seem never to have seen an engine before?'

'Can I trust you?' he asked in a piteously plaintive, half-terrified tone. 'If I tell you all about it, will you at least not aid in persecuting and imprisoning me?'

I was touched by his evident grief and terror. 'No,' I answered, 'you may trust me implicitly. I feel sure there is something in your history which entitles you to sympathy and protection.'

'Well,' he replied, grasping my hand warmly, 'I will tell you all my story; but you must be prepared for something almost too startling to be credible.'

'My name is Jonathan Spottiswood,' he began calmly.

Again I experienced a marvellous start: Jonathan Spottiswood was the name of my great-great-uncle, whose unaccountable disappearance from London just a century since had involved our family in so much protracted litigation as to the succession to his property. In fact, it was Jonathan Spottiswood's money which at that moment formed the bulk of my little fortune. But I would not interrupt him, so great was my anxiety to hear the story of his life.

'I was born in London,' he went on, 'in 1750. 'If you can hear me say that and yet believe that possibly I am not a madman, I will tell you the rest of my tale; if not, I shall go at once and for ever.'

'I suspend judgment for the present,' I answered. 'What you say is extraordinary, but not more extraordinary perhaps than the clear anachronism of your ignorance about locomotives in the midst of the present century.'

'So be it, then. Well, I will tell you the facts briefly in as few words as I can. I was always much given to experimental philosophy, and I spent most of my time in the little laboratory which I had built for myself behind my father's house in the Strand. I had a small independent fortune of my own, left me by an uncle who had made successful ventures in the China trade; and as I was indisposed to follow my father's profession of solicitor, I gave myself up almost entirely to the pursuit of natural philosophy, following the researches of the great Mr Cavendish, our chief English thinker in this kind, as well as of Monsieur Lavoisier, the ingenious French chemist, and of my friend Dr Priestley[4], the Birmingham philosopher, whose new theory of phlogiston[5] I have been much concerned to consider and to promulgate. But the especial subject to which I devoted myself was the elucidation of the nature of fixed air. I do not know how far you yourself may happen to have heard respecting these late discoveries in chemical science, but I dare venture to say that you are at least acquainted with the nature of the body to which I refer.'

'Perfectly,' I answered with a smile, 'though your terminology is now a little out of date. Fixed air was, I believe, the old-fashioned name for carbonic acid[6] gas.'

'Ah,' he cried vehemently, 'that accursed word again! Carbonic acid has undone me, clearly. Yes, if you will have it so, that seems to be what they call it in this extraordinary century; but fixed air was the name we used to give it in our time, and fixed air is what I must call it, of course, in telling you my story. Well, I was deeply interested in this curious question, and also in some of the results which I obtained from working with fixed air in combination with a substance I had produced from the essential oil of a weed known to us in England as lady's mantle, but which the learned Mr Carl Linnæus describes in his system as *Alchemilla vulgaris*[7]. From that weed I obtained an oil which I combined with a certain decoction of fixed air into a remarkable compound; and to this compound, from its singular properties, I proposed to give the name of Pausodyne. For some years I was almost wholly engaged in investigating the conduct of this remarkable agent; and lest I should weary you by entering into too much detail, I may as

well say at once that it possessed the singular power of entirely sus-
pending animation in men or animals for several hours together. It is
a highly volatile oil, like ammonia in smell, but much thicker in gravity; and when held to the nose of an animal, it causes immediate stop-
page of the heart's action, making the body seem quite dead for long
periods at a time. But the moment a mixture of the pausodyne with
oil of vitriol and gum resin is presented to the nostrils, the animal instantaneously revives exactly as before, showing no evil effects whatsoever from its temporary simulation of death. To the reviving mixture
I have given the appropriate name of Anegeiric.

'Of course you will instantly see the valuable medical applications
which may be made of such an agent. I used it at first for experimenting upon the amputation of limbs and other surgical operations. It
succeeded admirably. I found that a dog under the influence of pausodyne suffered his leg, which had been broken in a street accident, to
be set and spliced without the slightest symptom of feeling or discomfort. A cat, shot with a pistol by a cruel boy, had the bullet extracted
without moving a muscle. My assistant, having allowed his little finger
to mortify from neglect of a burn, permitted me to try the effect of my
discovery upon himself; and I removed the injured joints while he remained in a state of complete insensibility, so that he could hardly
believe afterwards in the actual truth of their removal. I felt certain
that I had invented a medical process of the very highest and greatest
utility.

'All this took place in or before the year 1781. How long ago that
may be according to your modern reckoning I cannot say; but to me
it seems hardly more than a few months since. Perhaps you would not
mind telling me the date of the current year. I have never been able to
ascertain it.'

'This is 1881,' I said, growing every moment more interested in his tale.

'Thank you. I gathered that we must now be somewhere near the close of the nineteenth century, though I could not learn the exact date with certainty. Well, I should tell you, my dear sir, that I had contracted an engagement about the year 1779 with a young lady of most remarkable beauty and attractive mental gifts, a Miss Amelia Spragg, daughter of the well-known General Sir Thomas Spragg, with whose achievements you are doubtless familiar. Pardon me, my friend of another age, pardon me, I beg of you, if I cannot allude to this subject without emotion after a lapse of time which to you doubtless seems like a century, but is to me a matter of some few months only at the utmost. I feel towards her as towards one whom I have but recently lost, though I now find that she has been dead for more than eighty years.' As he spoke, the tears came into his eyes profusely; and I could see that under the external calmness and quaintness of his eighteenth century language and demeanour his whole nature was profoundly stirred at the thought of his lost love.

'Look here,' he continued, taking from his breast a large, old-fashioned gold locket containing a miniature; 'that is her portrait, by Mr Walker, and a very truthful likeness indeed. They left me that when they took away my clothes at the Asylum, for I would not consent to part with it, and the physician in attendance observed that to deprive me of it might only increase the frequency and violence of my paroxysms. For I will not conceal from you the fact that I have just escaped from a pauper lunatic establishment.'

I took the miniature which he handed me, and looked at it closely. It was the picture of a young and beautiful girl, with the features and costume of a Sir Joshua. I recognized the face at once as that of a lady whose portrait by Gainsborough hangs on the walls of my uncle's dining-room at Whittingham Abbey. It was strange indeed to hear a living man speak of himself as the former lover of this, to me, historic personage.

'Sir Thomas, however,' he went on, 'was much opposed to our union, on the ground of some real or fancied social disparity in our positions; but I at last obtained his conditional consent, if only I could succeed in obtaining the Fellowship of the Royal Society, which might, he thought, be accepted as a passport into that fashionable circle of which he was a member. Spurred on by this ambition, and by the encouragement of my Amelia, I worked day and night at the perfectioning of my great discovery, which I was assured would bring not only honour and dignity to myself, but also the alleviation and assuagement of pain[8] to countless thousands of my fellow-creatures. I concealed the nature of my experiments, however, lest any rival investigator should enter the field with me prematurely, and share the credit to which I alone was really entitled. For some months I was successful in my efforts at concealment; but in March of this year—I mistake; of the year 1781, I should say—an unfortunate circumstance caused me to take special and exceptional precautions against intrusion.

'I was then conducting my experiments upon living animals, and especially upon the extirpation of certain painful internal diseases to which they are subject. I had a number of suffering cats in my laboratory, which I had treated with pausodyne, and stretched out on boards for the purpose of removing the tumours with which they were afflicted. I had no doubt that in this manner, while directly benefiting the animal creation, I should indirectly obtain the necessary skill to operate successfully upon human beings in similar circumstances. Already I had completely cured several cats without any pain whatsoever, and I was anxious to proceed to the human subject. Walking one morning in the Strand, I found a beggar woman outside a gin-shop, quite drunk, with a small, ill-clad child by her side, suffering the most excruciating torments from a perfectly remediable cause. I induced the mother to accompany me to my laboratory, and there I treated the poor little creature with pausodyne, and began to operate upon her with perfect confidence of success.

'Unhappily, my laboratory had excited the suspicion of many ill-disposed persons among the low mob of the neighbourhood. It was whispered abroad that I was what they called a vivisectionist; and these people, who would willingly have attended a bull-baiting or a prize fight, found themselves of a sudden wondrous humane when scientific procedure was under consideration. Besides, I had made myself unpopular by receiving visits from my friend Dr Priestley, whose religious opinions were not satisfactory to the strict orthodoxy of St Giles's. I was rumoured to be a philosopher, a torturer of live animals, and an atheist. Whether the former accusation were true or not, let others decide; the two latter, heaven be my witness, were wholly unfounded. However, when the neighbouring rabble saw a drunken woman with a little girl entering my door, a report got abroad at once that I was going to vivisect a Christian child. The mob soon collected in force, and broke into the laboratory. At that moment I was engaged, with my assistant, in operating upon the girl, while several cats, all completely anesthetised, were bound down on the boards around, awaiting the healing of their wounds after the removal of tumours. At the sight of such apparent tortures the people grew wild with rage, and happening in their transports to fling down a large bottle of the anegeiric, or reviving mixture, the child and the animals all at once recovered consciousness, and began of course to writhe and scream with acute pain. I need not describe to you the scene that ensued. My laboratory was wrecked, my assistant severely injured, and I myself barely escaped with my life.

'After this *contretemps* I determined to be more cautious. I took the lease of a new house at Hampstead, and in the garden I determined to build myself a subterranean laboratory where I might be absolutely free from intrusion. I hired some labourers from Bath for this purpose, and I explained to them the nature of my wishes, and the absolute necessity of secrecy. A high wall surrounded the garden, and here the workmen worked securely and unseen. I concealed my design even from my dear brother—whose grandson or great-grandson I suppose you must be—and when the building was finished, I sent my men back to Bath, with strict injunctions never to mention the matter to any one. A trap-door in the cellar, artfully concealed, gave access to the passage; a large oak portal, bound with iron, shut me securely in; and my air supply was obtained by means of pipes communicating through blank spaces in the brick wall of the garden with the outer atmosphere. Every arrangement for concealment was perfect; and I re-solved in future, till my results were perfectly established, that I would dispense with the aid of an assistant.

'I was in high spirits when I went to visit my Amelia that evening, and I told her confidently that before the end of the year I expected to gain the gold medal of the Royal Society. The dear girl was pleased at my glowing prospects, and gave me every assurance of the delight with which she hailed the probability of our approaching union.

'Next day I began my experiments afresh in my new quarters. I bolted myself into the laboratory, and set to work with renewed vig-our. I was experimenting upon an injured dog, and I placed a large bottle of pausodyne beside me as I administered the drug to his nos-trils. The rising fumes seemed to affect my head more than usual in that confined space, and I tottered a little as I worked. My arm grew weaker, and at last fell powerless to my side. As it fell it knocked down the large bottle of pausodyne, and I saw the liquid spreading over the floor. That was almost the last thing that I knew. I staggered toward the door, but did not reach it; and then I remember nothing more for a considerable period.'

He wiped his forehead with his sleeve—he had no handker-chief—and then proceeded.

'When I woke up again the effects of the pausodyne had worn themselves out, and I felt that I must have remained unconscious for at least a week or a fortnight. My candle had gone out, and I could not find my tinder-box. I rose up slowly and with difficulty, for the air of the room was close and filled with fumes, and made my way in the dark towards the door. To my surprise, the bolt was so stiff with rust that it would hardly move. I opened it after a struggle, and found my-self in the passage. Groping my way towards the trap-door of the cellar, I felt it was obstructed by some heavy body. With an immense effort, for my strength seemed but feeble, I pushed it up, and discovered that a heap of sea-coals lay on top of it. I extricated myself into the cellar, and there a fresh surprise awaited me. A new entrance had been made into the front, so that I walked out at once upon the open road, instead of up the stairs into the kitchen. Looking up at the exterior of my house, my brain reeled with bewilderment when I saw that it had dis-appeared almost entirely, and that a different porch and wholly unfa-miliar windows occupied its façade. I must have slept far longer than I at first imagined—perhaps a whole year or more. A vague terror pre-vented me from walking up the steps of my own home. Possibly my brother, thinking me dead, might have sold the lease; possibly some stranger might resent my intrusion into the house that was now his own. At any rate, I thought it safer to walk into the road. I would go towards London, to my brother's house in St Mary le Bone. I turned into the Hampstead Road, and directed my steps thitherward.

'Again, another surprise began to affect me with a horrible and ill-defined sense of awe. Not a single object that I saw was really familiar to me. I recognized that I was in the Hampstead Road, but it was not the Hampstead Road which I used to know before my fatal experiments. The houses were far more numerous, the trees were bigger and older. A year, nay, even a few years would not have sufficed for such a change. I began to fear that I had slept away a whole decade.

'It was early morning, and few people were yet abroad. But the costume of those whom I met seemed strange and fantastic to me. Moreover, I noticed that they all turned and looked after me with evident surprise, as though my dress caused them quite as much astonishment as theirs caused me. I was quietly attired in my snuff-coloured suit of small-clothes, with silk stockings and simple buckle shoes, and I had of course no hat; but I gathered that my appearance caused universal amazement and concern, far more than could be justified by the mere accidental absence of head-gear. A dread began to oppress me that I might actually have slept out my whole age and generation. Was my Amelia alive? and if so, would she be still the same Amelia I had known a week or two before? Should I find her an aged woman, still cherishing a reminiscence of her former love; or might she herself perhaps be dead and forgotten, while I remained, alone and solitary, in a world which knew me not?

'I walked along unmolested, but with reeling brain, through streets more and more unfamiliar, till I came near the St Mary le Bone Road. There, as I hesitated a little and staggered at the crossing, a man in a curious suit of dark blue clothes, with a grotesque felt helmet on his head, whom I afterwards found to be a constable, came up and touched me on the shoulder.

'"Look here," he said to me in a rough voice, "what are you a-doin' in this 'ere fancy-dress at this hour in the mornin'? You've lost your way home, I take it."

'"I was going," I answered, "to the St Mary le Bone Road."

'"Why, you image," says he rudely, "if you mean Marribon, why don't you say Marribon? What house are you a-lookin' for, eh?"

'"My brother lives," I replied, "at the Lamb, near St Mary's Church, and I was going to his residence."

'"The Lamb!" says he, with a rude laugh; "there ain't no public of that name in the road. It's my belief," he goes on after a moment, "that you're drunk, or mad, or else you've stole them clothes. Any way, you've got to go along with me to the station, so walk it, will you?"

'"Pardon me," I said, "I suppose you are an officer of the law, and I would not attempt to resist your authority"—"You'd better not," says he, half to himself—"but I should like to go to my brother's house, where I could show you that I am a respectable person."

'"Well," says my fellow insolently, "I'll go along of you if you like, and if it's all right, I suppose you won't mind standing a bob?"

'"A what?" said I.

'"A bob," says he, laughing; "a shillin', you know."

'To get rid of his insolence for a while, I pulled out my purse and handed him a shilling. It was a George II with milled edges, not like the things I see you use now. He held it up and looked at it, and then he said again, "Look here, you know, this isn't good. You'd better come along with me straight to the station, and not make a fuss about it. There's three charges against you, that's all. One is, that you're drunk. The second is, that you're mad. And the third is, that you've been trying to utter false coin. Any one of 'em's quite enough to justify me in takin' you into custody."

'I saw it was no use to resist, and I went along with him.

'I won't trouble you with the whole of the details, but the upshot of it all was, they took me before a magistrate. By this time I had begun to realize the full terror of the situation, and I saw clearly that the real danger lay in the inevitable suspicion of madness under which I must labour. When I got into the court I told the magistrate my story very shortly and simply, as I have told it to you now. He listened to me without a word, and at the end he turned round to his clerk and said, "This is clearly a case for Dr Fitz-Jenkins, I think."

'"Sir," I said, "before you send me to a madhouse, which I suppose is what you mean by these words, I trust you will at least examine the evidences of my story. Look at my clothing, look at these coins, look at everything about me." And I handed him my purse to see for himself.

'He looked at it for a minute, and then he turned towards me very sternly. "Mr Spottiswood," he said, "or whatever else your real name may be, if this is a joke, it is a very foolish and unbecoming one. Your dress is no doubt very well designed; your small collection of coins is interesting and well-selected; and you have got up your character re-markably well. If you are really sane, which I suspect to be the case, then your studied attempt to waste the time of this court and to make a laughing-stock of its magistrate will meet with the punishment it deserves. I shall remit your case for consideration to our medical of-ficer. If you consent to give him your real name and address, you will be liberated after his examination. Otherwise, it will be necessary to satisfy ourselves as to your identity. Not a word more, sir," he contin-ued, as I tried to speak on behalf of my story. "Inspector, remove the prisoner."

'They took me away, and the surgeon examined me. To cut things short, I was pronounced mad, and three days later the commissioners passed me for a pauper asylum. When I came to be examined, they said I showed no recollection of most subjects of ordinary education.

"'I am a chemist," said I; "try me with some chemical questions. You will see that I can answer sanely enough."

"'How do you mix a grey powder?" said the commissioner.

"'Excuse me," I said, "I mean a chemical philosopher, not an apothecary."

"'Oh, very well, then; what is carbonic acid?"

"'I never heard of it," I answered in despair. "It must be something which has come into use since—since I left off learning chemistry." For I had discovered that my only chance now was to avoid all reference to my past life and the extraordinary calamity which had thus unexpectedly overtaken me. "Please try me with something else."

"'Oh, certainly. What is the atomic weight of chlorine[9]?"

'I could only answer that I did not know.

"'This is a very clear case," said the commissioner. "Evidently he is a gentleman by birth and education, but he can give no very satisfactory account of his friends, and till they come forward to claim him we can only send him for a time to North Street."

"'For Heaven's sake, gentlemen," I cried, "before you consign me to an asylum, give me one more chance. I am perfectly sane; I remember all I ever knew; but you are asking me questions about subjects on which I never had any information. Ask me anything historical, and see whether I have forgotten or confused any of my facts."

'"I will do the commissioner the justice to say that he seemed anxious not to decide upon the case without full consideration. "Tell me what you can recollect," he said, "as to the reign of George IV."

'"I know nothing at all about it," I answered, terror-stricken, "but oh, do pray ask me anything up to the time of George III."

'"Then please say what you think of the French Revolution."

'I was thunderstruck. I could make no reply, and the commissioners shortly signed the papers to send me to North Street pauper asylum. They hurried me into the street, and I walked beside my captors towards the prison to which they had consigned me. Yet I did not give up all hope even so of ultimately regaining my freedom. I thought the rationality of my demeanour and the obvious soundness of all my reasoning powers would suffice in time to satisfy the medical attendant as to my perfect sanity. I felt sure that people could never long mistake a man so clear-headed and collected as myself for a madman.

'On our way, however, we happened to pass a churchyard where some workmen were engaged in removing a number of old tombstones from the crowded area. Even in my existing agitated condition, I could not help catching the name and date on one mouldering slab which a labourer had just placed upon the edge of the pavement. It ran something like this: "Sacred to the memory of Amelia, second daughter of the late Sir Thomas Spragg, knight, and beloved wife of Henry McAlister, Esq, by whom this stone is erected. Died May 20, 1799, aged 44 years." Though I had gathered already that my dear girl must probably have long been dead, yet the reality of the fact had not yet had time to fix itself upon my mind. You must remember, my dear sir, that I had but awaked a few days earlier from my long slumber, and that during those days I had been harassed and agitated by such a flood of incomprehensible complications, that I could not really grasp in all its fullness the complete isolation of my present position. When I saw the tombstone of one whom, as it seemed to me, I had loved passionately but a week or two before, I could not refrain from rushing to embrace it, and covering the insensible stone with my boiling tears. "Oh, my Amelia, my Amelia," I cried, "I shall never again behold thee, then! I shall never again press thee to my heart, or hear thy dear lips pronounce my name!"

'But the unfeeling wretches who had charge of me were far from being moved to sympathy by my bitter grief. "Died in 1799," said one of them with a sneer. "Why, this madman's blubbering over the grave of an old lady who has been buried for about a hundred years!" And the workmen joined in their laughter as my gaolers tore me away to the prison where I was to spend the remainder of my days.

'When we arrived at the asylum, the surgeon in attendance was informed of this circumstance, and the opinion that I was hopelessly mad thus became ingrained in his whole conceptions of my case. I remained five months or more in the asylum, but I never saw any chance of creating a more favourable impression on the minds of the authorities. Mixing as I did only with other patients, I could gain no clear ideas of what had happened since I had taken my fatal sleep; and whenever I endeavoured to question the keepers, they amused themselves by giving me evidently false and inconsistent answers, in order to enjoy my chagrin and confusion. I could not even learn the actual date of the present year, for one keeper would laugh and say it was 2001, while another would confidentially advise me to date my petition to the commissioners, "Jan 1, AD one million." The surgeon, who never played me any such pranks, yet refused to aid me in any way, lest, as he said, he should strengthen me in my sad delusion. He was convinced that I must be an historical student, whose reason had broken down through too close study of the eighteenth century; and he felt certain that sooner or later my friends would come to claim me.

He is a gentle and humane man, against whom I have no personal complaint to make; but his initial misconception prevented him and everybody else from ever paying the least attention to my story. I could not even induce them to make inquiries at my house at Hampstead, where the discovery of the subterranean laboratory would have partially proved the truth of my account.

'Many visitors came to the asylum from time to time, and they were always told that I possessed a minute and remarkable acquaintance with the history of the eighteenth century. They questioned me about facts which are as vivid in my memory as those of the present month, and were much surprised at the accuracy of my replies. But they only thought it strange that so clever a man should be so very mad, and that my information should be so full as to past events, while my notions about the modern world were so utterly chaotic. The surgeon, however, always believed that my reticence about all events posterior to 1781 was a part of my insanity. I had studied the early part of the eighteenth century so fully, he said, that I fancied I had lived in it; and I had persuaded myself that I knew nothing at all about the subsequent state of the world.'

The poor fellow stopped a while, and again drew his sleeve across his forehead. It was impossible to look at him and believe for a moment that he was a madman.

'And how did you make your escape from the asylum?' I asked.

'Now, this very evening,' he answered; 'I simply broke away from the door and ran down toward the Strand, till I came to a place that looked a little like St Martin's Fields, with a great column and some fountains, and near there I met you. It seemed to me that the best thing to do was to catch the York coach and get away from the town as soon as possible. You met me, and your look and name inspired me with confidence. I believe you must be a descendant of my dear brother.'

'I have not the slightest doubt,' I answered solemnly, 'that every word of your story is true, and that you are really my great-great-uncle. My own knowledge of our family history exactly tallies with what you tell me. I shall spare no endeavour to clear up this extraordinary matter, and to put you once more in your true position.'

'And you will protect me?' he cried fervently, clasping my hand in both his own with intense eagerness. 'You will not give me up once more to the asylum people?'

'I will do everything on earth that is possible for you,' I replied.

He lifted my hand to his lips and kissed it several times, while I felt hot tears falling upon it as he bent over me. It was a strange position, look at it how you will. Grant that I was but the dupe of a madman, yet even to believe for a moment that I, a man of well-nigh fifty, stood there in face of my own great-grandfather's brother, to all appearance some twenty years my junior, was in itself an extraordinary and marvellous thing. Both of us were too overcome to speak. It was a few minutes before we said anything, and then a loud knock at the door made my hunted stranger rise up hastily in terror from his chair.

'Gracious Heavens!' he cried, 'they have tracked me hither. They are coming to fetch me. Oh, hide me, hide me, anywhere from these wretches!'

As he spoke, the door opened, and two keepers with a policeman entered my room.

'Ah, here he is!' said one of them, advancing towards the fugitive, who shrank away towards the window as he approached.

'Do not touch him,' I exclaimed, throwing myself in the way. 'Every word of what he says is true, and he is no more insane than I am.'

The keeper laughed a low laugh of vulgar incredulity. 'Why, there's a pair of you, I do believe,' he said. 'You're just as mad yourself as t'other one.' And he pushed me aside roughly to get at his charge.

But the poor fellow, seeing him come towards him, seemed suddenly to grow instinct with a terrible vigour, and hurled off the keeper with one hand, as a strong man might do with a little terrier. Then, before we could see what he was meditating, he jumped upon the ledge of the open window, shouted out loudly, 'Farewell, farewell!' and leapt with a spring on to the embankment beneath.

All four of us rushed hastily down the three flights of steps to the bottom, and came below upon a crushed and mangled mass on the spattered pavement. He was quite dead. Even the policeman was shocked and horrified at the dreadful way in which the body had been crushed and mutilated in its fall, and at the suddenness and unexpectedness of the tragedy. We took him up and laid him out in my room; and from that room he was interred after the inquest, with all the respect which I should have paid to an undoubted relative. On his grave in Kensal Green Cemetery I have placed a stone bearing the simple inscription, 'Jonathan Spottiswood. Died 1881.' The hint I had received from the keeper prevented me from saying anything as to my belief in his story, but I asked for leave to undertake the duty of his interment on the ground that he bore my own surname, and that no other person was forthcoming to assume the task. The parochial authorities were glad enough to rid the ratepayers of the expense.

At the inquest I gave my evidence simply and briefly, dwelling mainly upon the accidental nature of our meeting, and the facts as to his fatal leap. I said nothing about the known disappearance of

Jonathan Spottiswood in 1781, nor the other points which gave credibility to his strange tale. But from this day forward I give myself up to proving the truth of his story, and realizing the splendid chemical discovery which promises so much benefit to mankind. For the first purpose, I have offered a large reward for the discovery of a trap-door in a coal-cellar at Hampstead, leading into a subterranean passage and laboratory; since, unfortunately, my unhappy visitor did not happen to mention the position of his house. For the second purpose, I have begun a series of experiments upon the properties of the essential oil of alchemilla, and the possibility of successfully treating it with carbonic anhydride[10]; since, unfortunately, he was equally vague as to the nature of his process and the proportions of either constituent. Many people will conclude at once, no doubt, that I myself have become infected with the monomania of my miserable namesake, but I am determined at any rate not to allow so extraordinary an anaesthetic to go unacknowledged, if there be even a remote chance of actually proving its useful nature. Meanwhile, I say nothing even to my dearest friends with regard to the researches upon which I am engaged.

---

[1] **Caspar [Kaspar] Hauser.** A German youth found wandering in the town of Nuremberg in 1828. He told a fantastic story of having been raised from birth in a dark cell, living entirely on bread and water supplied by unseen hands. Periodically he was given sleeping potions and tended to while asleep. The mystery of his origin, which was never solved, aroused much curiosity throughout Europe. He died of a stab wound, probably self-inflicted, in 1833, aged about 21.

[2] **the Seven Sleepers of Ephesus.** A legend, common to Christianity and Islam. In the usual version, seven youths fall asleep in a cave while escaping persecution, around AD250, and wake up in the reign of Theodosius, some 300 years later.

[3] **perhaps an Australian from the interior.** The name of the country came into common use between 1804 and 1824.

[4] **Cavendish … Lavoisier … Priestley.** Three great chemists of the later 18th century. Henry Cavendish (d.1810) ascertained the properties of hydrogen and established that air is mixture of gases. Antoine Lavoisier (d.1794), among many other discoveries, proved that water is a compound of two gases. Joseph Priestley (d.1804) was a polymath famous for several major discoveries in chemistry and electricity, including the discovery of oxygen. Like Spottiswood, his house and laboratory were burned down by a mob, in 1791. When Spottiswood falls asleep in 1781 all three were in mid-career and famous.

[5] **phlogiston.** A hypothetical substance, assumed to have negative weight, that was supposedly released during combustion and oxidation. Oxygen was first called 'dephlogisticated air' since it was supposed to lose its phlogiston as it reacted with other substances.

[6] **Carbonic acid.** The mild acid formed when carbon dioxide dissolves in water (now called soda water). It was first prepared around 1757. Carbon dioxide was identified by Joseph Black in 1754, but was known as 'fixed air' and then 'carbonic acid gas'.

[7] *Alchemilla vulgaris.* This is a real common plant, used by herbalists for mild pain relief. It was indeed given that name in the Linnaeus system, in 1753.

[8] **the alleviation and assuagement of pain.** The first use of anaesthetics (ether, nitrous oxide and chloroform) for surgical purposes dates to the 1840s.

[9] **atomic weight of chlorine.** This valuable concept was developed by John Dalton around 1803, but it was much refined by Berzelius, who prepared a fairly accurate table of the atomic weight of 54 elements in 1828.

[10] **carbonic anhydride.** Another obsolete name for carbon dioxide.

# THE BACKSLIDER

*The Backslider*, published anonymously in the *Cornhill* in August 1883, was Grant Allen's first contribution to that magazine, which had just acquired a new and demanding editor, and the story is more carefully developed than some of his earlier work.

For someone who was an avowed atheist, Allen took plenty of interest in religion—he was, after all, the son of an Irish minister. His attitude is nearly always humorously ironic, shading into satire, for he regarded all religious belief as an innate infection of the human mind, which only the strong disinfectant of scientific rationalism could hope to dispel.

The 'Gideonites' of the story are an invention of Allen's, and have nothing to do with the Gideons who distribute Bibles free (that movement was founded later, in 1898). But the Gideonites do have a lot in common with such real-life exemplars as the Salvation Army (1865), Christian Science (1879) and the Zion Watch Tower Tract Society [Jehovah's Witnesses] (1881). Such sects were essentially working- and lower-middleclass movements that, according to the narrator, 'spring up naturally in the outlying suburbs of great thinking centres'. With the passage of time, sects like these became more moderate and mainstream, but originally they were intransigent in their dealings with the rest of society—the 'Midianites', as they are called here.

How Allen acquired his working knowledge of such fringe Christian sects, it's hard to say: perhaps he went undercover to their meetings. At any rate, thanks to his prodigious knowledge of the Old and

New Testaments his imaginary Gideonites make a convincing picture of such a sect: not only its language, rituals and trappings, but its social psychology and the motivation of its leader and his disciples, with all the internal tensions and potential schisms that resulted.

It is appropriate that the final collapse of Paul Owen's faith results from his reading Herbert Spencer's *Sociology*. Spencer was arguably the most influential thinker in Victorian times, and for no one more than Grant Allen. For him no praise of Spencer could be too extravagant: he was 'the greatest philosopher that ever drew breath, the maximum brain on earth ... the greatest thinker of this or any other epoch.' The ten volumes of his vast 'synthetic Philosophy' elevated the theory of evolution far beyond its biological limits into a cosmic vision of inevitable progress. It was the most comprehensive of the rationalists' religion-substitutes. But Allen did not live to see Spencer's professional and popular reputation sink to near zero as the new century opened.

# 1.

THERE WAS much stir and commotion on the night of Thursday, January the 14th, 1874, in the Gideonite Apostolic Church, number 47, Walworth Lane, Peckham, S.E. Anybody could see at a glance that some important business was under consideration; for the Apostle was there himself, in his chair of presidency, and the twelve Episcops were there, and the forty-eight Presbyters, and a large and earnest gathering of the Gideonite laity. It was only a small bare school-room, fitted with wooden benches, was that headquarters station of the young Church; but you could not look around it once without seeing that its occupants were of the sort by whom great religious revolutions may be made or marred. For the Gideonites[1] were one of those strange enthusiastic hole-and-corner sects that spring up naturally in the outlying suburbs of great thinking centres. They gather around the marked personality of some one ardent, vigorous, half-educated visionary; and they consist for the most part of intelligent, half-reasoning people, who are bold enough to cast overboard the dogmatic beliefs of their fathers, but not so bold as to exercise their logical faculty upon the fundamental basis on which the dogmas originally rested. The Gideonites had thus collected around the fixed centre of their Apostle, a retired attorney, Murgess by name, whose teaching commended itself to their groping reason as the pure outcome of faithful Biblical research; and they had chosen their name because, though they were but three hundred in number, they had full confidence that when the time came they would blow their trumpets, and all the host of Midian[2] would be scattered before them. In fact, they divided the world generally into Gideonite and Midianite, for they knew that he that was not with them was against them. And no wonder, for the people of Peckham did not love the struggling Church. Its chief doctrine was one of absolute celibacy, like the Shakers[3] of America; and to this doctrine the

Church had testified in the Old Kent Road and elsewhere after a vigorous practical fashion that roused the spirit of South-eastern London into the fiercest opposition. The young men and maidens, said the Apostle, must no longer marry or be given in marriage; the wives and husbands must dwell asunder; and the earth must be made as an image of heaven. These were heterodox opinions, indeed, which South-eastern London could only receive with a strenuous counterblast of orthodox brickbats and sound Anglican road metal.[4]

The fleece of wool was duly laid upon the floor; the trumpet and the lamp were placed upon the bare wooden reading desk; and the Apostle, rising slowly from his seat, began to address the assembled Gideonites.[5]

'Friends,' he said, in a low, clear, impressive voice, with a musical ring tempering its slow distinctness, 'we have met together tonight to take counsel with one another upon a high matter. It is plain to all of us that the work of the Church in the world does not prosper as it might prosper were the charge of it in worthier hands. We have to contend against great difficulties. We are not among the rich or the mighty of the earth; and the poor whom we have always with us do not listen to us.[6] It is expedient, therefore, that we should set some one among us aside to be instructed thoroughly in those things that are most commonly taught among the Midianites at Oxford or Cambridge. To some of you it may seem, as it seemed at first to me, that such a course would involve going back upon the very principles of our constitution. We are not to overcome Midian by our own hand, nor by the strength of two and thirty thousand, but by the trumpet, and the pitcher, and the cake of barley bread. Yet, when I searched and inquired after this matter, it seemed to me that we might also err by overmuch confidence on the other side. For Moses, who led the people out of Egypt, was made ready for the task by being learned in all the learning[7] of the Egyptians. Daniel, who testified in the captivity, was cunning in knowledge[8], and understanding science, and instructed in the wisdom and tongue of the Chaldeans. Paul, who was the apostle of the Gentiles, had not only sat at the feet of Gamaliel[9], but was also able from their own poets and philosophers to confute the sophisms and subtleties of the Grecians themselves. These things show us that we should not too lightly despise even worldly learning and worldly science. Perhaps we have gone wrong in thinking too little of such dross, and being puffed up with spiritual pride. The world might listen to us more readily if we had one who could speak the word for us in the tongues understanded of the world[10].'

As he paused, a hum of acquiescence went round the room.

'It has seemed to me, then,' the Apostle went on, 'that we ought to choose some one among our younger brethren, upon whose shoulders the cares and duties of the Apostolate might hereafter fall. We are a poor people, but by subscription among ourselves we might raise a sufficient sum to send the chosen person first to a good school here in London, and afterwards to the University of Oxford. It may seem a doubtful and a hazardous thing thus to stake our future upon any one young man; but then we must remember that the choice will not be wholly or even mainly ours; we will be guided and directed as we ever are in the laying on of hands. To me, considering this matter thus, it has seemed that there is one youth in our body who is specially pointed out for this work. Only one child has ever been born into the Church: he, as you know, is the son of brother John Owen and sister Margaret Owen, who were received into the fold just six days before his birth. Paul Owen's very name seems to many of us, who take nothing for chance but all things for divinely ordered, to mark him out at once as a foreordained Apostle. Is it your wish, then, Presbyter John Owen, to dedicate your only son to this ministry?'

Presbyter John Owen rose from the row of seats assigned to the forty-eight, and moved hesitatingly towards the platform. He was an intelligent-looking, honest-faced, sunburnt working man, a mason by trade, who had come into the Church from the Baptist society; and he was awkwardly dressed in his Sunday clothes, with the scrupulous clumsy neatness of a respectable artisan who expects to take part in an important ceremony. He spoke nervously and with hesitation, but with all the transparent earnestness of a simple, enthusiastic nature.

'Apostle and friends,' he said, 'it ain't very easy for me to disentangle my feelin's on this subjec' from one another. I hope I ain't moved by any worldly feelin', an' yet I hardly know how to keep such considerations out, for there's no denyin' that it would be a great pleasure to me and to his mother to see our Paul becomin' a teacher in Israel, and receivin' an education such as you, Apostle, has pinted out. But we hope, too, we ain't insensible to the good of the Church and the advantage that it might derive from our Paul's support and preachin'. We can't help seein' ourselves that the lad has got abilities; and we've tried to train him up from his youth upward, like Timothy, for the furtherance of the right doctrine. If the Church thinks he's fit for the work laid upon him, his mother and me'll be glad to dedicate him to the service.'

He sat down awkwardly, and the Church again hummed its approbation in a suppressed murmur. The Apostle rose once more, and briefly called on Paul Owen to stand forward.

In answer to the call, a tall, handsome, earnest-eyed boy advanced timidly to the platform. It was no wonder that those enthusiastic Gideonite visionaries should have seen in his face the visible stamp of the Apostleship. Paul Owen had a rich crop of dark-brown glossy and curly hair, cut something after the Florentine Cinquecento fashion— not because his parents wished him to look artistic, but because that was the way in which they had seen the hair dressed in all the sacred pictures that they knew; and Margaret Owen, the daughter of some Wesleyan Spitalfields weaver folk[11], with the imaginative Huguenot blood still strong in her veins, had made up her mind ever since she became Convinced of the Truth (as their phrase ran) that her Paul was called from his cradle to a great work. His features were delicately chiselled, and showed rather natural culture, like his mother's, than rough honesty, like John Owen's, or strong individuality, like the masterful Apostle's. His eyes were peculiarly deep and luminous, with a far-away look which might have reminded an artist of the central boyish figure in Holman Hunt's picture of the Doctors in the Temple.[12] And yet Paul Owen had a healthy colour in his cheek and a general sturdiness of limb and muscle which showed that he was none of your nervous, bloodless, sickly idealists, but a wholesome English peasant boy of native refinement and delicate sensibilities. He moved forward with some natural hesitation before the eyes of so many people—ay, and what was more terrible, of the entire Church upon earth; but he was not awkward and constrained in his action like his father. One could see that he was sustained in the prominent part he took that morning by the consciousness of a duty he had to perform and a mission laid upon him which he must not reject.

'Are you willing, my son Paul,' asked the Apostle, gravely, 'to take upon yourself the task that the Church proposes?'

'I am willing,' answered the boy in a low voice, 'grace preventing me.'[13]

'Does all the Church unanimously approve the election of our brother Paul to this office?' the Apostle asked formally; for it was a rule with the Gideonites that nothing should be done except by the unanimous and spontaneous action of the whole body, acting under direct and immediate inspiration; and all important matters were accordingly arranged beforehand by the Apostle in private interviews with every member of the Church individually, so that everything that took place in public assembly had the appearance of being wholly unquestioned. They took counsel first with one another, and consulted the Scripture together; and when all private doubts were satisfied, they met as a Church to ratify in solemn conclave their separate conclusions. It was not often that the Apostle did not have his own way. Not only had he the most marked personality and the strongest will, but he alone also had Greek and Hebrew enough to appeal always to the original word; and that mysterious amount of learning, slight as it really was, sufficed almost invariably to settle the scruples of his wholly ignorant and pliant disciples. Reverence for the literal Scripture in its primitive language was the corner-stone of the Gideonite Church; and for all practical purposes, its one depositary and exponent for them was the Apostle himself. Even the Rev. Albert Barnes's *Commentary*[14] was held to possess an inferior authority.

'The Church approves,' was the unanimous answer.

'Then, Episcops, Presbyters, and brethren,' said the Apostle, taking up a roll of names, 'I have to ask that you will each mark down on this paper opposite your own names how much a year you can spare of your substance for six years to come as a guarantee fund for this great work. You must remember that the ministry of this Church has cost you nothing; freely I have received and freely given; do you now bear your part in equipping a new aspirant for the succession to the Apostolate.'

The two senior Episcops took two rolls from his hand, and went round the benches with a stylographic pen[15] (so strangely do the ages mingle—Apostles and stylographs) silently asking each to put down his voluntary subscription. Meanwhile the Apostle read slowly and reverently a few appropriate sentences of Scripture. Some of the richer members—well-to-do small tradesmen of Peckham—put down a pound or even two pounds apiece; the poorer brethren wrote themselves down for ten shillings or even five. In the end the guarantee list amounted to £195 a year. The Apostle reckoned it up rapidly to himself, and then announced the result to the assembly, with a gentle smile relaxing his austere countenance. He was well pleased, for the sum was quite sufficient to keep Paul Owen two years at school in London and then send him comfortably if not splendidly to Oxford. The boy had already had a fair education in Latin and some Greek, at the Birkbeck Schools[16]; and with two years' further study he might even gain a scholarship (for he was a bright lad), which would materially lessen the expense to the young Church. Unlike many prophets and enthusiasts, the Apostle was a good man of business; and he had taken pains to learn all about these favourable chances before embarking his people on so very doubtful a speculation. The Assembly was just about to close, when one of the Presbyters rose unexpectedly to put a question which, contrary to the usual practice, had not already been submitted for approbation to the Apostle. He was a hard-headed, thickset, vulgar-looking man, a greengrocer at Denmark Hill, and the Apostle always looked upon him as a thorn in his side, promoted by inscrutable wisdom to the Presbytery for the special purpose of keeping down the Apostle's spiritual pride.

'One more pint, Apostle,' he said abruptly, 'afore we close. It seems to me that even in the Church's work we'd ought to be business-like. Now, it ain't business-like to let this young man, Brother Paul, get his eddication out of us, if I may so speak afore the Church, on spec. It's all very well our sayin' he's to be eddicated and take on the Apostleship, but how do we know but what when he's had his eddication he may fall away and become a backslider, like Demas[17] and like others among ourselves that we could mention? He may go to Oxford among a lot of Midianites, and them of the great an' mighty of the earth too, and how do we know but what he may round upon the Church, and go back upon us after we've paid for his eddication? So what I want to ask is just this, can't we bind him down in a bond that if he don't take the Apostleship with the consent of the Church when it falls vacant he'll pay us back our money, so as we can eddicate up another as'll be more worthy?'

The Apostle moved uneasily in his chair; but before he could speak, Paul Owen's indignation found voice, and he said out his say boldly before the whole assembly, blushing crimson with mingled shame and excitement as he did so. 'If Brother Grimshaw and all the brethren think so ill of me that they cannot trust my honesty and honour,' he said, 'they need not be at the pains of educating me. I will sign no bond and enter into no compact. But if you suppose that I will be a backslider, you do not know me, and I will confer no more with you upon the subject.'

'My son Paul is right,' the Apostle said, flushing up in turn at the boy's audacity; 'we will not make the affairs of the Spirit a matter for bonds and earthly arrangements. If the Church thinks as I do, you will all rise up.'

All rose except Presbyter Grimshaw. For a moment there was some hesitation, for the rule of the Church in favour of unanimity was absolute; but the Apostle fixed his piercing eyes on Job Grimshaw, and after a minute or so Job Grimshaw too rose slowly, like one compelled by an unseen power, and cast in his vote grudgingly with the rest. There was nothing more said about signing an agreement.

## 2.

Meenie Bolton had counted a great deal upon her visit to Oxford, and she found it quite as delightful as she had anticipated. Her brother knew such a nice set of men, especially Mr Owen, of Christchurch. Meenie had never been so near falling in love with anybody in her life as she was with Paul Owen. He was so handsome and so clever, and then there was something so romantic about this strange Church they said he belonged to. Meenie's father was a country parson, and the way in which Paul shrank from talking about the rector, as if his office were something wicked or uncanny, piqued and amused her. There was an heretical tinge about him which made him doubly interesting to the Rector's daughter. The afternoon water party that eventful Thursday, down to Nuneham, she looked forward to with the deepest interest. For her aunt, the Professor's wife, who was to take charge of them, was certainly the most delightful and most sensible of chaperons.

'Is it really true, Mr Owen,' she said, as they sat together for ten minutes alone after their picnic luncheon, by the side of the weir under the shadow of the Nuneham beeches—'is it really true that this Church of yours doesn't allow people to marry?'

Paul coloured up to his eyes as he answered, 'Well, Miss Bolton, I don't know that you should identify me too absolutely with my Church. I was very young when they selected me to go to Oxford, and my opinions have decidedly wavered a good deal lately. But the Church certainly does forbid marriage. I have always been brought up to look upon it as sinful.'

Meenie laughed aloud; and Paul, to whom the question was no laughing matter, but a serious point of conscientious scruple, could hardly help laughing with her, so infectious was that pleasant ripple. He checked himself with an effort, and tried to look serious. 'Do you know,' he said, 'when I first came to Christchurch, I doubted even whether I ought to make your brother's acquaintance because he was a clergyman's son. I was taught to describe clergymen always as priests of Midian.' He never talked about his Church to anybody at Oxford, and it was a sort of relief to him to speak on the subject to Meenie, in spite of her laughing eyes and undisguised amusement. The other men would have laughed at him too, but their laughter would have been less sympathetic.

'And do you think them priests of Midian still?' asked Meenie.

'Miss Bolton,' said Paul suddenly, as one who relieves his over-burdened mind by a great effort, 'I am almost moved to make a confidante of you.'

'There is nothing I love better than confidences,' Meenie answered; and she might truthfully have added, 'particularly from you.'

'Well, I have been passing lately through a great many doubts and difficulties. I was brought up by my Church to become its next Apostle, and I have been educated at their expense both in London and here. You know,' Paul added with his innate love of telling out the whole truth, 'I am not a gentleman; I am the son of poor working people in London.'

'Tom told me who your parents were,' Meenie answered simply; 'but he told me, too, you were none the less a true gentleman born for that; and I see myself he told me right.'

Paul flushed again—he had a most unmanly trick of flushing up—and bowed a little timid bow. 'Thank you,' he said quietly. 'Well, while I was in London I lived entirely among my own people, and never heard anything talked about except our own doctrines. I thought our Apostle the most learned, the wisest, and the greatest of men. I had not a doubt about the absolute infallibility of our own opinions. But ever since I came to Oxford I have slowly begun to hesitate and to falter. When I came up first, the men laughed at me a good deal in a good-humoured way, because I wouldn't do as they did. Then I thought myself persecuted for the truth's sake, and was glad. But the men were really very kind and forbearing to me; they never argued with me or bullied me; they respected my scruples, and said nothing more about it as soon as they found out what they really were. That was my first stumbling-block. If they had fought me and debated with me, I might have stuck to my own opinions by force of opposition. But they turned me in upon myself completely by their silence, and mastered me by their kindly forbearance. Point by point I began to give in, till now I hardly know where I am standing.'

'You wouldn't join the cricket club at first, Tom says.'

'No, I wouldn't. I thought it wrong to walk in the ways of Midian. But gradually I began to argue myself out of my scruples, and now I positively pull six in the boat, and wear a Christchurch ribbon on my hat. I have given up protesting against having my letters addressed to me as Esquire (though I have really no right to the title), and I nearly went the other day to have some cards engraved with my name as 'Mr Paul Owen.' I am afraid I'm backsliding terribly.'

Meenie laughed again. 'If that is all you have to burden your conscience with,' she said, 'I don't think you need spend many sleepless nights.'

'Quite so,' Paul answered, smiling; 'I think so myself. But that is not all. I have begun to have serious doubts about the Apostle himself and the whole Church altogether. I have been three years at Oxford now; and while I was reading for Mods[18], I don't think I was so unsettled in my mind. But since I have begun reading philosophy for my Greats, I have had to go into all sorts of deep books—Mill, and Spencer, and Bain, and all kinds of fellows who really think about things, you know, down to the very bottom—and an awful truth begins to dawn upon me, that our Apostle is after all only a very third-rate type of a thinker. Now that, you know, is really terrible.'

'I don't see why,' Meenie answered demurely. She was beginning to get genuinely interested.

'That is because you have never had to call in question a cherished and almost ingrown faith. You have never realized any similar circumstances. Here am I, brought up by these good, honest, earnest people, with their own hard-earned money, as a pillar of their belief. I have been taught to look upon myself as the chosen advocate of their creed, and on the Apostle as an almost divinely inspired man. My whole life has been bound up in it; I have worked and read night and day in order to pass high and do honour to the Church; and now what do I begin to find the Church really is? A petty group of poor, devoted, enthusiastic, ignorant people, led blindly by a decently instructed but narrow-minded teacher, who has mixed up his own headstrong self-conceit and self-importance with his own peculiar ideas of abstract religion.' Paul paused, half surprised at himself, for, though he had doubted before, he had never ventured till that day to formulate his doubts, even to himself, in such plain and straightforward language.

'I see,' said Meenie, gravely; 'you have come into a wider world; you have mixed with wider ideas; and the wider world has converted you, instead of your converting the world. Well, that is only natural. Others beside you have had to change their opinions.'

'Yes, yes; but for me it is harder—oh! so much harder.'

'Because you have looked forward to being an Apostle?'

'Miss Bolton, you do me injustice—not in what you say, but in the tone you say it in. No, it is not the giving up of the Apostleship that troubles me, though I did hope that I might help in my way to make the world a new earth; but it is the shock and downfall of their hopes to all those good earnest people, and especially—oh! especially,

Miss Bolton, to my own dear father and mother.' His eyes filled with tears as he spoke.

'I can understand,' said Meenie, sympathetically, her eyes dimming a little in response. 'They have set their hearts all their lives long on your accomplishing this work, and it will be to them the disappointment of a cherished romance.'

They looked at one another a few minutes in silence.

'How long have you begun to have your doubts?' Meenie asked after the pause.

'A long time, but most of all since I saw you. It has made me—it has made me hesitate more about the fundamental article of our faith. Even now, I am not sure whether it is not wrong of me to be talking so with you about such matters.'

'I see,' said Meenie, a little more archly; 'it comes perilously near—' and she broke off, for she felt she had gone a step too far.

'Perilously near falling in love,' Paul continued boldly, turning his big eyes full upon her. 'Yes, perilously near.'

Their eyes met; Meenie's fell; and they said no more. But they both felt they understood one another. Just at that moment the Professor's wife came up to interrupt the *tête-à-tête*; 'for that young Owen,' she said to herself, 'is really getting quite too confidential with dear Meenie.'

That same evening Paul paced up and down his rooms in Peckwater with all his soul strangely upheaved within him and tossed and racked by a dozen conflicting doubts and passions. Had he gone too far? Had he yielded like Adam to the woman who beguiled him? Had he given way like Samson to the snares of Delilah? For the old Scripture phraseology and imagery, so long burned into his very nature, clung to him still in spite of all his faltering changes of opinion. Had he said more than he thought and felt about the Apostle? Even if he was going to revise his views, was it right, was it candid, was it loyal to the truth, that he should revise them under the biassing influence of Meenie's eyes? If only he could have separated the two questions—the Apostle's mission, and the something which he felt growing up within him! But he could not—and, as he suspected, for a most excellent reason, because the two were intimately bound up in the very warp and woof of his existence. Nature was asserting herself against the religious asceticism of the Apostle; it could not be so wrong for him to feel those feelings that had thrilled every heart in all his ancestors for innumerable generations.

He was in love with Meenie: he knew that clearly now. And this love was after all not such a wicked and terrible feeling; on the contrary, he felt all the better and the purer for it already. But then that might merely be the horrible seductiveness of the thing. Was it not always typified by the cup of Circe, by the song of the Sirens[19], by all that was alluring and beautiful and hollow? He paced up and down for half an hour, and then (he had sported his oak[20] long ago) he lit his little reading lamp and sat down in the big chair by the bay window. Running his eyes over his bookshelf, he took out, half by chance, Spencer's *Sociology*[21]. Then, from sheer weariness, he read on for a while, hardly heeding what he read. At last he got interested, and finished a chapter. When he had finished it, he put the book down, and felt that the struggle was over. Strange that side by side in the same world, in the same London, there should exist two such utterly different types of man as Herbert Spencer and the Gideonite Apostle. The last seemed to belong to the sixteenth century, the first to some new and hitherto uncreated social world. In an age which produced thinkers like that, how could he ever have mistaken the poor, bigoted, narrow, half-instructed Apostle for a divinely inspired teacher! So far as Paul Owen was concerned, the Gideonite Church and all that belonged to it had melted utterly into thin air.

Three days later, after the Eights[22] in the early evening, Paul found an opportunity of speaking again alone with Meenie. He had taken their party on to the Christchurch barge to see the race, and he was strolling with them afterwards round the meadow walk by the bank of the Cherwell. Paul managed to get a little in front with Meenie, and entered at once upon the subject of his late embarrassments.

'I have thought it all over since, Miss Bolton,' he said—he half hesitated whether he should say 'Meenie' or not, and she was half disappointed that he didn't, for they were both very young, and very young people fall in love so unaffectedly—'I have thought it all over, and I have come to the conclusion that there is no help for it: I must break openly with the Church.'

'Of course,' said Meenie, simply. 'That I understood.'

He smiled at her ingenuousness. Such a very forward young person! And yet he liked it. 'Well, the next thing is, what to do about it. You see, I have really been obtaining my education, so to speak, under false pretences. I can't continue taking these good people's money after I have ceased to believe in their doctrines. I ought to have faced the question sooner. It was wrong of me to wait until—until it was forced upon me by other considerations.'

This time it was Meenie who blushed. 'But you don't mean to leave Oxford without taking your degree?' she asked quickly.

'No, I think it will be better not. To stop here and try for a fellowship is my best chance of repaying these poor people the money which I have taken from them for no purpose.'

'I never thought of that,' said Meenie. 'You are bound in honour to pay them back, of course.'

Paul liked the instantaneous honesty of that 'of course.' It marked the naturally honourable character; for 'of course,' too, they must wait to marry (young people jump so) till all that money was paid off. 'Fortunately,' he said, 'I have lived economically, and have not spent nearly as much as they guaranteed. I got scholarships up to a hundred a year of my own, and I only took a hundred a year of theirs. They offered me two hundred. But there's five years at a hundred, that makes five hundred pounds—a big debt to begin life with.'

'Never mind,' said Meenie. 'You will get a fellowship, and in a few years you can pay it off.'

'Yes,' said Paul, 'I can pay it off. But I can never pay off the hopes and aspirations I have blighted. I must become a schoolmaster, or a barrister, or something of that sort, and never repay them for their self-sacrifice and devotion in making me whatever I shall become. They may get back their money, but they will have lost their cherished Apostle for ever.'

'Mr Owen,' Meenie answered solemnly, 'the seal of the Apostolate lies far deeper than that. It was born in you, and no act of yours can shake it off.'

'Meenie,' he said, looking at her gently, with a changed expression—'Meenie, we shall have to wait many years.'

'Never mind, Paul,' she replied, as naturally as if he had been Paul to her all her life long, 'I can wait if you can. But what will you do for the immediate present?'

'I have my scholarship,' he said; 'I can get on partly upon that; and then I can take pupils; and I have only one year more of it.'

So before they parted that night it was all well understood between them that Paul was to declare his defection from the Church at the earliest opportunity; that he was to live as best he might till he could take his degree; that he was then to pay off all the back debt; and that after all these things he and Meenie might get comfortably married whenever they were able. As to the Rector and his wife, or any other parental authorities, they both left them out in the cold as wholly as young people always do leave their elders out on all similar occasions.

'Maria's a born fool!' said the Rector to his wife a week after Meenie's return; 'I always knew she was a fool, but I never knew she was quite such a fool as to permit a thing like this. So far as I can get it out of Edie, and so far as Edie can get it out of Meenie, I understand that she has allowed Meenie to go and get herself engaged to some Dissenter fellow, a Shaker, or a Mormon, or a Communist, or something of the sort, who is the son of a common labourer, and has been sent up to Oxford, Tom tells me, by his own sect, to be made into a gentleman, so as to give some sort or colour of respectability to their absurd doctrines. I shall send the girl to town at once to Emily's, and she shall stop there all next season, to see if she can't manage to get engaged to some young man in decent society at any rate.'

## 3.

When Paul Owen returned to Peckham for the long vacation, it was with a heavy heart that he ventured back slowly to his father's cottage. Margaret Owen had put everything straight and neat in the little living room, as she always did, to welcome home her son who had grown into a gentleman; and honest John stood at the threshold beaming with pleasure to wring Paul's hand in his firm grip, just back unwashed from his day's labour. After the first kissings and greetings were over,

John Owen said rather solemnly, 'I have bad news for you, Paul. The Apostle is sick, even unto death.'

When Paul heard that, he was sorely tempted to put off the disclosure for the present; but he felt he must not. So that same night, as they sat together in the dusk near the window where the geraniums stood, he began to unburden his whole mind, gently and tentatively, so as to spare their feelings as much as possible, to his father and mother. He told them how, since he went to Oxford, he had learned to think somewhat differently about many things; how his ideas had gradually deepened and broadened; how he had begun to inquire into fundamentals for himself; how he had feared that the Gideonites took too much for granted, and reposed too implicitly on the supposed critical learning of their Apostle. As he spoke his mother listened in tearful silence; but his father murmured from time to time, 'I was afeard of this already, Paul; I seen it coming, now and again, long ago.' There was pity and regret in his tone, but not a shade of reproachfulness.

At last, however, Paul came to speak, timidly and reservedly, of Meenie. Then his father's eye began to flash a little, and his breath came deeper and harder. When Paul told him briefly that he was engaged to her, the strong man could stand it no longer. He rose up in righteous wrath, and thrust his son at arm's length from him. 'What!' he cried fiercely, 'you don't mean to tell me you have fallen into sin and looked upon the daughters of Midian! It was no Scriptural doubts that druv you on, then, but the desire of the flesh and the lust of the eyes that has lost you! You dare to stand up there, Paul Owen, and tell me that you throw over the Church and the Apostle for the sake of a girl, like a poor miserable Samson! You are no son of mine, and I have nothin' more to say to you.'

But Margaret Owen put her hand on his shoulder and said softly, 'John, let us hear him out.' And John, recalled by that gentle touch, listened once more. Then Paul pleaded his case powerfully again. He quoted Scripture to them; he argued with them, after their own fashion, and down to their own comprehension, text by text; he pitted his own critical and exegetical faculty against the Apostle's. Last of all, he turned to his mother, who, tearful still and heart-broken with disappointment, yet looked admiringly upon her learned, eloquent boy, and said to her tenderly, 'Remember, mother, you yourself were once in love. You yourself once stood, night after night, leaning on the gate, waiting with your heart beating for a footstep that you knew so well. You yourself once counted the days and the hours and the minutes till the next meeting came.' And Margaret Owen, touched to the heart by that simple appeal, kissed him fervently a dozen times over, the hot tears dropping on his cheek meanwhile; and then, contrary to all the rules of their austere Church, she flung her arms round her husband too, and kissed him passionately the first time for twenty years, with all the fervour of a floodgate loosed. Paul Owen's apostolate had surely borne its first fruit.

The father stood for a moment in doubt and terror, like one stunned or dazed, and then, in a moment of sudden remembrance, stepped forward and returned the kiss. The spell was broken, and the Apostle's power was no more. What else passed in the cottage that night, when John Owen fell upon his knees and wrestled in spirit, was too wholly internal to the man's own soul for telling here. Next day John and Margaret Owen felt the dream of their lives was gone; but the mother in her heart rejoiced to think her boy might know the depths of love, and might bring home a real lady for his wife.

On Sunday it was rumoured that the Apostle's ailment was very serious; but young Brother Paul Owen would address the Church. He did so, though not exactly in the way the Church expected. He told them simply and plainly how he had changed his views about certain matters; how he thanked them from his heart for the loan of their money (he was careful to emphasize the word *loan*), which had helped him to carry on his education at Oxford; and how he would repay them the principal and interest, though he could never repay them the kindness, at the earliest possible opportunity. He was so grave, so earnest, so transparently true, that, in spite of the downfall of their dearest hopes, he carried the whole meeting with him, all save one man. That man was Job Grimshaw. Job rose from his place with a look of undisguised triumph as soon as Paul had finished, and, mounting the platform quietly, said his say.

'I knew, Episcops, Presbyters, and Brethren,' he began, 'how this 'ere young man would finish. I saw it the day he was appinted. He's flushing up now the same as he flushed up then when I spoke to him; and it ain't sperritual, it's worldly pride and headstrongness, that's what it is. He's had our money, and he's had his eddication, and now he's going to round on us, just as I said he would. It's all very well talking about paying us back: how's a young man like him to get five hundred pounds, I should like to know. And if he did even, what sort o' repayment would that be to many of the brethren, who've saved and scraped for five year to let him live like a gentleman among the great and the mighty o' Midian? He's got his eddication out of us, and he can keep that whatever happens, and make a living out of it, too; and now he's going back on us, same as I said he would, and, having got all he can out of the Church, he's going to chuck it away like a sucked orange. I detest such backsliding and such ungratefulness.'

Paul's cup of humiliation was full, but he bit his lip till the blood almost came, and made no answer.

'He boasted in his own strength,' Job went on mercilessly, 'that he wasn't going to be a backslider, and he wasn't going to sign no bond, and he wasn't going to confer with us, but we must trust his honour and honesty, and such like. I've got his very words written down in my notebook 'ere; for I made a note of 'em, foreseeing this. If we'd 'a' bound him down, as I proposed, he wouldn't 'a' dared to go backsliding and rounding on us, and making up to the daughters of Midian, as I don't doubt but what he's been doing.' Paul's tell-tale face showed him at once that he had struck by accident on the right chord. 'But if he ever goes bringing a daughter of Midian here to Peckham,' Job continued, 'we'll show her these very notes, and ask her what she thinks of such dishonourable conduct. The Apostle's dying, that's clear; and before he dies I warrant he shall know this treachery.'

Paul could not stand that last threat. Though he had lost faith in the Apostle as an Apostle, he could never forget the allegiance he had once borne him as a father, or the spell which his powerful individuality had once thrown around him as a teacher. To have embittered that man's dying bed with the shadow of a terrible disappointment would be to Paul a lifelong subject of deep remorse. 'I did not intend to open my mouth in answer to you, Mr Grimshaw,' he said (for the first time breaking through the customary address of Brother), 'but I pray you, I entreat you, I beseech you, not to harass the Apostle in his last moments with such a subject.'

'Oh yes, I suppose so,' Job Grimshaw answered maliciously, all the ingrained coarseness of the man breaking out in the wrinkles of his face. 'No wonder you don't want him enlightened about your goings on with the daughters of Midian, when you must know as well as I do that his life ain't worth a day's purchase, and that he's a man of independent means, and has left you every penny he's got in his will, because he believes you're a fit successor to the Apostolate. I know it, for I signed as a witness, and I read it through, being a short one, while the other witness was signing. And you must know it as well as I do. I suppose you don't think he'll make another will now; but there's time enough to burn that one anyhow.'

Paul Owen stood aghast at the vulgar baseness of which this lewd fellow supposed him capable. He had never thought of it before; and yet it flashed across his mind in a moment how obvious it was now. Of course the Apostle would leave him his money. He was being educated for the Apostolate, and the Apostolate could not be carried on without the sinews of war. But that Job Grimshaw should think him guilty of angling for the Apostle's money, and then throwing the Church overboard—the bare notion of it was so horrible to him that he could not even hold up his head to answer the taunt. He sat down and buried his crimson face in his hands; and Job Grimshaw, taking up his hat sturdily, with the air of a man who has to perform an unpleasant duty, left the meeting-room abruptly without another word.

There was a gloomy Sunday dinner that morning in the mason's cottage, and nobody seemed much inclined to speak in any way. But as they were in the midst of their solemn meal, a neighbour who was also a Gideonite came in hurriedly. 'It's all over,' he said, breathless— 'all over with us and with the Church. The Apostle is dead. He died this morning.'

Margaret Owen found voice to ask, 'Before Job Grimshaw saw him?'

The neighbour nodded. 'Yes.'

'Thank heaven for that!' cried Paul. 'Then he did not die misunderstanding me!'

'And you'll get his money,' added the neighbour, 'for I was the other witness.'

Paul drew a long breath. 'I wish Meenie was here,' he said. 'I must see her about this.'

## 4.

A few days later the Apostle was buried, and his will was read over before the assembled Church. By earnest persuasion of his father, Paul consented to be present, though he feared another humiliation from Job Grimshaw. But two days before he had taken the law into his own hands, by writing to Meenie, at her aunt's in Eaton Place; and that very indiscreet young lady, in response, had actually consented to meet him in Kensington Gardens alone the next afternoon. There he sat with her on one of the benches by the Serpentine, and talked the whole matter over with her to his heart's content.

'If the money is really left to me,' he said, 'I must in honour refuse it. It was left to me to carry on the Apostolate, and I can't take it on any other ground. But what ought I to do with it? I can't give it over to the Church, for in three days there will be no Church left to give it to. What shall I do with it?'

'Why,' said Meenie, thoughtfully, 'if I were you I should do this. First, pay back everybody who contributed towards your support in full, principal and interest; then borrow from the remainder as much as you require to complete your Oxford course; and finally, pay back all that and the other money to the fund when you are able, and hand it over for the purpose of doing some good work in Peckham itself, where your Church was originally founded. If the ideal can't be fulfilled, let the money do something good for the actual.'

'You are quite right, Meenie,' said Paul, 'except in one particular. I will not borrow from the fund for my own support. I will not touch a penny of it, temporarily or permanently, for myself in any way. If it comes to me, I shall make it over to trustees at once for some good object, as you suggest, and shall borrow from them five hundred pounds to repay my own poor people, giving the trustees my bond to repay the fund hereafter. I shall fight my own battle henceforth un-aided.'

'You will do as you ought to do, Paul, and I am proud of it.'

So next morning, when the meeting took place, Paul felt some-what happier in his own mind as to the course he should pursue with reference to Job Grimshaw.

The Senior Episcop opened and read the last will and testament of Arthur Murgess, attorney-at-law. It provided in a few words that all his estate, real and personal, should pass unreservedly to his friend, Paul Owen, of Christchurch, Oxford. It was whispered about that, besides the house and grounds, the personalty might be sworn[23] at £8000, a vast sum to those simple people.

When the reading was finished, Paul rose and addressed the as-sembly. He told them briefly the plan he had formed, and insisted on his determination that not a penny of the money should be put to his own uses. He would face the world for himself, and thanks to their kindness he could face it easily enough. He would still earn and pay back all that he owed them. He would use the fund, first for the good of those who had been members of the Church, and afterwards for the good of the people of Peckham generally. And he thanked them from the bottom of his heart for the kindness they had shown him.

Even Job Grimshaw could only mutter to himself that this was not sperritual grace, but mere worldly pride and stubbornness, lest the lad should betray his evil designs, which had thus availed him nothing. 'He has lost his own soul and wrecked the Church for the sake of the money,' Job said, 'and now he dassn't touch a farden of it.'

Next John Owen rose and said slowly, 'Friends, it seems to me we may as well all confess that this Church has gone to pieces. I can't stop in it myself any longer, for I see it's clear agin nature, and what's agin nature can't be true.' And though the assembly said nothing, it was plain that there were many waverers in the little body whom the affairs of the last week had shaken sadly in their simple faith. Indeed, as a matter of fact, before the end of the month the Gideonite Church had melted away, member by member, till nobody at all was left of the whole assembly but Job Grimshaw.

'My dear,' said the Rector to his wife a few weeks later, laying down his *Illustrated*[24], 'this is really a very curious thing. That young fellow Owen, of Christchurch, that Meenie fancied herself engaged to, has just come into a little landed property and eight or nine thousand pounds on his own account. He must be better connected than Tom imagines. Perhaps we might make inquiries about him after all.'

The Rector did make inquiries in the course of the week, and with such results that he returned to the rectory in blank amazement. 'That fellow's mad, Amelia,' he said, 'stark mad, if ever anybody was. The leader of his Little Bethel, or Ebenezer[25], or whatever it may be, has left him all his property absolutely, without conditions; and the idiot of a boy declares he won't touch a penny of it, because he's ceased to believe in their particular shibboleth[26], and he thinks the leader wanted him to succeed him. Very right and proper of him, of course, to leave the sect if he can't reconcile it with his conscience, but perfectly Quixotic of him to give up the money and beggar himself outright. Even if his connection was otherwise desirable (which it is far from being), it would be absurd to think of letting Meenie marry such a ridiculous hair-brained fellow.'

Paul and Meenie, however, went their own way, as young people often will, in spite of the Rector. Paul returned next term to Oxford, penniless, but full of resolution, and by dint of taking pupils managed to eke out his scholarship for the next year. At the end of that time he took his first in Greats, and shortly after gained a fellowship[27]. From the very first day he began saving money to pay off that dead weight of five hundred pounds. The kindly ex-Gideonites had mostly protested against his repaying them at all, but in vain: Paul would not make his entry into life, he said, under false pretences. It was a hard pull, but he did it. He took pupils, he lectured, he wrote well and vigorously for the press, he worked late and early with volcanic energy; and by the end of three years he had not only saved the whole of the sum advanced by the Gideonites, but had also begun to put away a little nest-egg against his marriage with Meenie. And when the editor of a great morning paper in London offered him a permanent place upon the staff, at a large salary, he actually went down to Worcestershire, saw the formidable Rector himself in his own parish, and demanded Meenie outright in marriage. And the Rector observed to his wife that this young Owen seemed a well-behaved and amiable young man; that after all one needn't know anything about his relations if one didn't like; and that as Meenie had quite made up her mind, and was as headstrong as a mule, there was no use trying to oppose her any longer.

Down in Peckham, where Paul Owen lives, and is loved by half the poor of the district, no one has forgotten who was the real founder of the Murgess Institute, which does so much good in encouraging thrift, and is so admirably managed by the founder and his wife. He would take a house nowhere but at Peckham, he said. To the Peckham people he owed his education, and for the Peckham people he would watch the working of his little Institute. There is no better work being done anywhere in that great squalid desert, the east and south-east of London; there is no influence more magnetic than the founder's. John and Margaret Owen have recovered their hopes for their boy, only they run now in another and more feasible direction; and those who witness the good that is being done by the Institute among the poor

of Peckham, or who have read that remarkable and brilliant econom-
ical work lately published on 'The Future of Co-operation in the East
End, by P. O.,' venture to believe that Meenie was right after all, and
that even the great social world itself has not yet heard the last of young
Paul Owen's lay apostolate.

---

[1] **Gideonites.** An imaginary sect named after Gideon, a military hero of the
Israelites, who condemned and punished their idolatrous worship of Baal.
Ironically for the celibate Gideonites, he had a prodigious number of wives,
concubines and children.

[2] **the host of Midian.** Long-standing enemies of the Israelites; under Moses' leadership as directed by Jehovah, the Midianite women were all slaughtered and their young girls enslaved. Later the whole tribe was annihilated
by Gideon.

[3] **Shakers.** A sect founded in England by Ann Lee, but best known for its
American communities, now extinct; they were celibate and procreation was
forbidden.

[4] **brickbats ... road metal.** Fierce street-fighting using torn up cobble-
stones, *etc* was not unusual in the poor parts of London.

[5] **fleece ... trumpet ... lamp.** As told in Judges 7, these items played a big
part in Gideon's triumphs over the Midianites.

[6] **rich or the mighty ... the poor whom we have always with us.** Adaptation of Revelations 6:15 and of Jesus' words in Matthew 26:11.

[7] **learned in all the learning.** Said of Moses in Acts 7:22.

[8] **cunning in knowledge.** Attributes required of youths who were to be
taught Chaldean lore, in Daniel 1:4.

[9] **Gamaliel.** A Jewish rabbi and scholar, tutor of St Paul (Acts 22).

[10] **understanded of the world.** Phrase derived from the Thirty-nine Articles defining Anglican belief after the Reformation.

[11] **Spitalfields weaver folk.** French Protestants who fled France to avoid persecution and settled in this area as silk weavers.

[12] **Holman Hunt's picture.** Correctly titled *The Finding of the Saviour in the Temple* (1854-60), the figure in the centre is the 12-year old Jesus debating with the learned men at Jerusalem, an event told in Luke 2:21.

[13] **'grace preventing me.'** A formulaic phrase, meaning 'if God's grace prevents me from sinning'.

[14] **Albert Barnes's *Commentary*.** Barnes (*d*.1870) was an American theologian. His prolific sets of 'notes' on both the Old and New Testaments were huge bestsellers among Evangelicals, even though Barnes was once charged with heresy.

[15] **stylographic pen.** Then the most up-to-date fountain pen, with a hollow nib and a wire valve releasing the ink.

[16] **Birkbeck Schools.** What is now Birkbeck College of London University was originally a Mechanics' Institute offering part-time instruction.

[17] **backslider, like Demas.** In the Second Epistle to Timothy (usually assumed to be by St Paul) the disciple Demas is reported as having 'forsaken me, having loved this present world'.

[18] **reading for Mods.** Honour Moderations, the first examinations taken after five terms for the Classics degree at Oxford. The student then moved on to Greats for seven terms. The whole degree took four years.

[19] **the cup of Circe ... the song of the Sirens.** Both agents of seduction in Homer's *Odyssey*, luring Ulysses and his sailors to their doom.

[20] **he had sported his oak.** Closed the heavy outer door to his rooms, meaning do not disturb.

[21] **Spencer's *Sociology*.** Herbert Spencer's *Principles of Sociology*, in three volumes (1874-5) and much enlarged in his lifetime, was just one component of his enormously influential 'Synthetic Philosophy'.

[22] **after the Eights.** A regatta at Oxford held over four days in May.

[23] **the personalty might be sworn.** That is, movable property such as cash, furniture *etc*, as opposed to real estate. The sum in question is equivalent to about half a million pounds.

[24] **his *Illustrated*.** Presumably the *Illustrated London News*, a hugely popular weekly paper, with wood-cut pictures (and later photographs) on every page.

[25] **Little Bethel, or Ebenezer.** Both contemptuous terms for a Dissenting chapel or meeting-house.

[26] **shibboleth.** The specific beliefs or expressions of a group, often those considered to be unacceptable or outmoded. Used as a test-phrase by the Gileadites to identify their enemies the Ephraimites, whom they then slaughtered, in Judges 12.

[27] **shortly after gained a fellowship.** An Oxford fellowship at the time was worth about £300*pa*, but there were various ways of adding to it, including taking on extra college duties.

# THE CURATE OF CHURNSIDE

This story is one of a series that Allen wrote for the *Cornhill* magazine, where it appeared in September 1884. Allen said once that he had no problem giving his villains an occupation, because he made them all clergymen. A little exaggerated, perhaps, but it's true that his fictional men of the cloth do tend to be hypocrites, time-servers, fanatics and arsonists. Or, indeed, murderous psychopaths, like the Oxford-educated deacon in this story. What makes it the more impressive is that psychiatry was still an infant science in Allen's lifetime. As he noted himself, the sociopathic personality is 'less rare than many people will be inclined to imagine among the colder type of our own emancipated and cultivated classes.'

That is not to say, of course, that authors had not intuitively grasped the nature of such aberrant personalities earlier. Robert Browning had done so in his dramatic monologues like 'Porphyria's Lover' and 'My Last Duchess'. Browning's chilling monologues are voiced by the killers themselves; whereas in Allen's story the third person narration is from the standpoint of Walter Dene; or, more exactly, he uses a free indirect style so that even the descriptive passages are infused with Dene's sensibility. Allen captures well the arrogant belief that the moral code that others live by don't apply to him; and equally well caught is that peculiar mixture of cold-blooded brutality, high aesthetic sensibility and the creepy charm that often mark the homicidal psychopath. Nevertheless, there is much irony in the fact that

Dene, who considers himself cleverer and more cunning than everyone about him, has his murder plan go wrong from the start.

At the end of Browning's 'Porphyria's Lover' the murderer sits with his strangled victim, filled with horror and amazement that he has got away with it:

And thus we sit together now,/And all night long we have
not stirred,/And yet God has not said a word!

Walter Dene is troubled by no such sentiment. He does not merely evade the law; he lives happily afterwards, a good man in the eyes of all the world. His worst punishment is that he demeans himself in his own eyes by having to bribe the poacher to take what he knows off to Australia. But the effect even of that humiliation don't last long: 'As for the little episode,' the story ends, 'he himself has almost forgotten all about it.' That is not a message that Victorian readers of fiction expected to hear.

# 1.

WALTER DENE, deacon, in his faultless Oxford clerical coat and broad felt hat, strolled along slowly, sunning himself as he went, after his wont, down the pretty central lane of West Churnside. It was just the idyllic village best suited to the taste of such an idyllic young curate as Walter Dene. There were cottages with low-thatched roofs, thickly overgrown with yellow stonecrop and pink house-leek; there were trellis-work porches up which the scented dog-rose and the fainter honeysuckle clambered together in sisterly rivalry; there were pargeted gable-ends of Elizabethan farmhouses, quaintly varied with black oak joists and moulded plaster panels. At the end of all, between an avenue of ancient elm trees, the heavy square tower of the old church closed in the little vista—a church with a round Norman doorway and dogtooth arches, melting into Early English lancets in the aisle, and finishing up with a great Decorated east window by the broken cross and yew tree. Not a trace of Perpendicularity[1] about it anywhere, thank goodness: 'for if it were Perpendicular,' said Walter Dene to himself often, 'I really think, in spite of my uncle, I should have to look out for another curacy.'

Yes, it was a charming village, and a charming country; but, above all, it was rendered habitable and pleasurable for a man of taste by the informing presence of Christina Eliot. 'I don't think I shall propose to Christina this week after all,' thought Walter Dene as he strolled along lazily. 'The most delightful part of love-making is certainly its first beginning. The little tremor of hope and expectation; the half-needless doubt you feel as to whether she really loves you; the pains you take to pierce the thin veil of maidenly reserve; the triumph of detecting her at a blush or a flutter when she sees you coming—all these are delicate little morsels to be rolled daintily on the critical palate, and not to be swallowed down coarsely at one vulgar gulp. Poor child, she is on tenter-hooks of hesitation and expectancy all the time, I know; for I'm sure she loves me now, I'm sure she loves me; but I must wait a week yet: she will be grateful to me for it hereafter. We mustn't kill the goose that lays the golden eggs; we mustn't eat up all our capital at one extravagant feast, and then lament the want of our interest ever afterward. Let us live another week in our first fool's paradise before we enter on the safer but less tremulous pleasures of sure possession. We can enjoy first love but once in a lifetime; let us enjoy it now while we can, and not fling away the chance prematurely by mere childish haste and girlish precipitancy.' Thinking which thing, Walter Dene halted a moment by the churchyard wall, picked a long spray of scented wild thyme from a mossy cranny, and gazed into the blue sky above at the graceful swifts who nested in the old tower, as they curved and circled through the yielding air on their evenly poised and powerful pinions.

Just at that moment old Mary Long came out of her cottage to speak with the young parson. 'If ye plaze, Maister Dene,' she said in her native west-country dialect, 'our Nully would like to zee 'ee. She's main ill today, zur, and she be like to die a'most, I'm thinking.'

'Poor child, poor child,' said Walter Dene tenderly. 'She's a dear little thing, Mrs Long, is your Nellie, and I hope she may yet be spared to you. I'll come and see her at once, and try if I can do anything to ease her.'

He crossed the road compassionately with the tottering old grandmother, giving her his helping hand over the kerbstone, and following her with bated breath into the close little sick-room. Then he flung open the tiny casement with its diamond-leaded panes, so as to let in the fresh summer air, and picked a few sprigs of sweet-briar from the porch, which he joined with the geranium from his own button-hole to make a tiny nosegay for the bare bedside. After that, he sat and talked awhile gently in an undertone to pale, pretty little Nellie herself, and went away at last promising to send her some jelly and some soup immediately from the vicarage kitchen.

'She's a sweet little child,' he said to himself musingly, 'though I'm afraid she's not long for this world now; and the poor like these small attentions dearly. They get them seldom, and value them for the sake of the thoughtfulness they imply, rather than for the sake of the mere things themselves. I can order a bottle of calf's-foot at the grocer's, and Carter can set it in a mould without any trouble; while as for the soup, some tinned mock-turtle and a little fresh stock makes a really capital mixture for this sort of thing. It costs so little to give these poor souls pleasure, and it is a great luxury to oneself undeniably. But, after all, what a funny trade it is to set an educated man to do! They send us up to Oxford or Cambridge, give us a distinct taste for Aeschylus and Catullus, Dante and Milton, Mendelssohn and Chopin, good claret and *olives farcies*, and then bring us down to a country village, to look after the bodily and spiritual ailments of rheumatic old washerwomen! If it were not for poetry, flowers, and Christina, I really think I should succumb entirely under the infliction.'

'He's a dear, good man, that he is, is young passon,' murmured old Mary Long as Walter disappeared between the elm trees; 'and he do love the poor and the zick, the same as if he was their own brother. God bless his zoul, the dear, good vulla, vor all his kindness to our Nully.'

Halfway down the main lane Walter came across Christina Eliot. As she saw him she smiled and coloured a little, and held out her small gloved hand prettily. Walter took it with a certain courtly and graceful chivalry. 'An exquisite day, Miss Eliot,' he said; 'such a depth of sapphire in the sky, such a faint undertone of green on the clouds by the horizon, such a lovely humming of bees over the flickering hot meadows! On days like this, one feels that Schopenhauer is wrong after all, and that life is sometimes really worth living.'

'It seems to me often worth living,' Christina answered; 'if not for oneself, at least for others. But you pretend to be more of a pessimist than you really are, I fancy, Mr Dene. Any one who finds so much beauty in the world as you do can hardly think life poor or meagre. You seem to catch the loveliest points in everything you look at, and to throw a little literary or artistic reflection over them which makes them even lovelier than they are in themselves.'

'Well, no doubt one can increase one's possibilities of enjoyment by carefully cultivating one's own faculties of admiration and appreciation,' said the curate thoughtfully; 'but, after all, life has only a few chapters that are thoroughly interesting and enthralling in all its history. We oughtn't to hurry over them too lightly, Miss Eliot; we ought to linger on them lovingly, and make the most of their potentialities; we ought to dwell upon them like 'linked sweetness long drawn out'[2]. It is the mistake of the world at large to hurry too rapidly over the pleasantest episodes, just as children pick all the plums at once out of the pudding. I often think that, from the purely selfish and temporal point of view, the real value of a life to its subject may be measured by the space of time over which he has managed to spread the enjoyment of its greatest pleasures. Look, for example, at poetry, now.'

A faint shade of disappointment passed across Christina's face as he turned from what seemed another groove into that indifferent subject; but she answered at once, 'Yes, of course one feels that with the higher pleasures at least; but there are others in which the interest of plot is greater, and then one looks naturally rather to the end. When you begin a good novel, you can't help hurrying through it in order to find out what becomes of everybody at last.'

'Ah, but the highest artistic interest goes beyond mere plot inter-est. I like rather to read for the pleasure of reading, and to loiter over the passages that please me, quite irrespective of what goes before or what comes after; just as you, for your part, like to sketch a beautiful scene for its own worth to you, irrespective of what may happen to the leaves in autumn, or to the cottage roof in twenty years from this. By the way, have you finished that little water-colour of the mill yet? It's the prettiest thing of yours I've ever seen, and I want to look how you've managed the light on your foreground.'

'Come in and see it,' said Christina. 'It's finished now, and, to tell you the truth, I'm very well pleased with it myself.'

'Then I know it must be good,' the curate answered; 'for you are always your own harshest critic.' And he turned in at the little gate with her, and entered the village doctor's tiny drawing-room.

Christina placed the sketch on an easel near the window—a low window opening to the ground, with long lithe festoons of faint-scented jasmine encroaching on it from outside—and let the light fall on it aslant in the right direction. It was a pretty and a clever sketch certainly, with more than a mere amateur's sense of form and colour; and Walter Dene, who had a true eye for pictures, could conscien-tiously praise it for its artistic depth and fullness. Indeed, on that head at least, Walter Dene's veracity was unimpeachable, however lax in other matters; nothing on earth would have induced him to praise as good a picture or a sculpture in which he saw no real merit. He sat a little while criticizing and discussing it, suggesting an improvement here or an alteration there, and then he rose hurriedly, remembering all at once his forgotten promise to little Nellie. 'Dear me,' he said, 'your daughter's picture has almost made me overlook my proper du-ties, Mrs Eliot. I promised to send some jelly and things at once to poor little Nellie Long at her grandmother's. How very wrong of me to let my natural inclinations keep me loitering here, when I ought to have been thinking of the poor of my parish!' And he went out with just a gentle pressure on Christina's hand, and a look from his eyes that her heart knew how to read aright at the first glance of it.

'Do you know, Christie,' said her father, 'I sometimes fancy when I hear that new parson fellow talk about his artistic feelings, and so on, that he's just a trifle selfish, or at least self-centred. He always dwells so much on his own enjoyment of things, you know.'

'Oh no, papa,' cried Christina warmly. 'He's anything but selfish, I'm sure. Look how kind he is to all the poor in the village, and how much he thinks about their comfort and welfare. And whenever he's talking with one, he seems so anxious to make you feel happy and contented with yourself. He has a sort of little subtle flattery of manner about him that's all pure kindliness; and he's always thinking what he can say or do to please you, and to help you onward. What you say about his dwelling on enjoyment so much is really only his artistic sensibility. He feels things so keenly, and enjoys beauty so deeply, that he can't help talking enthusiastically about it even a little out of season. He has more feelings to display than most men, and I'm sure that's the reason why he displays them so much. A ploughboy could only talk enthusiastically about roast beef and dumplings; Mr Dene can talk about everything that's beautiful and sublime on earth or in heaven.'

Meanwhile, Walter Dene was walking quickly with his measured tread—the even, regular tread of a cultivated gentleman—down the lane toward the village grocer's, saying to himself as he went, 'There was never such a girl in all the world as my Christina. She may be only a country surgeon's daughter—a rosebud on a hedgerow bush—but she has the soul and the eye of a queen among women for all that. Every lover has deceived himself with the same sweet dream, to be sure—how over-analytic we have become nowadays, when I must needs half argue myself out of the sweets of first love!—but then they hadn't so much to go upon as I have. She has a wonderful touch in music, she has an exquisite eye in painting, she has an Italian charm in manner and conversation. I'm something of a connoisseur, after all, and no more likely to be deceived in a woman than I am in a wine or a picture. And next week I shall really propose formally to Christina, though I know by this time it will be nothing more than the merest formality. Her eyes are too eloquent not to have told me that long ago. It will be a delightful pleasure to live for her, and in order to make her happy. I frankly recognize that I am naturally a little selfish—not coarsely and vulgarly selfish; from that disgusting and piggish vice I may conscientiously congratulate myself that I'm fairly free; but still selfish in a refined and cultivated manner. Now, living with Christina and for Christina will correct this defect in my nature, will tend to bring me nearer to a true standard of perfection. When I am by her side, and then only, I feel that I am thinking entirely of her, and not at all of myself. To her I show my best side; with her, that best side would be always uppermost. The companionship of such a woman makes life something purer, and higher, and better worth having. The one thing that stands in our way is this horrid practical question of what to live upon. I don't suppose Uncle Arthur will be inclined to allow me anything, and I can't marry on my own paltry income and my curacy only. Yet I can't bear to keep Christina waiting indefinitely till some thick-headed squire or other chooses to take it into his opaque brain to give me a decent living.'

From the grocer's the curate walked on, carrying the two tins in his hand, as far as the vicarage. He went into the library, sat down by his own desk, and rang the bell. 'Will you be kind enough to give those things to Carter, John?' he said in his bland voice; 'and tell her to put the jelly in a mould, and let it set. The soup must be warmed with a little fresh stock, and seasoned. Then take them both, with my compliments, to old Mary Long the washerwoman, for her grandchild. Is my uncle in?'

'No, Master Walter,' answered the man—he was always 'Master Walter' to the old servants at his uncle's—'the vicar have gone over by train to Churminster. He told me to tell you he wouldn't be back till evening, after dinner.'

'Did you see him off, John?'

'Yes, Master Walter. I took his portmantew to the station.'

'This will be a good chance, then,' thought Walter Dene to himself. 'Very well, John,' he went on aloud: 'I shall write my sermon now. Don't let anybody come to disturb me.'

John nodded and withdrew. Walter Dene locked the door after him carefully, as he often did when writing sermons, and then lit a cigar, which was also a not infrequent concomitant of his exegetical labours. After that he walked once or twice up and down the room, paused a moment to look at his parchment-covered Rabelais and Villon on the bookshelf, peered out of the dulled glass windows with the crest in their centre, and finally drew a curious bent iron instrument out of his waistcoat pocket. With it in his hands, he went up quietly to his uncle's desk, and began fumbling at the lock in an experienced manner. As a matter of fact, it was not his first trial of skill in lock-picking; for Walter Dene was a painstaking and methodical man, and having made up his mind that he would get at and read his uncle's will, he took good care to begin by fastening all the drawers in his own bedroom, and trying his prentice hand at unfastening them again in the solitude of his chamber.

After half a minute's twisting and turning, the wards gave way gently to his dexterous pressure, and the lid of the desk lay open before him. Walter Dene took out the different papers one by one—there was no need for hurry, and he was not a nervous person—till he came to a roll of parchment, which he recognized at once as the expected will. He unrolled it carefully and quietly, without any womanish trembling or excitement—'thank Heaven,' he said to himself, 'I'm above such nonsense as that'—and sat down leisurely to read it in the big, low, velvet-covered study chair. As he did so, he did not forget to lay a notched foot-rest for his feet, and to put the little Japanese dish on the tiny table by his side to hold his cigar ash. 'And now,' he said, 'for the important question whether Uncle Arthur has left his money to me, or to Arthur, or to both of us equally. He ought, of course, to leave at least half to me, seeing I have become a curate on purpose to please him, instead of following my natural vocation to the Bar; but I shouldn't be a bit surprised if he had left it all to Arthur. He's a pig-headed and illogical old man, the vicar; and he can never forgive me, I believe, because, being the eldest son, I wasn't called after him by my father and mother. As if that was my fault! Some people's ideas of personal responsibility are so ridiculously muddled.'

He composed himself quietly in the arm-chair, and glanced rapidly at the will through the meaningless preliminaries till he came to the significant clauses. These he read more carefully. 'All my estate in the county of Dorset, and the messuage or tenement known as Redlands, in the parish of Lode, in the county of Devon, to my dear nephew, Arthur Dene,' he said to himself slowly: 'Oh, this will never do.' 'And I give and bequeath to my said nephew, Arthur Dene, the sum of ten thousand pounds, three per cent. consolidated annuities, now standing in my name.'—'Oh this is atrocious, quite atrocious! What's this?' 'And I give and bequeath to my dear nephew, Walter Dene, the residue of my personal estate'—'and so forth. Oh no. That's quite sufficient. This must be rectified. The residuary legatee would only come in for a few hundreds or so. It's quite preposterous. The vicar was always an ill-tempered, cantankerous, unaccountable person, but I wonder he has the face to sit opposite me at dinner after that.'

He hummed an air from Schubert, and sat a moment looking thoughtfully at the will. Then he said to himself quietly, 'The simplest thing to do would be merely to scrape out or take out with chemicals the name Arthur, substituting the name Walter, and vice versa. That's a very small matter; a man who draws as well as I do ought to be able easily to imitate a copying clerk's engrossing hand. But it would be madness to attempt it now and here; I want a little practice first. At the same time, I mustn't keep the will out a moment longer than is necessary; my uncle may return by some accident before I expect him; and the true philosophy of life consists in invariably minimizing the adverse chances. This will was evidently drawn up by Watson and Blenkiron, of Chancery Lane. I'll write tomorrow and get them to draw up a will for me, leaving all I possess to Arthur. The same clerk is pretty sure to engross it, and that'll give me a model for the two names on which I can do a little preliminary practice. Besides, I can try the stuff Wharton told me about, for making ink fade on the same parchment. That will be killing two birds with one stone, certainly. And now if I don't make haste I shan't have time to write my sermon.'

He replaced the will calmly in the desk, fastened the lock again with a delicate twirl of the pick, and sat down in his arm-chair to compose his discourse for tomorrow's evensong. 'It's not a bad bit of rhetoric,' he said to himself as he read it over for correction, 'but I'm not sure that I haven't plagiarized a little too freely from Montaigne and dear old Burton[3]. What a pity it must be thrown away upon a Churnside congregation! Not a soul in the whole place will appreciate a word of it, except Christina. Well, well, that alone is enough reward for any man.' And he knocked off his ash pensively into the Japanese ash-pan.

During the course of the next week Walter practised diligently the art of imitating handwriting. He got his will drawn up and engrossed at Watson and Blenkiron's (without signing it, *bien entendu*[4]); and he spent many solitary hours in writing the two names 'Walter' and 'Arthur' on the spare end of parchment, after the manner of the engrossing clerk. He also tested the stuff for making the ink fade to his own perfect satisfaction. And on the next occasion when his uncle was safely off the premises for three hours, he took the will once more deliberately from the desk, removed the obnoxious letters with scrupulous care, and wrote in his own name in place of Arthur's, so that even the engrossing clerk himself would hardly have known the difference. 'There,' he said to himself approvingly, as he took down quiet old George Herbert[5] from the shelf and sat down to enjoy an hour's smoke after the business was over, 'that's one good deed well done, anyhow. I have the calm satisfaction of a clear conscience. The vicar's proposed arrangement was really most unfair; I have substituted for it what Aristotle would have rightly called true distributive justice.[6] For though I've left all the property to myself, by the unfortunate necessity of the case, of course I won't take it all. I'll be juster than the vicar. Arthur shall have his fair share, which is more, I believe, than he'd have done for me; but I hate squalid money-grubbing. If brothers can't be generous and brotherly to one another, what a wretched, sordid little life this of ours would really be!'

Next Sunday morning the vicar preached, and Walter sat looking up at him reflectively from his place in the chancel. A beautiful clear-cut face, the curate's, and seen to great advantage from the doctor's pew, set off by the white surplice, and upturned in quiet meditation towards the elder priest in the pulpit. Walter was revolving many things in his mind, and most of all one adverse chance which he could not just then see his way to minimize. Any day his uncle might take it into his head to read over the will and discover the—ah, well, the rectification. Walter was a man of too much delicacy of feeling even to think of it to himself as a fraud or a forgery. Then, again, the vicar was not a very old man after all; he might live for an indefinite period, and Christina and himself might lose all the best years of their life waiting for a useless person's natural removal. What a pity that threescore was not the utmost limit of human life! For his own part, like the Psalmist, Walter had no desire to outlive his own highest tastes and powers of enjoyment. Ah, well, well, man's prerogative is to better and improve upon nature. If people do not die when they ought, then it becomes clearly necessary for philosophically minded juniors to help them on their way artificially.

It was an ugly necessity, certainly; Walter frankly recognized that fact from the very beginning, and he shrank even from contemplating it; but there was no other way out of the difficulty. The old man had always been a selfish bachelor, with no love for anybody or anything on earth except his books, his coins, his garden, and his dinner; he was growing tired of all except the last; would it not be better for the world at large, on strict utilitarian principles, that he should go at once? True, such steps are usually to be deprecated; but the wise man is a law unto himself, and instead of laying down the wooden, hard-and-fast lines that make conventional morality so much a rule of thumb, he judges every individual case on its own particular merits. Here was Christina's happiness and his own on the one hand, with many collateral advantages to other people, set in the scale against the feeble remnant of a selfish old man's days on the other. Walter Dene had a constitutional horror of taking life in any form, and especially of shedding blood; but he flattered himself that if anything of the sort became clearly necessary, he was not the man to shrink from taking the needful measures to ensure it, at any sacrifice of personal comfort.

All through the next week Walter turned over the subject in his own mind; and the more he thought about it, the more the plan gained in definiteness and consistency as detail after detail suggested itself to him. First he thought of poison. That was the cleanest and neatest way of managing the thing, he considered; and it involved the least unpleasant consequences. To stick a knife or shoot a bullet into any sentient creature was a horrid and revolting act; to put a little tasteless powder into a cup of coffee and let a man sleep off his life quietly was really nothing more than helping him involuntarily to a delightful euthanasia. 'I wish any one would do as much for me at his age, without telling me about it,' Walter said to himself seriously. But then the chances of detection would be much increased by using poison, and Walter felt it an imperative duty to do nothing which would expose Christina to the shock of a discovery. She would not see the matter in the same practical light as he did; women never do; their morality is purely conventional and a wise man will do nothing on earth to shake it. You cannot buy poison without the risk of exciting question. There remained, then, only shooting or stabbing. But shooting makes an awkward noise, and attracts attention at the moment; so the one thing possible was a knife, unpleasant as that conclusion seemed to all his more delicate feelings.

Having thus decided, Walter Dene proceeded to lay his plans with deliberate caution. He had no intention whatsoever of being detected, though his method of action was simplicity itself. It was only bunglers and clumsy fools who got caught; he knew that a man of his intelligence and ability would not make such an idiot of himself as— well, as common ruffians always do. He took his old American bowie-knife, bought years ago as a curiosity, out of the drawer where it had lain so long. It was very rusty, but it would be safer to sharpen it privately on his own hone and strop than to go asking for a new knife at a shop for the express purpose of enabling the shopman afterwards to identify him. He sharpened it for safety's sake during sermon-hour in the library, with the door locked as usual. It took a long time to get off all the rust, and his arm got quickly tired. One morning as he was polishing away at it, he was stopped for a moment by a butterfly which flapped and fluttered against the dulled window-panes. 'Poor thing,' he said to himself, 'it will beat its feathery wings to pieces in its struggles;' and he put a vase of Venetian glass on top of it, lifted the sash carefully, and let the creature fly away outside in the broad sunshine. At the same moment the vicar, who was strolling with his King Charlie on the lawn, came up and looked in at the window. He could not have seen in before, because of the dulled and painted diamonds.

'That's a murderous-looking weapon, Wally,' he said, with a smile, as his glance fell upon the bowie and hone. 'What do you use it for?'

'Oh, it's an American bowie,' Walter answered carelessly. 'I bought it long ago for a curiosity, and now I'm sharpening it up to help me in carving that block of walnut wood.' And he ran his finger lightly along the edge of the blade to test its keenness. What a lucky thing that it was the vicar himself, and not the gardener! If he had been caught by anybody else the fact would have been fatal evidence after all was over. '*Méfiez-vous des papillons*,' he hummed to himself, after Béranger[7], as he shut down the window. 'One more butterfly, and I must give up the game as useless.'

Meanwhile, as Walter meant to make a clean job of it—hacking and hewing clumsily was repulsive to all his finer feelings—he began also to study carefully the anatomy of the human back. He took down all the books on the subject in the library, and by their aid discovered exactly under which ribs the heart lay. A little observation of the vicar, compared with the plates in Quain's *Anatomy*[8] showed him precisely at what point in his clerical coat the most vulnerable interstice was situated. 'It's a horrid thing to have to do,' he thought over and over again as he planned it, 'but it's the only way to secure Christina's happiness.' And so, by a certain bright Friday evening in August, Walter Dene had fully completed all his preparations.

That afternoon, as on all bright afternoons in summer, the vicar went for a walk in the grounds, attended only by little King Charlie. He was squire and parson at once in Churnside, and he loved to make the round of his own estate. At a certain gate by Selbury Copse the vicar always halted to rest awhile, leaning on the bar and looking at the view across the valley. It was a safe and lonely spot. Walter remained at home (he was to take the regular Friday evensong) and went into the study by himself. After a while he took his hat, not without trembling, strolled across the garden, and then made the short cut through the copse, so as to meet the vicar by the gate. On his way he heard the noise of the Dennings in the farm opposite, out rabbit-shooting with their guns and ferrets in the warren. His very soul shrank within him at the sound of that brutal sport. 'Great heavens!' he said to himself, with a shudder; 'to think how I loathe and shrink from the necessity of almost painlessly killing this one selfish old man for an obviously good reason, and those creatures there will go out massacring innocent animals with the aid of a hideous beast of prey, not only without remorse, but actually by way of amusement! I thank Heaven I am not even as they are.'[9] Near the gate he came upon his uncle quietly and naturally, though it would be absurd to deny that at that supreme moment even Walter Dene's equable heart throbbed hard, and his breath went and came tremulously. 'Alone,' he thought to himself, 'and nobody near; this is quite providential,' using even then, in thought, the familiar phraseology of his profession.

'A lovely afternoon, Uncle Arthur,' he said as composedly as he could, accurately measuring the spot on the vicar's coat with his eye meanwhile. 'The valley looks beautiful in this light.'

'Yes, a lovely afternoon, Wally, my boy, and an exquisite glimpse down yonder into the churchyard.'

As he spoke, Walter half leaned upon the gate beside him, and adjusted the knife behind the vicar's back scientifically. Then, without a word more, in spite of a natural shrinking, he drove it home up to the haft, with a terrible effort of will, at the exact spot on the back that the books had pointed out to him. It was a painful thing to do, but he did it carefully and well. The effect of Walter Dene's scientific prevision was even more instantaneous than he had anticipated. Without a single cry, without a sob or a contortion, the vicar's lifeless body fell over heavily by the side of the gate. It rolled down like a log into the dry ditch beneath. Walter knelt trembling on the ground close by, felt the pulse for a moment to assure himself that his uncle was really dead, and having fully satisfied himself on this all-important point, proceeded to draw the knife neatly out of the wound. He had let it fall in the body, in order to extricate it more easily afterward, and not risk pulling it out carelessly so as to get himself covered needlessly by telltale drops of blood, like ordinary clumsy assassins. But he had forgotten to reckon with little King Charlie. The dog jumped piteously upon the body of his master, licked the wound with his tongue, and refused to allow Walter to withdraw the knife. It would be unsafe to leave it there, for it might be recognized. 'Minimize the adverse chances,' he muttered still; but there was no inducing King Charlie to move. A struggle might result in getting drops of blood upon his coat, and then, great heavens, what a terrible awakening for Christina! 'Oh, Christina, Christina, Christina,' he said to himself piteously, 'it is for you only that I could ever have ventured to do this hideous thing.' The blood was still oozing out of the narrow slit, and saturating the black coat, and Walter Dene with his delicate nerves could hardly bear to look upon it.

At last he summoned up resolution to draw out the knife from the ugly wound, in spite of King Charlie, and as he did so, oh, horror! the little dog jumped at it, and cut his left fore-leg against the sharp edge deep to the bone. Here was a pretty accident indeed! If Walter Dene had been a common heartless murderer he would have snatched up the knife immediately, left the poor lame dog to watch and bleed beside his dead master, and skulked off hurriedly from the mute witness to his accomplished crime. But Walter was made of very different mould from that; he could not find it in his heart to leave a poor dumb animal wounded and bleeding for hours together, alone and untended. Just at first, indeed, he tried sophistically to persuade himself his duty to Christina demanded that he should go away at once, and never mind the sufferings of a mere spaniel; but his better nature told him the next moment that such sophisms were indefensible, and his humane instincts overcame even the profound instinct of self-preservation. He sat down quietly beside the warm corpse. 'Thank goodness,' he said, with a slight shiver of disgust, 'I'm not one of those weak-minded people who are troubled by remorse. They would be so overcome by terror at what they had done that they would want to run away from the body immediately, at any price. But I don't think I could feel remorse. It is an incident of lower natures—natures that are capable of doing actions under one set of impulses, which they regret when another set comes uppermost in turn. That implies a want of balance, an imperfect co-ordination of parts and passions. The perfect character is consistent with itself; shame and repentance are confessions of weakness. For my part, I never do anything without having first deliberately decided that it is the best or the only thing to do; and having so done it, I do not draw back like a girl from the necessary consequences of my own act. No fluttering or running away for me. Still, I must admit that all that blood does look very ghastly. Poor old gentleman! I believe he really died almost without knowing it, and that is certainly a great comfort to one under the circumstances.'

He took King Charlie tenderly in his hands, without touching the wounded leg, and drew his pocket handkerchief softly from his pocket. 'Poor beastie,' he said aloud, holding out the cut limb before him, 'you are badly hurt, I'm afraid; but it wasn't my fault. We must see what we can do for you.' Then he wrapped the handkerchief deftly around it, without letting any blood show through, pressed the dog close against his breast, and picked up the knife gingerly by the reeking handle. 'A fool of a fellow would throw it into the river,' he thought, with a curl of his graceful lip. 'They always dredge the river after these incidents. I shall just stick it down a hole in the hedge a hundred yards off. The police have no invention, dull donkeys; they never dredge the hedges.' And he thrust it well down a disused rabbit burrow, filling in the top neatly with loose mould.

Walter Dene meant to have gone home quietly and said evensong, leaving the discovery of the body to be made at haphazard by others, but this unfortunate accident to King Charlie compelled him against his will to give the first alarm. It was absolutely necessary to take the dog to the veterinary at once, or the poor little fellow might bleed to death incontinently. 'One's best efforts,' he thought, 'are always liable to these unfortunate contretemps. I meant merely to remove a superfluous person from an uncongenial environment; yet I can't manage it without at the same time seriously injuring a harmless little creature that I really love.' And with one last glance at the lifeless thing behind him, he took his way regretfully along the ordinary path back towards the peaceful village of Churnside.

Halfway down the lane, at the entrance to the village, he met one of his parishioners. 'Tom,' he said boldly, 'have you seen anything of the vicar? I'm afraid he's got hurt somehow. Here's poor little King Charlie come limping back with his leg cut.'

'He went down the road, zur, 'arf an hour zince, and I arn't zeen him afterwards.'

'Tell the servants at the vicarage to look around the grounds, then; I'm afraid he has fallen and hurt himself. I must take the dog at once to Perkins's, or else I shall be late for evensong.'

The man went off straight toward the vicarage, and Walter Dene turned immediately with the dog in his arms into the village veterinary's.

## 2.

The servants from the vicarage were not the first persons to hit upon the dead body of the vicar. Joe Harley, the poacher, was out reconnoitring that afternoon in the vicar's preserves; and five minutes after Walter Dene had passed down the far side of the hedge, Joe Harley skulked noiselessly from the orchard up to the cover of the gate by Selbury Copse. He crept through the open end by the post (for it was against Joe's principles under any circumstances to climb over an obstacle of any sort, and so needlessly expose himself), and he was just going to slink off along the other hedge, having wires and traps in his pocket, when his boot struck violently against a soft object in the ditch underfoot. It struck so violently that it crushed in the object with the force of the impact; and when Joe came to look at what the object might be, he found to his horror that it was the bruised and livid face of the old parson. Joe had had a brush with keepers more than once, and had spent several months of seclusion in Dorchester Gaol; but, in spite of his familiarity with minor forms of lawlessness, he was moved enough in all conscience by this awful and unexpected discovery. He turned the body over clumsily with his hands, and saw that it had been stabbed in the back once only. In doing so he trod in a little blood, and got a drop or two on his sleeve and trousers; for the pool was bigger now, and Joe was not so handy or dainty with his fingers as the idyllic curate.

It was an awful dilemma, indeed, for a confirmed and convicted poacher. Should he give the alarm then and there, boldly, trusting to his innocence for vindication, and helping the police to discover the murderer? Why, that would be sheer suicide, no doubt; 'for who but would believe,' he thought, ''twas me as done it?' Or should he slink away quietly and say nothing, leaving others to find the body as best they might? That was dangerous enough in its way if anybody saw him, but not so dangerous as the other course. In an evil hour for his own chances Joe Harley chose that worse counsel, and slank off in his familiar crouching fashion towards the opposite corner of the copse.

On the way he heard John's voice holloaing for his master, and kept close to the hedge till he had quite turned the corner. But John had caught a glimpse of him too, and John did not forget it when, a few minutes later, he came upon the horrid sight beside the gate of Selbury Copse.

Meanwhile Walter had taken King Charlie to the veterinary's, and had his leg bound and bandaged securely. He had also gone down to the church, got out his surplice, and begun to put it on in the vestry for evensong, when a messenger came at hot haste from the vicarage, with news that Master Walter must come up at once, for the vicar was murdered.

'Murdered!' Walter Dene said to himself slowly half aloud; 'murdered! how horrible! Murdered!' It was an ugly word, and he turned it over with a genuine thrill of horror. That was what they would say of him if ever the thing came to be discovered! What an inappropriate classification!

He threw aside the surplice, and rushed up hurriedly to the vicarage. Already the servants had brought in the body, and laid it out in the clothes it wore, on the vicar's own bed. Walter Dene went in, shuddering, to look at it. To his utter amazement, the face was battered in horribly and almost unrecognizably by a blow or kick! What could that hideous mutilation mean? He could not imagine. It was an awful mystery. Great heavens! just fancy if any one were to take it into his head that he, Walter Dene, had done that—had kicked a defenceless old gentleman brutally about the face like a common London ruffian! The idea was too horrible to be borne for a moment. It unmanned him utterly, and he hid his face between his two hands and sobbed aloud like one broken-hearted. 'This day's work has been too much for my nerves,' he thought to himself between the sobs; 'but perhaps it is just as well I should give way now completely.'

That night was mainly taken up with the formalities of all such cases; and when at last Walter Dene went off, tired and nerve-worn, to bed, about midnight, he could not sleep much for thinking of the mystery. The murder itself didn't trouble him greatly; that was over and past now, and he felt sure his precautions had been amply sufficient to protect him even from the barest suspicion; but he couldn't fathom the mystery of that battered and mutilated face! Somebody must have seen the corpse between the time of the murder and the discovery! Who could that somebody have been? and what possible motive could he have had for such a horrible piece of purposeless brutality?

As for the servants, in solemn conclave in the hall, they had unanimously but one theory to account for all the facts: some poacher or other, for choice Joe Harley, had come across the vicar in the copse, with gun and traps in hand. The wretch had seen he was discovered, had felled the poor old vicar by a blow in the face with the butt-end of his rifle, and after he fell, fainting, had stabbed him for greater security in the back. That was such an obvious solution of the difficulty, that nobody in the servants' hall had a moment's hesitation in accepting it.

When Walter heard next morning early that Joe Harley had been arrested overnight, on John's information, his horror and surprise at the news were wholly unaffected. Here was another new difficulty, indeed. 'When I did the thing,' he said to himself, 'I never thought of that possibility. I took it for granted it would be a mystery, a problem for the local police (who, of course, could no more solve it than they could solve the *pons-asinorum*[10]), but it never struck me they would arrest an innocent person on the charge instead of me. This is horrible. It's so easy to make out a case against a poacher, and hang him for it, on suspicion. One's whole sense of justice revolts against the thing. After all, there's a great deal to be said in favour of the ordinary commonplace morality: it prevents complications. A man of delicate sensibilities oughtn't to kill anybody; he lets himself in for all kinds of unexpected contingencies, without knowing it.'

At the coroner's inquest things looked very black indeed for Joe Harley. Walter gave his evidence first, showing how he had found King Charlie wounded in the lane; and then the others gave theirs, as to the search for and finding of the body. John in particular swore to having seen a man's back and head slinking away by the hedge while they were looking for the vicar; and that back and head he felt sure were Joe Harley's. To Walter's infinite horror and disgust, the coroner's jury returned a verdict of wilful murder against the poor poacher. What other verdict could they possibly have given in accordance with such evidence?

The trial of Joe Harley for the wilful murder of the Reverend Arthur Dene was fixed for the next Dorchester Assizes. In the interval, Walter Dene, for the first time in his placid life, knew what it was to undergo a mental struggle. Whatever happened, he could not let Joe Harley be hanged for this murder. His whole soul rose up within him in loathing for such an act of hideous injustice. For though Walter Dene's code of morality was certainly not the conventional one, as he so often boasted to himself, he was not by any means without any code of morals of any sort. He could commit a murder where he thought it necessary, but he could not let an innocent man suffer in his stead. His ethical judgment on that point was just as clear and categorical as the judgment which told him he was in duty bound to murder his uncle. For Walter did not argue with himself on moral questions: he perceived the right and necessary thing intuitively; he was a law to himself, and he obeyed his own law implicitly, for good or for evil. Such men are capable of horrible and diabolically deliberate crimes; but they are capable of great and genuine self-sacrifices also.

Walter made no secret in the village of his disinclination to believe in Joe Harley's guilt. Joe was a rough fellow, he said, certainly, and he had no objection to taking a pheasant or two, and even to having a free fight with the keepers; but, after all, our game laws were an outrageous piece of class legislation, and he could easily understand how the poor, whose sense of justice they outraged, should be so set against them. He could not think Joe Harley was capable of a detestable crime. Besides, he had seen him himself within a few minutes before and after the murder. Everybody thought it such a proof of the young parson's generous and kindly disposition; he had certainly the charity which thinketh no evil[11]. Even though his own uncle had been brutally murdered on his own estate, he checked his natural feelings of resentment, and refused to believe that one of his own parishioners could have been

guilty of the crime. Nay, more, so anxious was he that substantial justice should be done the accused, and so confident was he of his innocence, that he promised to provide counsel for him at his own expense;
and he provided two of the ablest barristers on the Western circuit.

Before the trial, Walter Dene had come, after a terrible internal
struggle, to an awful resolution. He would do everything he could for
Joe Harley; but if the verdict went against him, he was resolved, then
and there, in open court, to confess, before judge and jury, the whole
truth. It would be a horrible thing for Christina; he knew that; but he
could not love Christina so much, 'loved he not honour more;'[12] and
honour, after his own fashion, he certainly loved dearly. Though he
might be false to all that all the world thought right, it was ingrained
in the very fibre of his soul to be true to his own inner nature at least.
Night after night he lay awake, tossing on his bed, and picturing to his
mind's eye every detail of that terrible disclosure. The jury would bring
in a verdict of guilty: then, before the judge put on his black cap, he,
Walter, would stand up, and tell them that he could not let another
man hang for his crime; he would have the whole truth out before
them; and then he would die, for he would have taken a little bottle of
poison at the first sound of the verdict. As for Christina—oh, Christina!—Walter Dene could not dare to let himself think upon that. It
was horrible; it was unendurable; it was torture a thousand times worse
than dying: but still, he must and would face it. For in certain phases,
Walter Dene, forger and murderer as he was, could be positively heroic.

The day of the trial came, and Walter Dene, pale and haggard
with much vigil, walked in a dream and faintly from his hotel to the
court-house. Everybody present noticed what a deep effect the shock
of his uncle's death had had upon him. He was thinner and more
bloodless than usual, and his dulled eyes looked black and sunken in

their sockets. Indeed, he seemed to have suffered far more intensely than the prisoner himself, who walked in firmer and more erect, and took his seat doggedly in the familiar dock. He had been there more than once before, to say the truth, though never before on such an errand. Yet mere habit, when he got there, made him at once assume the hang-dog look of the consciously guilty.

Walter sat and watched and listened, still in a dream, but without once betraying in his face the real depth of his innermost feelings. In the body of the court he saw Joe's wife, weeping profusely and ostentatiously, after the fashion considered to be correct by her class; and though he pitied her from the bottom of his heart, he could only think by contrast of Christina. What were that good woman's fears and sorrows by the side of the grief and shame and unspeakable horror he might have to bring upon his Christina? Pray Heaven the shock, if it came, might kill her outright; that would at least be better than that she should live long years to remember. More than judge, or jury, or prisoner, Walter Dene saw everywhere, behind the visible shadows that thronged the court, that one persistent prospective picture of heart-broken Christina.

The evidence for the prosecution told with damning force against the prisoner. He was a notorious poacher; the vicar was a game-preserver. He had poached more than once on the ground of the vicarage. He was shown by numerous witnesses to have had an animus against the vicar. He had been seen, not in the face, to be sure, but still seen and recognized, slinking away, immediately after the fact, from the scene of the murder. And the prosecution had found stains of blood, believed by scientific experts to be human, on the clothing he had worn when he was arrested. Walter Dene listened now with terrible, unabated earnestness, for he knew that in reality it was he himself who was upon his trial. He himself, and Christina's happiness; for if the poacher were found guilty, he was firmly resolved, beyond hope of respite, to tell all, and face the unspeakable.

The defence seemed indeed a weak and feeble theory. Somebody unknown had committed the murder, and this somebody, seen from behind, had been mistaken by John for Joe Harley. The blood-stains need not be human[13], as the cross-examination went to show, but were only known by counter-experts to be mammalian—perhaps a rabbit's. Every poacher—and it was admitted that Joe was a poacher—was liable to get his clothes blood-stained. Grant they were human, Joe, it appeared, had himself once shot off his little finger. All these points came out from the examination of the earlier witnesses. At last, counsel put the curate himself into the box, and proceeded to examine him briefly as a witness for the defence.

Walter Dene stepped, pale and haggard still, into the witness-box. He had made up his mind to make one final effort 'for Christina's happiness.' He fumbled nervously all the time at a small glass phial in his pocket, but he answered all questions without a moment's hesitation, and he kept down his emotions with a wonderful composure which excited the admiration of everybody present. There was a general hush to hear him. Did he see the prisoner, Joseph Harley, on the day of the murder? Yes, three times. When was the first occasion? From the library window, just before the vicar left the house. What was Joseph Harley then doing? Walking in the opposite direction from the copse. Did Joseph Harley recognize him? Yes, he touched his hat to him. When was the second occasion? About ten minutes later, when he, Walter, was leaving the vicarage for a stroll. Did Joseph Harley then recognize him? Yes, he touched his hat again, and the curate said, 'Good morning, Joe; a fine day for walking.' When was the third time? Ten minutes later again, when he was returning from the lane, carrying wounded little King Charlie. Would it have been physically possible for the prisoner to go from the vicarage to the spot where the murder was committed, and back again, in the interval between the first two occasions? It would not. Would it have been physically possible for the prisoner to do so in the interval between the second and third occasions? It would not.

'Then in your opinion, Mr Dene, it is physically impossible that Joseph Harley can have committed this murder?'

'In my opinion, it is physically impossible.'

While Walter Dene solemnly swore amid dead silence to this treble lie, he did not dare to look Joe Harley once in the face; and while Joe Harley listened in amazement to this unexpected assistance to his case—for counsel, suspecting a mistaken identity, had not questioned him too closely on the subject—he had presence of mind enough not to let his astonishment show upon his stolid features. But when Walter had finished his evidence in chief, he stole a glance at Joe; and for a moment their eyes met. Then Walter's fell in utter self-humiliation; and he said to himself fiercely, 'I would not so have debased and degraded myself before any man to save my own life—what is my life worth me, after all?—but to save Christina, to save Christina, to save Christina! I have brought all this upon myself for Christina's sake.'

Meanwhile, Joe Harley was asking himself curiously what could be the meaning of this new move on parson's part. It was deliberate perjury, Joe felt sure, for parson could not have mistaken another person for him three times over; but what good end for himself could parson hope to gain by it? If it was he who had murdered the vicar (as Joe strongly suspected), why did he not try to press the charge home against the first person who happened to be accused, instead of committing a distinct perjury on purpose to compass his acquittal? Joe Harley, with his simple everyday criminal mind, could not be expected to unravel the intricacies of so complex a personality as Walter Dene's.

But even there, on trial for his life, he could not help wondering what on earth young parson could he driving at in this business.

The judge summed up with the usual luminously obvious alternate platitudes. If the jury thought that John had really seen Joe Harley, and that the curate was mistaken in the person whom he thrice saw, or was mistaken once only out of the thrice, or had miscalculated the time between each occurrence, or the time necessary to cover the ground to the gate, then they would find the prisoner guilty of wilful murder. If, on the other hand, they believed John had judged hastily, and that the curate had really seen the prisoner three separate times, and that he had rightly calculated all the intervals, then they would find the prisoner not guilty. The prisoner's case rested entirely upon the alibi. Supposing they thought there was a doubt in the matter, they should give the prisoner the benefit of the doubt. Walter noticed that the judge said in every other case, 'If you believe the witness So-and-so,' but that in his case he made no such discourteous reservation. As a matter of fact, the one person whose conduct nobody for a moment dreamt of calling in question was the real murderer.

The jury retired for more than an hour. During all that time two men stood there in mortal suspense, intent and haggard, both upon their trial, but not both equally. The prisoner in the dock fixed his arms in a dogged and sullen attitude, the colour half gone from his brown cheek, and his eyes straining with excitement, but showing no outward sign of any emotion except the craven fear of death. Walter Dene stood almost fainting in the body of the court, his bloodless fingers still fumbling nervously at the little phial, and his face deadly pale with the awful pallor of a devouring horror. His heart scarcely beat at all, but at each long slow pulsation he could feel it throb distinctly within his bosom. He saw or heard nothing before him, but kept his aching eyes fixed steadily on the door by which the jury were to enter.

Junior counsel nudged one another to notice his agitation, and whispered that that poor young curate had evidently never seen a man tried for his life before.

At last the jury entered. Joe and Walter waited, each in his own manner, breathless for the verdict. 'Do you find the prisoner at the bar guilty or not guilty of wilful murder?' Walter took the little phial from his pocket, and held it carefully between his finger and thumb. The awful moment had come; the next word would decide the fate of himself and Christina. The foreman of the jury looked up solemnly, and answered with slow distinctness, 'Not guilty.' The prisoner leaned back vacantly, and wiped his forehead; but there was an awful cry of relief from one mouth in the body of the court, and Walter Dene sank back into the arms of the bystanders, exhausted with suspense and overcome by the reaction. The crowd remarked among themselves that young Parson Dene was too tender-hearted a man to come into court at a criminal trial. He would break his heart to see even a dog hanged, let alone his fellow-Christians. As for Joe Harley, it was universally admitted that he had had a narrow squeak of it, and that he had got off better than he deserved. The jury gave him the benefit of the doubt.

As soon as all the persons concerned had returned to Churnside, Walter sent at once for Joe Harley. The poacher came to see him in the vicarage library. He was elated and coarsely exultant with his victory, as a relief from the strain he had suffered, after the manner of all vulgar natures.

'Joe,' said the clergyman slowly, motioning him into a chair at the other side of the desk, 'I know that after this trial Churnside will not be a pleasant place to hold you. All your neighbours believe, in spite of the verdict, that you killed the vicar. I feel sure, however, that you did not commit this murder. Therefore, as some compensation for the suffering of mind to which you have been put, I think it well to send you and your wife and family to Australia or Canada, whichever you like best. I propose also to make you a present of a hundred pounds, to set you up in your new home.'

'Make it five hundred, passon,' Joe said, looking at him significantly.

Walter smiled quietly, and did not flinch in any way. 'I said a hundred,' he continued calmly, 'and I will make it only a hundred. I should have had no objection to making it five, except for the manner in which you ask it. But you evidently mistake the motive of my gift. I give it out of pure compassion for you, and not out of any other feeling whatsoever.'

'Very well, passon,' said Joe sullenly, 'I accept it.'

'You mistake again,' Walter went on blandly, for he was himself again now. 'You are not to accept it as terms; you are to thank me for it as a pure present. I see we two partially understand each other; but it is important you should understand me exactly as I mean it. Joe Harley, listen to me seriously. I have saved your life. If I had been a man of a coarse and vulgar nature, if I had been like you in a similar predicament, I would have pressed the case against you for obvious personal reasons, and you would have been hanged for it. But I did not press it, because I felt convinced of your innocence, and my sense of justice rose irresistibly against it. I did the best I could to save you; I risked my own reputation to save you; and I have no hesitation now in telling you that to the best of my belief, if the verdict had gone against you, the person who really killed the vicar, accidentally or intentionally, meant to have given himself up to the police, rather than let an innocent man suffer.'

THE STORIES OF GRANT ALLEN

'Passon,' said Joe Harley, looking at him intently, 'I believe as you're tellin' me the truth. I zeen as much in that person's face afore the verdict.'

There was a solemn pause for a moment; and then Walter Dene said slowly, 'Now that you have withdrawn your claim as a claim, I will stretch a point and make it five hundred. It is little enough for what you have suffered. But I, too, have suffered terribly, terribly.'

'Thank you, passon,' Joe answered. 'I zeen as you were turble anxious.'

There was again a moment's pause. Then Walter Done asked quietly, 'How did the vicar's face come to be so bruised and battered?'

'I stumbled up agin 'im accidental like, and didn't know I'd kicked 'un till I'd done it. Must 'a been just a few minutes after you'd 'a left 'un.'

'Joe,' said the curate in his calmest tone, 'you had better go; the money will be sent to you shortly. But if you ever see my face again, or speak or write a word of this to me, you shall not have a penny of it, but shall be prosecuted for intimidation. A hundred before you leave, four hundred in Australia. Now go.'

'Very well, passon,' Joe answered; and he went.

'Pah!' said the curate with a face of disgust, shutting the door after him, and lighting a perfumed pastille in his little Chinese porcelain incense-burner, as if to fumigate the room from the poacher's offensive presence. 'Pah! to think that these affairs should compel one to humiliate and abase one's self before a vulgar clod like that! To think that all his life long that fellow will virtually know—and misinterpret—my secret. He is incapable of understanding that I did it as a duty to Christina. Well, he will never dare to tell it, that's certain, for nobody would believe him if he did; and he may congratulate himself heartily that he's got well out of this difficulty. It will be the luckiest thing in the end that ever happened to him. And now I hope this little episode is finally over.'

When the Churnside public learned that Walter Dene meant to carry his belief in Joe Harley's innocence so far as to send him and his family at his own expense out to Australia, they held that the young parson's charity and guilelessness was really, as the doctor said, almost Quixotic. And when, in his anxiety to detect and punish the real murderer, he offered a reward of five hundred pounds from his own pocket for any information leading to the arrest and conviction of the criminal, the Churnside people laughed quietly at his extraordinary child-like simplicity of heart. The real murderer had been caught and tried at Dorchester Assizes, they said, and had only got off by the skin of his teeth because Walter himself had come forward and sworn to a quite improbable and inconclusive alibi. There was plenty of time for Joe to have got to the gate by the short cut, and that he did so everybody at Churnside felt morally certain. Indeed, a few years later a blood-stained bowie-knife was found in the hedge not far from the scene of the murder, and the gamekeeper 'could almost 'a took his Bible oath he'd zeen just such a knife along o' Joe Harley.'

That was not the end of Walter Dene's Quixotisms, however. When the will was read, it turned out that almost everything was left to the young parson; and who could deserve it better, or spend it more charitably? But Walter, though he would not for the world seem to cast any slight or disrespect upon his dear uncle's memory, did not approve of customs of primogeniture, and felt bound to share the estate equally with his brother Arthur. 'Strange,' said the head of the firm of Watson and Blenkiron to himself, when he read the little paragraph about this generous conduct in the paper; 'I thought the instructions were to leave it to his nephew Arthur, not to his nephew

Walter; but there, one forgets and confuses names of people that one does not know so easily.' 'Gracious goodness!' thought the engrossing clerk; 'surely it was the other way on. I wonder if I can have gone and copied the wrong names in the wrong places?' But in a big London business, nobody notes these things as they would have been noted in Churnside; the vicar was always a changeable, pernickety, huffy old fellow, and very likely he had had a reverse will drawn up afterwards by his country lawyer. All the world only thought that Walter Dene's generosity was really almost ridiculous, even in a parson. When he was married to Christina, six months afterwards, everybody said so charming a girl was well mated with so excellent and admirable a husband.

And he really did make a very tender and loving husband and father. Christina believed in him always, for he did his best to foster and keep alive her faith. He would have given up active clerical duty if he could, never having liked it (for he was above hypocrisy), but Christina was against the project, and his bishop would not hear of it. The Church could ill afford to lose such a man as Mr Dene, the bishop said, in these troubled times; and he begged him as a personal favour to accept the living of Churnside, which was in his gift. But Walter did not like the place, and asked for another living instead, which, being of less value—'so like Mr Dene to think nothing of the temporalities,'—the bishop even more graciously granted. He has since published a small volume of dainty little poems on uncut paper, considered by some critics as rather pagan in tone for a clergyman, but universally allowed to be extremely graceful, the perfection of poetical form with much delicate mastery of poetical matter. And everybody knows that the author is almost certain to be offered the first vacant canonry in his own cathedral. As for the little episode, he himself has almost forgotten all about it; for those who think a murderer must feel remorse his whole life long, are trying to read their own emotional nature into the wholly dispassionate character of Walter Dene.

---

[1] **Not a trace of Perpendicularity.** A late, plainer phase of the Gothic architecture of the Middle Ages. It fell out of favour and was little used in the 19th century Gothic Revival. The Houses of Parliament are an exception.

[2] **'linked sweetness long drawn out'.** From Milton's *L'Allegro*, a poem detailing how a happy man should live in the country.

[3] **plagiarized a little too freely from Montaigne and dear old Burton.** Michel de Montaigne's *Essays* of 1570-92 (his motto was 'What do I know?') and Robert Burton, author of *The Anatomy of Melancholy* (1621): both discursive works full of miscellaneous information, readily mined for quotations and examples.

[4] *bien entendu.* 'Naturally' or 'of course'.

[5] **quiet old George Herbert.** The religious Metaphysical poet (*d.*1633) and a man of saintly life.

[6] **Aristotle ... true distributive justice.** In his *Ethics* Aristotle defined this as the fair allocation of the wealth in a society, according to its prevailing norms.

[7] *'Méfiez-vous des papillons'* ... **Béranger.** 'Beware the butterflies', adapted from a song by the French songwriter Pierre-Jean de Béranger (*d.*1857).

[8] **the plates in Quain's *Anatomy*.** There were three medical Quains, all related, in the 19th century. The reference is probably to Quain & Wilson's *A Series of Anatomical Plates in Lithography* (1836–42).

[9] **I am not even as they are.** The Pharisee in Luke 18:11 was condemned by Jesus, after thanking God he was not like other sinful men.

[10] **than they could solve the *pons-asinorum*.** 'Bridge of donkeys'. A fairly complex geometrical proof, said to be called so because in Euclid's mathematical book it marks the point where the problems start to become difficult.

[11] **the charity which thinketh no evil.** A phrase from St Paul's First Epistle to the Corinthians.

[12] **'loved he not honour more'.** From Lovelace's poem 'To Lucasta, Going to the Warres': 'I could not love thee, dear, so much,/ Loved I not honour more'.

[13] **The blood-stains need not be human.** A forensic test specifically for human blood was devised in 1901, but it did not become fully reliable until some years later.

# THE CHILD OF THE PHALANSTERY

Francis Galton coined the word 'eugenics' in 1883 to describe 'the study of the agencies under social control, that improve or impair the racial qualities of future generations'. Forcible sterilisations in the United States and the killing of the 'unfit' by the Nazis in Germany eventually poisoned the debate over eugenics for ever, but throughout Grant Allen's working life it was a hot topic. Right up to the end of the 1930s, everyone had an opinion on eugenics: clergymen, social commentators and anthropologists; physiologists and philanthropists; economists and politicians of every stripe.

The model for Allen's 'Avondale Phalanstery' was probably the Oneida Community. It was founded in 1848, the year Allen was born, in New York State, not very far from his Canadian home town. Under its founder J.H. Noyes, it pursued a positive eugenical programme for ten years up to 1879, which was just when Allen's career was getting under way. At Oneida a committee selected which couples should breed, and fifty-eight children were born by this process, twelve of them sired by Noyes and his son. None of them proved exceptionally gifted.

Fictional interest in eugenics reached its apogee in Aldous Huxley's *Brave New World* (1932). Here there are no square pegs in round holes for the good reason that babies are bred to fit into the role predetermined for them. The State applies ruthlessly the mechanisms of both 'positive' and 'negative' eugenics. As foetuses, future rocket pilots are spun around in their breeding bottles so they will actually prefer life upside down; whereas the future Epsilon Semi-morons are starved of oxygen in their bottles to keep them 'below par'. After birth, Pavlovian conditioning and sleep-teaching reinforce their embryonic fate.

Grant Allen would have smiled grimly had he lived to read Huxley's dystopia. He wanted, not fewer of the unfit, but more of the fit, and saw nothing but harm and decadence in 'man-breeding' in the Oneidan manner. He thought the best way of ensuring the birth of sturdy, intelligent, superior children was to encourage women to be voluntary eugenic gatekeepers. He held that it was a woman's duty to find the best males to father her children. (If healthy she should be State-supported and aim to have four.) In the millennium she might, at different times, be attracted by 'this splendid athlete, by that profound thinker, by that nobly-moulded Adonis, by that high-souled poet.' That, he argued, was the best assurance against women becoming the mothers of 'a long family of scrofulous idiots'.

Naturally, writing for the *Belgravia* magazine in 1884, Allen could not even hint at any such arrangement. So he restricts himself to the case for the prosecution. Every sentence of his story is heavily ironical. His Olive and Eustace are as decorous and enervated a pair of Victorian lovers as the most puritanical reader could wish for—and there's the rub. Passionate young lovers don't waste time worrying about the future of 'divine humanity'. They act on pure impulsive instinct: they defy their parents, run away, outrage community conventions—in short, follow the 'internal divine motor' of Nature herself. The Avondale Phalanstery is decadent, and its people are slipping into what Allen called elsewhere 'a tame stereotyped pattern of amiable imbecility.' The feebly sentimental tone in which the story is told reflects this.

Allen thought there was empirical evidence that illegitimate children, born of lusty passion, are demonstrably healthier than others. He applied this to himself: he told H.G. Wells, half-jokingly perhaps, that his own semi-invalid state was due to his coming from too many generations of respectable married folk!

'*Poor little thing,*' said my strong-minded friend compassionately. '*Just look at her! Clubfooted. What a misery to herself and others! In a well-organised state of society, you know, such poor wee cripples as that would be quietly put out of their misery while they were still babies.*'

'*Let me think,*' said I, '*how that would work out in actual practice. I'm not so sure, after all, that we should be altogether the better or the happier for it.*'

## 1.

THEY SAT together in a corner of the beautiful phalanstery[1] garden, Olive and Clarence, on the marble seat that overhung the mossy dell where the streamlet danced and bickered among its pebbly stickles; they sat there, hand in hand, in lovers' guise, and felt their two bosoms beating and thrilling in some strange, sweet fashion, just like two foolish unregenerate young people of the old antisocial prephalansteric days. Perhaps it was the leaven of their unenlightened ancestors still leavening by heredity the whole lump[2]; perhaps it was the inspiration of the calm soft August evening and the delicate afterglow of the setting sun; perhaps it was the deep heart of man and woman vibrating still as of yore in human sympathy, and stirred to its innermost recesses by the unutterable breath of human emotion. But at any rate there they sat, the beautiful strong man in his shapely chiton, and the dainty fair girl in her long white robe with the dark green embroidered border, looking far into the fathomless depths of one another's eyes, in silence sweeter and more eloquent than many words. It was Olive's tenth day holiday from her share in the maidens' household duty of the community; and Clarence, by arrangement with his friend Germain, had made exchange from his own decade[3] (which fell on Plato) to this quiet Milton evening, that he might wander through the park and gardens with his chosen love, and speak his full mind to her now without reserve.

'If only the phalanstery will give its consent, Clarence,' Olive said at last with a little sigh, releasing her hand from his, and gathering up the folds of her stole from the marble flooring of the seat;—'if only the phalanstery will give its consent! but I have my doubts about it. Is it quite right? Have we chosen quite wisely? Will the hierarch and the elder brothers think I am strong enough and fit enough for the duties of the task? It is no light matter, we know, to enter into bonds with one another for the responsibilities of fatherhood and motherhood. I sometimes feel—forgive me, Clarence—but I sometimes feel as if I were allowing my own heart and my own wishes to guide me too exclusively in this solemn question: thinking too much about you and me, about ourselves (which is only an enlarged form of selfishness, after all), and too little about the future good of the community and— and'— blushing a little, for women will be women even in a phalanstery—'and of the precious lives we may be the means of adding to it. You remember, Clarence, what the hierarch said, that we ought to think least and last of our own feelings, first and foremost of the progressive evolution of universal humanity.'

'I remember, darling,' Clarence answered, leaning over towards her tenderly; 'I remember well, and in my own way, so far as a man can (for we men haven't the moral earnestness of you women, I'm afraid, Olive), I try to act up to it. But, dearest, I think your fears are greater than they need be: you must recollect that humanity requires for its higher development tenderness, and truth, and love, and all the softer qualities, as well as strength and manliness; and if you are a trifle less strong than most of our sisters here, you seem to me at least (and I really believe to the hierarch and to the elder brothers too) to make up for it, and more than make up for it, in your sweet and lovable inner nature. The men of the future mustn't all be cast in one unvarying stereotyped mould; we must have a little of all good types combined, in order to make a perfect phalanstery.'

Olive sighed again. 'I don't know,' she said pensively. 'I don't feel sure. I hope I am doing right. In my aspirations every evening I have desired light on this matter, and have earnestly hoped that I was not being misled by my own feelings; for, oh, Clarence, I do love you so dearly, so truly, so absorbingly, that I half fear my love may be taking me unwittingly astray. I try to curb it; I try to think of it all as the hierarch tells us we ought to; but in my own heart I sometimes almost fear that I may be lapsing into the idolatrous love of the old days, when people married and were given in marriage, and thought only of the gratification of their own personal emotions and affections, and nothing of the ultimate good of humanity. Oh, Clarence, don't hate me and despise me for it; don't turn upon me and scold me; but I love you, I love you, I love you; oh, I'm afraid I love you almost idolatrously!'

Clarence lifted her small white hand slowly to his lips, with that natural air of chivalrous respect which came so easily to the young men of the phalanstery, and kissed it twice over fervidly with quiet reverence. 'Let us go into the music-room, Olive dearest,' he said as he rose; 'you are too sad tonight. You shall play me that sweet piece of Marian's that you love so much; and that will quiet you, darling, from thinking too earnestly about this serious matter.'

## 2.

Next day, when Clarence had finished his daily spell of work in the fruit-garden (he was third under-gardener to the community), he went up to his own study, and wrote out a little notice in due form to be posted at dinner-time on the refectory door: 'Clarence and Olive ask leave of the phalanstery to enter with one another into free contract of holy matrimony.' His pen trembled a little in his hand as he framed that familiar set form of words (strange that he had read it so often with so little emotion, and wrote it now with so much: we men are so selfish!); but he fixed it boldly with four small brass nails on the regulation notice-board, and waited, not without a certain quiet confidence, for the final result of the communal council.

'Aha!' said the hierarch to himself with a kindly smile, as he passed into the refectory at dinner-time that day, 'has it come to that, then? Well, well, I thought as much; I felt sure it would. A good girl, Olive: a true, earnest, lovable girl: and she has chosen wisely, too; for Clarence is the very man to balance her own character as man's and wife's should do. Whether Clarence has done well in selecting her is another matter. For my own part, I had rather hoped she would have joined the celibate sisters, and have taken nurse-duty for the sick and the children. It's her natural function in life, the work she's best fitted for; and I should have liked to see her take to it. But, after all, the business of the phalanstery is not to decide vicariously for its individual members—not to thwart their natural harmless inclinations and wishes; on the contrary, we ought to allow every man and girl the fullest liberty to follow their own personal taste and judgment in every possible matter. Our power of interference as a community, I've always felt and said, should only extend to the prevention of obviously wrong and immoral acts, such as marriage with a person in ill-health, or of inferior mental power, or with a distinctly bad or insubordinate temper. Things of that sort, of course, are as clearly wicked as idling in work-hours, or marriage with a first cousin[4]. Olive's health, however, isn't really bad, nothing more than a very slight feebleness of constitution, as constitutions go with us; and Eustace, who has attended her medically from her babyhood (what a dear crowing little thing she used to be in the nursery, to be sure!), tells me she's perfectly fitted for the duties of her proposed situation. Ah well, ah well; I've no doubt they'll be perfectly happy; and the wishes of the whole phalanstery will go with them in any case, that's certain.'

Everybody knew that whatever the hierarch said or thought was pretty sure to be approved by the unanimous voice of the entire community. Not that he was at all a dictatorial or dogmatic old man; quite the contrary; but his gentle kindly way had its full weight with the brothers; and his intimate acquaintance, through the exercise of his spiritual functions, with the inmost thoughts and ideas of every individual member, man or woman, made him a safe guide in all difficult or delicate questions, as to what the decision of the council ought to be. So when, on the first Cosmos, the elder brothers assembled to transact phalansteric business, and the hierarch put in Clarence's request with the simple phrase, 'In my opinion, there is no reasonable objection,' the community at once gave in its adhesion, and formal notice was posted an hour later on the refectory door, 'The phalanstery approves the proposition of Clarence and Olive, and wishes all happiness to them and to humanity from the sacred union they now contemplate.' 'You see, dearest,' Clarence said, kissing her lips for the first time (as unwritten law demanded), now that the seal of the community had been placed upon their choice, 'you see, there can't be any harm in our contract, for the elder brothers all approve it.'

Olive smiled and sighed from the very bottom of her full heart, and clung to her lover as the ivy clings to a strong supporting oak-tree. 'Darling,' she murmured in his ear, 'if I have you to comfort me, I shall not be afraid, and we will try our best to work together for the advancement and the good of divine humanity.'

Four decades later, on a bright Cosmos morning in September, those two stood up beside one another before the altar of humanity, and heard with a thrill the voice of the hierarch uttering that solemn declaration, 'In the name of the Past, and of the Present, and of the Future, I hereby admit you, Clarence and Olive, into the holy society of Fathers and Mothers, of the United Avondale Phalanstery, in trust for humanity, whose stewards you are. May you so use and enhance the good gifts you have received from your ancestors that you may hand them on, untarnished and increased, to the bodies and minds of your furthest descendants.' And Clarence and Olive answered humbly and reverently, 'If grace be given us, we will.'

## 3.

Brother Eustace, physiologist to the phalanstery, looked very grave and sad indeed as he passed from the Mothers' Room into the Conversazione[5] in search of the hierarch. 'A child is born into the phalanstery,' he said gloomily; but his face conveyed at once a far deeper and more pregnant meaning than his mere words could carry to the ear.

The hierarch rose hastily and glanced into his dark keen eyes with an inquiring look. 'Not something amiss?' he said eagerly, with an infinite tenderness in his fatherly voice. 'Don't tell me that, Eustace. Not ... oh, not a child that the phalanstery must not for its own sake permit to live! Oh, Eustace, not, I hope, idiotic! And I gave my consent too; I gave my consent for pretty gentle little Olive's sake! Heaven grant I was not too much moved by her prettiness and her delicacy; for I love her, Eustace, I love her like a daughter.'

'So we all love the children of the phalanstery, Cyriac, we who are elder brothers,' said the physiologist gravely, half smiling to himself nevertheless at this quaint expression of old-world feeling on the part even of the very hierarch, whose bounden duty it was to advise and persuade a higher rule of conduct and thought than such antique phraseology implied. 'No, not idiotic; not quite so bad as that, Cyriac; not absolutely a hopeless case, but still, very serious and distressing for all that. The dear little baby has its feet turned inward. She'll be a cripple for life, I fear, and no help for it.'

Tears rose unchecked into the hierarch's soft grey eyes. 'Its feet turned inward,' he muttered sadly, half to himself. 'Feet turned inward! Oh, how terrible! This will be a frightful blow to Clarence and to Olive. Poor young things! their first-born, too. Oh, Eustace, what an awful thought that, with all the care and precaution we take to keep all causes of misery away from the precincts of the phalanstery, such trials as this must needs come upon us by the blind workings of the unconscious Cosmos! It is terrible, too terrible!'

'And yet it isn't all loss,' the physiologist answered earnestly. 'It isn't all loss, Cyriac, heart-rending as the necessity seems to us. I sometimes think that if we hadn't these occasional distressful objects on which to expend our sympathy and our sorrow, we in our happy little communities might grow too smug, and comfortable, and material, and earthly. But things like this bring tears into our eyes, and we are the better for them in the end, depend upon it, we are the better for them. They try our fortitude, our devotion to principle, our obedience to the highest and the hardest law. Every time some poor little waif like this is born into our midst, we feel the strain of old prephalansteric emotions and fallacies of feeling dragging us steadily and cruelly down. Our first impulse is to pity the poor mother, to pity the poor child, and in our mistaken kindness to let an unhappy life go on indefinitely to its own misery and the preventable distress of all around it. We have to make an effort, a struggle, before the higher and more abstract pity conquers the lower and more concrete one. But in the end we are all the better for it: and each such struggle and each such victory, Cyriac, paves the way for that final and truest morality when we shall do right instinctively and naturally, without any impulse on any side to do wrong in any way at all.'

'You speak wisely, Eustace,' the hierarch answered with a sad shake of his head, 'and I wish I could feel like you. I ought to, but I can't. Your functions make you able to look more dispassionately upon these things than I can. I'm afraid there's a great deal of the old Adam lingering wrongfully in me yet. And I'm still more afraid there's a great deal of the old Eve lingering even more strongly in all our mothers. It'll be a long time, I doubt me, before they'll ever consent without a struggle to the painless extinction of necessarily unhappy and imperfect lives. A long time: a very long time. Does Clarence know of this yet?'

'Yes, I have told him. His grief is terrible. You had better go and console him as best you can.'

'I will, I will. And poor Olive! Poor Olive! It wrings my heart to think of her. Of course she won't be told of it, if you can help, for the probationary four decades?'

'No, not if we can help it: but I don't know how it can ever be kept from her. She will see Clarence, and Clarence will certainly tell her.'

The hierarch whistled gently to himself. 'It's a sad case,' he said ruefully, 'a very sad case; and yet I don't see how we can possibly prevent it.'

He walked slowly and deliberately into the anteroom where Clarence was seated on a sofa, his head between his hands, rocking himself to and fro in his mute misery, or stopping to groan now and then in a faint feeble inarticulate fashion. Rhoda, one of the elder sisters, held the unconscious baby sleeping in her arms, and the hierarch took it from her like a man accustomed to infants, and looked ruefully at the poor distorted little feet. Yes, Eustace was evidently quite right. There could be no hope of ever putting those wee twisted ankles back straight and firm into their proper place again like other people's.

He sat down beside Clarence on the sofa, and with a commiserating gesture removed the young man's hands from his pale white face. 'My dear, dear friend,' he said softly, 'what comfort or consolation can we try to give you that is not a cruel mockery? None, none, none. We can only sympathise with you and Olive: and perhaps, after all, the truest sympathy is silence.'

Clarence answered nothing for a moment, but buried his face once more in his hands and burst into tears. The men of the phalanstery were less careful to conceal their emotions than we old-time folks in these early centuries. 'Oh, dear hierarch,' he said, after a long sob, 'it is too hard a sacrifice, too hard, too terrible! I don't feel it for the baby's sake: for her 'tis better so: she will be freed from a life of misery and dependence; but for my own sake, and oh, above all, for dear Olive's! It will kill her, hierarch; I feel sure it will kill her!'

The elder brother passed his hand with a troubled gesture across his forehead. 'But what else can we do, dear Clarence?' he asked pathetically. 'What else can we do? Would you have us bring up the dear child to lead a lingering life of misfortune, to distress the eyes of all around her, to feel herself a useless encumbrance in the midst of so many mutually helpful and serviceable and happy people? How keenly she would realise her own isolation in the joyous, busy, labouring community of our phalansteries! How terribly she would brood over her own misfortune when surrounded by such a world of hearty, healthy, sound-limbed, useful persons! Would it not be a wicked and a cruel act to bring her up to an old age of unhappiness and imperfection? You have been in Australia, my boy, when we sent you on that plant-hunting expedition, and you have seen cripples with your own eyes, no doubt, which I have never done—thank Heaven!—I who have never gone beyond the limits of the most highly civilised Euramerican countries. You have seen cripples, in those semi-civilised old colonial societies, which have lagged after us so slowly in the path of progress; and would you like your own daughter to grow up to such a life as that, Clarence? would you like her, I ask you, to grow up to such a life as that?'

Clarence clenched his right hand tightly over his left arm, and answered with a groan, 'No, hierarch; not even for Olive's sake could I wish for such an act of irrational injustice. You have trained us up to know the good from the evil, and for no personal gratification of our deepest emotions, I hope and trust, shall we ever betray your teaching or depart from your principles. I know what it is: I saw just such a cripple once, at a great town in the heart of Central Australia—a child of eight years old, limping along lamely on her heels by her mother's side; a sickening sight: to think of it even now turns the blood in one's arteries; and I could never wish Olive's baby to live and grow up to be a thing like that. But, oh, I wish to heaven it might have been otherwise: I wish to heaven this trial might have been spared us both. Oh, hierarch, dear hierarch, the sacrifice is one that no good man or woman would wish selfishly to forgo; yet for all that, our hearts, our hearts are human still; and though we may reason and may act up to our reasoning, the human feeling in us—relic of the idolatrous days, or whatever you like to call it—it will not choose to be so put down and stifled: it will out, hierarch, it will out for all that, in real hot, human tears. Oh, dear, dear kind father and brother, it will kill Olive: I know it will kill her!'

'Olive is a good girl,' the hierarch answered slowly. 'A good girl, well brought up, and with sound principles. She will not flinch from doing her duty, I know, Clarence; but her emotional nature is a very delicate one, and we have reason indeed to fear the shock to her nervous system. That she will do right bravely, I don't doubt: the only danger is lest the effort to do right should cost her too dear. Whatever can be done to spare her shall be done, Clarence. It is a sad misfortune for the whole phalanstery, such a child being born to us as this: and we all sympathise with you: we sympathise with you more deeply than words can say.'

The young man only rocked up and down drearily as before, and murmured to himself, 'It will kill her, it will kill her! My Olive, my Olive, I know it will kill her.'

## 4.

They didn't keep the secret of the baby's crippled condition from Olive till the four decades were over, nor anything like it. The moment she saw Clarence, she guessed at once with a woman's instinct that something serious had happened; and she didn't rest till she had found out from him all about it. Rhoda brought her the poor wee mite, carefully wrapped, after the phalansteric fashion, in a long strip of fine flannel, and Olive unrolled the piece until she came at last upon the small crippled feet, that looked so soft and tender and dainty and waxen in their very deformity. The young mother leant over the child a moment in speechless misery. 'Spirit of Humanity,' she whispered at length feebly, 'oh, give me strength to bear this terrible, unutterable trial! It will break my heart. But I will try to bear it.'

There was something so touching in her attempted resignation that Rhoda, for the first time in her life, felt almost tempted to wish she had been born in the old wicked prephalansteric days, when they would have let the poor baby grow up to womanhood as a matter of course, and bear its own burden through life as best it might. Presently, Olive raised her head again from the crimson silken pillow. 'Clarence,' she said, in a trembling voice, pressing the sleeping baby hard against her breast, 'when will it be? How long? Is there no hope, no chance of respite?'

'Not for a long time yet, dearest Olive,' Clarence answered through his tears. 'The phalanstery will be very gentle and patient with us, we know; and brother Eustace will do everything that lies in his power, though he's afraid he can give us very little hope indeed. In any case, Olive darling, the community waits for four decades before deciding anything: it waits to see whether there is any chance for physiological or surgical relief: it decides nothing hastily or thoughtlessly: it waits for every possible improvement, hoping against hope till hope itself is hopeless. And then, if at the end of the quartet, as I fear will be the case—for we must face the worst, darling, we must face the worst—if at the end of the quartet it seems clear to brother Eustace, and the three assessor physiologists from the neighbouring phalansteries, that the dear child would be a cripple for life, we're still allowed four decades more to prepare ourselves in: four whole decades more, Olive, to take our leave of the darling baby. You'll have your baby with you for eighty days. And we must wean ourselves from her in that time, darling. We must try to wean ourselves. But oh Olive, oh Rhoda, it's very hard: very, very, very hard.'

Olive answered not a word, but lay silently weeping and pressing the baby against her breast, with her large brown eyes fixed vacantly upon the fretted woodwork of the panelled ceiling.

'You mustn't do like that, Olive dear,' sister Rhoda said in a half-frightened voice. 'You must cry right out, and sob, and not restrain yourself, darling, or else you'll break your heart with silence and repression. Do cry aloud, there's a dear girl: do cry aloud and relieve yourself. A good cry would be the best thing on earth for you. And think, dear, how much happier it will really be for the sweet baby to sink asleep so peacefully than to live a long life of conscious inferiority and felt imperfection! What a blessing it is to think you were born in a phalansteric land, where the dear child will be happily and painlessly rid of its poor little unconscious existence, before it has reached the age when it might begin to know its own incurable and inevitable misfortune! Oh, Olive, what a blessing that is, and how thankful we ought all to be that we live in a world where the sweet pet will be saved so much humiliation, and mortification, and misery!'

At that moment, Olive, looking within into her own wicked, rebellious heart, was conscious, with a mingled glow, half shame, half indignation, that so far from appreciating the priceless blessings of her own situation, she would gladly have changed places then and there with any barbaric woman of the old semi-civilised prephalansteric days. We can so little appreciate our own mercies. It was very wrong and anti-cosmic, she knew; very wrong indeed, and the hierarch would have told her so at once; but in her own woman's soul she felt she would rather be a miserable naked savage in a wattled hut, like those one saw in old books about Africa before the illumination, if only she could keep that one little angel of a crippled baby, than dwell among all the enlightenment, and knowledge, and art, and perfected social arrangements of phalansteric England without her child—her dear, helpless, beautiful baby. How truly the Founder himself had said, 'Think you there will be no more tragedies and dramas in the world when we have reformed it, nothing but one dreary dead level of monotonous content? Ay, indeed, there will; for that, fear not; while the heart of man remains, there will be tragedy enough on earth and to spare for a hundred poets to take for their saddest epics.'

Olive looked up at Rhoda wistfully. 'Sister Rhoda,' she said in a timid tone, 'it may be very wicked—I feel sure it is—but do you know, I've read somewhere in old stories of the unenlightened days that a mother always loved the most afflicted of her children the best. And I can understand it now, sister Rhoda; I can feel it here,' and she put her hand upon her poor still heart. 'If only I could keep this one dear crippled baby, I could give up all the world beside—except you, Clarence.'

'Oh, hush, darling!' Rhoda cried in an awed voice, stooping down half alarmed to kiss her pale forehead. 'You mustn't talk like that, Olive dearest. It's wicked; it's undutiful. I know how hard it is not to repine and to rebel; but you mustn't, Olive, you mustn't. We must each strive to bear our own burdens (with the help of the community), and not to put any of them off upon a poor, helpless, crippled little baby.'

'But our natures,' Clarence said, wiping his eyes dreamily; 'our natures are only half attuned as yet to the necessities of the higher social existence. Of course it's very wrong and very sad, but we can't help feeling it, sister Rhoda, though we try our hardest. Remember, it's not so many generations since our fathers would have reared the child without a thought that they were doing anything wicked—nay, rather, would even have held (so powerful is custom) that it was positively wrong to save it by preventive means from a certain life of predestined misery. Our conscience in this matter isn't yet fully formed. We feel that it's right, of course; oh yes, we know the phalanstery has ordered everything for the best; but we can't help grieving over it; the human heart within us is too unregenerate still to acquiesce without a struggle in the dictates of right and reason.'

Olive again said nothing, but fixed her eyes silently upon the grave, earnest portrait of the Founder over the carved oak mantelpiece, and let the hot tears stream their own way over her cold, white, pallid, bloodless cheek without reproof for many minutes. Her heart was too full for either speech or comfort.

## 5.

Eight decades passed away slowly in the Avondale Phalanstery; and day after day seemed more and more terrible to poor, weak, disconsolate Olive. The quiet refinement and delicate surroundings of their placid life seemed to make her poignant misery and long anxious term of waiting only the more intense in its sorrow and its awesomeness. Every day the younger sisters turned as of old to their allotted round of pleasant housework; every day the elder sisters, who had earned their leisure, brought in their dainty embroidery, or their drawing materials, or their other occupations, and tried to console her, or rather to condole with her, in her great sorrow. She couldn't complain of any unkindness; on the contrary, all the brothers and sisters were sympathy itself; while Clarence, though he tried hard not to be too idolatrous to her (which is wrong and antisocial, of course), was still overflowing with tenderness and consideration for her in their common grief. But all that seemed merely to make things worse. If only somebody would have been cruel to her; if only the hierarch would have scolded her, or the elder sisters have shown any distant coldness, or the other girls have been wanting in sisterly sympathy, she might have got angry or brooded over her wrongs; whereas, now, she could do nothing save cry passively with a vain attempt at resignation. It was nobody's fault; there was nobody to be angry with, there was nothing to blame except the great impersonal laws and circumstances of the Cosmos, which it would be rank impiety and wickedness to question or to gainsay. So she endured in silence, loving only to sit with Clarence's hand in hers, and the dear doomed baby lying peacefully upon the stole in her lap. It was inevitable, and there was no use repining; for so profoundly had the phalanstery schooled the minds and natures of those two unhappy young parents (and all their compeers), that grieve as they might, they never for one moment dreamt of attempting to relax or set aside the fundamental principles of phalansteric society in these matters.

By the kindly rule of the phalanstery, every mother had complete freedom from household duties for two years after the birth of her child; and Clarence, though he would not willingly have given up his own particular work in the grounds and garden, spent all the time he could spare from his short daily task (every one worked five hours every lawful day, and few worked longer, save on special emergencies) by Olive's side. At last, the eight decades passed slowly away, and the fatal day for the removal of little Rosebud arrived. Olive called her Rosebud because, she said, she was a sweet bud that could never be opened into a full-blown rose. All the community felt the solemnity of the painful occasion; and by common consent the day (Darwin, December 20) was held as an intra-phalansteric fast by the whole body of brothers and sisters.

On that terrible morning Olive rose early, and dressed herself carefully in a long white stole with a broad black border of Greek key pattern. But she had not the heart to put any black upon dear little Rosebud; and so she put on her fine flannel wrapper, and decorated it instead with the pretty coloured things that Veronica and Philomela had worked for her, to make her baby as beautiful as possible on this its last day in a world of happiness. The other girls helped her and tried to sustain her, crying all together at the sad event. 'She's a sweet little thing,' they said to one another as they held her up to see how she looked. 'If only it could have been her reception today instead of her removal!' But Olive moved through them all with stoical resignation—dry-eyed and parched in the throat, yet saying not a word save for necessary instructions and directions to the nursing sisters. The iron of her creed had entered into her very soul.

After breakfast, brother Eustace and the hierarch came sadly in their official robes into the lesser infirmary. Olive was there already, pale and trembling, with little Rosebud sleeping peacefully in the hollow of her lap. What a picture she looked, the wee dear thing, with the hothouse flowers from the conservatory that Clarence had brought to adorn her fastened neatly on to her fine flannel robe! The physiologist took out a little phial from his pocket, and began to open a sort of inhaler of white muslin. At the same moment, the grave, kind old hierarch stretched out his hands to take the sleeping baby from its mother's arms. Olive shrank back in terror, and clasped the child softly to her heart. 'No, no, let me hold her myself, dear hierarch,' she said, without flinching. 'Grant me this one last favour. Let me hold her myself.' It was contrary to all fixed rules; but neither the hierarch nor any one else there present had the heart to refuse that beseeching voice on so supreme and spirit-rending an occasion.

Brother Eustace poured the chloroform solemnly and quietly on to the muslin inhaler. 'By resolution of the phalanstery,' he said, in a voice husky with emotion, 'I release you, Rosebud, from a life for which you are naturally unfitted. In pity for your hard fate, we save you from the misfortune you have never known, and will never now experience.' As he spoke he held the inhaler to the baby's face, and watched its breathing grow fainter and fainter, till at last, after a few minutes, it faded gradually and entirely away. The little one had slept from life into death, painlessly and happily, even as they looked.

Clarence, tearful but silent, felt the baby's pulse for a moment, and then, with a burst of tears, shook his head bitterly. 'It is all over,' he cried with a loud cry. 'It is all over; and we hope and trust it is better so.'

But Olive still said nothing.

The physiologist turned to her with an anxious gaze. Her eyes were open, but they looked blank and staring into vacant space. He took her hand, and it felt limp and powerless. 'Great heaven!' he cried, in evident alarm, 'what is this? Olive, Olive, our dear Olive, why don't you speak?'

Clarence sprang up from the ground, where he had knelt to try the dead baby's pulse, and took her unresisting wrist anxiously in his. 'Oh, brother Eustace,' he cried passionately, 'help us, save us; what's the matter with Olive? she's fainting, she's fainting! I can't feel her heart beat, no, not ever so little.'

Brother Eustace let the pale white hand drop listlessly from his grasp upon the pale white stole beneath, and answered slowly and distinctly: 'she isn't fainting, Clarence; not fainting, my dear brother. The shock and the fumes of chloroform together have been too much for the action of the heart. She's dead too, Clarence; our dear, dear sister; she's dead too.'

Clarence flung his arms wildly round Olive's neck, and listened eagerly with his ear against her bosom to hear her heart beat. But no sound came from the folds of the simple black-bordered stole; no sound from anywhere save the suppressed sobs of the frightened women who huddled closely together in the corner, and gazed horror-stricken upon the two warm fresh corpses.

'She was a brave girl,' brother Eustace said at last, wiping his eyes and composing her hands reverently. 'Olive was a brave girl, and she died doing her duty, without one murmur against the sad necessity that fate had unhappily placed upon her. No sister on earth could wish to die more nobly than by thus sacrificing her own life and her own weak human affections on the altar of humanity for the sake of her child and of the world at large.'

143

'And yet, I sometimes almost fancy,' the hierarch murmured, with a violent effort to control his emotions, 'when I see a scene like this, that even the unenlightened practices of the old era may not have been quite so bad as we usually think them, for all that. Surely an end such as Olive's is a sad and a terrible end to have forced upon us as the final outcome and natural close of all our modern phalansteric civilisation.'

'The ways of the Cosmos are wonderful,' said brother Eustace solemnly; 'and we, who are no more than atoms and mites upon the surface of its meanest satellite, cannot hope so to order all things after our own fashion that all its minutest turns and chances may approve themselves to us as right in our own eyes.'

The sisters all made instinctively the reverential genuflexion. 'The Cosmos is infinite,' they said together, in the fixed formula of their cherished religion. 'The Cosmos is infinite, and man is but a parasite upon the face of the least among its satellite members. May we so act as to further all that is best within us, and to fulfil our own small place in the system of the Cosmos with all becoming reverence and humility! In the name of universal Humanity. So be it.'

---

[1] **Phalanstery.** A proposed utopian community based on the ideas of Charles Fourier (1772-1837), the word being a combination of 'phalanx' and 'monastery'. For esoteric reasons, each phalanstery was to comprise exactly 1620 people. Fourier's ideas were sexually radical—he proposed the community should keep a card-index to facilitate residents' choice of partners—but eugenic practices as such did not figure. Several phalansteries had a brief existence in the United States in the mid-19th century, notably Brook Farm in the 1840s, fictionalised by Hawthorne in *The Blithedale Romance*. No such community, as far as is known, sanctioned the murder of disabled children, as in the story.

[2] **leavening ... the whole lump.** A metaphor from St Paul's Epistle to the Galatians 5.

[3] **his own decade.** Reorganising the week into 10 days named after great historical figures is Allen's invention.

[4] **marriage with a first cousin.** An anxiety-making practice much discussed by biologists in Victorian times, although never illegal in Britain. Both Darwin and Queen Victoria married their cousins. A question on such marriages was considered for the census of 1871 but dropped.

[5] **Conversazione.** Allen's invented term for what Fourier called a *seristère*, a large hall with adjacent small rooms in the phalanstery for social interactions.

# THE MYSTERIOUS OCCURRENCE IN PICCADILLY

Grant Allen prided himself on spotting topics of public interest that might become material for his fiction. Like many authors, he kept notebooks in which to jot down anecdotes, gossip and stray items of information that might stir his imagination, always being anxious, as he said, 'to keep pace with every changing breath of popular favour'. This story is a good example of that. It appeared under a pen-name in the *Belgravia* magazine in May 1884.

Spiritualism and the holding of *séances*, together with increasing interest in related phenomena like telepathy, ghost-hunting, apparitions, *etc.* had been building up in the 1870s, and this led in February 1882 to the founding in London of the Society for Psychical Research. Among its members were some of Britain's most eminent names in science, philosophy and literature. The aim of the SPR was to investigate scientifically several possibly fruitful areas of the paranormal and follow the findings wherever they might lead. No doubt Allen, who was interested in everything but had no time for supernaturalism in any form, followed its early activities with amused and sceptical attention.

There is an interesting sidenote to this story. The month *after* it was published there appeared an article in the *Nineteenth Century* magazine by two of the top investigators of the SPR. Titled 'Visible Apparitions', it cited a letter from a distinguished judge in Shanghai, Sir Edmund Hornby, recounting a remarkable experience he had had in January 1875—that is, nearly ten years earlier. The apparition of a journalist, he claimed, had appeared at his bedside in the middle of the night, it being revealed the next day that the man had unexpectedly died at that very same time. When this issue of the magazine got back to Shanghai, an enterprising editor soon discovered that none of the details of this weird tale could possibly be true. What gave them an extra piquancy was Hornby's claim that his wife woke up just after the ghostly visitant had left their bedroom, whereupon he told her what had happened. However, it emerged that at the date in question Hornby was unmarried. He did marry (for the third time), but only some months later. He was fifty. His bride was thirty years younger. Much hilarity ensued.

It is possible that Allen had knowledge of Hornby's letter well before publication. One of his friends was the philosopher-psychologist George Croom Robertson, who was a member of a circle including Edmund Gurney, co-author of the 'Apparitions' article.

Whether this is so or not, Allen gives a pitch-perfect imitation, in Prof. W. Bryce Murray's account of the Piccadilly 'mystery', of the pompous, orotund style—what his disrespectful son-in-law says mockingly is his 'admirable and perspicuous language'—that Hornby used. In its early days the Achilles heel of the SPR was what the historian Roger Luckhurst has called 'the regular invocation of gentlemanly guarantee'—that is to say, its undue readiness to take at face value, without much or any investigation, accounts of weird events when they came from high-status informants like Hornby.

*A Mysterious Occurrence* employs a simple device to generate an apparently inexplicable situation—one which might well have had the earnest seekers of the SPR at a loss for a rational explanation, just like Professor Bryce Murray. It relies, of course, on the rapidity and efficiency of late-Victorian communications, and it must be admitted that Allen pushed them to their limit and perhaps beyond to make his ingenious plot work. For a modern reader, the most 'supernatural' element might be that it was then possible to post a letter in Oxford around 6.30 *pm* and have it collected, sorted, transported and delivered in London by the last post that same evening!

# 1.

I REALLY never felt so profoundly ashamed of myself in my whole life as when my father-in-law, Professor W. Bryce Murray, of Oriel College, Oxford, sent me the last number of the *Proceedings of the Society for the Investigation of Supernatural Phenomena*[1]. As I opened the pamphlet, a horrible foreboding seized me that I should find in it, detailed at full length, with my name and address in plain printing (not even asterisks), that extraordinary story of his about the mysterious occurrence in Piccadilly. I turned anxiously to page 14, which I saw was neatly folded over at the corner; and there, sure enough, I came upon the Professor's remarkable narrative, which I shall simply extract here, by way of introduction, in his own admirable and perspicuous language.

'I wish to communicate to the Society,' says my respected relation, 'a curious case of wraiths or doubles, which came under my own personal observation, and for which I can vouch on my own authority, and that of my son-in-law, Dr Owen Mansfield, keeper of Accadian Antiquities at the British Museum. It is seldom, indeed, that so strange an example of a supernatural phenomenon can be independently attested by two trustworthy scientific observers, both still living.

'On the 12th of May, 1873—I made a note of the circumstance at the time, and am therefore able to feel perfect confidence as to the strict accuracy of my facts—I was walking down Piccadilly about four o'clock in the afternoon, when I saw a simulacrum or image approaching me from the opposite direction, exactly resembling in outer appearance an undergraduate of Oriel College, of the name of Owen Mansfield. It must be carefully borne in mind that at this time I was not related or connected with Mr Mansfield in any way, his marriage with my daughter having taken place some eleven months later: I only knew him then as a promising junior member of my own College. I was just about to approach and address Mr Mansfield, when a most singular and mysterious event took place. The simulacrum appeared spontaneously to glide up towards me with a peculiarly rapid and noiseless motion, waved a wand or staff which it bore in its hands thrice round my head, and then vanished hastily in the direction of an hotel which stands at the corner of Albemarle Street. I followed it quickly to the door, but on inquiry of the porter, I learned that he himself had observed nobody enter. The simulacrum seems to have dissipated itself or become invisible suddenly in the very act of passing through the folding glass portals which give access to the hotel from Piccadilly.

'That same evening, by the last post[2], I received a hastily-written note from Mr Mansfield, bearing the Oxford postmark, dated Oriel College, *5pm*, and relating the facts of an exactly similar apparition which had manifested itself to him, with absolute simultaneity of occurrence. On the very day and hour when I had seen Mr Mansfield's wraith in Piccadilly, Mr Mansfield himself was walking down the Corn Market in Oxford, in the direction of the Taylor Institute[3]. As he approached the corner, he saw what he took to be a vision or image of myself, his tutor, moving towards him in my usual leisurely manner. Suddenly, as he was on the point of addressing me with regard to my Aristotle lecture the next morning, the image glided up to him in a rapid and evasive manner, shook a green silk umbrella with a rhinoceros-horn handle three times around his head, and then disappeared incomprehensibly through the door of the Randolph Hotel. Returning to college in a state of breathless alarm and surprise, at what he took to be an act of incipient insanity or extreme inebriation on my part, Mr Mansfield learnt from the porter, to his intense astonishment, that I was at that moment actually in London. Unable to conceal his amazement at this strange event, he wrote me a full account of the facts while they were still fresh in his memory: and as I preserve his note to this day, I append a copy of it to my present communication, for publication in the Society's *Transactions*.

'There is one small point in the above narrative to which I would wish to call special attention, and that is the accurate description given by Mr Mansfield of the umbrella carried by the apparition he observed in Oxford. This umbrella exactly coincided in every particular with the one I was then actually carrying in Piccadilly. But what is truly remarkable, and what stamps the occurrence as a genuine case of supernatural intervention, is the fact that *Mr Mansfield could not possibly ever have seen that umbrella in my hands, because I had only just that afternoon purchased it at a shop in Bond Street.* This, to my mind, conclusively proves that no mere effort of fancy or visual delusion based upon previous memories, vague or conscious, could have had anything whatsoever to do with Mr Mansfield's observation at least. It was, in short, distinctly an objective apparition, as distinguished from a mere subjective reminiscence or hallucination.'

As I laid down the *Proceedings* on the breakfast table with a sigh, I said to my wife (who had been looking over my shoulder while I read): 'Now, Nora, we're really in for it. What on earth do you suppose I'd better do?'

Nora looked at me with her laughing eyes laughing harder and brighter than ever. 'My dear Owen,' she said, putting the *Proceedings* promptly into the waste paper basket, 'there's really nothing on earth possible now, except to make a clean breast of it.'

I groaned. 'I suppose you're right,' I answered, 'but it's a precious awkward thing to have to do. However, here goes.' So I sat down at once with pen, ink, and paper at my desk, to draw up this present narrative as to the real facts about the 'Mysterious Occurrence in Piccadilly.'

## 2.

In 1873 I was a fourth-year man, going in for my Greats[4] at the June examination. But as if Aristotle and Mill and the affair of Corcyra[5] were not enough to occupy one young fellow's head at the age of twenty-three, I had foolishly gone and fallen in love, undergraduate fashion, with the only really pretty girl (I insist upon putting it, though Nora has struck it out with her pen) in all Oxford. She was the daughter of my tutor, Professor Bryce Murray, and her name (as the astute reader will already have inferred) was Nora.

The Professor had lost his wife some years before, and he was left to bring up Nora by his own devices, with the aid of his sister, Miss Lydia Amelia Murray, the well-known advocate of female education, woman's rights, anti-vaccination, vegetarianism, the Tichborne claimant[6], and psychic force. Nora, however, had no fancy for any of these multifarious interests of her aunt's: I have reason to believe she takes rather after her mother's family: and Miss Lydia Amelia Murray early decided that she was a girl of no intellectual tastes of any sort, who had better be kept at school at South Kensington as much as possible. Especially did Aunt Lydia hold it to be undesirable that Nora should ever come in contact with that very objectionable and wholly antagonistic animal, the Oriel undergraduate. Undergraduates were well known to laugh openly at woman's rights, to devour underdone beefsteaks with savage persistence, and to utter most irreverent and ribald jests about psychic force.

Still, it is quite impossible to keep the orbit of a Professor's daughter from occasionally crossing that of a stray meteoric undergraduate. Nora only came home to Oxford in vacation time: but during the preceding Long I had stopped up for the sake of pursuing my Accadian studies[7] in a quiet spot, and it was then that I first quite accidentally met Nora. I was canoeing on the Cherwell one afternoon, when I came across the Professor and his daughter in a punt, and saw the prettiest girl in all Oxford actually holding the pole in her own pretty little hands, while that lazy old man lolled back at his ease with a book, on the luxurious cushions in the stern. As I passed the punt, I capped the Professor, of course, and looking back a minute later I observed that the pretty daughter had got her pole stuck fast in the mud, and couldn't, with all her force, pull it out again. In another minute she had lost her hold of it, and the punt began to drift of itself down the river towards Iffley.

Common politeness naturally made me put back my canoe, extricate the pole, and hand it as gracefully as I could to the Professor's daughter. As I did so, I attempted to raise my straw hat cautiously with one hand, while I gave back the pole with the other: an attempt which of course compelled me to lay down my paddle on the front of the canoe, as I happen to be only provided with two hands, instead of four like our earlier ancestors. I don't know whether it was my instantaneous admiration for Nora's pretty blush, which distracted my attention from the purely practical question of equilibrium, or whether it was her own awkwardness and modesty in taking the pole, or finally whether it was my tutor's freezing look that utterly disconcerted me, but at any rate, just at that moment, something unluckily (or rather luckily) caused me to lose my balance altogether. Now, everybody knows that a canoe is very easily upset: and in a moment, before I knew exactly where I was, I found the canoe floating bottom upward about three yards away from me, and myself standing, safe and dry, in my tutor's punt, beside his pretty blushing daughter. I had felt the canoe turning over as I handed back the pole, and had instinctively jumped into the safer refuge of the punt, which saved me at least the ignominy of appearing before Miss Nora Murray in the ungraceful attitude of clambering back, wet and dripping, into an upset canoe.

The inexorable logic of facts had thus convinced the Professor of the impossibility of keeping all undergraduates permanently at a safe distance: and there was nothing open for him now except resignedly to acquiesce in the situation so created for him. However much he might object to my presence, he could hardly, as a Christian and a gentleman, request me to jump in and swim after my canoe, or even, when we had at last successfully brought it alongside with the aid of the pole, to seat myself once more on the soaking cushions. After all, my mishap had come about in the endeavour to render him a service: so he was fain with what grace he could to let me relieve his daughter of the pole, and punt him back as far as the barges, with my own moist and uncomfortable bark trailing casually from the stern.

As for Nora, being thus thrown unexpectedly into the dangerous society of that gruesome animal, the Oriel undergraduate, I think I may venture to say (from my subsequent experience) that she was not wholly disposed to regard the creature as either so objectionable or so ferocious as she had been previously led to imagine. We got on together so well that I could see the Professor growing visibly wrathful about the corners of the mouth: and by the time we reached the barges, he could barely be civil enough to say Good Morning to me when we parted.

An introduction, however, no matter how obtained, is really in these matters absolutely everything. As long as you don't know a pretty girl, you don't know her, and you can't take a step in advance without an introduction. But when once you do know her, heaven and earth and aunts and fathers may try their hardest to prevent you, and yet whatever they try they can't keep you out. I was so far struck with Nora, that I boldly ventured whenever I met her out walking with her father or her aunt, to join myself to the party: and though they never hesitated to show me that my presence was not rapturously welcomed, they couldn't well say to me point-blank, 'Have the goodness, Mr Mansfield, to go away and not to speak to me again in future.' So the end of it was, that before the beginning of October term, Nora and I understood one another perfectly, and had even managed, in a few minutes' *tête-à-tête* in the parks, to whisper to one another the ingenuous vows of sweet seventeen and two-and-twenty.

When the Professor discovered that I had actually written a letter to his daughter, marked 'Private and Confidential,' his wrath knew no bounds. He sent for me to his rooms, and spoke to me severely. 'I've half a mind, Mansfield,' he said, 'to bring the matter before a college meeting. At any rate, this conduct must not be repeated. If it is, Sir,'— he didn't finish the sentence, preferring to terrify me by the effective figure of speech which commentators describe as an aposiopesis[8]: and I left him with a vague sense that if it *was* repeated I should probably incur the penalties of *præmunire* (whatever they may be), or be hanged, drawn, and quartered, with my head finally stuck as an adornment on the acute wings of the Griffin, *vice* Temple Bar[9] removed.

Next day, Nora met me casually at a confectioner's in the High, where I will frankly confess that I was engaged in experimenting upon the relative merits of raspberry cream and lemon water ices. She gave me her hand timidly, and whispered to me half under her breath, 'Papa's so dreadfully angry, Owen, and I'm afraid I shall never be able to meet you any more, for he's going to send me back this very afternoon to South Kensington, and keep me away from Oxford altogether in future.' I saw her eyes were red with crying, and that she really thought our little romance was entirely at an end.

'My darling Nora,' I replied in an undertone, 'even South Kensington is not so unutterably remote that I shall never be able to see you there. Write to me whenever you are able, and let me know where I can write to you. My dear little Nora, if there were a hundred papas and a thousand Aunt Lydias interposed in a square between us, don't you know we should manage all the same to love one another and to overcome all difficulties?'

Nora smiled and half cried at once, and then discreetly turned to order half a pound of *glacé* cherries. And that was the last that I saw of her for the time at Oxford.

During the next term or two, I'm afraid I must admit that the relations between my tutor and myself were distinctly strained, so much so as continually to threaten the breaking out of open hostilities. It wasn't merely that Nora was in question, but the Professor also suspected me of jeering in private at his psychical investigations. And if the truth must be told, I will admit that his suspicions were not wholly without justification. It began to be whispered among the undergraduates just then that the Professor and his sister had taken to turning *planchettes*[10], interrogating easy-chairs, and obtaining interesting details about the present abode of Shakespeare or Milton from intelligent and well-informed five-o'clock tea-tables. It had long been well known that the Professor took a deep interest in haunted houses, considered that the portents recorded by Livy[11] must have something in them, and declared himself unable to be sceptical as to facts which had convinced such great men as Plato, Seneca, and Samuel Johnson. But the table-turning was a new fad, and we noisy undergraduates occasionally amused ourselves by getting up an amateur *séance*, in imitation of the Professor, and eliciting psychical truths, often couched in a surprisingly slangy or even indecorous dialect, from a very lively though painfully irreverent spirit, who discoursed to us through the material intervention of a rickety what-not. However, as the only mediums we employed were the very unprofessional ones of two plain decanters, respectively containing port and sherry, the Professor (who was a teetotaller, and who paid five guineas a *séance* for the services of that distinguished psychical specialist, Dr Grade) considered the interesting results we obtained as wholly beneath the dignity of scientific inquiry. He even most unworthily endeavoured to stifle research by gating us all one evening when a materialized spirit, assuming the outer form of the junior exhibitioner, sang a comic song of the period in a loud voice with the windows open, and accompanied itself noisily with a psychical tattoo on the rickety what-not. The Professor went so far as to observe sarcastically that our results appeared to him to be rather spirituous than spiritual.

On May 11, 1873 (I will endeavour to rival the Professor in accuracy and preciseness), I got a short note from dear Nora, dated from South Kensington, which I, too (though not from psychical motives), have carefully preserved. I will not publish it, however, either here or in the Society's *Proceedings*, for reasons which will probably be obvious to any of my readers who happen ever to have been placed in similar circumstances themselves. Disengaging the kernel of fact from the irrelevant matter in which it was imbedded, I may state that Nora wrote me somewhat to this effect. She was going next day to the Academy with the parents of some schoolfellow; could I manage to run up to town for the day, go to the Academy myself, and meet her 'quite accidentally, you know, dear,' in the Water-colour room about half-past eleven?

This was rather awkward; for next day, as it happened, was precisely the Professor's morning for the Herodotus lecture; but circumstances like mine at that moment know no law. So I succeeded in excusing myself from attendance somehow or other (I hope truthfully) and took the 9*am* express up to town. Shortly after eleven I was at the Academy, and waiting anxiously for Nora's arrival. That dear little hypocrite, the moment she saw me approach, assumed such an inimitable air of infantile surprise and innocent pleasure at my unexpected appearance that I positively blushed for her wicked powers of deception.

'You here, Mr Mansfield!' she cried in a tone of the most apparently unaffected astonishment, 'why, I thought it was full term time; surely you ought to be up at Oriel.'

'so I am,' I answered, 'officially; but in my private capacity I've come up for the day to look at the pictures.'

'Oh, how nice!' said that shocking little Nora, with a smile that was childlike and bland. 'Mr Mansfield is such a great critic, Mrs Worplesdon; he knows all about art, and artists, and so on. He'll be able to tell us which pictures we ought to admire, you know, and which aren't worth looking at. Mr Worplesdon, let me introduce you; Mrs Worplesdon—Miss Worplesdon. How very lucky we should have happened to come across you, Mr Mansfield!'

The Worplesdons fell immediately, like lambs, into the trap so ingenuously spread for them. Indeed, I have always noticed that ninety-nine per cent of the British public, when turned into an art-gallery, are only too glad to accept the opinion of anybody whatsoever, who is bold enough to have one, and to express it openly. Having thus been thrust by Nora into the arduous position of critic by appointment to the Worplesdon party, I delivered myself *ex cathedrâ* forthwith upon the merits and demerits of the entire exhibition; and I was so successful in my critical views that I not only produced an immense impression upon Mr Worplesdon himself, but also observed many ladies in the neighbourhood nudge one another as they gazed intently backward and forward between wall and catalogue, and heard them whisper audibly among themselves, 'A gentleman here says the flesh tones on that shoulder are simply marvellous;' or, 'That artist in the tweed suit behind us thinks the careless painting of the ferns in the foreground quite unworthy of such a colourist as Daubiton.' So highly was my criticism appreciated, in fact, that Mr Worplesdon even invited me to lunch with Nora and his party at a neighbouring restaurant, where I spent the most delightful hour I had passed for the last half-year, in the company of that naughty mendacious little schemer.

About four o'clock, however, the Worplesdons departed, taking Nora with them to South Kensington; and I prepared to walk back in the direction of Paddington, meaning to catch an evening train, and return to Oxford. I was strolling in a leisurely fashion along Piccadilly towards the Park, and looking into all the photographers' windows, when suddenly an awful apparition loomed upon me—the Professor himself, coming round the corner from Bond Street, folding up a new rhinoceros-handled umbrella as he walked along. In a moment I felt that all was lost. I was up in town without leave; the Professor would certainly see me and recognize me; he would ask me how and why I had left the University, contrary to rules; and I must then either tell him the whole truth, which would get Nora into a fearful scrape, or else run the risk of being sent down in disgrace, which might prevent me from taking a degree, and would at least cause my father and mother an immense deal of unmerited trouble.

Like a flash of lightning, a wild idea shot instantaneously across my brain. Might I pretend to be my own double? The Professor was profoundly superstitious on the subject of wraiths, apparitions, ghosts, brain-waves, and supernatural appearances generally; if I could only manage to impose upon him for a moment by doing something outrageously uncommon or eccentric, I might succeed in stifling further inquiry by setting him from the beginning on a false track which he was naturally prone to follow. Before I had time to reflect upon the consequences of my act, the wild idea had taken possession of me, body and soul, and had worked itself out in action with all the rapidity of a mad impulse. I rushed frantically up to the Professor, with my eyes fixed in a vacant stare on a point in space somewhere above the tops of the chimney-pots: I waved my stick three times mysteriously around his head; and then, without giving him time to recover from his surprise or to address a single word to me, I bolted off in a Red Indian dance to the nearest corner.

There was an hotel there, which I had often noticed before, though I had never entered it; and I rushed wildly in, meaning to get out as best I could when the Professor (who is very short-sighted) had passed on along Piccadilly in search of me. But fortune, as usual, favoured the bold. Luckily, it was a corner house, and, to my surprise, I found when I got inside it, that the hall opened both ways, with a door on to the side street. The porter was looking away as I entered; so I merely ran in one door and out of the other, never stopping till I met a hansom, into which I jumped and ordered the man to drive to Paddington. I just caught the 4.35 to Oxford[12], and by a little over six o'clock I was in my own rooms at Oriel.

It was very wrong of me, indeed; I acknowledge it now; but the whole thing had flashed across my undergraduate mind so rapidly that I carried it out in a moment, before I could at all realize what a very foolish act I was really committing. To take a rise out of the Professor, and to save Nora an angry interview, were the only ideas that occurred to me at the second: when I began to reflect upon it afterwards, I was conscious that I had really practised a very gross and wicked deception. However, there was no help for it now; and as I rolled along in the train to Oxford, I felt that to save myself and Nora from utter disgrace, I must carry the plot out to the end without flinching. It then occurred to me that a double apparition would be more in accordance with all recognized principles of psychical manifestation than a single one. At Reading, therefore, I regret to say, I bought a pencil, and a sheet of paper, and an envelope; and before I reached Oxford station, I had written to the Professor what I now blush to acknowledge as a tissue of shocking fables, in which I paralleled every particular of my own behaviour to him by a similar imaginary piece of behaviour on his part to me, only changing the scene to Oxford. It was awfully wrong, I admit. At the time, however, being yet but little more than a school-boy, after all, I regarded it simply in the light of a capital practical joke. I informed the Professor gravely how I had seen him at four o'clock in the Corn Market, and how astonished I was when I found him waving his green silk umbrella three times wildly, around my head.

The moment I arrived at Oxford, I dashed up to college in a han-som, and got the Professor's address in London from the porter. He had gone up to town for the night, it seemed, probably to visit Nora, and would not be back in college till the next morning. Then I rushed down to the post-office, where I was just in time (with an extra stamp) to catch the last post for that night's delivery. The moment the letter was in the box, I repented, and began to fear I had gone too far: and when I got back to my own rooms at last, and went down late for dinner in hall, I confess I trembled not a little, as to the possible effect of my quite too bold and palpable imposition.

Next morning by the second post I got a long letter from the Pro-fessor, which completely relieved me from all immediate anxiety as to his interpretation of my conduct. He rose to the fly with a charming simplicity which showed how delighted he was at this personal confir-mation of all his own most cherished superstitions. 'My dear Mans-field,' his letter began, 'now hear what, at the very self-same hour and minute, happened to me in Piccadilly.' In fact, he had swallowed the whole thing entire, without a single moment's scepticism or hesitation.

From what I heard afterwards, it was indeed a lucky thing for me that I had played him this shocking trick, for Nora believes he was then actually on his way to South Kensington on purpose to forbid her most stringently from holding any further communication with me in any way. But as soon as this mysterious event took place, he began to change his mind about me altogether. So remarkable an apparition could not have happened except for some good and weighty reason, he argued: and he suspected that the reason might have something to do with my intentions towards Nora. Why, when he was on his way to warn her against me, should a vision, bearing my outer and bodily shape, come straight across his path, and by vehement signs of displeasure, endeavour to turn him from his purpose, unless it were clearly well for Nora that my attentions should not be discouraged?

From that day forth the Professor began to ask me to his rooms and address me far more cordially than he used to do before: he even, on the strength of my singular adventure, invited me to assist at one or two of his psychical *séances*. Here, I must confess, I was not entirely successful: the distinguished medium complained that I exerted a repellent effect upon the spirits, who seemed to be hurt by my want of generous confidence in their good intentions, and by my suspicious habit of keeping my eyes too sharply fixed upon the legs of the tables. He declared that when I was present, an adverse influence seemed to pervade the room, due, apparently, to my painful lack of spiritual sympathies. But the Professor condoned my failure in the regular psychical line, in consideration of my brilliant success as a beholder of wraiths and visions. After I took my degree that summer, he used all his influence to procure me the post of keeper of the Accadian Antiquities at the Museum, for which my previous studies had excellently fitted me: and by his friendly aid I was enabled to obtain the post, though I regret to say that, in spite of his credulity in supernatural matters, he still refuses to believe in the correctness of my conjectural interpretation of the celebrated Amalekite cylinders[13] imported by Mr Ananias, which I have deciphered in so very simple and satisfactory a manner. As everybody knows, my translation may be regarded as perfectly certain, if only one makes the very modest assumption that the cylinders were originally engraved upside down by an Aztec captive, who had learned broken Accadian, with a bad accent, from a Chinese exile, and who occasionally employed Egyptian hieroglyphics in incorrect senses, to piece out his own very imperfect idiom and doubtful spelling of the early Babylonian language. The solitary real doubt in the matter is whether certain extraordinary marks in the upper left-hand corner of the cylinder are to be interpreted as accidental scratches, or as a picture representing the triumph of a king over seven bound prisoners, or, finally, as an Accadian sentence in cuneiforms which may be translated either as 'To the memory of Om the Great,' or else as 'Pithor the High Priest dedicates a fat goose to the family dinner on the 25th of the month of midwinter.' Every candid and unprejudiced mind must admit that these small discrepancies or alternatives in the opinions of experts can cast no doubt at all upon the general soundness of the method employed. But persons like the Professor, while ready to accept any evidence at all where their own prepossessions are concerned, can never be induced to believe such plain and unvarnished statements of simple scientific knowledge.

However, the end of it all was that before I had been a month at the Museum, I had obtained the Professor's consent to my marriage with Nora: and as I had had Nora's own consent long before, we were duly joined together in holy matrimony early in October at Oxford, and came at once to live in Hampstead. So, as it turned out, I finally owed the sweetest and best little wife in all Christendom to the mysterious occurrence in Piccadilly.

[1] *Proceedings of the Society for the Investigation* ... Allen's fictional version of the Society for Psychical Research, founded in 1882.

[2] **by the last post.** The last delivery in central London was as late as 9*pm*.

[3] **Taylor Institute.** A fine neo-classical building in the heart of Oxford, then used as an overflow library for the Bodleian.

[4] **my Greats.** The colloquial name for the undergraduate degree in Classics at Oxford.

[5] **the affair of Corcyra.** The allusion is to a dispute between Corinth and Corcyra (Corfu) which led to the Second Peloponnesian War and the downfall of Athens.

[6] **the Tichborne claimant.** A prolonged and expensive legal case which riveted Victorian England, in which the Claimant (usually identified as Arthur Orton from Australia) claimed to be the heir to the valuable Tichborne estates. Orton eventually served a long sentence for fraud and was released in the year of this story. He had many supporters before and after his imprisonment.

[7] **the preceding Long ... my Accadian studies.** The summer vacation at Oxford, here spent studying an obscure ancient language of Mesopotamia, written in cuneiform.

[8] **an aposiopesis.** In rhetoric, leaving a sentence unfinished to produce a dramatic effect.

[9] **Griffin ... *vice* Temple Bar removed.** There is a winged gargoyle on the front of Oriel College on which a decapitated head might be stuck, as was formerly the practice on Temple Bar on the Strand, before it was removed in 1878.

[10] *planchettes* ... **table-turning.** Two means of calling up spirits, both popular domestic activities in this period. The first used a flat wooden plate on castors, with a vertical pen to record messages; for the second, several people sat around a table which might tilt or turn, spelling a message when the alphabet was called out.

[11] **recorded by Livy.** In a passage in his *History of Rome* (Book 21) many 'prodigies' are recorded, including men in shining garments, showers of pebbles, *etc.*

[12] **I just caught the 4.35 to Oxford.** In 1895 the journey took about an hour and twenty minutes, but there were only eight trains a day. If he left the train at Reading to buy stationery and then took the next one, could Manning have arrived at Oriel shortly after 6 *pm*?

[13] **Amalekite cylinders.** The Amalekites were longstanding foes of the Israelites and were wiped out by the latter at God's command. Allen is probably thinking of the famous Cyrus Cylinder, acquired by the British Museum in 1880.

# The Pot-boiler

*The Pot-boiler* appeared in *Longman's Magazine* in October 1892 and was never reprinted after Allen's death. More of a fable than a story— an account of an artist's predicament and a temptation set aside—the subject is one to which Allen often returned in both his fiction and his essays. Clearly, the name of the hero, Ernest Grey, is meant to evoke Oscar Wilde's *The Picture of Dorian Gray* (1890). In this novel, Dorian is tempted into sin by the wicked Lord Henry Wotton. Bernard Hume, armed with a copy of Browning's dramatic monologue 'Andrea del Sarto', fills the same role.

Allen's own situation was not quite the same as Ernest Grey's. He had no strong creative impulse. He was more interested in ideas than people. He regarded himself chiefly as a scientific and philosophical writer and, on social questions, a controversialist with strong opinions, especially about marriage and sexual morality in general. But like Grey he did have a wife and child and he was a semi-invalid. He could afford to take no risks. His first priority was his family. 'I never cared for the chance of literary reputation except as a means of making a livelihood for Nellie and the boy', he wrote to a friend when his career started to look promising. 'I can now make a livelihood easily: and I ought to turn to whatever will make it best'. He sought to make a lot of money quickly, and soon discovered that the best returns came from novels— at one point he published seven in two years—and short stories. Popular novels were especially lucrative if a magazine chose to serialise them, and stories could be syndicated world-wide and then collected into anthologies and sold again.

That was all well and good; but Allen chafed inwardly at the restraints placed on him. He said he had written nothing he *did not* believe in, but pressure from editors and publishers forced him to be silent about much that he *did* believe in. That was the discipline to which he submitted for much of his career. But *The Pot-boiler* belongs to the last decade of his life when he had accumulated a nest-egg of capital and at last felt freer to explore the plight, as he saw it, of the freelance writer with much to say who is chained to the domestic 'simmering saucepan'. His public assumption of the role of a serious writer who had hitherto been fettered by 'the views of blushing sixteen in the rectory drawing-room' made him the target for some ill-natured mirth, such as this anonymous assault from the *National Observer*:

> You make soap for so much a year; for so much a year less
> you could make pictures. You go on making soap, and
> complain that you are not rich enough to make pictures.
> Truly, a just and manly complaint. Yet are you better than
> he who, making soap, yet clamours for the credit for making pictures.

That was the main offence: that a literary 'soap-maker' like Grant Allen should have the effrontery to insist on the privileges of the true artist, when he 'writes stuff which has no more concern with literature than his tailor's bills!' Allen, cut to the quick by this sneer, wrote a pained response to the editor, but either he did not send it or it wasn't published.

The moral of *The Pot-boiler* is, of course, conservative. Filled with self-hatred at his temporary weakness, Grey slashes to pieces his Pre-Raphaelite fantasy just as his Wildean namesake slashes his loathsome portrait. But henceforward Allen himself, buoyed up by money in the bank, took a more defiant course. He wrote several inflammatory essays about sexual morality, more fables about struggling artists, and his polemical feminist novel *The Woman Who Did.* He had to endure much criticism but his standing with editors was not much affected and his prosperity continued to rise in the few years remaining to him.

ERNEST GREY was an inspired painter. Therefore he was employed to paint portraits of insipid little girls[1] in black-silk stockings, and to produce uninteresting domestic groups, of which a fat and smiling baby of British respectability formed the central figure.

He didn't like it, of course. Pegasus[2] never does like being harnessed to the paternal go-cart. But being a philosopher in his way, and having a wife and child to keep, he dragged it none the less, with as good a grace as could reasonably be expected from such celestial mettle. The wife, in fact, formed the familiar model for the British mother in his Academy[3] pictures, while little Joan (with bare legs) sat placidly for the perennial and annual baby. Each year, as observant critics might have noticed, that baby grew steadily a twelvemonth older. But there were no observant critics for Ernest Grey's pictures: the craft were all too busy inspecting the canvas of made reputations to find time on hand for spying out merit in the struggling work of unknown beginners. It's an exploded fallacy of the past to suppose that insight and initiative are the true critic's hallmark. Why go out of your way to see good points in unknown men, when you can earn your three guineas so much more surely and simply by sticking to the good points that everybody recognizes? The way to gain a reputation for critical power nowadays is, to say in charming and pellucid language what everybody regards as the proper thing to say about established favourites. You voice the popular taste in the very best English.

But Ernest Grey had ideals, for all that. How poor a creature the artist must be who doesn't teem with unrealized and unrealizable ideals! All the while that he painted the insipid little girls in the impeccable stockings, very neatly gartered, he was feeding his soul with a tacit undercurrent of divine fancy. He had another world than this of ours, in which he lived by turns—a strange world of pure art[4], where all was profound, mysterious, magical, beautiful. Idylls of Celtic fancy floated visible on the air before his mind's eye. Great palaces reared themselves like exhalations on the waste ground by Bedford Park. Fair white maidens moved slow, with measured tread, across his imagined canvas. What pictures he might paint—if only somebody would pay him for painting them! He revelled in designing these impossible works. His scenery should all lie in the Lost Land of Lyonesse. A spell as of Merlin should brood, half-seen, over his dreamy cloisters. The carved capitals of his pilasters should point to something deeper than mere handicraftsman's workmanship; his brocades and his fringes should breathe and live; his arabesques and his fretwork, his tracery and his moulding, should be instinct with soul and with indefinite yearning. The light that never was on sea or land should flood his landscape. [5] In the pictures he had never painted, perhaps never would paint, ornament and decoration were lavished in abundance; design ran riot; onyx and lapis lazuli, chrysolite and chalcedony, beryl and jacinth, studded his jewelled bowls and his quaintly-wrought scabbards; but all to enrich and enforce one fair central idea, to add noble attire and noble array to that which was itself already noble and beautiful. No frippery should intrude. All this wealth of detail should be subservient in due place to some glorious thought, some ray of that divine sadness that touches nearest the deep heart of man.

So he said to himself in his day-dreams. But life is not day-dream. Life, alas! is very solid reality. While Ernest Grey nourished his secret soul with such visions of beauty, he employed his deft fingers in painting spindle legs, ever fresh in number, yet ever the same in kind, and unanimously clad in immaculate spun-silk stockings[6]. No hosier was better up in all the varieties of spun silk than that inspired painter. 'Tis the way of the world, you know—our industrial world of supply and demand—to harness its blood-horses to London hansoms.

After all, he was working for Baby Joan and Bertha. (Bertha was the sort of name most specially in vogue when his wife was a girl; it had got to Joan and Joyce by the date of the baby.) They lived together in a very small house at Bedford Park[7]—so small, Bertha said, that when a visitor dropped in they bulged out at the windows.

But Ernest Grey had a friend better off than himself—a man whose future was already assured him—a long-haired proprietor[8] who wrote minor verse which the world was one day to wake up and find famous[9]. He was tall and thin, and loosely knit, and looked as if he'd been run up by contract. His name was Bernard Hume; he claimed indirect descent from the philosopher[10] who demolished everything. Unlike his collateral ancestor, however, Bernard Hume had faith, a great deal of faith—first of all in himself, and after that in every one else who shared the honour of his acquaintance. This was an amiable trait on Bernard's part, for, as a rule, men who believe in themselves complete their simple creed with that solitary article. With Bernard Hume, on the contrary, egotism took a more expanded and expansive form—it spread itself thin over the entire entourage. He thought there was always a great deal in any one who happened to inspire him with a personal fancy. 'I like this man,' he said to himself virtually, 'therefore he must be a very superior soul, else how could he have succeeded in attracting the attention of so sound a critic and judge of human nature?'

Of all Bernard Hume's friends, however, there was not one in whom he believed more profoundly than the inspired painter. 'Ernest Grey,' he used to say, 'if only he'd retire from the stocking-trade and give free play to his fancy, would bring the sweat[11], I tell you, into that brow of Burne-Jones's. (You think the phrase vulgar? Settle the question by all means, then, with Browning, who invented it!) He's a born idealist, is Grey—a direct descendant of Lippi and Botticelli, pitchforked, by circumstances over which he has no control, into the modern hosiery business. If only he could *paint* those lovely things he draws so beautifully! Why, he showed me some sketches the other day for unrealized pictures, first studies for dreams of pure form and colour—fair virgins that flit, white-armed, through spacious halls—plaintive, melancholy, passionate, mystical. One of them was superb. An Arthurian uncertainty enveloped the scene. The touch of a wizard had made all things in it suffer a beautiful change. It was life with the halo on—life as the boy in Wordsworth's "Ode on Immortality"[12] must surely have seen it—life in the glow of a poet's day-dream. A world of pure phantasy, lighted up from above with glancing colour. A world whose exact date is *once upon a time.* A world whose precise place is in the left-hand corner of the land of fairy-tales. If only Ernest Grey would paint like that, he might fail for today; he might fail for tomorrow; his wife and child might starve and die; he might fall himself exhausted in the gutter—but his place hereafter would be among the immortals.'

Ernest heard him talk so at times—and went on with the detail of the left stocking. It's easy enough to let some other divine genius's wife and child starve to death for the sake of posterity; but when it comes to your own, *pardi!*[13] it's by no means so simple. Posterity then becomes a very small affair, bar one component member. But Bernard Hume was a bachelor.

One afternoon Ernest was smoking his meditative pipe in the bare, small studio—he allowed himself a pipe; 'twas his one slight luxury—when Bernard Hume, all fiery-eyed, strolled in unexpectedly. Bernard Hume was a frequent and a welcome visitor. 'Tis not in human nature not to like deft flattery, especially on the points you believe to be your strongest. You may be ever so modest a man in the abstract, and under normal conditions of opposition and failure; but when a friend begins to praise your work to your face, and to find in it the qualities you like the best yourself, why, hang it all! you stand back a bit, and gaze at it with your head just a trifle on one side, and say to your own soul in an unuttered aside, 'Well, after all, I'm a diffident sort of a fellow, and I distrust my own products, but it's quite true what he says—there *is* a deal of fine feeling and fine painting in the reflection of those nude limbs in that limpid water; and what could be more exquisite, though I did it myself, than the gracious curl of those lithe festoons of living honeysuckle?'

So Bernard was a favourite at the little house in Bedford Park. Even Bertha liked him, and was proud of his opinion of Ernest's genius, though she wished he didn't try to distract dear Ernest so much from serious work to mere speculative fancies.

On this particular afternoon, however, Bernard had dropped in of *malice prepense*[14], and in pursuance of a deep-laid scheme against Bertha's happiness. The fact is, he had been reading Browning's 'Andrea del Sarto' the night before, and, much impressed by that vigorous diatribe against all forms of pot-boiling, he had come round to put out poor Bertha's smouldering kitchen-fire for ever. He knew the moment had now arrived when Ernest should be goaded on into letting his wife and child starve for the benefit of humanity; and he felt like a missionary sent out on purpose, by some Society for the Propagation of the Aesthetic Gospel, to convert the poor benighted pot-boiler from the whole base cult of the scullery pipkin.

He came, indeed, at a propitious moment. Ernest had just dismissed the model who sat for the elder daughter in his new Academy picture of 'Papa's Return,' and was then engaged in adding a few leisurely touches haphazard to little Joan's arms as the crowing baby. (Papa himself stood outside the frame; not even the worship of the simmering saucepan itself could induce Ernest Grey to include in his canvas the jocund figure of the regressive stockbroker.) Bernard Hume sat down, and after the usual interchange of meteorological opinion, drew forth from his pocket a small brown-covered volume. Bertha trembled in her chair; she knew well what was in store for them: 'twas the 'selections from Browning,'—homeopathic dose[15] for the general public. *Habitués* absorb him whole in fifteen volumes.

'I was reading a piece of Browning's[16] last night,' Bernard began tentatively; 'his "Andrea del Sarto"—do you know it, Mrs Grey?—it impresses me immensely. I was so struck with it, indeed, that I wanted to come round and read it over to Ernest this afternoon. I thought it might be—well, suggestive to him in his work, don't you know.' And he glanced askance at that hostile Bertha. So very unreasonable of a genius's wife not to wish to starve, with her baby in her arms, for the sake of high art, and her husband, and posterity!

Bertha nodded a grudging assent; and Bernard, drawing breath, settled down in a chair and began to read that famous poem, which was to act, he hoped, as a goad to Ernest Grey's seared artistic conscience.

Once or twice, to be sure, Bernard winced not a little at the words he had to read—they were so *very* personal:—

Some women do so. Had the mouth there urged,

'God and the glory: never care for gain!

The present by the future, what is that?

Live for fame, side by side with Agnolo![17]

Rafael is waiting: up to God all three!'

I might have done it for you. So it seems.

Perhaps not. All is as God overrules.

Besides, incentives come from the soul's self;

The rest avail not. Why do I need you?

What wife had Rafael or has Agnolo?

In this world, who can do a thing will not;

And who would do it cannot, I perceive.


That was tolerably plain—almost rude, he felt[18], now he came to read it with Bertha actually by his side. Yet still he persisted through all that magnificent special pleading of the case for posterity and high art against wife and children—persisted to the bitter end, in spite of everything. He never flinched one moment. He read it all out—all, all—every word of it—'We might have risen to Rafael, you and I,' and all the rest of it. His voice quivered a little—only a little—as he poured forth those last few lines:—

Four great walls in the New Jerusalem,

Meted on each side by the angel's reed,[19]

For Leonard, Rafael, Agnolo, and me

To cover—the three first without a wife,

While I have mine. So—still they overcome,

Because there's still Lucrezia,—as I choose.


But he read it out for all that, with eyes glancing askance (at the commas) on Bertha's fiery face, and lips that trembled with the solemnity of the occasion.

The pot-boiler's heart was touched. For, mind you, it's easy to touch every artist's artistic conscience. You only ask him to do the thing he best loves doing.

When Bernard Hume ceased there was a pause for a few minutes—a terrible pause. Then Bertha rose slowly, and went over to her husband. In spite of Bernard's presence, she kissed him twice on the forehead. Then she burst into tears, and rushed from the room wildly.

All that night she hardly slept. Next morning she rose, determined, whatever she did, never for one moment to interfere with Ernest's individuality.

Throughout the day she avoided the studio studiously. At eleven the model who sat for the elder sister in 'Papa's Return' came in as usual.

She was very much surprised to find Ernest Grey engaged on a large drawing which had been lying about the studio for months unfinished. It represented, as she remarked to herself, among a crowd of other figures, a male model in armour pushing his way through a dense wood towards a floating female model in insufficient drapery. But Ernest himself called it 'The Quest of the Ideal.'

She stood for a minute irresolute. Ernest Grey meanwhile surveyed her critically. Yes, he thought so—she would do. No more the elder sister in 'Papa's Return,' but the Elusive herself in 'The Quest of the Ideal.'

The model looked at him in surprise. She was a beautiful girl, with a face of refined and spiritual beauty. 'Why, Mr Grey,' she cried, taken aback, 'you don't mean to say you're not goin' on with your Academy picture?'

'This *is* my Academy picture,' Ernest Grey answered gravely. 'I've discarded the other one. It never was really mine. I'm giving up the hosiery business.'

The model looked aghast. 'And it *was* so lovely!' she cried, all re-grets. 'That dear, sweet baby! and her so pleased, too, at her pa coming 'ome again!'

Ernest answered only by bringing out a piece of thin, creamy-white drapery. 'I shall want you to wear this,' he said; 'just so, as in the sketch. I think you'll do admirably for the central figure.'

The model demurred a little—the undress was rather more than she had yet been used to. She sat for head and shoulders or draped figure only. 'I think,' she said with decision, 'you'd better get another lady.'

But Ernest insisted. He was hot for high art now; and after a short hesitation, the model consented. It was no more, he pointed out, than evening-dress permits the most modest maiden. All on fire with his new departure, Ernest began a study of her head and shoulders then and there—the head and shoulders of the Eternal Elusive.

He wrought at it with a will. He was inspired and eager. To be sure, it was an awkward moment to begin an experiment, with the rent just due and no cash in hand to pay it, while the baker was clamouring hard for his last month's money. 'But things like that, you know, must be/ *Before* a famous victory!'[20] Nothing venture, nothing have. There would still be just time to complete the study, at least, before Sending-in Day; and if somebody took a fancy to his very first attempt at a serious picture, why—farewell for ever to the spun-silk stocking trade!

For a week he worked away by himself in the studio. Bertha never came near the room, though she shuddered to herself to think what Ernest was doing. But she had made up her mind, once for all, after hearing Bernard Hume read Browning's 'Andrea,' never again to in-terfere with her husband's individuality. As for the model, her grief was simple and unaffected. She couldn't think how Mr Grey, and him so clever, too, could ever desert that dear, sweet baby in 'Papa's Return' for all them dreadful gashly men and un'olesome women. He was making such a fright of her for his figger of the Eloosive[21] as she'd be ashamed to acknowledge to any of her friends it was her that sat to him for it. A pretty girl don't like to be painted into a fright like that, with her 'air all streamin' loose like a patient at Colney 'Atch[22], and her clothes fallin' off, quite casual-like, be'ind her!

About Friday Bernard Hume called in. The model expected him to disapprove most violently. But when he saw the drawing, and still more the study, as far as it had gone—for Ernest, knowing exactly what effect he meant to produce, had worked at the head and arms with surprising rapidity—he was in visible raptures. He stood long and gazed at it. 'Why, Grey,' he cried, standing back a little, and shading his eyes with his hand, 'it's simply and solely the incarnate spirit of the nineteenth century. The nineteenth century in its higher and purer avatar; deep-questioning, mystic, uncertain, rudderless. Faith gone; humanity left; heaven lost; earth realized as man's true home and sole hope for the future! Those sad eyes of your wan maidens gaze forth straight upon the infinite. Those bronzed faces of your mailed knights have confronted strange doubts and closed hard with nameless terrors. There's a pathos in it all—a—what shall I call it?—a something inexpressible; a pessimism, a meliorism, an obstinate questioning of invisible things, that no age but this age of ours could possibly have compassed. Who, save you, could have put so much intense spirituality into the broidery of a robe, could have touched with such sacred and indefinable sadness the frayed fringe of a knightly doublet?'

As he spoke, Ernest gazed at his own work, in love with it. The criticism charmed him. It was just the very thing he'd have said of it himself, if it had been somebody else's; only he couldn't have put it in such glowing language.[23] It's delightful to hear your work so justly appraised by a sympathetic soul; it makes a modest man think a great deal better than he could ever otherwise think of his own poor little performances. But most modest men, alas! have no Bernard Hume at hand to applaud their efforts. The Bernard Humes of this world are all busily engaged in booming the noisy, successful self-advertisers.

The model looked up with a dissatisfied air. 'I don't like it,' she said, grumbling internally. 'It makes me look as if I wanted a blue-pill[24]. It ain't 'arf so pretty as 'Papa's Return,' and it's my belief it ain't 'arf so sellin' either.'

'Pretty!' Bernard Hume responded with profound contempt. 'Well, the sole object of art is not, I should say, to be merely pretty. And as for selling—well, no, I dare say it won't *sell*. But what does that matter? It's a beautiful work, and it does full justice to Mr Grey's imaginative faculty. There's not another man in England today who could possibly paint it.'

The model said nothing, but she thought the more. She thought, among other things, that to her it *did* matter; for, in the first place, a painter who doesn't sell isn't likely to be able to pay his models; and, in the second place, no self-respecting girl cares to sit very long for unsaleable pictures. It interferes, of course, with her market value. Who's going to employ an unsuccessful man's model?

For a week Ernest toiled on almost without stopping, but it was easy toil compared to the stocking trade. The study grew apace under his eager fingers; the model declared confidentially to her family he was ruining her prospects. 'I'm as yellow as a guinea,'[25] she said; 'and as for expression, why, you'd think I was goin' to die in about three weeks in a gallopin' consumption.' Not such the elder sister in 'Papa's Return'—that rosy-cheeked, round-faced, English middle-class girl whom Ernest had elaborated by his Protean art[26] out of the features and form of the self-same model.

At the end of the week he was working hard in his studio one evening to save the last ray of departing sunlight, when Bertha burst in suddenly with a very scared face. 'Oh, Ernest!' she cried, 'do come up and look at Joan. She seems so ill. I can't think what's the matter with her.'

Ernest flung down his brush, and forgot in a moment, as a father will, all about the Elusive. It eluded him instantly. He followed Bertha to the little room at the top of the house that served as nursery. ('Keep your child always,' he used to say, 'as near as you can to heaven.') Little Joan, just three years old at that time, lay listless and glassy-eyed in the nurse's arms. Ernest looked at her with a vague foreboding of evil. He saw at once she was very ill. 'This is serious,' he said in a low voice. 'I must go for the doctor.'

When the doctor came, discreetly uncertain, he shook his head and looked wise, and declined to commit himself. He was rather of opinion, though, it might turn out to be scarlet fever[27].

Scarlet fever! Bertha's heart stood still in her bosom, and so did Ernest's. For the next ten days the model had holiday; the Elusive was permitted to elude unchased; the studio was forsaken day and night for the nursery. It was a very bad case, and they fought it all along the line, inch by inch, unflinchingly. Poor little Joan was very ill indeed. It made Ernest's heart bleed to see her chubby small face grow so thin and yet so fiery. Night after night they sat up and watched. What did Ernest care now for art or the ideal? That one little atomy of solid round flesh was more to him than all the greatest pictures in Christendom. 'Rafael did this, Andrea painted that!' Ah, God! what did it matter, with little Joan's life hanging poised in the balance between life and death, and little Joan's unseeing eyes turned upward, white between the eyelids, toward the great blank ceiling? If Joan were to die, what would be art or posterity? The sun in the heavens might shine on as before, but the sun in Ernest and Bertha's life would have faded out utterly.

At last the crisis came. 'If she gets through tonight,' the doctor said in his calm way, as though he were talking of somebody else's baby, 'the danger's practically over. All my patients in the present epidemic who've passed this stage have recovered without difficulty.'

They watched and waited through that livelong night in breathless suspense and terror and agony. You who are parents know well what it means. Why try to tell others? *They* could never understand; and if they could, why, heaven forbid we should harrow them as we ourselves have been harrowed.

At last, towards morning, little Joan dropped asleep. A sweet, deep sleep. Her breathing was regular. Father and mother fell mute into one another's arms. Their tears mingled. They dared not utter one word, but they cried long and silently.

From that moment, as the doctor had predicted, little Joan grew rapidly stronger and better. In a week she was able to go out for a drive—in a hansom, of course—no carriages for the struggling! Exchequer, much depleted by expenses of illness, felt even that hansom a distinct strain[28] upon it.

Next morning Ernest had heart enough to begin work again. He sent word round accordingly to the model.

In the course of the day Bernard Hume dropped in. He was anxious to see how the Ideal and the Elusive got on after the crisis. He surprised Ernest at his easel. 'Hullo!' he cried with a little start, straightening his long spine, 'what does all this mean, Grey? You don't mean to say you're back at 'Papa's Return'? Have you yielded once more to Gath and Askelon[29]?'

'No,' Ernest answered firmly, looking him back in the face, 'I've yielded to Duty. You can go now, Miss Baker. I've done about as much as I'm good for today. My hand's too shaky. And now, Hume, I'll speak out to you. All these days and nights while little Joan's been ill I've thought it all over and realized to myself which is the truest heroism. It's very specious and very fine to talk in deep bass about the talents that God has bestowed upon one in trust for humanity. I can talk all that stuff any day with the best of you. But I've married Bertha, and I've helped to put little Joan into the world, and I'm responsible to them for their daily bread, their life and happiness. It may be heroic to despise comfort and fame and wealth and security for the sake of high art and the best that's in one. I dare say it is; but I'm sure it's a long way more heroic still to do work one doesn't want to do for wife and children. It's easy enough to follow one's own natural bent: I was perfectly happy—serenely happy—those seven days I painted away at the Elusive. But it's very hard indeed to give all that up for the sake of Duty. What you came to preach to me was only a peculiarly seductive form of self-indulgence—the indulgence of one's highest and truest self, but still self-indulgence. If I'd followed you, everybody would have praised and admired my single-hearted devotion to the cause of art; but Joan and Bertha would have paid for it. No man can make a public for anything new and personal in any art whatever without waiting and educating his public for years. If he's rich, he can afford to wait and educate it, as your own friend Browning did. If he's a bachelor, rich or poor, he can still afford to do it, because nobody but himself need suffer for it with him. But if he's poor and married—ah, then it's quite different. He has given hostages to fortune[30]; he has no right to think first of anything at all but the claims of his wife and children upon him. I call it more heroic, then, to work at any such honest craft as will ensure their livelihood, than to go astray after the Ashtaroth of specious ideals[31] such as you set before me.'

Bernard Hume's lip curled. This was what the Church knows as Invincible Ignorance[32]. He had done his best for the man, and the old Adam[33] had conquered. 'And what are you going to do,' he asked with a contemptuous smile, 'about 'The Quest of the Ideal'?'

Ernest laid down his palette, and thrust his hand silently into his trousers pocket. He drew forth a knife, and opened it deliberately. Then, without a single word, he walked across the floor to the Study of the Elusive. With one ruthless cut he slashed the canvas across from corner to corner. Then he slashed the two cut pieces again transversely. After that he took down the drawing of the design from the smaller easel, and solemnly thrust it into the studio fire. It burnt by slow degrees, for the cardboard was thick. His heart beat hard. As long as it smouldered he watched it intently. As the last of the mailed knights disappeared in white smoke up the studio chimney he drew a long breath. 'Good-bye,' he said in a choking voice; 'Good-bye to the Ideal.'

'And good-bye to *you*,' Bernard Hume made answer, 'for I call it desecration.'

Bernard Hume is now of opinion that he used once vastly to overrate Ernest Grey's capabilities. The man had talent, perhaps—some grain of mere talent—but never genius. As for Ernest, he has toiled on ever since, more or less contentedly (probably less), at the hosiery business, and makes quite a decent living now out of his portraits of children and his domestic figure-pieces. The model considers them all really charming.

It's everybody's case, of course; but still—it's a tragedy.

---

[1] **portraits of insipid little girls.** An obvious dig at the famous painter J.E. Millais, who was accused of prostituting his talent to support his large

family, with pictures like *Cherry Ripe* and *Little Miss Muffet*. He permitted his picture *Bubbles* (1886) to be used to advertise soap.

[2] **Pegasus.** The winged stallion of Greek mythology: wherever he stamped the ground with a hoof a magical spring of creativity in which artists could bathe gushed forth.

[3] **Academy.** For the Royal Academy's Summer Exhibition any artist could submit two works to its Hanging Committee. Its choices were often condemned as expressing a 'safe' view of artistic taste.

[4] **a strange world of pure art.** What follows describes paintings of the Pre-Raphaelite school in its later medieval-mythological phase, as represented by Rossetti, Burne-Jones, Waterhouse, *etc.*

[5] **light that never was on sea or land.** A line from Wordsworth's poem 'Peele Castle, in a Storm'.

[6] **Spun-silk stockings.** Cheaper ones made of inferior, waste silk fibres, as opposed to quality 'thrown' silk.

[7] **house at Bedford Park.** A garden suburb in west London, laid out in the 1870s and for a while very popular with the fashionable-artistic set.

[8] **long-haired proprietor.** Hume's 'artistic' interests are financed by rented property.

[9] **to wake up and find famous.** Sarcastic adaptation of Byron's remark that 'I woke up one morning and found myself famous' when his long poem *Childe Harold* first appeared.

[10] **descent from the philosopher.** David Hume (*d.*1776), a notorious sceptic who denied miracles and was accused of atheism.

[11] **bring the sweat …** A phrase from 'Andrea del Sarto': in the poem the artist who would 'sweat' when he grasped Andrea's talent is Raphael.

[12] **the boy in Wordsworth's 'Ode on Immortality'.** The poem 'Intimations of Immortality from Recollections of Early Childhood' tells how a child has memories of his antenatal existence, until 'Shades of the prison-house begin to close/Upon the growing Boy'.

[13] *pardi!* A minor French oath; roughly, 'damn it!'

[14] **of *malice prepense.*** In law, a premeditated criminal act.

[15] **homeopathic dose.** That is, with a tiny quantity of 'poetic' ingredient: Browning was a hugely prolific and sometimes obscure writer.

[16] **a piece of Browning's.** One of the most skilled of Browning's famous dramatic monologues in blank verse, 'Andrea del Sarto (Called "The Faultless Painter")' was published in 1855.

[17] **Agnolo.** Michelangelo. Unlike Andrea, neither he nor Raphael nor Leonardo were burdened with a family.

[18] **Almost rude, he felt.** Not surprisingly, for in the poem Browning took over a contemporary description of Andrea's wife Lucrezia as faithless, jealous and a vixen.

[19] **angel's reed.** According to the Book of Revelations, the stupendous walls of the heavenly New Jerusalem will be laid out by an angel with a measuring rod.

[20] ***Before* a famous victory!'** An adaptation of the ironical refrain 'But 'twas a famous victory' in Southey's poem about a battlefield, 'After Blenheim'.

[21] **figger of the Eloosive.** Allen's attempt at the cockney speech of the model. Most painters' female models were from the respectable working-class and usually were careful of their reputations.

[22] **Colney 'Atch.** In its heyday, the biggest lunatic asylum in Europe. The name was often used as a synonym for insanity.

[23] **such glowing language.** Probably an exaggerated amalgam of the writings of Oscar Wilde, Walter Pater and Andrew Lang, three influential critics much given to 'purple prose'.

[24] **a blue-pill.** Generic name for any quack medicine, originally containing mercury, used to treat everything from constipation to depression and tuberculosis.

[25] **yellow as a guinea.** A proverbial phrase: the bright gold guinea coin was long out of circulation.

[26] **Protean art.** Suggesting variety and flexibility, from Proteus, the shape-shifting sea-god.

[27] **scarlet fever.** A feared childhood bacterial disease, for which there was no effective treatment before antibiotics.

[28] **even that hansom a distinct strain.** Hansom cabs were not cheap—they cost from sixpence to a shilling per mile, too much for many people.

[29] **Gath and Askelon.** An allusion to a verse in the Second Book of Samuel that Allen was fond of: 'Tell it not in Gath, publish it not in the streets of Askelon; lest the daughters of the Philistines rejoice'.

[30] **Hostages to fortune.** A phrase from an essay by Francis Bacon, where he defines a wife and children as 'impediments to great enterprises'.

[31] **Ashtaroth of specious ideals.** In the Bible, another name for the pagan goddess Astarte, tempting the Jews away from their jealous god Jehovah.

[32] **Invincible Ignorance.** In Roman Catholic theology, failings which a person cannot amend due to their condition (*eg* infants) or by innate, incurable disposition.

[33] **old Adam.** A phrase from the ceremony of baptism in *The Book of Common Prayer,* alluding to man's state of original sin.

# THE GREAT RUBY ROBBERY: A DETECTIVE STORY

This classic early detective story appeared in the *Strand* magazine in October 1892. The *Strand* was a British imitation of smart American papers like *Harper's*, offering light articles and stories with lavish illustrations and lavish payments to those contributors who could meet its high standards. The *Strand's* popularity was ensured by Allen's friend Arthur Conan Doyle. Doyle's first series of twelve Sherlock Holmes stories ran there from June 1891 (*A Scandal in Bohemia*) until June 1892 (*The Adventure of the Copper Beeches*). They were enormously successful and made Doyle famous, and the editor immediately commissioned a further series, which was eagerly anticipated. However, they did not start until that December, so no doubt readers welcomed Allen's contribution in the meantime.

Allen was no stranger in the *Strand*. He had a story in its very first issue, in January 1891, and was rarely out of its pages afterwards. In fact he contributed sixty-six pieces to it to his considerable profit, sometimes having both fiction and popular science articles running in the same issue. Among other things, he adapted Doyle's idea of having the central characters and settings reappear in each successive story. Allen went a little further by introducing a thin narrative thread connecting all the separate stories. These were collected as *An African*

*Millionaire*, starring a confidence trickster, and were followed by two series starring female detectives, *Miss Cayley's Adventures* and *Hilda Wade*, both of which have been frequently reprinted. Allen showed remarkable ingenuity in devising plots for these 'adventures', though he occasionally fell into inconsistencies and the 'trick ending', which Doyle despised. In the present story, for example, the reader must wonder why the thief was so reckless as to receive a certain letter from Amsterdam at Lady Maclure's house, thereby bringing about the *dénouement* of the case, and an arrest.

# 1.

PERSIS REMANET was an American heiress. As she justly remarked, this was a commonplace profession for a young woman nowadays; for almost everybody of late years has been an American and an heiress. A poor Californian, indeed, would be a charming novelty in London society. But London society, so far, has had to go without one.

Persis Remanet was on her way back from the Wilcoxes' ball. She was stopping, of course, with Sir Everard and Lady Maclure at their house at Hampstead. I say 'of course' advisedly; because if you or I go to see New York, we have to put up at our own expense (five dollars a day, without wine or extras) at the Windsor or the Fifth Avenue; but when the pretty American comes to London (and every American girl is *ex officio* pretty, in Europe at least; I suppose they keep their ugly ones at home for domestic consumption) she is invariably the guest either of a dowager duchess or of a Royal Academician, like Sir Everard, of the first distinction. Yankees visit Europe, in fact, to see, among other things, our art and our old nobility; and by dint of native persistence they get into places that you and I could never succeed in penetrating, unless we devoted all the energies of a long and blameless life to securing an invitation.

Persis hadn't been to the Wilcoxes with Lady Maclure, however. The Maclures were too really great to know such people as the Wilcoxes, who were something tremendous in the City, but didn't buy pictures; and Academicians, you know, don't care to cultivate City people—unless they're customers. ('Patrons,' the Academicians more usually call them; but I prefer the simple business word myself, as being a deal less patronizing.) So Persis had accepted an invitation from Mrs Duncan Harrison, the wife of the well-known member for the Hackness Division of Elmetshire, to take a seat in her carriage to and from the Wilcoxes. Mrs Harrison knew the habits and manners of

American heiresses too well to offer to chaperon Persis; and indeed, Persis, as a free-born American citizen, was quite as well able to take care of herself, the wide world over, as any three ordinary married Englishwomen.

Now, Mrs Harrison had a brother, an Irish baronet, Sir Justin O'Byrne, late of the Eighth Hussars, who had been with them to the Wilcoxes, and who accompanied them home to Hampstead on the back seat of the carriage. Sir Justin was one of those charming, ineffective, elusive Irishmen whom everybody likes and everybody disapproves of. He had been everywhere, and done everything—except to earn an honest livelihood. The total absence of rents during the sixties and seventies had never prevented his father, old Sir Terence O'Byrne, who sat so long for Connemara in the unreformed Parliament, from sending his son Justin in state to Eton, and afterwards to a fashionable college at Oxford. 'He gave me the education of a gentleman,' Sir Justin was wont regretfully to observe 'but he omitted to give me also the income to keep it up with.'

Nevertheless, society felt O'Byrne was the sort of man who must be kept afloat somehow and it kept him afloat accordingly in those mysterious ways that only society understands, and that you and I, who are not society, could never get to the bottom of if we tried for a century. Sir Justin himself had essayed Parliament, too, where he sat for a while behind the great Parnell[1] without for a moment forfeiting society's regard even in those early days when it was held as a prime article of faith by the world that no gentleman could possibly call himself a Home-Ruler. 'Twas only one of O'Byrne's wild Irish tricks, society said, complacently, with that singular indulgence it always extends to its special favourites, and which is, in fact, the correlative of that unsparing cruelty it shows in turn to those who happen to offend against its unwritten precepts. If Sir Justin had blown up a Czar or two in a fit of political exuberance, society would only have regarded the escapade as 'one of O'Byrne's eccentricities.' He had also held a commission for a while in a cavalry regiment, which he left, it was understood, owing to a difference of opinion about a lady with the colonel; and he was now a gentleman-at-large on London society, supposed by those who know more about everyone than one knows about oneself, to be on the look-out for a nice girl with a little money.

Sir Justin had paid Persis a great deal of attention that particular evening; in point of fact, he had paid her a great deal of attention from the very first whenever he met her; and on the way home from the dance he had kept his eyes fixed on Persis's face to an extent that was almost embarrassing. The pretty Californian leaned back in her place in the carriage and surveyed him languidly. She was looking her level best that night in her pale pink dress, with the famous Remanet rubies in a cascade of red light setting off that snowy neck of hers. 'Twas a neck for a painter. Sir Justin let his eyes fall regretfully more than once on the glittering rubies. He liked and admired Persis, oh! quite immensely. Your society man who has been through seven or eight London seasons could hardly be expected to go quite so far as falling in love with any woman; his habit is rather to look about him critically among all the nice girls trotted out by their mammas for his lordly inspection, and to reflect with a faint smile that this, that, or the other one might perhaps really suit him—if it were not for—and there comes in the inevitable *But* of all human commendation. Still, Sir Justin admitted with a sigh to himself that he liked Persis ever so much; she was so fresh and original! and she talked so cleverly! As for Persis, she would have given her eyes (like every other American girl) to be made 'my lady'; and she had seen no man yet, with that auxiliary title in his gift, whom she liked half so well as this delightful wild Irishman.

At the Maclures' door the carriage stopped. Sir Justin jumped out and gave his hand to Persis. You know the house well, of course; Sir Everard Maclure's: it's one of those large new artistic mansions, in red brick and old oak, on the top of the hill; and it stands a little way back from the road, discreetly retired, with a big wooden porch, very convenient for leave-taking. Sir Justin ran up the steps with Persis to ring the bell for her; he had too much of the irrepressible Irish blood in his veins to leave that pleasant task to his sister's footman. But he didn't ring it at once; at the risk of keeping Mrs Harrison waiting outside for nothing, he stopped and talked a minute or so with the pretty American. 'You looked charming tonight, Miss Remanet,' he said, as she threw back her light opera wrap for a moment in the porch and displayed a single flash of that snowy neck with the famous rubies; 'those stones become you so.'

Persis looked at him and smiled. 'You think so?' she said, a little tremulous, for even your American heiress, after all, is a woman. 'Well, I'm glad you do. But it's good-bye tonight, Sir Justin, for I go next week to Paris.'

Even in the gloom of the porch, just lighted by an artistic red and blue lantern in wrought iron, she could see a shade of disappointment pass quickly over his handsome face as he answered, with a little gulp, 'No! you don't mean that? Oh, Miss Remanet, I'm so sorry!' Then he paused and drew back: 'And yet ... after all,' he continued, 'perhaps—,' and there he checked himself.

Persis looked up at him hastily. 'Yet, after all, what?' she asked, with evident interest.

The young man drew an almost inaudible sigh. 'Yet, after all—nothing,' he answered, evasively.

'That might do for an Englishwoman,' Persis put in, with American frankness, 'but it won't do for me. You must tell me what you mean by it.' For she reflected sagely that the happiness of two lives might depend upon those two minutes; and how foolish to throw away the chance of a man you really like (with a my-ladyship to boot), all for the sake of a pure convention!

Sir Justin leaned against the woodwork of that retiring porch. She was a beautiful girl. He had hot Irish blood. ... Well, yes; just for once—he would say the plain truth to her.

'Miss Remanet,' he began, leaning forward, and bringing his face close to hers, 'Miss Remanet—Persis—shall I tell you the reason why? Because I like you so much. I almost think I love you!'

Persis felt the blood quiver in her tingling cheeks. How handsome he was—and a baronet!

'And yet you're not altogether sorry,' she said, reproachfully, 'that I'm going to Paris!'

'No, not altogether sorry,' he answered, sticking to it; 'and I'll tell you why, too, Miss Remanet. I like you very much, and I think you like me. For a week or two, I've been saying to myself, 'I really believe I *must* ask her to marry me.' The temptation's been so strong I could hardly resist it.'

'And why do you want to resist it?' Persis asked, all tremulous.

Sir Justin hesitated a second; then with a perfectly natural and instinctive movement (though only a gentleman would have ventured to make it) he lifted his hand and just touched with the tips of his fingers the ruby pendants on her necklet. 'This is why,' he answered simply, and with manly frankness. 'Persis, you're so rich! I never dare ask you.'

'Perhaps you don't know what my answer would be,' Persis murmured very low, just to preserve her own dignity.

'Oh yes, I think I do,' the young man replied, gazing deeply into her dark eyes. 'It isn't that; if it were only that, I wouldn't so much mind it. But I think you'd take me.' There was moisture in her eye. He went on more boldly: 'I know you'd take me, Persis, and that's why I don't ask you. You're a great deal too rich, and *these* make it impossible.'

'Sir Justin,' Persis answered, removing his hand gently, but with the moisture growing thicker, for she really liked him, 'it's most unkind of you to say so; either you oughtn't to have told me at all, or else—if you did—' She stopped short. Womanly shame overcame her.

The man leaned forward and spoke earnestly. 'Oh, don't say that!' he cried, from his heart. 'I couldn't bear to offend you. But I couldn't bear, either, to let you go away—well—without having ever told you. In that case you might have thought I didn't care at all for you, and was only flirting with you. But, Persis, I've cared a great deal for you— a great, great deal—and had hard work many times to prevent myself from asking you. And I'll tell you the plain reason why I haven't asked you. I'm a man about town, not much good, I'm afraid, for anybody or anything; and everybody says I'm on the look-out for an heiress— which happens not to be true; and if I married you, everybody'd say, 'Ah, there! I told you so!' Now, I wouldn't mind that for myself; I'm a man, and I could snap my fingers at them; but I'd mind it for *you*, Persis, for I'm enough in love with you to be very, very jealous, indeed, for your honour. I couldn't bear to think people should say, 'There's that pretty American girl, Persis Remanet that was, you know; she's thrown herself away upon that good-for- nothing Irishman, Justin O'Byrne, a regular fortune-hunter, who's married her for her money.'

So for your sake, Persis, I'd rather not ask you; I'd rather leave you for some better man to marry.'

'But I wouldn't,' Persis cried aloud. 'Oh, Sir Justin, you must believe me. You must remember—'

At that precise point, Mrs Harrison put her head out of the carriage window and called out rather loudly—

'Why, Justin, what's keeping you? The horses'll catch their deaths of cold; and they were clipped this morning. Come back at once, my dear boy. Besides, you know, *les convenances*!'

'All right, Nora,' her brother answered; 'I won't be a minute. We can't get them to answer this precious bell. I believe it don't ring! But I'll try again, anyhow.' And half forgetting that his own words weren't strictly true, for he hadn't yet tried, he pressed the knob with a vengeance.

'Is that your room with the light burning, Miss Remanet?' he went on, in a fairly loud official voice, as the servant came to answer. 'The one with the balcony, I mean? Quite Venetian, isn't it? Reminds one of Romeo and Juliet. But most convenient for a burglar, too! Such nice low rails! Mind you take good care of the Remanet rubies!'

'I don't want to take care of them,' Persis answered, wiping her dim eyes hastily with her lace pocket-handkerchief, 'if they make you feel as you say, Sir Justin. I don't mind if they go. Let the burglar take them!'

And even as she spoke, the Maclure footman, immutable, sphinx-like, opened the door for her.

## 2.

Persis sat long in her own room that night before she began undressing. Her head was full of Sir Justin and these mysterious hints of his.

At last, however, she took her rubies off, and her pretty silk bodice. 'I don't care for them at all,' she thought, with a gulp, 'if they keep from me the love of the man I'd like to marry.'

It was late before she fell asleep; and when she did, her rest was troubled. She dreamt a great deal; in her dreams, Sir Justin, and dance music, and the rubies, and burglars were incongruously mingled. To make up for it, she slept late next morning; and Lady Maclure let her sleep on, thinking she was probably wearied out with much dancing the previous evening—as though any amount of excitement could ever weary a pretty American! About ten o'clock she woke with a start. A vague feeling oppressed her that somebody had come in during the night and stolen her rubies. She rose hastily and went to her dressing-table to look for them. The case was there all right; she opened it and looked at it. Oh, prophetic soul![2] the rubies were gone, and the box was empty!

Now, Persis had honestly said the night before the burglar might take her rubies if he chose, and she wouldn't mind the loss of them. But that was last night, and the rubies hadn't then as yet been taken. This morning, somehow, things seemed quite different. It would be rough on us all (especially on politicians) if we must always be bound by what we said yesterday. Persis was an American, and no American is insensible to the charms of precious stones; 'tis a savage taste which the European immigrants seem to have inherited obliquely from their Red Indian predecessors. She rushed over to the bell and rang it with feminine violence. Lady Maclure's maid answered the summons, as usual. She was a clever, demure-looking girl, this maid of Lady Maclure's; and when Persis cried to her wildly, 'send for the police at once, and tell Sir Everard my jewels are stolen!' she answered, 'Yes, miss,' with such sober acquiescence that Persis, who was American, and therefore a bundle of nerves, turned round and stared at her as an incomprehensible mystery. No Mahatma could have been more un-moved.[3] She seemed quite to expect those rubies would be stolen, and to take no more notice of the incident than if Persis had told her she wanted hot water.

Lady Maclure, indeed, greatly prided herself on this cultivated imperturbability of Bertha's; she regarded it as the fine flower of English domestic service. But Persis was American, and saw things otherwise; to her, the calm repose with which Bertha answered, 'Yes, miss; certainly miss; I'll go and tell Sir Everard,' seemed nothing short of exasperating.

Bertha went off with the news, closing the door quite softly; and a few minutes later Lady Maclure herself appeared in the Californian's room, to console her visitor under this severe domestic affliction. She found Persis sitting up in bed, in her pretty French dressing jacket (pale blue with *revers* of fawn colour), reading a book of verses. 'Why, my dear!' Lady Maclure exclaimed, 'then you've found them again, I suppose? Bertha told us you'd lost your lovely rubies!'

'So I have, dear Lady Maclure,' Persis answered, wiping her eyes; 'they're gone. They've been stolen. I forgot to lock my door when I came home last night, and the window was open; somebody must have come in, this way or that, and taken them. But whenever I'm in trouble, I try a dose of Browning. He's splendid for the nerves. He's so consoling, you know; he brings one to anchor.'

She breakfasted in bed; she wouldn't leave the room, she declared, till the police arrived. After breakfast she rose and put on her dainty Parisian morning wrap—Americans have always such pretty bedroom things for these informal receptions—and sat up in state to await the police officer. Sir Everard himself, much disturbed that such a mishap should have happened in his house, went round in person to fetch the official. While he was gone, Lady Maclure made a thorough search of the room, but couldn't find a trace of the missing rubies.

'Are you sure you put them in the case, dear?' she asked, for the honour of the household.

And Persis answered: 'Quite confident, Lady Maclure; I always put them there the moment I take them off; and when I came to look for them this morning, the case was empty.'

'They were *very* valuable, I believe?' Lady Maclure said, inquiringly.

'Six thousand pounds was the figure in your money, I guess,' Persis answered, ruefully. 'I don't know if you call that a lot of money in England, but we do in America.'

There was a moment's pause, and then Persis spoke again—

'Lady Maclure,' she said abruptly, 'do you consider that maid of yours a Christian woman?'

Lady Maclure was startled. That was hardly the light in which she was accustomed to regard the lower classes.

'Well, I don't know about that,' she said slowly; 'that's a great deal, you know, dear, to assert about *anybody*, especially one's maid. But I should think she was honest, quite decidedly honest.'

'Well, that's the same thing, about, isn't it?' Persis answered, much relieved. 'I'm glad you think that's so; for I was almost half afraid of her. She's too quiet for my taste, somehow; so silent, you know, and inscrutable.'

'Oh, my dear,' her hostess cried, 'don't blame her for silence; that's just what I like about her. It's exactly what I chose her for. Such a nice, noiseless girl; moves about the room like a cat on tiptoe; knows her proper place, and never dreams of speaking unless she's spoken to.'

'Well, you may like them that way in Europe,' Persis responded frankly; 'but in America, we prefer them a little bit human.'

Twenty minutes later the police officer arrived. He wasn't in uniform. The inspector, feeling at once the gravity of the case, and recognizing that this was a Big Thing, in which there was glory to be won, and perhaps a promotion, sent a detective at once, and advised that if possible nothing should be said to the household on the subject for the present, till the detective had taken a good look round the premises. That was useless, Sir Everard feared, for the lady's-maid knew; and the lady's-maid would be sure to go down, all agog with the news, to the servants' hall immediately. However, they might try; no harm in trying; and the sooner the detective got round to the house, of course, the better.

The detective accompanied him back—a keen-faced, close-shaven, irreproachable-looking man, like a vulgarized copy of Mr John Morley[4]. He was curt and business-like. His first question was, 'Have the servants been told of this?'

Lady Maclure looked inquiringly across at Bertha. She herself had been sitting all the time with the bereaved Persis, to console her (with Browning) under this heavy affliction.

'No, my lady,' Bertha answered, ever calm (invaluable servant, Bertha!), 'I didn't mention it to anybody downstairs on purpose, thinking perhaps it might be decided to search the servants' boxes.'

The detective pricked up his ears. He was engaged already in glancing casually round the room. He moved about it now, like a conjurer, with quiet steps and slow. 'He doesn't get on one's nerves,' Persis remarked approvingly, in an undertone to her friend; then she added, aloud: 'What's your name, please, Mr Officer?'

The detective was lifting a lace handkerchief on the dressing-table at the side. He turned round softly. 'Gregory, madam,' he answered, hardly glancing at the girl, and going on with his occupation.

'The same as the powders!'[5] Persis interposed, with a shudder. 'I used to take them when I was a child. I never could bear them.'

'We're useful, as remedies,' the detective replied, with a quiet smile; 'but nobody likes us.' And he relapsed contentedly into his work once more, searching round the apartment.

'The first thing we have to do,' he said, with a calm air of superiority, standing now by the window, with one hand in his pocket, 'is to satisfy ourselves whether or not there has really, at all, been a robbery. We must look through the room well, and see you haven't left the rubies lying about loose somewhere. Such things often happen. We're constantly called in to investigate a case, when it's only a matter of a lady's carelessness.'

At that Persis flared up. A daughter of the great republic isn't accustomed to be doubted like a mere European woman. 'I'm quite sure I took them off,' she said, 'and put them back in the jewel case. Of that I'm just confident. There isn't a doubt possible.'

Mr Gregory redoubled his search in all likely and unlikely places. 'I should say that settles the matter,' he answered blandly. 'Our experience is that whenever a lady's perfectly certain, beyond the possibility of doubt, she put a thing away safely, it's absolutely sure to turn up where she says she didn't put it.'

Persis answered him never a word. Her manners had not that repose that stamps the caste of Vere de Vere[6]; so, to prevent an outbreak, she took refuge in Browning.

Mr Gregory, nothing abashed, searched the room thoroughly, up and down, without the faintest regard to Persis's feelings; he was a detective, he said, and his business was first of all to unmask crime, irrespective of circumstances. Lady Maclure stood by, meanwhile, with the imperturbable Bertha. Mr Gregory investigated every hole and cranny, like a man who wishes to let the world see for itself he performs a disagreeable duty with unflinching thoroughness. When he had finished, he turned to Lady Maclure. 'And now, if you please,' he said blandly, 'we'll proceed to investigate the servants' boxes.'

Lady Maclure looked at her maid. 'Bertha,' she said, 'go downstairs, and see that none of the other servants come up, meanwhile, to their bedrooms.' Lady Maclure was not quite to the manner born, and had never acquired the hateful aristocratic habit of calling womenservants by their surnames only.

But the detective interposed. 'No, no,' he said sharply. 'This young woman had better stop here with Miss Remanet—strictly under her eye—till I've searched the boxes. For if I find nothing there, it may perhaps be my disagreeable duty, by-and-by, to call in a female detective to search her.'

It was Lady Maclure's turn to flare up now. 'Why, this is my own maid,' she said, in a chilly tone, 'and I've every confidence in her.'

'Very sorry for that, my lady,' Mr Gregory responded, in a most official voice; 'but our experience teaches us that if there's a person in the case whom nobody ever dreams of suspecting, that person's the one who has committed the robbery.'

'Why, you'll be suspecting myself next!' Lady Maclure cried, with some disgust.

'Your ladyship's just the last person in the world I should think of suspecting,' the detective answered, with a deferential bow—which, after his previous speech, was to say the least of it equivocal.

Persis began to get annoyed. She didn't half like the look of that girl Bertha, herself; but still, she was there as Lady Maclure's guest, and she couldn't expose her hostess to discomfort on her account.

'The girl shall *not* be searched,' she put in, growing hot. 'I don't care a cent whether I lose the wretched stones or not. Compared to human dignity, what are they worth? Not five minutes' consideration.'

'They're worth just seven years,' Mr Gregory answered, with professional definiteness. 'And as to searching, why, that's out of your hands now. This is a criminal case. I'm here to discharge a public duty.'

'I don't in the least mind being searched,' Bertha put in obligingly, with an air of indifference. 'You can search me if you like— when you've got a warrant for it.'

The detective looked up sharply; so also did Persis. This ready acquaintance with the liberty of the subject in criminal cases impressed her unfavourably. 'Ah! we'll see about that,' Mr Gregory answered, with a cool smile. 'Meanwhile, Lady Maclure, I'll have a look at the boxes.'

<h2 style="text-align:center">3.</h2>

The search (strictly illegal) brought out nothing. Mr Gregory returned to Persis's bedroom, disconsolate. 'You can leave the room,' he said to Bertha; and Bertha glided out. 'I've set another man outside to keep a constant eye on her,' he added in explanation.

By this time Persis had almost made her mind up as to who was the culprit; but she said nothing overt, for Lady Maclure's sake, to the detective. As for that immovable official, he began asking questions— some of them, Persis thought, almost bordering on the personal. Where had she been last night? Was she sure she had really worn the rubies? How did she come home? Was she certain she took them off? Did the maid help her undress? Who came back with her in the carriage?

To all these questions, rapidly fired off with cross-examining acuteness, Persis answered in the direct American fashion. She was sure she had the rubies on when she came home to Hampstead, because Sir Justin O'Byrne, who came back with her in his sister's carriage, had noticed them the last thing, and had told her to take care of them.

At mention of that name the detective smiled meaningly. (A meaning smile is stock-in-trade to a detective.) 'Oh, Sir Justin O'Byrne!' he repeated, with quiet self-constraint. '*He* came back with you in the carriage, then? And did he sit the same side with you?'

Lady Maclure grew indignant (that was Mr Gregory's cue). 'Really, sir,' she said angrily, 'if you're going to suspect gentlemen in Sir Justin's position, we shall none of us be safe from you.'

'The law,' Mr Gregory replied, with an air of profound deference, 'is no respecter of persons.'

'But it ought to be of characters,' Lady Maclure cried warmly. 'What's the good of having a blameless character, I should like to know, if—if—'

'If it doesn't allow you to commit a robbery with impunity?' the detective interposed, finishing her sentence his own way. 'Well, well, that's true. That's perfectly true—but Sir Justin's character, you see, can hardly be called blameless.'

'He's a gentleman,' Persis cried, with flashing eyes, turning round upon the officer; 'and he's quite incapable of such a mean and despicable crime as you dare to suspect him of.'

'Oh, I see,' the officer answered, like one to whom a welcome ray of light breaks suddenly through a great darkness. 'Sir Justin's a friend of yours! Did he come into the porch with you?'

'He did,' Persis answered, flushing crimson; 'and if you have the insolence to bring a charge against him—'

'Calm yourself, madam,' the detective replied coolly. 'I do nothing of the sort—at this stage of the proceedings. It's possible there may have been no robbery in the case at all. We must keep our minds open for the present to every possible alternative. It's—it's a delicate matter to hint at; but before we go any further—do you think, perhaps, Sir Justin may have carried the rubies away by mistake, entangled in his clothes?—say, for example, his coat-sleeve?'

It was a loophole of escape; but Persis didn't jump at it.

'He had never the opportunity,' she answered, with a flash. 'And I know quite well they were there on my neck when he left me, for the last thing he said to me was, looking up at this very window: "That balcony's awfully convenient for a burglary. Mind you take good care of the Remanet rubies." And I remembered what he'd said when I took them off last night; and that's what makes me so sure I really had them.'

'*And* you slept with the window open!' the detective went on, still smiling to himself. 'Well, here we have all the materials, to be sure, for a first-class mystery!'

## 4.

For some days more, nothing further turned up of importance about the Great Ruby Robbery. It got into the papers, of course, as everything does nowadays, and all London was talking of it. Persis found herself quite famous as the American lady who had lost her jewels.

People pointed her out in the park; people stared at her hard through their opera-glasses at the theatre. Indeed, the possession of the celebrated Remanet rubies had never made her half so conspicuous in the world as the loss of them made her. It was almost worth while losing them, Persis thought, to be so much made of as she was in society in consequence. All the world knows a young lady must be somebody when she can offer a reward of five hundred pounds for the recovery of gewgaws valued at six thousand.

Sir Justin met her in the Row one day. 'Then you don't go to Paris for awhile yet—until you get them back?' he inquired very low.

And Persis answered, blushing, 'No, Sir Justin; not yet; and—I'm almost glad of it.'

'No, you don't mean that!' the young man cried, with perfect boyish ardour. 'Well, I confess, Miss Remanet, the first thing I thought myself when I read it in *The Times* was just the very same: 'Then, after all, she won't go yet to Paris!''

Persis looked up at him from her pony with American frankness. 'And I,' she said, quivering, 'I found anchor in Browning. For what do you think I read?'

And I learn to rate a true man's heart

Far above rubies.[7]

'The book opened at the very place; and *there* I found anchor!'

But when Sir Justin went round to his rooms that same evening his servant said to him, 'A gentleman was inquiring for you here this afternoon, sir. A close-shaven gentleman. Not very prepossessin'. And it seemed to me somehow, sir, as if he was trying to pump me.'

Sir Justin's face was grave. He went to his bedroom at once. He knew what that man wanted; and he turned straight to his wardrobe,

looking hard at the dress coat he had worn on the eventful evening.
Things may cling to a sleeve, don't you know—or be entangled in a
cuff—or get casually into a pocket! Or some one may put them there.

## 5.

For the next ten days or so Mr Gregory was busy, constantly busy.
Without doubt, he was the most active and energetic of detectives. He
carried out so fully his own official principle of suspecting everybody,
from China to Peru[8], that at last poor Persis got fairly mazed with his
web of possibilities. Nobody was safe from his cultivated and highly
trained suspicion—not Sir Everard in his studio, nor Lady Maclure in
her boudoir, nor the butler in his pantry, nor Sir Justin O'Byrne in his
rooms in St James's. Mr Gregory kept an open mind against everybody
and everything. He even doubted the parrot, and had views as to the
intervention of rats and terriers. Persis got rather tired at last of his
perverse ingenuity; especially as she had a very shrewd idea herself who
had stolen the rubies. When he suggested various doubts, however,
which seemed remotely to implicate Sir Justin's honesty, the sensitive
American girl 'felt it go on her nerves,' and refused to listen to him,
though Mr Gregory never ceased to enforce upon her, by precept and
example, his own pet doctrine that the last person on earth one would
be likely to suspect is always the one who turns out to have done it.

A morning or two later, Persis looked out of her window as she
was dressing her hair. She dressed it herself now, though she was an
American heiress, and, therefore, of course, the laziest of her kind; for
she had taken an unaccountable dislike, somehow, to that quiet girl
Bertha. On this particular morning, however, when Persis looked out,
she saw Bertha engaged in close, apparently very intimate, conversation with the Hampstead postman. This sight disturbed the unstable
equilibrium of her equanimity not a little. Why should Bertha go to

the door to the postman at all? Surely it was no part of the duty of Lady Maclure's maid to take in the letters! And why should she want to go prying into the question of who wrote to Miss Remanet? For Persis, intensely conscious herself that a note from Sir Justin lay on top of the postman's bundle—she recognized it at once, even at that distance below, by the peculiar shape of the broad rough envelope—jumped to the natural feminine conclusion that Bertha must needs be influenced by some abstruse motive of which she herself, Persis, was, to say the very least, a component element. 'Tis a human fallacy. We're all of us prone to see everything from a personal standpoint; indeed, the one quality which makes a man or woman into a possible novelist, good, bad, or indifferent, is just that special power of throwing himself or herself into a great many people's personalities alternately. And this is a power possessed on an average by not one in a thousand men or not one in ten thousand women.

Persis rang the bell violently. Bertha came up all smiles: 'Did you want anything, miss?' Persis could have choked her. 'Yes,' she answered, plainly, taking the bull by the horns, 'I want to know what you were doing down there, prying into other people's letters with the postman?'

Bertha looked up at her, ever bland; she answered at once, without a second's hesitation: 'The postman's my young man, miss; and we hope before very long now to get married.'

'Odious thing!' Persis thought. 'A glib lie always ready on the tip of her tongue for every emergency.'

But Bertha's full heart was beating violently. Beating with love and hope and deferred anxiety.

A little later in the day Persis mentioned the incident casually to Lady Maclure—mainly in order to satisfy herself that the girl had been lying. Lady Maclure, however, gave a qualified assent:—

'I *believe* she's engaged to the postman,' she said. 'I *think* I've heard so; though I make it a rule, you see, my dear, to know as little as I can of these people's love affairs. They're so very uninteresting. But Bertha certainly told me she wouldn't leave me to get married for an indefinite period. That was only ten days ago. She said her young man wasn't just yet in a position to make a home for her.'

'Perhaps,' Persis suggested grimly, 'something has occurred meanwhile to better her position. Such strange things crop up. She may have come into a fortune!'

'Perhaps so,' Lady Maclure replied languidly. The subject bored her. 'Though, if so, it must really have been very sudden; for I think it was the morning before you lost your jewels she told me so.'

Persis thought that odd, but she made no comment.

Before dinner that evening she burst suddenly into Lady Maclure's room for a minute. Bertha was dressing her lady's hair. Friends were coming to dine—among them Sir Justin. 'How do these pearls go with my complexion, Lady Maclure?' Persis asked rather anxiously; for she specially wished to look her best that evening, for one of the party.

'Oh, charming!' her hostess answered, with her society smile. 'Never saw anything suit you better, Persis.'

'Except my poor rubies!' Persis cried rather ruefully, for coloured gewgaws are dear to the savage and the woman. 'I wish I could get them back! I wonder that man Gregory hasn't succeeded in finding them.'

'Oh! my dear,' Lady Maclure drawled out, 'you may be sure by this time they're safe at Amsterdam. That's the only place in Europe now to look for them.'

'Why to Amsterdam, my lady?' Bertha interposed suddenly, with a quick side-glance at Persis.

Lady Maclure threw her head back in surprise at so unwonted an intrusion. 'What do you want to know that for, child?' she asked, somewhat curtly. 'Why, to be cut, of course. All the diamond-cutters in the world are concentrated in Amsterdam; and the first thing a thief does when he steals big jewels is to send them across, and have them cut in new shapes so that they can't be identified.'

'I shouldn't have thought,' Bertha put in, calmly, 'they'd have known who to send them to.'

Lady Maclure turned to her sharply. 'Why, these things,' she said, with a calm air of knowledge, 'are always done by experienced thieves, who know the ropes well, and are in league with receivers the whole world over. But Gregory has his eye on Amsterdam, I'm sure, and we'll soon hear something.'

'Yes, my lady,' Bertha answered, in her acquiescent tone, and relapsed into silence.

## 6.

Four days later, about nine at night, that hard-worked man, the posty on the beat, stood loitering outside Sir Everard Maclure's house, openly defying the rules of the department, in close conference with Bertha.

'Well, any news?' Bertha asked, trembling over with excitement, for she was a very different person outside with her lover from the demure and imperturbable model maid who waited on my lady.

'Why, yes,' the posty answered, with a low laugh of triumph. 'A letter from Amsterdam! And I think we've fixed it!'

Bertha almost flung herself upon him. 'Oh, Harry!' she cried, all eagerness, 'this is too good to be true! Then in just one other month we can really get married!'

There was a minute's pause, inarticulately filled up by sounds unrepresentable through the art of the type-founder. Then Harry spoke again. 'It's an awful lot of money!' he said, musing. 'A regular fortune! And what's more, Bertha, if it hadn't been for your cleverness we never should have got it!'

Bertha pressed his hand affectionately. Even ladies'-maids are human.

'Well, if I hadn't been so much in love with you,' she answered frankly, 'I don't think I could ever have had the wit to manage it. But, oh! Harry, love makes one do or try anything!'

If Persis had heard those singular words, she would have felt no doubt was any longer possible.

## 7.

Next morning, at ten o'clock, a policeman came round, post haste, to Sir Everard's. He asked to see Miss Remanet. When Persis came down, in her morning wrap, he had but a brief message from head-quarters to give her: 'Your jewels are found, miss. Will you step round and identify them?'

Persis drove back with him, all trembling. Lady Maclure accompanied her. At the police-station they left their cab, and entered the ante-room.

A little group had assembled there. The first person Persis distinctly made out in it was Sir Justin. A great terror seized her. Gregory had so poisoned her mind by this time with suspicion of everybody and everything she came across, that she was afraid of her own shadow. But next moment she saw clearly he wasn't there as prisoner, or even as witness; merely as spectator. She acknowledged him with a hasty bow, and cast her eye round again. The next person she definitely distinguished was Bertha, as calm and cool as ever, but in the very centre of the group, occupying as it were the place of honour which naturally belongs to the prisoner on all similar occasions. Persis was not surprised at that; she had known it all along; she glanced meaningly at Gregory, who stood a little behind, looking by no means triumphant. Persis found his dejection odd; but he was a proud detective, and perhaps some one else had effected the capture!

'These are your jewels, I believe,' the inspector said, holding them up; and Persis admitted it.

'This is a painful case,' the inspector went on. 'A very painful case. We grieve to have discovered such a clue against one of our own men; but as he owns to it himself, and intends to throw himself on the mercy of the Court, it's no use talking about it. He won't attempt to defend it; indeed, with such evidence, I think he's doing what's best and wisest.'

Persis stood there, all dazed. 'I—I don't understand,' she cried, with a swimming brain. 'Who on earth are you talking about?'

The inspector pointed mutely with one hand at Gregory; and then for the first time Persis saw he was guarded. She clapped her hand to her head. In a moment it all broke in upon her. When she had called in the police, the rubies had never been stolen at all. It was Gregory who stole them!

She understood it now, at once. The real facts came back to her. She had taken her necklet off at night, laid it carelessly down on the dressing-table (too full of Sir Justin), covered it accidentally with her lace pocket-handkerchief, and straightway forgotten all about it. Next day she missed it, and jumped at conclusions. When Gregory came, he spied the rubies askance under the corner of the handkerchief—of course, being a woman, she had naturally looked everywhere except in the place where she had laid them—and knowing it was a safe case he had quietly pocketed them before her very eyes, all unsuspected. He felt sure nobody could accuse him of a robbery which was committed before he came, and which he had himself been called in to investigate.

'The worst of it is,' the inspector went on, 'he had woven a very ingenious case against Sir Justin O'Byrne, whom we were on the very point of arresting today, if this young woman hadn't come in at the eleventh hour, in the very nick of time, and earned the reward by giving us the clue that led to the discovery and recovery of the jewels. They were brought over this morning by an Amsterdam detective.'

Persis looked hard at Bertha. Bertha answered her look. 'My young man was the postman, miss,' she explained, quite simply; 'and after what my lady said, I put him up to watch Mr Gregory's delivery for a letter from Amsterdam. I'd suspected him from the very first; and when the letter came, we had him arrested at once, and found out from it who were the people at Amsterdam who had the rubies.'

Persis gasped with astonishment. Her brain was reeling. But Gregory in the background put in one last word—

'Well, I was right, after all,' he said, with professional pride. 'I told you the very last person you'd dream of suspecting was sure to be the one that actually did it.'

Lady O'Byrne's rubies were very much admired at Monte Carlo last season. Mr Gregory has found permanent employment for the next seven years at Her Majesty's quarries on the Isle of Portland.

Bertha and her postman have retired to Canada with five hundred pounds to buy a farm. And everybody says Sir Justin O'Byrne has beaten the record, after all, even for Irish baronets, by making a marriage at once of money and affection.

---

[1] **the great Parnell.** The 'uncrowned king of Ireland' was one of GA's political heroes. He had fallen from power in the wake of a scandal and died in 1891, taking any immediate hope of Irish Home Rule with him. Allen's airy dismissal in the *Fortnightly Review* of Parnell's adultery as a 'breach of etiquette' equivalent to breaking one's breakfast egg at the wrong end, outraged many of his readers.

[2] **Oh, prophetic soul!** Hamlet's outburst when the Ghost confirms his suspicion that Uncle Claudius has murdered his father.

[3] **No Mahatma could have been more unmoved.** At this time the 'mahatmas' were key figures in the cult of Theosophy, popular in the 1880s. The best-known of these adepts was 'Koot Hoomi', supposedly a Tibetan who dispensed oracular sayings and was reported as sinking into trances lasting months.

[4] **Mr John Morley.** A Radical politician and editor of the *Fortnightly Review* and the *Pall Mall Gazette*, both of which published Allen's work. His wife was judged unacceptable in high society, which also endeared him to the author. According to an infamous anecdote, when Morley was asked who the father was of his stepson, he replied, 'I don't know, and I doubt if she knows either.'

[5] **The same as the powders.** Gregory's Powder, a patent medicine containing rhubarb and ginger, was a popular laxative given to children.

[6] **The caste of Vere de Vere.** An allusion to the poem 'Lady Clara Vere de Vere' by Alfred Tennyson. Lady Clara is the very type of the arrogant, bored aristocrat.

[7] **And learn to rate a true man's heart/Far above rubies.** To impress Sir Justin, Persis has apparently invented this quotation by adapting an apt phrase about a 'virtuous woman' from Proverbs in the Bible.

[8] **From China to Peru.** Samuel Johnson, *The Vanity of Human Wishes*: 'Survey mankind, from China to Peru.'

# THE MISSING LINK

Grant Allen was a professional author who prided himself on meeting the demands of the market, and he rarely allowed himself to come into conflict with the censorious demands of editors and publishers. He was therefore mortified when not a single magazine editor would take this story of the loss of a doctor's Christian faith under the shattering impact of a unique fossil discovery. His practice with unsellable work up to then, he wrote later, had been to cremate 'all such stillborn children of my imagination'; but that after his trouble with this one he resolved to 'keep their poor little corpses by my side, and embalm them from time to time in an experimental volume of Rejected Efforts'. But as things turned out it achieved print for the first and only time when his publisher friend Andrew Chatto allowed it to appear without demur in the collection *Ivan Greet's Masterpiece, Etc* in 1893.

One can speculate as to why the story was so universally rejected. There is the fact that most magazine readers were middlebrow and middle class, and they wanted to be entertained, not have their prejudices upset. Grant Allen, it was coming to be known, was a freethinker with alarming notions about all sorts of things. So perhaps the mockery directed against earnest institutions like the YMCA jarred on editors' sensibilities. Or perhaps it was the ironical treatment of Dr Hawkins' belief that as long as the anthropoid origin of humanity was concealed, sexual morality would be preserved and 'our wives and daughters might yet live pure and good'. Perhaps it was simply that the doctor's melodramatic ravings—with much citation of Holy Writ—over what is, after all, a mere fossil were found distasteful.

215

Certainly, the theological issues dramatized in the story were acute enough. By the 1890s belief in the inerrancy of the Bible, particularly the account of creation in Genesis, had weakened under the onslaughts from impressively learned controversialists like T.H. Huxley. As the vicar in the story reminds Dr Hawkins, under the impact of geology the Church had been forced to capitulate over the six literal 'days' of creation. (Somewhat inconsistently, the hidebound Dr Hawkins does not hold to the belief, once commonplace and based on Biblical chronology, that the Earth is just 6,000 years old.) But powerful elements within the Church—and some reputable scientists too— were fighting a rear guard action against Darwinism. Where, they demanded, is the evidence that intermediate forms between ape and man had ever existed at all? To the discomfiture of many, an apparent answer to that came with the discovery of some fossils of 'Java Man' (now known to be *H. erectus*) in 1892. This was at once proclaimed to be the 'missing link', although that was hotly contested for many years afterward. It was surely this discovery that provided Allen with the immediate impetus for his story.

Finally, it should be noted that if pre-human remains were discovered in British Pliocene deposits like crag pits they would cause just as much perturbation among palaeontologists today as they do in Dr Hawkins' breast. The Pliocene is the geological epoch extending from roughly five million and two and a half million years ago. Several species of hominids lived in Africa during the Pliocene, most famously 'Lucy', excavated in 1974, whose partial skeleton is around 3.2m years old. Which of these hominids evolved much later into *Homo sapiens* and spread out across the world is still a matter of debate, and in this sense the 'missing link' is still missing, although the phrase is never used scientifically now. But the very oldest British physical remains, a shin bone and two teeth, found at Boxgrove—fossils of what the

Victorians would have called an 'ape man' had they known of them—
are far younger, at about 500,000 years. Somewhat older are the footprints in hardened mud recently revealed by coastal erosion, probably
made by a wandering party of the species *H. antecessor*, some 850,000
years ago. But this is still very far short of the Pliocene. By coincidence
the footprints were discovered at Happisburgh, only about 60 miles
north of the site of the fictional town of Dimthorpe in the story.

RICHARD HAWKINS was the Dimthorpe doctor. You've heard of Dimthorpe, no doubt—that stranded little village on the low Suffolk coast, bounded on the north by a salt-marsh, on the south by a sand-bank, on the right by a spreading East Anglian broad, and on the left by the wild waves of the German Ocean. As you tack along that flat shore, in a lumbering lugger, you see a faint streak of land and a squat church tower on your weather bow; and if you ask the Southwold skipper who navigates your boat what place that is, he'll answer you offhand, 'Yon's the hill at Dimthorpe.' He says it's a hill, you know, because it rises full eight feet high above sea-level at spring tides. Any-where else in the world but in the Suffolk marshes, you'd laugh at the notion of calling that a hill. In Suffolk the wise man accepts elevations at the native estimate.

All the doctors who ever came to Dimthorpe before Richard Hawkins, had taken to drink; except one, his predecessor, and *he* took to opium-eating. There was nothing else for an educated man to do in the place, people said. Perhaps it was the lowness and dampness of that marshy islet, and the depressing climate. But anyhow, in the marshes, men begin with quinine, for their first six weeks, to ward off fever and ague; take next, after twelve months, to brandy or gin; and end, after a year or two, with injections of morphia. That's the regular round, if a man lives long enough; but most of them die off before they reach the opiate stage.

Richard Hawkins, however, was a religious man: a secretary of Young Men's Christian Associations and Bible Society Auxiliaries[1]: so he took instead to the pursuit of science. He had taken to it, indeed, long before he bought the retiring opium-eater's practice at Dimthorpe. The Christian Young Men have a taste for magic lanterns and for the wonders of creation. They like to glance curiously at a creature under the microscope, and to say as they pass on, with an unctuous air, 'The handicraft of God is very marvellous.' Early in life, therefore, Richard Hawkins undertook to supply that felt want of the Christian Young Men by Wednesday evening lectures. As a student, he had paid particular attention to botany, comparative anatomy, geology; as a full-fledged medical man, he managed to find time still in the intervals of his practice, for these favourite studies. He had an adamantine constitution, which enabled him to go his rounds all day in his dog-cart or on his short-legged cob, and to be up again, fossil-hunting in the crag pits[2] by the river, at five o'clock next morning. A clean-shaven man, stubborn, pig-headed, conscientious, honest; the father of a family, blest with many twins, and ruling his own house well; one of those solid, stolid cast-iron Britons who know they're in the right, and will go to the stake gladly for their dearest prejudices rather than swerve an inch to the right or to the left from the path of truth as their eyes envisage it.

At Dimthorpe, Richard Hawkins gained universal respect. A doctor who didn't drink was indeed a novelty there. A doctor who served his turn in due time as churchwarden: a doctor who had means of his own, and paid his bills weekly: a doctor who lectured on the errors of Darwinism to the budding East Anglian grocer's assistant: a doctor who buttressed the tottering fabric of orthodoxy with magic-lantern slides, and combated the growing scepticism of this Erastian age with the two-edged sword of the Bible and Science—that was a rare treasure. The vicar congratulated himself on so useful an ally, though with an undercurrent of terror lest Dr Hawkins should suggest more doubts than he laid, and should rouse by his apologies more questions than he answered, in the candid minds of the young ladies of Dimthorpe. For the young should be shielded from the very shadow of error.

But these are, alas! unbelieving days. Now, Dimthorpe was cursed with a very bad man—'a blaspheming cobbler,' the mild-eyed curate called him—one Job Whittingham by name, a shrunken little creature, who took the *National Reformer* and the *Secularist*[3] for his intellectual diet, and who had read wicked books by Colenso, Huxley, Spencer, and Tyndall.[4] Nourishing his spare soul on these indigestible morsels, the cobbler in time waxed fat and kicked, intellectually speaking: for corporally, he was as lean and miserable as a scarecrow. He was a fearful radical too, folks thought, that cobbler: he feared neither squire nor parson, God nor devil. And therefore, at one of Richard Hawkins's Wednesday Evenings for the People—the Reverend the Vicar in the Chair as usual—he rose in his seat when all was done, and, humming and hawing somewhat in his native modesty, yet with much vehement oratory, as is the fashion of the British working-man when he speaks in public, he ventured, he said, 'umbly to call in question some of our learned lecturer's most 'ardy conclusions.

Richard Hawkins smiled. With that ample consciousness of intellectual superiority which the right use of the aspirate always gives to an educated man, face to face with the objections of an uneducated opponent, he leaned with both hands on the little table before him, and ejaculated blandly in a very soft voice, 'Which ones, pray? Which ones?'

'With Dr 'Awkins's permission, sir,' the cobbler answered sturdily, addressing himself with a fine sense of propriety to the vicar in the chair, 'I would like to offer an observation or two on his cumulative argament against the hanimal origin of the 'uman species.'

The vicar frowned faintly. This was just as he feared. When once you begin to reason about matters of faith, you open the floodgates of unbelief, and there's no knowing in what abysses of doubt you may be finally landed. (The vicar's metaphors were always rather exuberant than strictly consistent.) Besides, to give a common cobbler a chance of airing his infidel opinions at a public meeting was a thing not to be dreamed of. 'I think, Whittingham,' the vicar said coldly—it was a matter of principle with the vicar to keep the lower orders in that station in life to which,—and so forth; so he carefully abstained from addressing an unbelieving cobbler as *Mister* Whittingham: 'I think any public discussion on these delicate questions is out of order at our meetings. If there are points on which you'd like Dr Hawkins to instruct you further'—with a very marked stress upon the good word *instruct*—'you'd better inquire about them privately of him in the vestry—I mean, in his study—afterwards.'

For the vicar wasn't one to encourage brawling, nor did he think it seemly that an unwashed cobbler[5] should be heard in the assembly before the faces of his superiors.

Richard Hawkins, however, was made of other mould. Unlike the vicar, he had no sneaking undercurrent of terror in his inmost soul lest the religion of his fathers might be worsted and laid low in a hand-to-hand encounter with a journeyman shoemaker. A good man and true, he trusted his own cause, and he leapt into the fray as a knight armed at all points might leap upon the defenceless body of his Paynim assailant. He loved fair play; he loved free speech; he loved to see every man have a right to his opinion. And besides, he knew well he could crush that cobbler to earth in a second with the dead weight of his knowledge, his learning, his logical faculty.

'I think, Mr Chairman,' he interposed, still bland, still smiling his condescending smile, and fingering his smooth chin, 'if Mr Whittingham will state his objections to my views outright, I may be able to here and now to dispel his difficulties.'

The vicar's face was black. The vicar's eye was glassy. He shuffled uneasily in his chair of office. 'As you will, Dr Hawkins,' he answered, without attempting to conceal his grave disapproval. In the doctor's own house, even the priest of the parish could hardly prevent the doctor from letting his guests have their say if they would. But it was certainly unseemly that he, a beneficed clergyman of the Church of England, should be presiding over a meeting where an unbelieving cobbler was allowed to vent his vulgar infidelity unchecked before the faces of his betters. Still, politeness too has its laws. *Noblesse oblige.* Against his better judgment, the vicar bowed to his host's decision.

Then the cobbler, still swaying there awkwardly in his Sunday clothes, and waiting in some anxiety for the chairman's leave, with his head craned forward, and his little black eyes screwed up inquiringly under his projecting eyebrows,—the cobbler, I say, fell to with a will upon his destructive argument. He orated, of course—the British workman is nothing if not oratorical; his one idea of a speech is to declaim, full-mouthed; rhetoric is to him the soul of debate; he warms up as he goes, and launches forth, fiercely vehement. Dust pours from the slapped thighs of his Sunday trousers. But still, for all that, the cobbler pressed his professional opponent hard in argument. He combatted the doctrine, he said, of any distinct creation of the 'uman species. He believed, with 'Erbert Spencer, in the principles of evolutionism and gradual development. He saw no necessary limits imposed by nature on the action of them laws. They were eternal, all-pervading, inevitable, self-hacting. Warming up with his subject as he went, he proceeded to quote from memory in very long screeds what 'Uxley had said of man's place in nature. He appealed to Darwin, he appealed to 'Ackel, he appealed even to the partially adverse opinions of Mr Awlfred Russel Wallace[6]. He showed how shallow and sophistical, how devoid of solid basis, were the arguments advanced by Dr 'Awkins against them. He demolished Dr 'Awkins, indeed, with anatomy and physiology, with phylogeny and embryology, with the gorilla and the chimpanzee, with *ay priory* reasoning and *ay posteriory* facts[7]. IL was a triumphant vindication. The cobbler waxed warm over it, and mopped his bald forehead more than once by the way with the corner of his best red silk pocket-handkerchief.

But the audience—well, the audience just stared and tittered. In their well-bred ignorance— for most of them belonged to the local gentry and professional classes of the mud-bank islet—they felt the genial tolerance of superiority for the cobbler's facts and the cobbler's theories. It was nothing to them that Job Whittingham knew ten thousand times more about the question at issue than any one of themselves did. It was nothing to them that his logic was acute and his reasons convincing; nothing that his knowledge, though second- hand, was really in its way both wide and accurate. The man dropped his h's; that was quite enough for Dimthorpe. What science can you expect from the lips of a man who misplaces the very letters of the English alphabet? As Job grew warmer, and mopped his face more vigorously, the audience tittered louder at each absentee aspirate. As he finished, the chartered wag of Dimthorpe turned round to the vicar's second daughter with a broad smile on his face, and suggested in an audible aside that to judge from the speaker's words the Missing Link of 'umanity was the letter H.

Then Richard Hawkins, never heeding these rude allusions, but with the sweet smile of superiority on his smug clean-shaven face, rose once more from his seat, and expanding his white shirt-front with obtrusive respectability, addressed himself in the calm and courteous tone of the experienced lecturer to the Reverend the Chairman. That was a crushing answer. As the cobbler afterwards described it in a conversation with a friend, 'Awkins pounced down upon him like an 'awk; he was simply scarified. Not that the doctor could really reply to any one of his unlearned opponent's cogent arguments; but the doctor's aspirates were as firm as a rock, and the doctor's delivery was after the manner of a man who demonstrates to a beginner well-ascertained certainties.

'I ain't a-arguin' with you,' said a public-house orator one day to a foolish objector: 'I'm only a-tellin' of you.' And Richard Hawkins didn't argue either; he only told Job Whittingham where and how he was in error. Against Huxley and Darwin, the lecturer quoted with impressive effect (raising his voice as he spoke) that great and venerated anatomist, Sir Richard Owen[8]; and the audience, thrilling to the title, as in duty bound, felt instinctively that just as a member of the Royal College of Physicians is a better authority on science than a common cobbler, so a professor who had received the dignity of knighthood at the hands of most sacred majesty itself, must be a better authority on comparative anatomy than a brace of plain misters. It stood to reason, of course, that the Queen must know best on a question of abstruse scientific opinion.

In short, Richard Hawkins beat down his cobbler antagonist by sheer dint of authority and of social position. It was white-tie and swallow-tail against Sunday suit; it was academical English against sound common sense and quaint homespun rhetoric, with no h's to boast of.

As soon as the doctor had wagged his forefinger for the last time at a demonstrative period, the chairman, still wriggling uneasily in his chair, but with a pleasing consciousness that orthodoxy had now been amply vindicated, dissolved the meeting at once without waiting for Job Whittingham. The right of final reply, he said, rested always with the lecturer. That was a rule of debate. Dr Hawkins had replied. We would now adjourn, and meet again in this place on Wednesday fortnight: subject, The Evidences supplied by the Geological Record as to the Authenticity and Truth of Holy Scripture.

And for the next three days nobody talked of anything at the tea-tables of Dimthorpe, except the cheek of the cobbler, and the way Dr

Hawkins had banged the breath out of his body. He hadn't a leg to stand upon, the mild-eyed curate opined—not a leg to stand upon; he was simply extinguished.

But Job Whittingham went away, scratching what hair remained on his shock-headed poll, and feeling vaguely conscious that in spite of the doctor's long words—his crushing allusions to the *hippocampus major*[9] and the *flexor pollicis longus*[10]— Darwin and Huxley were right after all, and Richard Hawkins was but a shallow middle-class sciolist. It was his ample shirt-front that had carried the day. 'A working-man ain't got no chance,' Job remarked to himself, with philosophic resignation, 'agin the respectability and the social prestige of the black-coated classes. That's just where it is, don't you see? He ain't got no chance agin 'em.'

It was on Saturday of that week that Richard Hawkins, going his rounds on foot in the poor part of the town, saw one of Job Whittingham's eight starveling youngsters sitting on the doorstep of the cobbler's house; for though the radical philosopher was in theory a stalwart Malthusian, in practice his quiver was very full[11] of them. The boy was sucking a bone, which immediately attracted the doctor's trained attention. It wasn't a fresh bone, and it had no trace of meat on it. But the thing that made Richard Hawkins give a start of surprise at sight of it was the fact that—not to mince matters too fine—the bone was human. His anatomical eye told him that in a moment. The second or middle joint of a human forefinger!

He drew back, astonished. Not that there was here any faint flavour of romantic cannibalism. The bone, though human, was old and long buried. His interest in it was antiquarian and scientific, not living and medical. No suspicion of murder about this strange relic; no case of infanticide and back-garden interment. With facts like those, Richard Hawkins was only too familiar. He knew the ways of the poor and the evils of illegitimacy. But this bone was dry, very antique, thoroughly mineralized. He took it from the boy sharply, and looked hard at it awhile with the naked eye. Ha! what was this? Why, traces of crag on the sides and knuckle! Now, crag is the loose red Pliocene deposit of the hill at Dimthorpe; and as every geologist or antiquary knows, it antedates by many, many thousands of years the supposed first appearance of man on our planet. If the bone really came from a layer of the crag—Richard Hawkins drew back in unspeakable horror. He didn't even dare to formulate to himself his instinctive conclusions.

If the bone really came from the crag, then the age of man on the earth must be pushed back a couple of million years at least, to the Pliocene time—and Heaven only knows what might be the remote consequences to the cause of orthodoxy.

'Where did you get this finger, boy?' he asked the lad sharply.

And little Ted, looking up, made answer with a jerk of his thumb over his right side, 'Down yon: by Wood's crag-pit.'

'Dug it out?' the doctor asked in a very short voice.

And the boy nodded assent. 'Dug it out there,' he answered.

The doctor put the bone in his pocket hurriedly, gave the boy a ha'penny—for he was a saving man—and walked away to the next patient's house, much perturbed and preoccupied. He could hardly attend to the symptoms in the case—a mere ordinary development of acute brain-fever, in the stage of collapse—so interested and excited was he by that momentous question. What did it matter, in fact, whether one more poor old woman lived or died, when the whole fabric of theology, the whole future hopes of the human race, trembled tottering in the balance?

As soon as he decently could, he got away from his patients, home by himself, and, locking the door of the consulting-room, as often happened when people had to be examined, he took out his little plat-yscopic lens, and gazed long and anxiously at that tell-tale forefinger. Fragments of crag were embedded on it all round. It was to some extent mineralized by removal of bony particles and their replacement through filtration of iron compounds. Richard Hawkins peered at it in blank dismay. If this were indeed a bone of Pliocene date—then the whole fabric of his philosophy must topple over, helter-skelter, in one awful collapse, from base to coping-stone.

But no! Impossible! Incredible! The thing couldn't be. By sure and certain warranty of Holy Scripture, he knew it wasn't so; he knew it; he *knew* it. Man was fashioned direct, in the shape that we see him, by the finger of the Creator (whatever that may mean), without any Missing Link or other intermediate developmental form between himself and the soulless anthropoids. The bone must have been buried by accident in the crag, or deliberately interred there in ancient British times, and must have got mineralized in a comparatively short period by the action of water. Tomorrow morning he would go and examine the crag-pit. Till then, he'd put the bone back safe in his waistcoat pocket.

But he felt uneasy about it, all the same, for the rest of the day; that uncanny fragment! how annoying of it to come in with its disturbing implications, to upset the snug edifice of his cut-and-dried system! Bones shouldn't be allowed to get craggy like that! They should be kept in their place; they should be retained on the surface; they should be confined entirely to their proper strata. As the vicar with Job Whittingham, so the doctor with that digital.

That evening the vicar called round for an amiable chat with Dr Hawkins in his private study. The twins never came there, and he could see his friend quietly. They had a cigar together, and discussed the last lecture. The doctor was more positive that night than ever. He gazed at the illustrative casts of mammalian skulls in the cabinet opposite—man's, the gorilla's, the chimpanzee's, the gibbon's—and remarked complacently that for his part he pinned his faith on Specific Distinctions. If ever the affiliation of man on the Anthropoid Apes became a Proved Fact, then he didn't see how they could any longer resist the plain conclusion: on the special creation of man rested the Immortal Soul; and with the Immortal Soul went the whole complex system of orthodox theology.

The vicar, on the other hand, holding his coffee half sipped, was far more cautious and far less dogmatic. It didn't do, the vicar thought, for Christian men to base their faith too much upon any particular scientific or mere human opinion. Facts might be too strong for them in the end, any day, and they might have to reconsider their ideas and eat their own words, if they spoke too positively. 'Remember how we stuck at first to the six literal days of creation,' the vicar said softly, twirling two fat thumbs upon his ample knee. 'And we had to give them up after all. We had to go back upon it. Geology taught us they were only six epochs. For my part, Hawkins, if I were you, I wouldn't lay so much stress upon any one mode of interpreting scripture—especially Genesis. Genesis is a *very* hard nut to crack. While insisting strongly on the general close correspondence between the book of God and the book of nature, I wouldn't tie myself down to any special theory as to the *mode* of the coincidence between them—wouldn't nail a particular little flag to my mast, and pledge myself before the world to stand or fall by it.' For the parson was one of those prudent men who believe in the saving grace of hedging. The vicarage of Bray[12] would exactly have suited him. He took his stand, of course, on the Impregnable Rock of Holy Scripture: but he insisted that no one individual fragment of it had any necessary connection with the stability of the entire structure.

Richard Hawkins, however, with his scientific ideas, and his logical intellect, would hear of no such paltering with eternal and immutable Truth. More orthodox than the parson, he hated these latitudinarian views. 'No, no,' he said with warmth, fingering the bone in his pocket uneasily as he spoke: 'I can't admit that. I won't play fast and loose with the plain words of the Book. If God made man in His own image, and breathed into his nostrils the breath of life on the Sixth Day of Creation, then I can understand all the rest: the Immortal Soul; Free Will; the Plan of Salvation; the difference that marks us off from the lower animals; the existence within us of a divinely-sent conscience. But if ever it can be shown conclusively, shown beyond the shadow of a doubt, we're descended from an ape, then I give up all. We can be nothing more than the beasts that perish.[13] For at what point in the series of evolving monkeys can the Immortal Soul first come in? How can we ever say where the ape leaves off, and the man begins? Once admit the existence of a continuous chain of life, and you abandon the citadel. Either man is created in the image of God, or else he is a direct descendant of the monkey, the lizard, the ascidian, the jelly-fish. What is true of them is true also of him. The soul, the conscience, eternal life, depend entirely on direct creation.'

The vicar knocked off his ash pensively, and perused his boots. Logically, he had nothing to answer to the doctor's argument; but practically, he knew in his own soul that if evolutionism were to prove man's animal origin beyond the shadow of a doubt tomorrow morning, he'd stick to the vicarage of Dimthorpe still, and debate us hotly as ever at the diocesan synod over apostolic succession[14] and the eastward position[15]. So he held his silence, like a wise man, and stared hard at the fireplace.

All that night long, Richard Hawkins hardly slept a wink. The bone was indeed a bone of contention to him. Early in the morning, he rose up betimes, and betook himself in the grey dawn to the crag-pit by the river. Mrs Hawkins, the mother of many twins, was little surprised at his eccentric movements. A doctor's wife is accustomed to night alarms. She took it for granted he was called up to attend some patient.

Sunday morning though it was—no fit day for fossilizing—Richard Hawkins began to peer about in the pit, to see if he could find any trace of the owner of the forefinger. He wasn't long in discovering it. It was easy enough to find. His heart stood still within him as he gazed at the spot. A hand half protruded from the face of the cutting, where the workmen had left it exposed without ever discovering it. Or perhaps Ted Whittingham had grubbed it out after they went away from their work for the evening. The doctor's practised eye took in the facts at once. A significant glance at the lie of the strata told him this was indeed no ancient British interment. All the beds were undisturbed. The skeleton, if there was one, lay there *in situ*.

A few minutes' work succeeded in convincing him there *was* a skeleton. Egging away with his knife at the soft stone, he gradually unearthed a palm and fore-arm. He started afresh at the sight. Human, no doubt; yes, distinctly human! But how curiously proportioned, too! How unusually shaped! How strangely ape-like!

As he looked, a vague horror came over him suddenly. Why, this was an accursed thing, a work of the devil! He saw what it all meant already, and shrank from it with a deadly shrinking, an unspeakable repugnance. His first impulse, indeed, was to cover it all up, and rush away from the spot, and let the unclean thing remain buried for ever. But what use would that be? In a day or two's time, the workmen would reach it as they dug, and all England would ring with the hateful discovery. Second thoughts told him better. This was the Lord's doing. How lucky it was Sunday! Thank Heaven, in England, we remember the sabbath day to keep it holy still! The workmen wouldn't come to dig it out today. And how lucky it was a Christian who had first discovered it! In an agony of haste, he wrenched the fore-arm and wrist from the crag with a jerk, and wrapped them up with care in his white silk pocket-handkerchief. Then he turned and fled from that unhallowed pit. All the devils in hell hooted after him in derision.

That morning, Richard Hawkins didn't go to church. He was in no humour for prayer. He locked himself up in his own study, and sat examining those hateful bones with minute anatomical care. The more he looked at them, the less he liked them. Gratiolet's plates[16] lay open by his side. He compared the things with the normal skeleton in his cabinet—much to their disadvantage. Human; yes, human; undoubtedly human; but oh, how ape-like in effect, how intermediate in character! They were ghastly in their reminiscence of the great anthropoids. No Hottentot or Bushman was one twentieth so simian.

How he got through the day, he hardly knew. Dinner time came, and he ate his food mechanically. But horrible thoughts surged and seethed in his soul. The universe was tottering to its centre that day. The cosmos stood tremulous on the brink of an abyss. God himself was being weighed in the balance, and perhaps found wanting.[17] The existence of order, creation, a deity, depended upon the undisclosed remainder of that hateful skeleton. If the rest was as monkey-like as the fragment he had unearthed, then the Bible was a lie; the Creator was a dream; religion was a figment; the universe rolled black down the ages to hell: there never was, there never had been, a God its ruler.

So Richard Hawkins thought. Perhaps he thought right. Perhaps he thought wrong. But at any rate, he thought so. Too logical to palter with petty reconciliations, he stood by his guns manfully in this last extremity. He had erected for himself early in life a well-rounded philosophy, a system of things; and on that system he had based himself through all the years of his manhood. On the Impregnable Rock of Holy Scripture he had taken his stand. Now a moral earthquake shook and assailed that Rock. It trembled before his very eyes. If it staggered and fell, the solid ground would have failed beneath him. He had no place left in which to lay his head. Hell yawned open beside him. He must plunge into it and be satisfied.

Yet, born man of science that he was for all that, he could never be untrue to the Facts, could never ignore Evidence. Though that skeleton were to overthrow his God and his philosophy at once, he must unearth it still: he must find out the Truth: let it cost what it might, he must stand even with Realities. At nine o'clock he rose, and took out his lantern. His wife looked astonished. 'Where are you going, Richard?' she asked. And for the first time in his life, that perturbed and troubled soul told her guiltily a deliberate lie. 'A midwifery case,' he answered, shuffling. 'Poor woman out Ness way. I mayn't be back till morning.'

And he went out by himself towards the crag-pit by the river.

It rained hard that night, but for hours he stood there in the cold and wet, digging away with all his might, digging feverishly, madly. At all hazards, he must dig out that accursed thing. Never should it affront an innocent world with its godless face. Never should it laugh its mute laugh at purity and goodness. No workman should unearth it, and exhibit it in a glass case at the British Museum. If it was all that he feared, no human eye but his own should ever behold the atheistical grin on its mocking skull. He alone should pass through that fiery furnace. He alone should know by positive proof his Bible a lie and his God a delusion.

Two million years ago, some black and hairy creature, shambling along half erect on crouching knees through the woodland, had been suddenly carried away by a wild rush of water from a bursting tree-dam, and, after one hideous yell of rage and despair, had been drowned and buried in sand on the spot that is now the Hill at Dimthorpe. Alone among his kind, his skeleton was thus preserved, by the pure accident of geology, for our age to look upon. Richard Hawkins had discovered the one surviving specimen of the ancestor of man, as he roamed the dense woods of a Pliocene Britain.

Bit by bit he uncovered the thing—head, feet, trunk, shoulders. In the dark and under the rain, by the dim light of his lantern, he could hardly form any just anatomical opinion upon its form and affinities. But he saw quite enough even so to know his worst fears were hideously confirmed. With the energy of despair— the energy of a man who works body and soul against fearful odds to save the community from some unknown cataclysm, Richard Hawkins dug on, all heedless of rain and cold and darkness. His one terror was now lest any man should come up before dawn and interrupt him. That *he* should have learned that ghastly secret of the rocks was bad enough in all conscience: but that all the world should know it, and sink into the hopeless slough of infidelity and vice,—that was more than Richard Hawkins could bear to contemplate.

At last he finished his task. Every bone of the entire skeleton was there, unbroken. He thrust the precious fossils carefully into his sack, extinguished his lantern, and trudged wearily home through the rain, a disillusioned unbeliever.

Any other discoverer with half Richard Hawkins's scientific knowledge would have gone home rejoicing that he had found the most wonderful geological relic ever unearthed on the surface of our planet. But to Richard Hawkins, the whole episode envisaged itself quite otherwise. The iron of the Young Men's Christian Association had entered into his soul[18]. For years he had preached, with all the solid, stolid square-headed logic of his British middle-class mind, that morality, decency, the well-being of our race depended absolutely upon the religious life, and that the religious life depended absolutely upon implicit acceptance of the Bible story as he himself interpreted it:—and was he going now to turn back upon the creed of a lifetime, merely because he found the facts of the world had gone against him? Never, never, never! Nobly consistent in his way, Richard Hawkins admitted himself fairly beaten. The book of nature and the book of God, contrary to all belief, were plainly at variance. There *was* no God; there *was* no Immortal Soul: infidelity and vice had things all their own way: one moral shone clear from that evening's bad work—Let us eat and drink, for tomorrow we die![19] Let us wallow, if we would be logical, in the foul sty of licentiousness!

He had preached it so long, he had reiterated it so often, that he firmly believed it himself. If only the world knew what he carried in his bag, the world would in twenty-four hours from that time be a seething mass of sin like Sodom and Gomorrah.

With such thoughts surging fiercely in his feverish brain, he reached his home at last, let himself in with his latch-key, and deposited the sack in his own study. It was three in the morning, and he was wet to the skin. But the internal heat of a great disillusion kept him fiery hot in spite of it. Most men would have grown cold with it: Richard Hawkins went feverish. He took out the bones and examined them one by one. That skull—oh, how horrible! how loathsome! how disgusting! Human, human; vaguely, prophetically human: room for large hemispheres in it, a thinking brain; but what a low-browed scowl, what huge bony ridges over the deep-set eyes, what a massive lower jaw, what savage and snarling canines! The creature that owned that head-piece was a man in intelligence—of the lowest and most degraded Digger Indian type[20]—but a brute in moral sense, in fiendish cruelty, in fierce fighting instincts, in ungovernable passions. Richard

Hawkins reconstructed the fellow mentally for himself at a single glance—a peering, scowling, hairy-browed, heavy-jawed, shambling, scurrying, long-limbed savage—a bully all fists and tusks and brutal battles with his kind—a transmitter of the ape into the veins of what we had fondly hoped was rather the archangel ruined[21].

Richard Hawkins hid his face in his hands, not sobbing, but mute and horror-struck. Then he was an ape himself, and if he did as he ought to do on his own frequent showing, he should go straight upstairs, garden hatchet in hand, and dash out the brains of Mary and the children. Must he stultify himself before the faces of the Christian Young Men? Must he go back on his own oft-repeated philosophy?

Slowly he rose, after a long pause for thought, and lighted a huge fire in the study grate. His mind was made up now. He knew just what to do. Duty shone clear as a lamp before him. It was destroying the Evidence, to be sure. Well, never mind for that! There *was* no God. There *was* no Immortal Soul. But Heaven forbid the world should ever find it out through him. The words of Holy Scripture rang still in his ears—the words of that divine, that delusive Book on which he had pinned his life-long faith in vain—'It were better for that man that a millstone were fastened round his neck and he were cast into the sea.'[22] Let the universe roll on down its godless course; let fortuitous atoms[23] clash and clang for ever in unholy strife; but he at least, Richard Hawkins, would be guiltless of disclosing the loathsome secret. Not on *his* head would the blood of humanity rest. He would save society still from the demon of Atheism.

There *was* no God: but what of that? what of that? The world, the world could never get along without Him. We must believe in Him still, even though He be not. Why, he himself, Richard Hawkins, no solitary man, was left wholly rudderless before the blast by that accidental discovery. And how could the whole race survive the disillusion? Should he let loose rapine and uncleanness and massacre upon the earth, to go about like raging lions, seeking whom they might devour,[24] by telling the hideous truth to babes and sucklings[25]? Perish the thought! Far sooner than that, he would go down quick into the pit himself, and let the conscious earth close over him in silence[26].

One by one, he thrust the dry bones of the only specimen of Pliocene man into the fire, remorselessly. He stirred them with the poker, like the devils in some mediaeval Italian hell. He watched them crumble. He gloated over their destruction. Those atheistical fossils, doubly damned, had destroyed his peace of mind, and would have destroyed the world's, but for his own active and prompt intervention. In that burning fiery furnace, heated seven times hot[27], they mouldered away to ashes. As the last of them disappeared, he drew a deep breath. Religion was saved! The Bible might still be accounted true. Infidelity couldn't stalk triumphant through the land. Our wives and daughters might yet live pure and good. He had deserved well of the State. He had rescued humanity.

It was all a vast Lie, a triumph of priest-craft. But they would believe it still. They wouldn't stand out in the dark and cold as he did. Dark! why, the universe rolled black as pitch before him! Cold! why, not a ray of sunshine from heaven came to warm up anywhere its chilly expanse. He shuddered to realize it. There was no God; and the world was a vile cock-pit of jarring elements.

Well, well; he had done his duty to his kind, and after that he could go. 'Lord, now lettest Thou Thy servant depart in peace.'[28] Ah me, the irony of it! His eyes had beheld, not salvation, but the downfall of all hope, all faith, all charity. Profoundly religious to the core, as he understood religion, Richard Hawkins couldn't consent to live any longer in a godless and polluted world. He had found it all out. Henceforth it was no fit home for him. Born an heir of the Kingdom, he couldn't endure to abjure his birthright and dwell now for a brief space in the tents of iniquity.[29]

But he had one more duty to perform before he went hence. The cobbler! Job Whittingham! For duty was still the pole-star of that wrecked and sinking bark. Like an honest man that he was, and a sincere Christian, Richard Hawkins must allow when he was fairly beaten. As soon as day broke, he rose once more from his chair, let himself silently out, and walked along the cold grey streets to the cobbler's doorstep.

There, he knocked and waited. The cobbler, half-dressed, let him in, and yawned. Richard Hawkins's face was as white as a sheet. 'Good Lord, sir, what's the matter?' the cobbler asked, half terrified.

'Matter enough,' Richard Hawkins answered in a hollow voice, sinking heavily into a seat. His coat was still damp, and his eyes were haggard. 'Whittingham, I argued against you the other day at my lecture, that man couldn't possibly be descended from an ape-like ancestor. Well, since then, I've had positive proof that's not the truth. Man is descended after all from a monkey—a hideous, grinning, leering, horrible monkey. I know it. I've seen it. With my own very eyes I've found it all out. ... You were right. ... I was wrong. ... As a Christian man, I've come today to acknowledge it.' The cobbler stared hard at him. Was Dr 'Awkins mad? 'Wy, wot's made yer change yer mind?' he asked at last, much wondering.

'No matter,' Richard Hawkins answered, with lips like death. 'I've had reason to change. That's enough for us two. Whittingham, this morning I stand before you, an atheist like yourself. But not a contented one. I can't live so, for long. It's impossible, unhuman. I know now there's no God. Tonight in the long watches I've found God out. But I can't do without Him. For in Him, as the apostle truly says, we live and move and have our being.'[30]

The cobbler stared still harder. What strange mixture of faith and unbelief was this? His working-man mind couldn't fathom it at all. The despair of a wrecked system was too deep for his plummet to sound.[31] 'I don't see what you're a-drivin' at,' he blurted out bluntly.

Richard Hawkins drew his hand across his brow like one stunned. 'I dare say not, my friend,' he answered, in the voice of a man who speaks in a dream. 'I dare say not. But I mean it for all that. I mean it, every word of it. I couldn't bear to die without coming to acknowledge my change of view to you. I feel I wronged you. And I ought to have recanted as openly as I spoke. I ought to have made you a public restitution. If I wrong any man in ought, I would wish, like Zacchaeus, to repay him twofold.[32] But I can't, I can't. For the sake of a groping world, of all those good innocent Christian souls who still believe, as I did, I haven't the heart to do it. I haven't the heart to disillusion them. And I ask you yet one thing, my friend. For God's sake— though there *is* no God—but, there! one says it instinctively—for God's sake, speak not a word of this episode to anybody. Whittingham, you don't know what it costs me to make such a confession—to deny my God: to proclaim myself an atheist. Lock it up in your own soul! Say no syllable to any one.'

The cobbler, screwing up his small face, and peering eagerly out at him, took in by degrees the fact that his visitor's heart was stirred to the profoundest depths,—and had pity upon him. 'I will say not a word, sir,' he answered, after a moment's hesitation.

Richard Hawkins grasped his hand, rose in solemn silence, and staggered out once more. At the door he paused again. 'No God! No God!' he cried, nodding his head twice or thrice and half turning a second time to the astonished cobbler. Then he went out into the street, his hat in his hand, and walked hurriedly homeward. After all, why debate? All was well at home. Mary was provided for: the children wouldn't want. Of what use was he now in the world—that godless world? He couldn't bear the weight of such a secret for years and years. Any day he might blab. And ten drops of Prussic acid would end all so easily!

In his own study, he knelt down and prayed earnestly, fervently, to the God that never was, that never had been. You can't conquer in a day the habits of a lifetime. Then he unlocked his medicine chest, and took from it a phial.

The jury brought it in 'temporary insanity,' of course. People said, much learning had made him mad,[33] like Paul. He had worked too hard at once at science and his profession.

---

[1] **Young Men's Christian Associations ... Bible Society Auxiliaries.** The YMCA was and is a worldwide movement founded in 1844 to promote a healthy Christian lifestyle. The Bible Society was founded in 1804 to make Bibles readily available, and its auxiliaries were set up in many towns at home and abroad with the same object. Both movements had strong Evangelical origins, and were subject to hostile attacks and mockery by atheistic rationalists like Grant Allen.

[2] **crag pits.** A geological formation unique to East Anglia, made up of soft, pebbly sandstone, crushed shells and some fossils, dating to the Pliocene epoch.

[3] *National Reformer ... Secularist.* Two Radical, aggressively atheistic weekly periodicals, both strongly supportive of Malthusianism (contraception). The *Secularist* was more inclined to political Socialism, but lasted only one year under that exact title (1876-7).

[4] **Colenso, Huxley, Spencer, and Tyndall.** Bishop John Colenso was a biblical scholar who publicly doubted the literal truth of portions of the Bible; Thomas Henry Huxley, the formidable zoologist and controversialist known as 'Darwin's bulldog'; Herbert Spencer, who built his entire

philosophical system around evolutionism; John Tyndall, physicist and effective proponent of rationalism and the scientific world-view.

[5] **unwashen cobbler.** 'Unwashen' appears in the KJV translation of the Bible, where Jesus condemns ritual handwashing as typical of the Pharisees' hypocrisy.

[6] **'Ackel ... Awlfred Russel Wallace.** Ernst Haeckel, biologist and philosopher, the most able promoter of Darwinism in Germany in the late 19th century; A.R. Wallace was the co-discoverer with Darwin of the theory of natural selection, but later denied that it was capable of explaining the higher human faculties.

[7] *ay priory* **reasoning and** *ay posteriory* **facts.** Whittingham's pronunciation of *a priori* and *a posteriori*, meaning knowledge not requiring experience (*eg* theorems in maths), and empirical knowledge (*eg* most of science).

[8] **Sir Richard Owen.** Famous palaeontologist and anti-Darwinian; a highly controversial, slippery figure and great enemy of T.H. Huxley.

[9] *hippocampus major.* Apparently a slip, deliberate or not, for *hippocampus minor.* A brain structure which Owen wrongly claimed is unique to humans. A lengthy and vituperative public debate with Huxley followed, which caught the public fancy for a while.

[10] *flexor pollicis longus.* Muscle controlling the thumb, not found in other primates, a fact supposedly reinforcing the anti-Darwinian case.

[11] **in practice his quiver was very full.** The cobbler believes in birth control, but is 'blessed' with many children. The metaphor is from Psalm 127.

[12] **vicarage of Bray.** An allusion to a clergyman of that village in a popular 18th century satirical song, who is ready to adapt himself to any and all swings in religious orthodoxy, just as long as he can retain his preferment.

[13] **the beasts that perish.** A phrase from Psalm 49, alluding to the fate of those who 'understandeth not' God's word.

[14] **apostolic succession.** A debate among Protestants about whether Christian teaching had been properly handed down in an unbroken chain of bishops since the original apostles.

[15] **eastward position.** After the Reformation, the Church abandoned the practice of the priest facing east with his back to the congregation while celebrating Mass. The ensuing controversy was briefly revived in the mid-19th century by the Oxford Movement.

[16] **Gratiolet's plates.** Louis Pierre Gratiolet (*d.*1865) was a zoologist and comparative anatomist who specialised in the structure of the brain, both human and anthropoid. His work led him to strongly racist views about the intellectual capacities of different peoples.

[17] **God himself was being weighed in the balance.** In the Book of Daniel, the Babylonian king Belshazzar was, by God's judgement, weighed and 'found wanting' according to a miraculous inscription on his palace wall.

[18] **The iron ... had entered his soul.** A phrase from *The Book of Common Prayer*, mistranslated from Psalm 105.

[19] **Let us eat and drink, for tomorrow we die!** A phrase found twice in the Bible, first in Isaiah 22 and by St Paul in his Epistle to the Corinthians: a sentiment signifying a reckless indifference to one's future fate.

[20] **degraded Digger Indian type.** A derogatory term for a Californian hunter-gatherer tribe which did not farm but foraged for edible roots, *etc.*

[21] **the archangel ruined.** Satan is so described in Milton's *Paradise Lost*, Book 1.

[22] **'It were better for that man that a millstone were fastened round his neck ...'** Jesus' condemnation of those who offend against the 'little ones' (Luke 17).

[23] **fortuitous atoms.** Usually quoted as 'a fortuitous concourse of atoms'— Jonathan Swift's expression of incredulity that there should be no design in nature.

[24] **seeking whom they might devour.** According to the First Epistle of Peter it is the devil, metaphorically a roaring lion, who acts in this way.

[25] **babes and sucklings.** A phrase from Psalm 8.

---

[26] **he would go down quick into the pit himself, and let the conscious earth close over him in silence.** Adapted from the fate of Moses' enemies, as recorded in the Book of Numbers 16.

[27] **In that burning fiery furnace, heated seven times hot.** In the Book of Daniel, three young Jews are thrown into a furnace by King Nebuchadnezzar for refusing to worship an idol. They are miraculously unharmed.

[28] **'Lord, now lettest Thou Thy servant depart in peace.'** Opening line of the 'Nunc dimittis' or Song of Simeon, who gave praise that he had lived to see the birth of Jesus, in Luke 15.

[29] **the tents of iniquity.** A phrase of one of Job's accusers, in the Book of Job 11.

[30] **we live and move and have our being.** A phrase from St Paul's address to the Athenians, Acts 17.

[31] **was too deep for his plummet to sound.** 'And deeper than did ever plummet sound/I'll drown my book.' Prospero abjures his magic in the last Act of *The Tempest*.

[32] **If I wrong any man in ought, I would wish, like Zacchaeus, to repay him twofold.** The tax-collector in Luke 19 who boasts that he 'restore(s)' 'fourfold' any money he has falsely collected.

[33] **much learning had made him mad.** So St Paul is accused, in a hearing before the Roman rulers Marcus Agrippa and Festus, Acts 25.

# MAJOR KINFAUN'S
# MARRIAGE

This black comedy appeared anonymously in the *Cornhill* magazine in March 1894 and was never reprinted. It's a neat twist on the theme of the 'biter bit', drawing on the fact, exploited by many novelists, that the signals of social breeding and economic status can be difficult to interpret when in foreign places—with consequences ranging from the disconcerting to the catastrophic. It's told from the cynical perspective of a fortune-hunting cavalry officer, and is set on the louche Riviera, specifically at the Hotel du Cap, Antibes, which the semi-invalid Grant Allen himself frequented most winters with his family in his more prosperous years. Thanks to the power of sterling, living was very cheap in the South of France in the 1890s. Britons of many types had settled like migrating birds in the hotels and pensions of Grasse, Cannes and Menton: mostly invalids recuperating in the mild winters and the elderly pensioned, but with a good sprinkling of more dubious parasites—the idle rich, pseudo-artists, husband- and fortune-hunters, fraudsters and 'adventuresses'. Angus Kinfaun is a typical type of that era. A major in the cavalry earned round £365 a year on active service, but since Kinfaun apparently has no duties he is presumably a reservist on half-pay, not enough to maintain convincingly the status of a gentleman at home.

The time of the story's setting isn't given, but we deduce it must be after the Married Women's Property Act of 1893 by which, for the first time, women retained full ownership of property they acquired both before and after marriage. The new Act made fortune-hunting by men of Kinfaun's stamp a trickier proposition than it had been. However, men of middle rank and above who married heiresses or rich widows could, without social odium, ask for and expect a prenuptial settlement in their favour. Amy takes it as a 'signal proof' of her husband's love that he refrains from requesting one.

'TWAS A terrible nemesis that befell poor Major Kinfaun. He deserved it, no doubt—if every man had his deserts, indeed, which
would 'scape whipping?[1] But who that sees Kinfaun today, for all
that, can refrain from pitying him?

He met her, when anemones bloom, at Antibes, at that charming
hotel on the Cape, pushed far out into the sea, where you look way
across the Baie des Anges towards Nice and Bordighera, and the other
way, across the Golfe Juan and the Isles, towards jagged outline of the
rearing Esterel. Not that Kinfaun himself cared two straws in his heart
for any of these things. Anemones and dandelions were all one to him.

It was the rich young widow, or the young widow reputed to be
rich, that brought the politic soldier to Antibes. For himself, he vastly
preferred Cannes—that worldly Cannes, where the breath of princes
hangs heavy on the air, and grand-dukes and bankers pullulate by the
score upon every bristling hillside. That was the sort of atmosphere
that Kinfaun loved; he drank it in, princely carbonic acid[2] and all, with
pure delight. It made him feel happier to pass a man in the street and
be told he was really a small crowned head; it made him stand higher
in his neat walking shoes to tread the same pavement worn smooth by
the soles of so much Serene and Imperial Altitude.

But Kinfaun had always a keen nose for an heiress, and taking
walks abroad between Califomie and the Croisette[3], he scented the
young widow at Antibes afar off. For the sake of being near her, he
was ready, like a thorough-going strategist that he was, to scorn the
noisy delights of Cannes, and live ignoble days,[4] through a brief court-
ship at least, by the water-worn cliffs and dashing breakers of the Cap
d'Antibes. So he drove across with his portmanteau one March morning from the Prince de Galles, where he had been spending the winter;
drove across, characteristically enough, in the young Comte de Kérouac's high dog-cart; for no ever knew better how to make the best use

of all his friends than Angus Kinfaun. The whole plan fitted in so neatly together. De Kérouac suffered severely from the fashionable *anglomanie*; he dressed himself in very loud sporting tweeds, chequered like a chess-board, and owned a dog-cart; to him, nothing could be in better form or better keeping than to have an English officer seated beside him in the machine as he drove; he regarded it as *tout ce qu'il y a de plus sportsman*[5]. Kinfaun, on the other hand, considered that he couldn't make a better first impression on the widow's hotel than by dashing up to the door in a neat turn-out, with a Breton count in stentorian tweeds by his side and the trimmest of trim close-shaven French grooms stuck bolt upright behind, arms crossed severely on his swelling breast, and face like a sphinx in the act of ruminating upon her own riddles. Things get about so quickly at hotels in these twaddling, gossiping winter stations. Everybody would say to the widow at *table d'hôte* that evening, 'Have you seen the new arrival who came over from Cannes by road today? He wears an orchid in his buttonhole, and De Kérouac of the Réunion wheeled him across by the Pines in his dog-cart.'

The value of a first impression in affairs of the heart cannot be over-estimated. And Kinfaun was indeed a man to make good impression at first sight. Tall, well-knit, with his soldierly imperial and twirled moustache just becomingly grizzled by the first snows of the forties, he looked and stood every inch a gentleman. Those keen grey eyes and that well-bred nose of his showed just enough of their owner's cynical temperament to be merely piquant. His manner was frank, yet delicately deferential: the manner of a man of the world who knows well how to please, and who has ample reasons of his own for the wish to be pleasing. If Kinfaun had made up his mind to win the widow, everybody said—why, then the widow must be hard indeed to win if she resisted Kinfaun.

Fortune favours the brave. He came upon her by accident in a lucky moment, the very first afternoon he spent at the Cape. He had wandered out after lunch to enjoy the fine aroma of his cigar in the grounds, among the scent of the pine woods, and strolled down to the little bay by the craggy promontory where the sea always dashes high, one side or the other, no matter what wind may happen to be blowing. There, in a nook of the cliffs—for they descend by natural steps in the living rock to sea-level—a vision of delight met his enraptured eye. He knew at once it was the widow; it could only be she, according to description. She was thirty-five, to be sure, but round-faced and gracious-looking; a taking smile played enticingly round the corners of her full red lips, though she was quite alone; she was fishing up sea-anemones out of a pool with her parasol as she sat: the sun shone on the sea, and the waves danced merrily. Kinfaun gazed down on her intently for a minute before she was aware of being perceived. It brought the colour into her cheek when, looking up, she saw a man stand by the edge of the cliff, gazing upon her hard, yet with a sympathetic curve about the corners of his mouth; but she smiled once more that taking smile, and to his immense delight, being taken off her guard, spoke to him unaccosted.

'It's a beautiful spot, this,' she said, 'so quiet and retired.' She said it to cover her confusion, he knew, half out of the mere bashfulness of having been caught, alone, in that childish attitude, fishing in the pool with her parasol; but he counted it all to the good for his scheme nevertheless. For a woman to speak first to you of her own accord is the best of all possible introductions.

Kinfaun flung away his cigar at once. He flung it into the sea; not ostentatiously, yet with such a deferential little air of instinctive courtesy that the widow could hardly fail to notice the graceful action. As a rule, you may smoke when you talk to a lady; to smoke is mannish;

247

but on first acquaintance, it looks well, nevertheless, as a matter of form, to abjure your tobacco. It shows that you value a stray moment of the lady's conversation far more than you value any ephemeral joy to be derived from the best half of a prime Havana. And besides, it's chivalrous. For the first few stages chivalry pays; after them, a certain bold and even obtrusive masculinity has the greater attraction. The veriest old maids will sometimes confess they like the smell of tobacco; it shows there's a man about the house, and to have a man about the house is eminently respectable.

'Delightful,' he answered from under that grizzled moustache, with his own most charming responsive smile, as he flung the cigar away. 'So far from all the bustle and noise of Cannes! The very kind of place for people who love calm and quiet,' for he saw at a glance what was the widow's line. 'So breezy and open, and with such lovely views too.' And he lifted his eyes from hers quite naturally for a second towards the long jagged line of that indented Esterel.

It was just as he did so that the cigar struck the water.

'Oh, I'm so sorry you've thrown it away,' Mrs Roupell cried, watching the splash where it fell.

Kinfaun came down tentatively a couple of steps along the broken ledges towards where she sat; he felt the sacrifice of so much good tobacco entitled him at least to make that further advance in her direction. To have thrown it away was an earnest of good-will. Then he leant against his stick behind him and gazed down with peering eyes into the pool.

'What wonderful creatures one always finds in these rock-basins,' he went on abstractedly; though, to say the truth, he had never hunted them since he was a boy in knickerbockers, wading on the sands. 'And what lovely colours they take on the Mediterranean seaboard here!'

Mrs Roupell dipped down her parasol into the fishery once more, and hooked out some sea-mats. She seemed by no means indisposed, for her part, to continue the conversation. 'You've only just come?' she said interrogatively, as she examined her find with half-affected interest.

'Drove over from Cannes this morning,' the major answered, still leaning back on his stick and gazing down intently into the shallow basin. 'I was tired of the eternal round of tea and tennis, gout and gossip, so I thought I'd come over here for the strolls and the scrambles.'

'I saw you come,' Mrs Roupell went on, spreading out the sea-mat on the rock by her side; and Kinfaun scored one internally with joy that the dog-cart and the groom had not passed unnoted. 'You're quite right. The walks here are charming: especially in and out, in and out, round the coast. Such endless little bays and points and headlands. If scrambling's what you like, you've come to the right place for it.'

'I adore scrambling,' Kinfaun answered, with a glance at those neat walking shoes, descending just a step, and poking his stick into the pool in turn in search of anemones. 'This seems quite an ideal hotel for anyone to stop at who loves nature.'

'And you should see the flowers in the woods!' Mrs Roupell replied with enthusiasm.

So at the end of ten minutes, by perfectly natural gradations, Kinfaun was seated on the rocks opposite the pretty widow, and deeply engaged in profound conversation on scenery, Keats, and the human affections. For Kinfaun was a clever fellow at bottom in spite of his society airs and graces; and though his knowledge of men and books was by no means deep, it was as wide as it was shallow. He could mould his talk to suit his hearer with an accommodating versatility which many abler but less shifty talkers might well have envied him.

Before they got up from the rocks that afternoon, Kinfaun had succeeded in making his impression. The pretty little widow, reputed rich, thought him a most charming and sympathetic man, and the pleasantest companion she had met since she came to Antibes.

That same evening Kinfaun found himself alone in the billiard room, over a cigar and a brandy and soda, with Marindin of the Record Office—the very man who had given him the first stray hint as to the existence of a wealthy young woman, now unattached, awaiting siege at the hotel on the promontory.

'Pretty little body enough, that Mrs Roupell,' he remarked casually, as he knocked about the billiard-balls for pure practice (he was a first-rate player). 'Middle-aged, of course, but extremely well-preserved. I like what I've seen of her. And her smile's so pleasant.'

'Yes, we're all immensely taken with her,' Marindin answered languidly, between the long slow puffs. 'She's such a nice little thing, so kind-hearted and good-natured. She takes my little girl out driving almost every afternoon. Polly's quite in love with her.'

Kinfaun pricked up his ears at the sound. 'Driving,' he repeated. 'Then she drives a good deal, does she? Has she got a carriage?'

'Hires one from Cannes by the month,' Marindin replied laconically. 'Neat turn-out: couple of greys, coachman in livery.'

Kinfaun pretended to be profoundly absorbed in a difficult cannon he was endeavouring to pull off by a miracle of rebounds, and walked round the billiard table in the most leisurely fashion to survey the best point from which to accomplish it. 'Then she's really well off?' he said, with insinuating inquiry, as the balls kissed and glided off gently at the exact angle required.

'Oh, I s'pose so,' Marindin answered, throwing back his head and blowing out a long round stream of tobacco smoke. 'She's never told *me*. The precise amount of her income is, no doubt, a question that lies only between herself and the Commissioners of Inland Revenue. But to judge by what she spends, I should say she can't be penniless.'

To judge by what she spends indeed! What a fatuous criterion! Kinfaun totted up the total mentally. After all, it needn't mean so very much. Mrs Roupell herself, her maid, and no children: first floor rooms, *table d'hôte*, and salon: say eleven pounds a week, all told, for hotel-bill. Well, she might live like that, carriage and dress and travelling expenses included—a lone lorn woman[6]—for a trifle over seven or eight hundred a year, he fancied. It wasn't princely, but still—it was a competence. And a competence, you know, is always something. Kinfaun didn't feel sure that he cared to chuck himself away this time for so little. It was all very well, sentiment, when you were young and foolish; but when the first snows of the forties begin to grizzle your well-waxed moustache—by Jove! sir, a man begins to know his market worth, and determines to sell himself at the highest current quotation for cavalry officers. For Kinfaun, too, had once been young, and like all the rest of us had committed a youthful indiscretion. He had married for love at three-and-twenty. His wife, to be sure, had a couple of hundred a year or so of her own in consols[7]; but what was that to Kinfaun? A man of his tastes finds two hundred a year and one's pay mere beggary. Ah, well! poor Mrs Kinfaun was dead and gone long since, however—died a twelvemonth ago at Cannes, where he had come for her health, for in his way he was fond of her; and now that the year of decent mourning was fairly over, and the Kinfaun moustaches were once more in the market, he hadn't the slightest intention of repeating in maturer years that one error of an otherwise blameless and strictly prudent existence.

So he surveyed the balls again, with his head on one side, deliberative of point and twist and impetus; then he remarked at last, after he had taken his stroke and scored once more, 'You've no idea what part of the world she comes from, have you?'

'Not the slightest,' Marindin answered with perfect unconcern. 'That's the oddest part of it all. She's a lady, obviously, well-bred and well-educated; but not a soul in the place knows anything of her antecedents. We only gather from casual allusions in her talk that her father was a parson somewhere down in the Midlands, that the late lamented Roupell made money in the City, and that she has a house of her own somewhere or other in England. But she seems anxious not to let one know too much. My own idea is'—and Marindin fixed his glassy eye hard upon Kinfaun—'that she wants to keep out of the clutches of fortune-hunters.' Kinfaun's hand never faltered in the least, though this was a most difficult stroke with the cue behind one's back; but he went on quietly: 'Ah! I shouldn't be surprised. So many fellows are on the trail of money. And the other little woman, with the invalid husband—Mrs Percival, I think they called her—what sort is she, now? So the talk glided off imperceptibly by gradual degrees into less important channels.

But for the next three weeks or so poor Kinfaun was sedulously engaged in playing a very distracting and disquieting double game. On the one hand, he didn't want to begin advances towards Mrs Roupell unless he could find out whether or not she was really worth marrying; and, on the other hand, he didn't want to throw away a chance which might not again occur under such favourable circumstances. Those lonely walks and up-and-down scrambles among the cliffs and rocks, with their quiet little nooks where two human souls could sit alone together so long unperceived, seemed as if absolutely predestined by nature for the precise purposes of love-making and flirtation. But

Kinfaun felt he mustn't be too precipitate. For aught he knew to the contrary, the woman might be nothing more after all than the merest adventuress. She might be living on her wits—perhaps on tick, perhaps on false pretences. One must be very cautious at these foreign watering-places and winter stations. One never knows what society one may be thrown among. So different from the pure and guileless drawing-rooms of our immaculate London!

So Kinfaun was prudent, consummately prudent. He played his hand dexterously in this dangerous double game of his. He went on getting deeper and deeper into Mrs Roupell's confidence—picking anemones and grubbing up fern roots—while he prosecuted his researches privately into her position and history with the utmost care, and at the same time avoided too overtly committing himself to anything which couldn't be explained away at moment's notice as the merest flirtation or botanical interest, should the result of his inquiries prove unsatisfactory to the widow's chance of meriting so great a prize in the matrimonial lottery.

But with all his caution and all his careful searching, Kinfaun after all could find out nothing. Nobody anywhere knew aught worth hearing. Hints, doubts, suspicions, exaggerations by the score, but not one ounce of solid fact or assured certainty. She worth nothing; she was worth a hundred thousand; those were the conflicting items of evidence that baffled a poor unoffending fortune-hunter. Kinfaun almost gave up the quest in despair. He couldn't bear to let the young widow, reputed rich, slip through his fingers; but he couldn't bear, either, to commit Angus Kinfaun and all his fortunes to so profound an uncertainty.

As for Mrs Roupell, confiding and childlike in everything else, on that point of her money value she was a perfect marvel of feminine silence. No matter how delicately Kinfaun approached the crucial question of her private means, by graceful lateral avenues or quick flank surprises, she seemed to descry from a distance whither all his gentle advances tended, and to erect at once between problem and solution some subtle impalpable stockade of womanly reticence. All he could gather, and that dimly, from her infrequent hints, was that her marriage with the late Mr Roupell had been a marriage of convenience, arranged for her by her parents, whence it might perhaps be fairly inferred that the late Mr Roupell was a man of substance—else why should those worthy parents have selected him as the convenience in question for their own daughter? But had the late Mr Roupell inserted in his will any ugly clause about 'so long as my said wife shall continue to live unmarried'? That was the doubt that chiefly tortured poor Kinfaun's mind, as the widow grew every day more and more visibly and demonstrably in love with him.

For the widow *was* in love; of that there could be no question. A gentle, shrinking, womanly little woman, who seemed as though her heart had been too long repressed, she accepted Kinfaun frankly as just the man he put himself forward to be (anemones and all) and gave him her confidence (in all other matters) as freely as he asked for it. And since love is catching, even with men of Kinfaun's temperament, that middle-aged cynic began before long to avow to himself, somewhat shamefacedly indeed, yet none the less candidly, that he was really very fond of that pretty simple little smiling woman. One wild hope he clung to, as he floundered deeper and deeper in the slough of entanglement with a person of unascertained wealth and indeterminate position; surely so sweet a little soul, who was so unaffectedly in love with him, could never dream of deceiving him about her worldly prospects! And though she implied nothing else, she always implied she had enough to live upon, which left a vague sense in the background of infinite possibilities unspecified and unhinted.

Once, on the rocks, as he sat alone behind a jutting point, Kinfaun overheard her saying to Mrs Marindin, 'Oh, yes, indeed; if ever I married again, I should like to feel my husband married me for no other reason than because he loved me.'

Then she must be rich; rich enough to attract the attention fortune-hunters!

So at last that very afternoon, ten minutes later, Kinfaun felt a crisis had arisen where he must madly plunge or give up the widow for ever. Nothing venture, nothing have; and he decided on plunging. Brave soldier that he was, he took his life in his hand, and asked the little widow for her hand and heart, not only gracefully, but even poetically. As he spoke, Mrs Roupell blushed rosy red, like a girl of fifteen, and her bosom heaved and fell; but she turned to him with all a true woman's confidingness, and she answered him 'Yes,' like one whose life-dream has at last come true after many long days watching and waiting.

And before Kinfaun knew how things would turn out, it was all arranged for, almost without his willing it—a consular marriage, and that day fortnight. He had plunged indeed, and the next two weeks were weeks, for him, of suspense and torture. For as soon as everybody knew- how all was arranged, everybody began to indulge in shrugs and hints and sinister suggestions which nearly threw poor Kinfaun's mind clear off its balance. Or, what was still worse, they asked him questions—inconvenient questions that he couldn't answer. Where was Mrs Roupell's place? Who was Mrs Roupell's first husband? What was Mrs Roupell herself worth? and other equally rude and impertinent inquiries. Kinfaun kept his temper under these inflictions as best he could; or, what was still better policy, pretended to lose it with becoming dignity. But in his heart how he wished he could only answer them! So the fortnight drifted away, and on the very day before the one that was fixed for the marriage, Kinfaun as yet had found out nothing worth speaking of about his future wife.

In his anxiety to secure the rich young widow, as she was reputed to be, he had pushed matters forward a little too hurriedly, and now he was beginning to regret his precipitancy.

That day, to get over the tedium of waiting, he went into the Réunion at Cannes for half an hour. On the tennis-lawn he met Richard Goldwin, fresh arrived from London, and new to the gossip and scandal of the Riviera. They foregathered awhile about various acquaintances, but before Kinfaun had time modestly to break the news of his own approaching matrimonial projects, Sir Richard remarked in a dubious tone, 'At Antibes, are you? Dear me, why little Mrs Roupell is there. Have you made her acquaintance?' He asked the question with so strange a smile that Kinfaun drew himself up and answered stiffly, yet full of curiosity, 'I have, Sir Richard. Do you know anything about her?'

The baronet smiled again and again mysteriously. 'Why, rather,' he answered, with an amused air. 'Last autumn in town I met her at the Fitzgibbons'. She calls herself the widow of some man Roupell, who was something in the City. But who the dickens Roupell was, or whether there ever was a Roupell at all, or how or why she became a Mrs, nobody seems to know. And where the money comes from, I always wonder: but heaven only can tell whether there's any money in the case at all, or whether the good lady lives by her wits and that pretty smile of hers. It's my belief she's the very same woman who did that famous diamond swindle at Paris last season.'

'What famous diamond swindle?' Kinfaun asked faintly, without having the courage to cut him short. And then Goldwin told him in brief outline that whole long story, so famous at the clubs in the year of its occurrence.

As soon as he'd finished, Kinfaun drew himself up and walked away with just a cold 'good-bye.' He was either too proud or too great a coward to tell the whole truth and shame Sir Richard, so he sneaked off, undecided, and went back to Antibes again.

On the way—with many throes—he had time to make up his mind. The risk was too great. He would break it all off, let it cost what it might. He couldn't afford to throw himself away like that on a woman who might turn out to be the merest adventuress.

At Antibes he went straight to Amy's room. It was Amy and Angus between them now; and he really liked her. In a sort of way he admired the woman's pluck and cleverness in so taking him in. But marry the diamond-swindler! Incredible, impossible!

He sat down, and tried to bring things gently to an explanation. But Amy Roupell looked blank into his eyes every time he tried to approach the subject gracefully, and he slank back disarmed. The tears half started to her lashes at the mere tone of his greeting. 'Oh, Angus!' she cried, as she took his hand in hers; and it thrilled through and through him. Wish as he might, he hadn't the courage so much as to hint to that beautiful, innocent, guileless child of thirty-five that some one suspected her of being the Paris diamond swindler. He sat long irresolute, while Mrs Roupell grew sorer and sorer perplexed; then he rose, much dissatisfied at his own weakness. He went to his own rooms, and left the little widow sobbing alone in hers, and wondering to herself what on earth could ever have come over Angus.

All night long he tossed and turned, sleepless. How on earth to extricate himself from this deadly fix he couldn't imagine.

It was an awful night of vile and selfish fears—an unmanly night; but he lived through it somehow. Next morning he felt it was too late to turn back now. Let her be who she might, he couldn't help but marry Amy.

And marry her he did, in fear and trembling. He hated himself for having been so weak a fool; but marry her he did, without even a settlement. On that she remarked once or twice herself on her wedding day. She seemed to take it as a signal proof of his genuine attachment that he should marry her without making any inquiry as to settlements.

And then, as soon as they were irrevocably married, and no way out of it, it being now full May, Mrs Kinfaun proposed they should return to England. She was anxious to take her husband down to her place in the country, she said; and Kinfaun, for his part, though tremulous for the upshot, was by no means sorry to investigate the whereabouts of that half-mythical estate, whose very existence he had more than once doubted.

On the journey Mrs Kinfaun was perfectly happy—quietly happy, not like a person, Kinfaun thought to himself, who is just going to be unmasked in a great deception. But still, even now, her references to her place were singularly enigmatical and wanting in precision. All he could learn was that this mysterious place lay in a well-known village of Essex, some thirty or forty mile from town, and with that vague information he was fain perforce to console his mind during the long night he spent in doubt and suspense at the Metropole in London. She had money enough in hand, anyhow, he reflected with pleasure, to stop royally in good rooms at the Metropole.

Next day Kinfaun rose feverish with excitement. That morning was to set its seal upon his future fate. He would be rich or a dupe, as the event decided. Trembling with anticipations of good and evil, he took his seat in a first-class carriage at Liverpool Street, and was whirled down rapidly to the Essex village.

At the country station a porter came up to the window, all timid respect, and touched his hat to Mrs Kinfaun with a deferential air of submissive recognition. Kinfaun breathed more freely, and handed him the black bag in even a lordlier style than usual—for he was always lordly. The porter took it, and at the same moment a footman approached with the proper degree of servility which betokens a gentleman's servant in a first-class family. Kinfaun drew a long breath, relieved, but threw his rugs and wraps across the footman's arm like one used to such attendance, and strode blindly out, following his wife, who led the way, with a certain air of half-conscious triumph, to a carriage at the exit. As they passed, the station-master bowed low before them, and the boy at the gate said 'Ticket, sir; thank you,' in that hushed voice with which our labouring class are wont to approach their pastors and masters.

Kinfaun's head reeled as he went. 'This is a very nice carriage, Amy,' he murmured feebly, as he leaned back on the cushions, too much taken aback to speak much. And Mrs Kinfaun, with that sweet smile growing deeper as she said it, answered, like a child whose little ruse has fully succeeded, 'I'm glad you like it, Angus. I wouldn't tell you anything about the Knoll beforehand, for fear of disappointing you.'

The footman took his seat beside the coachman on the box. 'Home,' Mrs Kinfaun said, and they rolled along smoothly on those comfortable C-springs. The horse-chestnuts were just coming into the first full leaf, and the flower buds were big almost to bursting on the scented lilacs.

'It's all very beautiful,' Kinfaun said faintly, as at a big entrance the lodge-keeper, watching, flung open wide a massive iron gate. 'I'd no idea, Amy, your place would be anything like so fine as this.'

The tears were standing in Mrs Kinfaun's eyes, as she bent closer to his ear and whispered low, 'I wanted whoever married me, Angus, to marry me for myself. I know you never once wanted to ask me a single question—except if I loved you.'

But Kinfaun could hardly answer her yet. His heart was too full—in its sordid way. They were driving up through grounds that made his pulse bound and his breath come and go in short spasmodic jerks. Suburban, new, just fifteen years' growth—no time-honoured oaks, but money, every inch of it. Not so much land, indeed—ten acres or so at best—but laid out in perfect order, as rich men in the city lay out their pet places within easy reach of town, whither they run up daily. A couple of gardeners, with four fellows to help them, Kinfaun estimated roughly. Six thousand a year, at least, if it meant a penny. And how nearly he had been fooled by that croaker Goldwin!

His heart came up into his mouth with horror, to think of the narrow escape he had had not quite a week ago!

The carriage drew up at last in front of the house. Two more men-servants stood there awaiting it. High porch, broad stair-case, suburban mansion. Not the fine old ancestral place in the country by any means—large, new-fangled, Queen Anne, red-bricky; but oh, what wealth! What outward and visible signs of it. The late Mr Roupell must have been rolling in money! Kinfaun put up his hand to his dazed brow. His brain whirled. Everything was new, decorated, and polished throughout. The very steps and porch, with their great Vallauris taz-zas[8] and hot-house palms, seemed to reek with riches. The place was magnificent. It dazzled and appalled him.

He followed his wife, faltering, up the broad stairs and into the entrance-hall. Six thousand a year, indeed! It was nearer twenty! The late Mr Roupell (who, as a matter of fact, had been an importer of tobacco in a well-known firm that bears an older name) had feathered his nest like a bird of Paradise. Kinfaun felt his knees sink bodily under him. The moneyed splendour of the thing, in its ostentatious Philistine way, had fairly overpowered him. He looked at his wife, who turned round to him for his applause, like a simple child that she was; then he murmured in a strangely dazed and far-away voice, 'This is a fine house. I'd no idea your house would be like this, Amy.'

With a tottering tread, he mooned from room to room; hall, ante-chamber, drawing-room, all was money, money, money. He gazed at the walls; they were hung thick with pictures, bearing well-known names, and bought, he couldn't doubt, at fancy prices. As in a dream, he strolled on into the billiard-room, all amazed. Mechanically, he touched the bell, he knew not why; a servant in knee-breeches and powdered hair came in with respectful mien, obedient to his summons. Kinfaun stammered out something about a brandy and soda; he felt faint and ill; so much grandeur took his breath away.

His wife bent over him tenderly. 'You're tired with the journey,' she said. 'Come out into the open air. That'll revive you, Angus.'

'No, no,' Kinfaun answered, rising again and rousing himself. 'It's so sudden, so unexpected.' And he nodded his head strangely. 'I didn't anticipate at all so fine a place as this is, Amy.'

He followed her out into the garden. She led him on from plot to plot, from parterre to parterre. Neat jam-tart crescents, all of them, in smooth stretches of lawn, mown close with velvety sward, in the best and most moneyed style of horticulture. His wife looked at him now and again, half tenderly, half inquiringly. Kinfaun murmured at every turn, 'This is fine, very fine! Such beautiful turf! Such well-kept gardens!'

Beyond, there were hot-houses, stables, outbuildings, the appurtenances and belongings of a great domain. Peaches blossomed on the walls; vines were leafing in the vinery. Kinfaun moved through it all, still dazed and still dreamy. From time to time, he murmured some brief word of approbation. But it was clear he was hardly more than half himself. This glamour of wealth seemed to stun and unman him.

Slowly, by devious paths, through shrubbery and garden, they returned to the house. Kinfaun sat for awhile and tried to talk, but words failed him. He could speak of nothing but the beauty of the rooms, the ground, the pictures. Mrs Kinfaun looked pleased; she was glad in her heart dear Angus was so satisfied. Before long, it was time for him to dress for dinner. He went up to his dressing-room. Everything there was of the best, the richest, the costliest. Kinfaun looked every inch a gentleman in evening clothes. He walked down the stairs to dinner, gazing to right and left at the expensive decorations—William Morris, every scrap of them, and Morris is expensive. A Burne-Jones hung incongruously with one by its side; but what of that? Kinfaun knew they both cost money. He gave his wife his arm with stately dignity. The dinner was excellent; a first-rate cook; good clear soup; nice smelts; a capital glass of sherry. When the hock came up, Kinfaun sipped it with gusto and rolled it on his palate. 'Your wines are most choice, Amy,' he said with an effort, for he was lethargic still, 'This is exquisite Johannisberg. I never tasted better.'

Mrs Kinfaun fairly beamed. If dear Angus was pleased, she was more than happy. He praised the sweetbreads, the asparagus, the hothouse strawberries. They were all of them excellent—and they all meant money.

After dinner, he rose, and gazed blankly at the wall. He paced round the room and examined each picture separately. Then he gazed at the plate, the furniture, the powdered footmen. His head shook strangely. He turned to his wife for support. He staggered, and stood still. She gave him her arm. He looked at her and murmured, 'This is a very fine place—a very fine place indeed. Such splendid plate! such beautiful furniture!'

He doddered as he spoke. His wife gazed at him, terrified. She led him into the drawing-room, and he sank into an easy chair.

'You're ill, Angus,' she cried.

'Oh, no,' he answered faintly, wagging his head up and down, with his mouth half-open, and his eyes staring blankly at the wall before him. 'But this is a very fine place, indeed; a beautiful place. I didn't expect at all so fine a place as this, Amy.'

He looked so strangely unhinged, so changed, as if by magic, that his wife grew alarmed. She rang the bell. 'Send for Dr Wolcott, James,' she cried to the servant hastily. 'Major Kinfaun is ill. The journey has fatigued him.'

When Dr Wolcott came Kinfaun looked up at him with a stupid dull look in those keen grey eyes, and hung his chin once more like a confirmed imbecile. 'This is a fine place, doctor,' he drawled out idiotically. 'I didn't expect to find it at all so fine. It must have cost a great deal of money.'

The sudden reversion, the wild access of wealth, had thrown his intellect entirely off its balance. And to this day, if you venture into the grounds of the big square house where poor Mrs Kinfaun, that sweet lady in black, with the sad childish face and the great red eyes, lives with her mad husband, you may chance to stumble across a slouching tall man, with grizzled moustache and open doddering mouth (accompanied by a keeper), who will stop you and, pointing to the well-kept flower-beds and the pillared porch, will murmur pathetically, 'This is a fine place—a very fine place. I didn't expect to find it so fine. My wife must be worth a terrible lot of money.'

[1] **which would 'scape whipping?** Hamlet's response to Polonius: 'use every man/ After his desert, and who should 'scape whipping?'

[2] **princely carbonic acid.** That is, the carbon dioxide which the exalted residents exhaled.

[3] **Califomie and the Croisette.** Respectively an expensive suburb and (then) the main street in Cannes.

[4] **scorn the noisy delights ... and live ignoble days.** An ironic version of a line from Milton's *Lycidas*: 'to scorn delights and live laborious days'.

[5] *tout ce qu'il y a de plus sportsman.* Everything that makes for the true sporting man.

[6] **a lone lorn woman.** Mrs Gummidge in Dickens's *David Copperfield* regularly refers to herself as 'a lone lorn creetur', and the phrase became proverbial.

[7] **consols.** Very safe government bonds paying around 3%*pa*, much favoured by the prudent middle-classes.

[8] **Vallauris tazzas.** Decorative bowls made by a famous ceramics factory on the Riviera, where Picasso worked later.

# EVELYN MOORE'S POET

This story appeared in *Longman's Magazine* in March 1895. Although Grant Allen drew many a psychopathic or monomaniacal character in his fiction, this time he set himself quite a challenge in making a truly bizarre situation credible. His heroine is a reasonably intelligent and a tolerably educated woman—a solicitor's daughter, in fact—as she has to be in order to be impressed by the Poet's high-flown conversation at all. Could such a woman be so incredibly naïve? Allen solved it by making her a product of the Clapham sect, a loose group of Evangelical Christians associated with that London suburb. The great days of their campaign for the emancipation of slaves were long over by this date, and for political and social Radicals like Allen they now stood for an unhealthy puritanism which frowned on frivolity and popular amusements like the theatre. They were given, rather, to founding numerous societies to reform social ills, a tendency wickedly mocked by Wilkie Collins' invention of a 'servants' Sunday Sweethearts Supervision Society'. The product of such an environment might well not recognise a single line of Shakespeare, not even the opening lines of *Twelfth Night*.

In truth, though, it's immaterial that the reader will guess the mystery of 'William Sperling' after a couple of pages. The story is really about a mutually uncomprehending, doubly misguided relationship; a situation perfectly reflected in the Venetian setting before the age of mass tourism—a city of melancholy decay, of decadence and illusions, of mingled glamour and squalor, very much like Mann's *Death in Venice* a little later. Victorian readers liked a touch of travelogue in their stories, especially descriptions of picturesque places they could not expect to visit themselves, and Allen delivers plenty of that sort of intriguing detail. He recycled some of it in the last of his highbrow *Historical Guides* (1898), though in his story he refrains from mentioning his warning in the *Guide to Venice* that the interior of the Campanile is 'sadly malodorous'.

# 1.

SHE MET him at Venice, in the gallery of the Campanile in the Piazza of St Mark's.

Her mother had refused to go up to the summit with her. 'My dear Evelyn,' Mrs Moore said testily, with the querulousness of old age, 'how can you ever expect me, at my time of life, to get to the top of that dreadful tower?'

'I *don't* expect you, mother dear,' Evelyn answered with a sigh— she was twenty-seven and romantic; 'but how can you expect me to go away from Venice without having seen the view from the Campanile? You can sit on one of those nice chairs by the Café over yonder, and watch the crowd. I won't be gone long; just look about, and wait for me.'

It was Evelyn's first visit to Venice, and she was charmed with everything—the gondolas, the pigeons, St Mark's, the Doge's Palace, the dark women in the streets, the red sails, the green water. So she mounted the Campanile with eager feet; such an easy ascent, too—no horrid stone steps, but a continuous inclined plane of smooth-worn bricks, gently winding round and round, and so very well lighted. At the top she emerged on the square gallery of the platform. All Venice glowed at her feet in refulgent sunshine—the five cupolas of St Mark's, the red tower of San Giorgio, the myriad spires of the town, the vast dome of the Salute. For a moment Evelyn held her breath, dazed with excess of pleasure. It was all so lovely! The Oriental magnificence of the golden mosaics, the fantastic effect of the gilt-winged angels on the Gothic pinnacles, the Byzantine glories of the vast façade, the arcades of the loggia, the twin pillars of the Piazzetta—bursting upon her all at once, they fairly made her heart stop. And then the serpentine curve of the Grand Canal, Fortuna's gilded ball on the Dogana di Mare,

Nero's gilt horses above the portal of the great church, the Giudecca stretching map-like over the lagoon to the south, the snowy dells and pencilled lines of the Tyrolese Alps, sun-smitten, to northward! It was too much for one first view. She drew back, half-paralysed by it.

'How lovely!' she murmured, half aloud, gazing down from the parapet at the roofs and domes of the magic city, threaded by silver lanes of gleaming water. 'How perfect! How exquisite!'

'Yes, it *is* exquisite,' a clear and cultivated English voice broke in beside her. 'Especially this afternoon. A divine October day! Such glorious sunshine; such unusual clearness! I come up here twice a week; but never before, in three years of Venice, have I seen the Istrian Mountains, beyond the Adriatic, with their furrowed snows so magnificently lighted up by the pale rose of sunset.'

'It's my first visit,' Evelyn answered, leaning for support on the parapet, and just glancing at the stranger. He was a comely young man, say thirty or thereabouts, with light straw-coloured beard, cut daintily to a point, and a supple, thin figure, very tall and athletic-looking.

'Oh, indeed!' the stranger answered, drawing his beard through his hand and caressing it gently; 'then you're fortunate in your first glimpse of this glorious view. Such pink light is rare, even here in Titian's Venice.'

'How lucky!' Evelyn replied, turning away toward the other side, partly because she wanted to take in the whole bird's-eye picture undisturbed; but partly, too, from a vivid sense of British respectability. The perfect lady mustn't yield to conversation with a casual stranger in a brown tweed suit, no matter how handsome, well-bred, and gentlemanly, whom she meets by pure chance on the top of a campanile. She was a pretty woman; and she knew how to take care of herself.

But the young man with the pointed beard was not thus to be baulked of his new acquaintance.

'You have no glasses,' he said, following her, and offering her his own, which were of bright aluminium. 'These are very powerful. If you've never been up here before, you won't know the different buildings, or the lagoons and islands. So many of the churches seem quite different from above. From the canals and *campi* you see only the doorways and the marble façades; from this height, on the other hand, you look down upon nothing but brick walls and tiled cupolas.'

Evelyn accepted the proffered glasses with somewhat doubtful grace. She wasn't quite certain whether it was quite proper to take them. She had been brought up at Clapham, in the strictest sect of their religion, a Grundyite[1]. But the young man was so attentive, and had such a sweet, suave voice, that she hardly thought it could be so wrong after all to talk to him. As she gazed through the glasses from point to point, he kept following the direction of her glance with his eyes, and describing to her one by one the different islets and channels.

'That's San Lazzaro over yonder,' he said, 'with the Armenian monastery: such an interesting place—has an Oriental library. The smaller islands in the foreground are Sant' Elena and San Servolo; and beyond them you can just see the high bank of the Lido. The church on the nearest island, with the basin in front, is San Giorgio Maggiore. I always admire its red-brick campanile, so honest and workmanlike, with the bells showing through, and the marble top stuck just where it's wanted for constructive effect to complete the picture. They call it Maggiore, you see, to distinguish it from the other one, San Giorgio degli Schiavoni, Saint George of the Slavonians, over yonder to eastward. He was always a great saint here in Venice, was St George— Oriental, you know, very. That's St George of the Greeks with the slender campanile jutting out just in front of it. Plenty of Georges, big, little, or middle-sized, everywhere that Byzantine influence penetrates; and Venice, of course, is essentially a bit of the Byzantine Empire, isolated by pure chance on this side of the Adriatic. There's the Saint himself (you can make him out, I dare say), in gilded armour flamboyant in the sun on top of the dome of San Giorgio Maggiore; he's always in armour—a most warlike man of God, representing the Church militant, exactly as you know him on our own crowns, engaged with his short sword in demolishing the dragon. You've read about him in Gibbon, no doubt, I suppose.[2] What! no? Well, you ought to, then. It's all most interesting.'

This was just the sort of conversation Evelyn loved to hear. It flattered her vanity. Without being quite above her range of comprehension, it gave her a vague sense of moving for the moment in literary society. She felt she was really learning something. The stranger was well-informed, and obviously eager to impart his information to a ready listener. He teemed with facts about Sansovino and Bellini. Before he had finished he had told his pretty friend at full length what Gibbon had to say about the knightly saint, and what the orthodox critics had to say about Gibbon's theory. He had explained to her Clermont-Ganneau's abstruse affiliation[3] of the Cappadocian George on the Egyptian Horus. He had discoursed most pleasantly of the Slavonian merchants who gave their name in old time to one of the many St Georges, and to the Riva degli Schiavoni. He had waxed eloquent on the mediaeval Venetian trade with the ports of the Black Sea and the Esterlings of the Baltic. He had taught her so much, in fact, that Evelyn's poor head was in a perfect whirl with it. She carried away from all he said some vague flitting phantasmagoria of Doge Dandolo's cap[4] and Queen Catherine of Cyprus[5], of Romanesque arches and Venetian Gothic, of the porphyry knights at the corner of the Piazzetta and the Runic inscriptions on the lions[6] of the Arsenal. Yet the stranger was so pleasant and so soft-toned withal that, as she listened, she thought she must remember every word of it. He had put everything so gracefully and in such simple words that even the unlearned and untravelled like herself could easily understand him.

Just at the last, when Evelyn was beginning to feel she really *must* go now, or mother would be so angry, the stranger, looking down upon the carved capitals of the columns in the Piazza below, quoted, half to himself, some melodious lines of English poetry. They were beautiful, Evelyn thought; and, indeed, she was right; many critics of fine taste, both before and since, have stamped them with their approval. 'How lovely!' she said timidly, glancing back at his frank face as he passed the pale straw-coloured beard through his hand once more, and looked curiously hard at her. 'Whose are they, I wonder?'

The handsome young man gave a faint little start of surprise and pleasure. 'My own,' he said simply. 'I'm so glad you like them.'

Evelyn drew back, and cast down her hazel eyes, half-alarmed. She was unaccustomed as yet to the society of authors. 'Your own?' she repeated, taken by surprise. 'Oh, how awfully nice! Then I suppose you're a poet?'

'I write verses,' the young man answered with modest reserve— 'verses and plays. They have been favourably received in London and elsewhere. Very favourably indeed. ...Well, yes, I suppose I may even go so far as to call myself a poet.'

He said it with such evident native bashfulness, yet with an undercurrent of manly and not unbecoming pride, that Evelyn, for her part, was simply charmed with him. Little as she was accustomed to trust her own judgment in matters of art, she felt sure in her own mind the verses the young man had just recited to her were genuine poetry. And, emboldened by his modesty, she said so, frankly.

The young man's eye flashed unspoken gratitude. 'Oh! I'm so glad you think them good,' he answered, leaning across towards her and beaming. 'It's encouraging to be praised. Praise is the best spur. It leads one on to do more. We none of us get too much of it.'

'But you said your poems and plays had been so well received,' Evelyn interposed, half doubtful.

The young man drew himself up very proud and erect, and a shade passed momentarily over his handsome features. 'Oh, yes, *well received*,' he said, with a curious emphasis—'very well received—indeed. Most cordially applauded. ... But that, after all—well, you know that's not everything.'

He let his soft voice drop, with a studied air of mystery. Every syllable sounded as distinct as a bell. Evelyn was longing to know what his words could mean—especially as he looked at her with a pathetic glance that invited inquiry and the chance of explanation. But just at that moment her eye fell by accident on her mother below, gazing about among the dense crowd with fidgety apprehension. The daughter's conscience pricked her. 'I must go,' she said hurriedly, handing the young man back his luxurious opera-glasses. 'My mother's waiting for me below. I've left her too long. I'm so much obliged to you for the use of these, and for the very kind way you've pointed everything out to me.'

The stranger looked disappointed. His face fell suddenly. He had missed one chance. But he raised his hat none the less with a born courtier's grace. 'Good afternoon,' he said, bowing low; and his bow was instinct with old-fashioned courtesy. 'I'm glad to have been of service to a lady in any way.' He paused for a second; then he added, with grave dignity, 'Perhaps I may be fortunate enough to meet so appreciative a critic again tomorrow.'

'Perhaps,' Evelyn answered with an inclination of the head, hardly knowing if she did right to encourage him so far—though she feared it wasn't likely. And, indeed, she descended the inclined plane with a passing pang of distinct regret at the thought that she would probably never again meet him while she lived—that charming poet!

## 2.

Evelyn's mind was full of the young man with the pointed beard for the whole of the evening, and all night long. To say the truth, her path had not hitherto been strewn with poets; and now she had found one she was inclined to make the most of him. She regretted so much she hadn't asked him his name. She might have ordered his poems and plays from London. Or perhaps they were in the Tauchnitz[7]; and, if so, of course, she could even have got them without delay in Venice. But now the chance was gone, the critical moment was lost; and the uncertainty as to who the unknown singer might be would pursue her for a lifetime.

He was somebody; of that, at least, she was perfectly sure. Quite undoubtedly somebody. There was an impressiveness in his grave smile, a solemn dignity in his pointed beard, a modesty in his clear and well-modulated voice, that at once acclaimed him something above the mere common poetaster. Only a man of mark could have admitted with such frank grace, with such conscious worth, yet with such retiring simplicity, the gentle impeachment of being a real live poet. And a real live poet he was, so Evelyn said to herself a hundred times over between one and three in the morning. His figure had by that time assumed heroic proportions. Quite unconsciously to herself, indeed, Evelyn was falling in love with him.

Next day, after her early coffee, she strolled out by herself (as her Baedeker bid) into the square of St Mark's. Her mother was tired, and didn't want to walk till after luncheon. So, red guidebook in hand, Evelyn made her way dutifully, by devious paths, into the marvellous atrium of that queen of churches, and began spelling out with honest care, as best she might, the meaning of the mosaics in the outer vestibule. For, in her own blind way, like most others of her kind, she was eager after culture, and wished to learn all she could from this one Italian tour, the first and last, in all likelihood, that would ever be vouchsafed to her. But oh! how curt and lifeless good Herr Baedeker seemed[8], with his cut-and-dried facts, after the rich living voice of yesterday evening on the Campanile. In vain she tried to solve those quaint riddles in gilt glass. They evaded her elusively. She longed for the handsome stranger with the straw-coloured beard to read for her the enigma of those world old cupolas!

As she stood there, puzzling hard over Noah and his vine, her eyes rooted on the ceiling, a delicate voice at her side made her start with astonishment. 'You should begin at the far right,' it said in bell-like tones, '*not* to the left, as usual. The history's told the opposite way from the way you read: it begins at the end there. The Creation's in the first dome, the Deluge in the second, father Abraham in the third, and so on through the rest of the Old Testament legend.'

Evelyn's face shone with unaffected delight. This was really providential. She greeted the stranger like an old friend recovered, as he paused and raised his hat, half-surprised himself at his own temerity in so boldly accosting her. 'Oh, how nice!' she said, frankly holding out one gloved hand. 'Now you'll be able to tell me what it's all of it driving at. That's the making of Adam, I can see, overhead; but she doesn't look like Eve, the winged figure beside him.'

'Oh no!' the young man answered, gazing above with eager eyes at the stiff and beautiful old Byzantine figures. 'Why should Eve have wings? She was a woman just like you, only—not half so interesting.

Besides, if you look close, you'll see Eve's being taken, a little farther on, out of Adam's right side, in a separate compartment. This is earlier in the scenes. That's the Lord, you notice, who had made Adam with his hands out of plastic clay, exactly like a sculptor; and the little winged figure he holds to Adam's mouth is the soul of man, as yet untabernacled. The Lord is just going to breathe into Adam's nostrils the breath of life, and man will then become a living soul, as you read in the Scriptures. See how frankly and naïvely the old artificers conceived the gist of the passage. The Lord stuffs the soul down Adam's throat in as literal a sense as one might stuff down a bolus.'

Evelyn saw he was right at once—though she herself would never have guessed it. But the knowledge delighted her. Quite willingly she committed herself into the stranger's hands to be led about the building. He had nothing to do, he said, and would be charmed to show her round, and explain what he could to her. 'I can diverge,' he said, laughing; 'I know almost every stone in St Mark's by heart, and if you care to hear, I shall be proud of such a listener.'

Evelyn felt raised in her own esteem by the handsome stranger's apparent partiality. Young men at home, at Clapham, with less than half his brains (not to speak of the pointed beard), affected to think lightly of her feminine intellect. This clever young poet, the ablest and nicest man she had ever yet met, was all courtly deference and polite appreciation. Nothing pleases a woman so much as to find she can talk her best to the cleverest men. Their quickness to seize and to put into words what she leaves half-unexpressed makes her seem abler than she is, and so flatters her soul with the subtlest flattery.

She followed him round the portico, drinking in at every pore the knowledge he flashed in upon her. He made her see everything. The strange old figures in Byzantine attitudes seemed to live at his word upon their golden backgrounds. The stories in dumb show on the pictured arches seemed to enact themselves afresh at his explanations. The animals that waddled, two and two, into the Ark; the dove that flew, wooden, across the solid waters; the builders who fell out over the Tower of Babel—she read them all now with the true eye of faith in their twelfth-century simplicity. Then her poet, nothing loth, led her passive round the church, inside and out—chapels, sacristy, and gallery. He paused by the spiral alabaster column that came from Solomon's Temple at Jerusalem; he showed her the golden pall that covers the very bones of the second Evangelist; he pointed out the short, square pillars, deeply scored with inscriptions in mystic Greek characters 'conveyed, the wise call it,' he said, with a queer smile, 'from the demolished church of St Saba at Ptolemais.'9 Evelyn drank it all in with wondering delight; 'twas so charming to be treated on terms of such perfect intellectual equality by so learned a personage.

'How well you know Venice,' she exclaimed at last, as she stood with her back to the Doge's palace, gazing up at the ornate south front of St Mark's, with its encrusted portico. 'You seem to me to have learnt every stone of it.'

'Why, of course,' the young man answered, looking almost half-surprised at so simple a remark. 'I almost consider the Rialto my own; the scene of one of my very best-known plays is laid in the city.'

'*Not The Gondoliers?*' Evelyn put in, somewhat hastily, glancing with vague alarm at so distinguished a playwright. Mr Gilbert must surely be much more than thirty.

'No, *not The Gondoliers*,' the young man replied, with a half-contemptuous smile. 'Though it's had a longer run,' he added after a pause, 'on the London boards than any of those slight things of Gilbert and Sullivan's.'

He spoke with such confidence and such a studied air of high intellectual disdain that Evelyn was half-afraid her suggestion had offended him. Clearly, she thought to herself, he must be somebody *very* distinguished. And, indeed, in the course of the morning the young man quoted more than once a few verses of his own, from one of his Italian dramas, which she recognised as possessing the truest and highest ring of dramatic poetry. So eager was she to discover his identity, indeed, that she was quite relieved when at parting he asked her politely if he might learn her name. Evelyn gave it him, all trembling, with a droop of the long dark lashes. The young man in return pulled out a Russia-leather card-case, and presented her with a card. She gazed on it, hardly knowing what distinguished poet she ought most to expect. 'Twas with a faint little start of surprise and disappointment that she read the simple words, 'Mr William Sperling.'

She had never even heard of him!

For a moment she regretted it was no better-known name. Next instant her heart, loyal to him already, had made answer to her doubts: 'What matters his name? What matters his fame? Those are both extraneous. He is what he is. If not famous as yet, he must be one day. Or if never at all, still none the less great because not famous.'

Swiftly as all this passed though her mind, however, her poet yet noted it with the instinctive quickness of the poetic temperament. 'You never heard my name before?' he said, looking down at her hurriedly with a strange air of anxiety.

Evelyn rose to the occasion. 'No, I never heard it before,' she answered, with a frank smile; 'and I was so perfectly sure you were someone very great, both from your verses and your talk, that I fully expected to recognise it at once as very familiar. All the more so as I'm sure I've heard or read somewhere some of the lovely verses you repeated to me this morning.'

The young man was standing, hat in hand, in the Piazzetta to bid her adieu. He ran his fingers for a moment through his light chestnut hair, and flung it picturesquely off his high white forehead. 'I expected as much,' he said, with an abstracted air, fixing his clear blue eyes on her. 'I'm seldom recognised—indeed, I may almost with truth say, never.' Then he added, after a short pause, 'But that's not the name under which I publish my poems and plays. I adopt a pseudonym.'

'What is it?' Evelyn cried, now burning with curiosity.

She could remember no playwright of the present day—especially one so young—who seemed to her mind to fulfil for a moment all the requirements of the situation. But then she knew so little of the world of literature.

The young man, however, only smiled once more that enigmatic smile of his, and handed her with grave and deferential care into the gondola he had called for her. 'Ah! no,' he said, smiling, and shaking his head with grave solemnity. 'That would be to tell you too much, and too soon, I think. Some other day, perhaps'—he waved his hand gracefully.

'Whither, signor? the gondolier asked, looking up at him and bowing.

'Whither, signora?' the poet echoed, with a laugh.

'To the Hotel Britannia,' Evelyn answered, with half a blush, feeling vaguely ashamed of so prosaic an address in that romantic Venice.

'And I,' the young man answered, as if to complete the introduction, 'have apartments of my own, very nice little rooms, on the Fondamenta delle Zattere.'

He raised his hat once more with a regretful air. He *was* so handsome! As the gondola glided away by the Royal Gardens Evelyn saw him still standing there, bareheaded and abstracted. She was really in love with him now—no use in denying the fact; and it occurred to her in a flash that he too—well, perhaps he too was in love with her. She was pretty and intelligent; and then, of course, a poet's fancy!

## 3.

At the Britannia that evening Evelyn was sitting at *table d'hôte*, a little disconsolate at the thought that she might never again, perhaps, behold her unknown singer. Her mother sat next her, with a little black shawl round her ample shoulders; and Evelyn had turned towards her, to combat for the twentieth time since they crossed the Channel the maternal suspicions against the soup of the Continent. While she was engaged on that hopeless task somebody glided in, unperceived, along the parquetry floor, and took the vacant seat next her. When she turned to her place again, she gave a start of surprise, while a conscious flush rose hot to her very forehead. 'What! you, Mr Sperling!' she cried, scarcely able to contain herself. 'I thought you said you had permanent rooms of your own on the Fondamenta delle Zattere.'

'So I have,' the poet answered, with apologetic shyness, fixing his eyes on his napkin—'very nice little rooms, which I've furnished and decorated. But I fancied—well, you see, Miss Moore, it's lonely to be always by myself in lodgings, so I decided just for once to come to the hotel and seek a little society.'

'Then you're dining here tonight?' Evelyn asked, secretly flattered.

The poet looked embarrassed. 'I've taken rooms here for the present,' he answered, playing idly with his bread. 'I—eh—I mean to keep them on as long—as long as I find it comfortable.'

He glanced meaningly at Evelyn as he spoke. She understood him perfectly. Her heart gave one wild bound. This was too good to be true. Her poet meant to stop there as long as she did.

All through dinner that night Evelyn lived and moved in the seventh heavens. How cold and formal it seemed, that conventional introduction. 'Mother dear, this is Mr Sperling, who I told you was so kind to me at St Mark's this morning.' Her mother, turning round, took him in from head to foot with a stony matronly British stare. But what was that to Evelyn? Her singer had come there on purpose that he might sit by her side; and he talked to her all through dinner. Ah! Heaven, how he talked! She knew now what it meant, that Biblical phrase about speaking with the tongues of men and angels.

For his voice was low and sweet, and his words were exquisite.

After dinner they went into the *salon*. Mrs Moore took up *Galignani*[10], and ensconced herself comfortably in an easy-chair. *Galignani*, indeed, in place of the poet's bright talk! Yet Evelyn was glad of it. She wanted him all to herself, in the corner of the garden that opens out upon the Grand Canal and the moonlit water. She wanted him, and she got him. He sat and talked to her in his melodious voice. Through the trellised window they could just catch glimpses now and again of wandering gondolas upon the silvery channel, gondolas that glided by with coloured lanterns at their prows, and women in light wraps stretched voluptuously at full length beneath the lazy *felze*. Santa Maria loomed large against the twilight sky; vague sounds of singing voices floated in upon them, as they sat, from a *barca* just opposite[11].

'How long will you stop here?' Evelyn asked at a pause in the conversation. She trembled for the answer,

'How long will *you*?' the poet answered, growing bold, and gazing across at her inquiringly.

Evelyn's heart beat high. Her full bosom heaved and fell.

'I don't quite know,' she answered, dropping her voice. 'We *intended* a week. But perhaps—if we like the place, I might persuade my mother to stop a little longer.'

'Then *I* stop as long as *you* stop,' the poet said boldly. 'Do, please, be persuasive.' He was feeling his wings now. This one woman understood him.

The *barca* drew nearer, with Chinese lanterns all aglow; it paused, pensive, just in front; women's voices floated soft across the waters of the canal, singing gay Venetian serenades, with just an occasional undertone of Italian melancholy. Evelyn and the poet broke off their talk and listened. What more seductive than music, heard at night, by two together? At last, as the voices finished, the poet burst in once more. 'You sing yourself,' he said confidently. 'I'm sure of it. I can see it untold. There's a fullness in your throat that always betrays the born songstress.'

'Yes, I sing—a little,' Evelyn answered, well pleased that he should have noticed her peculiarities so close; and without further demand, not waiting for the airs and graces of Clapham society, she rose from her chair at once and sat herself down at the hotel piano. Oh, how glad she was she had spent so many weary years in cultivating what voice kind Nature had bestowed upon her! For she sang really well, and tonight, under pressure of so unwonted a stimulus, her throat seemed to flow and trill as she herself had never before known it. Love is a mighty master of music to mortals.

As for the poet, he leant over her, drinking it in, delighted. When she finished, his eyes met hers and murmured a mute 'Thank you.' For a moment he said nothing; then he bent down and uttered in a very low voice three lines of poetry:

If music be the food of love, play on;
Give me excess of it, that, surfeiting,
The appetite may sicken, and so die.[12]

Evelyn glanced up at him with one hand just quivering over the notes on the keyboard.

'Your own?' she asked in a tremulous voice.

The poet nodded assent.

'From one of my best plays,' he said. 'You've never seen it?'

'I don't think so,' Evelyn answered, arching her eyebrows in doubt. 'But tell me the name of it.'

The poet shook his head.

'No, not yet,' he said slowly, with a very resigned air. 'It wouldn't do just now. You might be just like the others.' And he relapsed for a moment into meditative silence.

## 4.

The next five days were for Evelyn a time of unalloyed happiness. She spent the greater part of them in exploring Venice, side by side with her poet. He lent them his own gondola for the purpose, with two romantic yellow-girdled attendants. Her mother went with them—in the back seat for the most part, to be sure; but what did that matter? Mrs Moore disliked getting in and out at the steps so much that she was content on the whole to take her Venice passively leaning back on the padded black cushions in the luxurious sunlight. The Grand Canal, the palaces, the life, the bustle, the movement, were quite enough for her, she said. At her time of life she didn't want to go climbing up steps and campaniles. So she lounged outside on the leather-covered seats, while Evelyn and Mr Sperling explored the churches, the palazzi, the galleries. And, to do them justice, they took their time about it.

Evelyn was in no hurry to tear herself away from the Frari or the Redentore, with such a guide as her poet to explain it all at full length to her.

'You love Italy,' she said once to him as he stepped, half-reluctantly, with eyes still loitering, away from the carved capitals of the Doge's palace.

'Yes, I love it,' her new friend said earnestly, with that strange, grave air she so often noticed. 'The scene of half my plays is laid somewhere or other in Italy: Venice, Padua, Verona, Rome, Syracuse, Naples. I prefer my Italian plays to all others I have written. They're more real, more vivid. The passion of the South seems to inspire me as I write them.' He paused one second, then he added, musingly, 'Yes, yes, I love Italy—almost as much as I love *you*, Evelyn.'

Evelyn's heart gave a fierce bound. 'Twas the very first time he had called her by her Christian name—the very first time he had openly avowed his growing love for her.

'Then you love me?' she cried, trembling and tingling at his words. 'You really love me?' The poet leaned over towards her as earnestly as he dared on the open Riva.

'Why, of course I love you, Evelyn,' he said, gazing tenderly down at her. 'You must have known it long since; you must surely have felt it.'

'I think I guessed it,' Evelyn answered very low. Then her wonder and joy found vent in words. 'But oh! Mr Sperling,' she cried, turning round towards him suddenly, 'what on earth can you have seen in me to make you love me?'

She said it quite seriously, earnestly, doubtfully. She felt him in many ways so far above her level. The verses he had recited to her were so beautiful and so true. She was sure in her own soul he was a very great poet.

But her lover, flushing rosy red in that handsome face of his, made answer at once, with a charming smile:

'What have I found in you to make me love you? Why, Evelyn, sympathy.'

They were alone on the Piazza steps. He beckoned his gondoliers.

'To the Giudecca!' he cried. 'We can talk better here under the covering, Evelyn.'

Then he spoke with burning energy:

'I wanted to tell you so,' he went on in a quivering voice as they sank behind the cabin. 'I wanted to tell you why it is. You're so different in every way from all the others. Other women, when I talk to them, may like me very well; they may be polite to my verses; they may admire them and praise them, and say kind things of them, but they laugh at *me* myself; I can see at a glance they don't believe in me. Now, *you* believe in me. I could tell from the very first moment you really believed in me. That made me love you; for love, you know, is in essence sympathy.' He leaned across to her, under cover of the great black *felze*. 'Love has always something egotistic in it,' he went on, fixing her with his blue eyes. 'I admit that freely. I've never pretended for one moment to ignore it. That you appreciate me, that I appreciate you, is to each of us half the reason for loving one another. But *you* must often have enjoyed that luxury, Evelyn—'tis a pretty woman's right. To *me*, on the contrary, it's a new sensation. Never, till I met you, my own dear child, have I found one woman on earth to believe in me!'

He took her hand as he spoke. He smoothed it tenderly. Evelyn's heart leapt up at the pressure, and throbbed high in her breast. She didn't attempt to prevent him. She returned his caress. She leant over to him eagerly.

'But oh! Mr Sperling,' she cried, in a choking voice. 'I can't understand that. You're so great, so sweet, so true and deep a poet!'

'Yes, they all allow *that*,' he answered, with a sad, low cadence— 'as to the verses themselves, they all allow it. But as to *me*—ah! no, that's quite another thing. You're the very first woman that has ever believed in me.'

He broke off suddenly, and began to repeat at once, in soft musical tones, a sonnet of his own making. 'I wrote it last night,' he said, still smoothing her hand with his own; 'I think you can guess whose face it was that inspired it.'

Evelyn listened, too proud and delighted for words. It was like a dream to her to think she should have given the impulse to such noble poetry. One line in particular burnt itself at once into her heart and brain: 'swift as a shadow, short as any dream.'[13]

She felt instinctively that was a master's handicraft. And she told him so in broken words, so pleased and happy was she.

Her poet drew back, and gazed at her tenderly. 'You remind me of four lines I once wrote in a book,' he said, with the simple self-confidence of a great soul:

Things base and vile, holding no quantity,

Love can transpose to form and dignity;

Love looks not with the eyes, but with the mind;

And therefore is winged Cupid painted blind.[14]

'That's the case with you, I'm afraid, dear Evelyn. You love me, and therefore you think all I do and all I write perfection.' He toyed for a moment with the rings on her finger, unreproved. 'And yet,' he went on slowly, 'that's far better than the rest. 'Tis nobler to see me through those deceptive eyes of purblind Cupid than to laugh at me, as the others do, and misread me altogether.'

'I can't think how anybody could ever possibly laugh at you,' Evelyn said, looking up into the calm grave face, whose lips almost touched her. 'You seem to me too high, too noble to laugh at.'

'But I haven't told you all yet,' her poet answered, with a tremulous cadence. 'I must *know* you love me first before I tell you my secret. Say you will be mine, Evelyn; say you will be mine in spite of everything. Don't think me too hasty.

Nay, trust me, lady; I will prove more true

Than those that have more cunning to be strange.'[15]

Evelyn let her eyes drop. 'I will be yours,' she murmured, with a thrill of ecstasy. Their lips met in the gondola. For a moment those two were supremely happy.

## 5.

That evening, as Evelyn played on the piano in the *salon*, the poet leant over her and listened, enraptured. 'I've made up some lines as you sat there,' he whispered in her ear. 'I mean to put them into the new Italian play I'm writing:

What you do

Still betters what is done. When you speak, sweet,

I'd have you do it ever; when you sing,

I'd have you buy and sell so; so give alms;

Pray so; and, for the ordering your affairs,

To sing them too.'[16]

Evelyn's face glowed with unaffected transport. How wonderful that she, a simple solicitor's daughter from Clapham, should fire a true poet's soul with such beautiful verses! She thought so in her own heart, and she said so to him frankly.

Her lover smiled a quiet, self-restrained smile.

'And I, too,' he said, 'sometimes think to myself, seeing how rare and precious a thing it is to be a poet, why should I, of all men, just chance to be born one? But, Evelyn, you're more a thousand times than that: you are already all that poets feign. You are more than a poet, seeing that you must needs draw poetry from whoever sees you.'

Evelyn went to bed that night very, very happy. Though her poet would not tell her by what name he was known to the outer world, she had no doubts on that score. You had only to talk with him to feel his greatness.

Next day Mrs Moore stopped at home with a bad cold. Without being unfilial, Evelyn thought it most opportune. She had all that long day to herself—and Willie. He made her call him Willie now, and it seemed quite natural. When she said so, he smiled.

'Why, of course,' he exclaimed, 'love *is* natural to humanity. You may bury your Miranda in an enchanted isle, yet, trust me, when her Ferdinand once drifts ashore she will take to him as naturally as Eve took to Adam!'

Evelyn felt he was right. This new love that had sprung up so suddenly within her was yet so deep-rooted, so native, so instinctive, that she somehow felt as if she had always belonged to him.

In the course of that day the poet took her on foot to many unvisited, strange nooks of Venice. He dived down short courts and under darkling doorways. Evelyn liked that even better than gliding in a gondola along the Grand Canal, or by the narrow waterways that intersect the city. Her lover led her through a labyrinth of intricate lanes or sunless *calli*, paved with slabs of worn stone, and shut in on either hand by high walls of houses. Quaint little bridges, single-arched, iron-railed, carried them every here and there across some tiny *rio*, where brown-faced women with big gold earrings sat washing soiled clothes in still dirtier water. Dusky bargemen floated by with cigarettes in mouth, and chaffed the girls good-humouredly in their soft Venetian dialect. Now and again the poet emerged for a moment on the paved little *campo* of some sequestered church, whose florid façade and tall brick campanile gave picturesque dignity to their squalid surroundings. Red petticoats hung drying from mysterious balconies. Children played barefooted in the sun-smitten squares; girls drew water from carved spouts at the marble fountains into hammered copper pails; men lounged, and talked, and gesticulated fiercely, and discussed the flaring electoral posters displayed in red and green on the bare walls of the dead monasteries. It was quite another Venice from the Venice of the tourists who lolled back at their ease in the cushioned gondolas, yet none the less replete with light and life and colour for all that. The clear notes of church bells floated vaguely overhead; beneath, came the low plash of unseen oars in the waterway. Musical cries of 'stali!' 'Premè!'[17] rang round darkling corners from invisible boatmen. All else was silent, save for the hurry of frequent feet upon the narrow pavement. A stillness as of death seemed to pervade the city.

The poet led her on through strange ways and back alleys where, alone, she would hardly have dared to penetrate. He plunged down lonely lanes, through the heart of the native town, past Santa Maria Formosa and the Ponte del Paradiso, by whose quay flat boats laden with firewood were discharging their cargo into arcaded magazines. On and on they went, through queer alleys which smelt of dried fish, and sour wine, and garlic. From church portals, as they passed, came close fumes of incense. Here and there the poet paused for a moment in his headlong course to point out some Gothic arch, some Romanesque pillar, some Renaissance doorway. By endless small bridges and strange zigzag detours, past courtyards and *campi*, across stagnant canals, he led her, unresisting, towards the quarter of the Ghetto. At last they reached a fantastic little red-washed square, far from the centre of life, where one broader channel debouched full front in a sort of small harbour upon the open lagune.

So queer a little square Evelyn never had seen during her whole long life of eight days in Venice. 'Twas a deserted *campo*. The buildings around it were plastered with orange and pink distemper; many of them had balconies of old white marble balustrades in the last crumbling stage of decay and dilapidation. Medallions stood encrusted in the palazzo walls; oval windows with dusty gratings opened out on the canal; the stucco, peeling off, revealed underneath a mouldering substratum of water-worn brickwork. All was picturesque and antique and untidy. The very flags were untrodden, save for two or three yellow-haired Venetian children, and a woman in a flaming vermilion shawl, by the porch of the great house, who was performing her toilet most innocently *al fresco*. At the far end, by the lagoon, a funny red church rose high in the air, with a Byzantine dome and a great square belfry. The poet turned to Evelyn with an undercurrent of proprietary pride in his voice. 'This is untouched Venice,' he said, with a wave of his hand towards the tumbledown Romanesque doorway—'Venice as it was before the tourists and the steamboats spoiled it.'

'It's very picturesque,' Evelyn said, half shrinking. 'Twas the most she could honestly say, for to her English eye the whole place sadly needed repairs and whitewash.

The poet gazed up at the squat square tower with paternal affection. 'I consider this campanile as good as my own,' he said, smiling.

'I give the man who takes care of it ten francs a week to let me go up there whenever I choose, and write verses on the summit. I've written the best part of my new Italian play there. Its scenes are laid in Venice—and you know its heroine. I can't compose it in a dingy, stingy, close-walled room; I need the open air, the expanse, the broad horizon. You must come up to the top and see the view from my study, as I call it. Nobody knows it but me, and yet it's the finest picture to be found in Venice.'

Evelyn drew back, half-alarmed, as he opened the rusty door. 'The stairs look so shaky,' she said, shrinking; 'do you think they'll bear me?'

Her lover laughed lightly. 'Bear you?' he cried, much amused; 'what, a featherweight like you? Why, you're light as gossamer. 'Twould bear a round hundred of such Ariels easily. The steps are solid stone; there isn't a stabler or firmer-set square old tower today in Venice.'

At the sound of his musical voice the old custodian in the sacristy sallied forth to greet him with Italian suavity. 'Good morning, signor,' he cried, rubbing his withered hands; 'and good morning, signora. The view today is magnificent, superb, delicious, inexpressible. You take the signora to the top to see it? You are lucky in such a day; not for a week have I seen the snow-mountains so beautiful.'

The poet nodded and smiled, and dropped a piece of twenty francs in good yellow gold into the wrinkled and expectant hand stretched forth to him. Evelyn was far too truly and purely in love to harbour for a moment one mercenary thought of him. Yet she noted, half-unconsciously, as she had noted before, that her Willie was both rich and lavishly generous. He gave to all who asked with reckless profusion; and his rooms, where she had gone with her mother to tea, were furnished with taste and with reputed Donatellos.

The poet gave her his hand up the dark and tortuous staircase. When she reached the top step she felt at once he had not exaggerated the beauty of the prospect. The tower looked down sheer into the green water below; beneath, lay the little church with the Byzantine dome, the quaint pink square, the crowded houses of the Ghetto. On one side stood the city, steepled and turreted from end to end; on the other side, the lagoon, the broad plain, the distant white mountains. The poet pointed with one delicate white hand towards a range of purple heights in the middle distance. 'Do you know what those are?' he asked eagerly. 'They're the Euganean hills, the divinely touched Euganeans. You remember them in Shelley:

'Mid the mountains Euganean

I stood listening to the paean

With which the legioned rooks did hail

The sun's uprise majestical.[18]

'And at their foot, you know, lies Padua, which you've read about, of course, in *The Merchant of Venice*.'

'Oh yes, I remember,' Evelyn put in with spirit, overjoyed to bear her part in this literary conversation. 'It was Portia who lived there.'

The poet drew her to a seat; then, for the first time, she noticed that the platform of the tower was fitted up in rude state as an outdoor study. It had springy metal chairs, and a long garden-seat, and a painted iron table, with pens and inkbottle. A tiled canopy overhead just protected them from the weather. The poet threw himself on the bench and drew Evelyn down beside him. 'Now that was just the very thing I wanted to speak to you about,' he said earnestly. 'I brought you here on purpose.' His face of a sudden grew most grave and anxious. 'Before we go any further, Evelyn,' he went on, 'I want us to understand one another clearly about this matter. I want now, in short—to tell you my secret.'

Evelyn trembled violently. She couldn't conceal from herself the fact that she longed to learn it. And yet she dreaded it. 'Whatever it may be, dear,' she faltered, leaning across to him tenderly, and seizing his hand in hers with a woman's impulse, 'I shall love you all the same; I shall always be true to you.'

He looked at her doubtfully. 'I wish I could think so,' he said, with a deep-drawn sigh; 'I only wish I could think so! But where none of the rest will believe me, how can I hope that you will? They all fall away—as soon as ever they learn it.'

Evelyn gazed into those clear blue eyes, in which no guile lurked unseen, and felt sure, whatever it might be, she could really trust him. 'Oh no!' she cried, pressing his hand in return. 'Not with *me*, dear Willie. I love you; I trust you; I shall always believe in you.'

He paused for a moment, as though he hardly knew how he should begin to break it to her. Then he went on with quiet dignity. 'In the first place,' he said, bracing himself up, as it were, against a possible disappointment, 'I want to ask you seriously one thing. Have you ever heard, or read, or seen in a book any of my lines before? Did they sound at all familiar to you?'

'Well, I've fancied at times,' Evelyn answered, with truth, 'I must certainly have read or heard them somewhere.'

'Yes, yes; but did they recall any name to you distinctly?'

'No, nothing distinctly. I've only a sort of vague impression in the background of my mind that I must have known *them* before—sometime, somewhere.'

The poet's face fell. He must try another tack. So far, it was clear, she hadn't yet discovered, or even doubted, his identity.

292

'Well, I must begin all over again,' he continued, passing his hand across his brow with a weary gesture. 'Those sonnets that I read to you at the Britannia one night—you had never before seen them?'

'No, never,' Evelyn answered, too honest to say yes, yet sorry to disappoint him. 'We live so very little in the world of letters, you see. But I'm sure, at any rate, they were exquisite poetry.'

'Oh yes, everybody says *that*,' he answered, with such evident chagrin that it quite took away from the seeming conceit of so open an avowal. 'I don't mind about *that*; it's the question of the authorship alone that troubles me.'

'Why, what about the authorship?' Evelyn asked, astonished. Who that heard him could doubt 'twas he indeed that wrote them?

Her lover drew himself up with a very embarrassed air, and leaned one arm carelessly on the mouldering red parapet. 'Well, I'm rich,' he said slowly; 'I have lots of money. My father was a wealthy manufacturer in Birmingham. He left me everything. When a man's rich, he has always relations by the score who'll move heaven and earth to get his estate away from him. And when a man passes under an assumed name or publishes under a pseudonym it's always difficult for him to reclaim his own work when he will, especially if he's let many years elapse before he makes the reclamation. Those two things, you see, have been sadly against me.'

'But under what name did you publish?' Evelyn asked, all eagerness.

The poet leaned forward with his clasped hands clenched and his earnest eyes fixed hard on her. 'Evelyn, my darling!' he cried excitedly, with trembling lips—'my own heart's darling, my queen, my empress, forgive me if in one thing I have wittingly deceived you. The name under which I publish is my own real name. It's the one I gave you which alone is an assumed one.'

Evelyn drew back in alarm. 'Then why did you give me it?' she exclaimed, taken aback at his excitement.

'I had every excuse,' her lover answered penitently. 'It's the name I go by—have always gone by in the world. I can't do otherwise. If I assumed my own, don't you see, my relations would be down upon me and would seize my fortune.'

'But your plays,' Evelyn cried; 'they're acted and published in your own right name, I suppose? At least, so you told me.'

'Oh yes, and that's just why nobody will believe I wrote them.'

'And your real name is—' She trembled like an aspen-leaf.

'Can't you guess?'

'No, I can't.'

'What! a writer of famous plays, the scenes of many of them laid in Italy?'

Evelyn shook her head, still in a maze. This mystification puzzled her.

The poet turned round to her with a great glow on his face. He was transformed—transfigured. The tall white brow, the straw-coloured beard, the clear blue eyes, the expressive mouth, all were lighted up now with the intensest emotion. 'My name,' he said solemnly, 'is— William Shakespeare!'

'And your plays?' Evelyn gasped, hardly daring to ask it.

'*The Merchant of Venice, Othello, Romeo and Juliet, The Tempest.* All those are Italian. On Northern themes, *King Lear, Macbeth, Hamlet, Cymbeline.*'

# 6.

There was a long, deep pause for several seconds. And during that pause each lived over and unlived again their whole previous acquaintance.

Evelyn grasped at one glance the whole horror of the situation. Her poet, her lover, her king, was a monomaniac! Cultivated, learned, able, intelligent, literary—but still a monomaniac! The lines he had written to her, the passages he had quoted to her, were not one of them his own, but every word of them Shakespeare's. And yet he was a poet still, a born poet in fibre; a man of culture, a man of fancy, a thinker, a phrase-maker. He was the cleverest talker, the widest reader, the best-informed scholar she had ever yet come across. His conversation itself was brilliant and wise and eloquent; no wonder she had thought him capable of writing, as he had said he did, those Shakespearean gems he was constantly showering upon her. She had loved him before, and she loved him still; yet the bitterest element in all this terrible disillusion was the painful thought that her own ignorance alone had made him fall in love with her. A better-read woman would have detected at once the truth, that the lines he recited were simply Shakespeare's, and would have laughed at him, as he said, for his mad claim to their authorship. He had fallen in love with her because she failed to detect their source, because she thought they were his, because, as he put it himself, she gave him her sympathy.

And yet, at the same time, Evelyn couldn't help feeling in her heart of hearts the whole pitiful pathos of it. He longed to be loved; but he must only be loved as William Shakespeare. And as such, in effect, for eight days she had loved him. The face, the voice, the straw-coloured beard, each counting for something; but 'twas the poet himself, the singer of sweet songs, that most of all had attracted her. And now she knew the poet was dead for three centuries, and the verses she fancied he had written to herself were common property in every house in England!

As for her lover, he watched her face all this time with intensest interest. As each thought passed across it, he read it like a woman. He was tremulous for the result of that appalling disclosure—the disclosure that had already cost him so many valued friendships. At last he spoke, but 'twas in a saddened voice. 'Well, you don't believe me,' he said slowly, as if with a knife in his throat. 'You think it isn't so. You're just like the other ones.'

Evelyn leaned forward on the table with hands clasped and bloodless. Even then she was true to him. The disillusion had stunned her, but had not shaken her trust. She knew he was a madman; she knew she was alone with him on that lonely tower; but she wasn't afraid of him. Mad or sane, she felt at once he was a gentleman—too gentle a creature to do willing harm to her or to anyone.

'Willie,' she cried looking across at him with real pathos in her eyes, 'I believe in you still; I love you dearly!'

But her poet drew back as she approached, and held his left hand in front of him, palm outward, as if to forbid her touching him till she had answered his next question. 'That's not enough,' he said hoarsely. 'You must tell me more than that. Do you or don't you believe I wrote *Macbeth*, *Othello*, *Hamlet?*'

Evelyn's lips trembled hard. 'Twas a terrible position. But still, even so, she would be true to herself, and true to her poet. 'I can't believe it,' she answered, with an ashen face. 'Dear Willie, I believe you're every thing on earth that's great and good and beautiful. You *could* have written them if you liked. You could write what you would. But you didn't write them.'

The unhappy man turned away from her with a wild gesture of despair. 'They're all the same!' he cried bitterly. 'They're all the same at a pinch! They'll give me everything else, except the one thing I want from them—sympathy!'

Evelyn seized his hand once more. 'Oh! sympathy you shall have, dear,' she cried. 'As much as ever man's soul can want of sympathy. I know how this has happened.' She paused a moment, for she realised to the full how this hungry human heart, cut off by its monomania from all intercourse with its kind on what touched it nearest, yearned and longed for companionship. 'I see how it's come about. You are a poet yourself, with a poet's nature; and you've read and drunk in your Shakespeare so long, you've understood it so well, you've felt it out so completely, that you've come at last to believe you wrote it all—as, indeed, you might have done.'

The young man rose and gazed at her fixedly. 'You have said the word,' he answered, with a solemn gesture. 'They all say it sooner or later—either mocking me or pitying me. But I will not be mocked, and I will not be pitied. I am far above either. I am myself a great poet, the greatest dramatist in the world. I want a woman to love me, to sympathise with me, to believe in me. Unless she will marry me as William Shakespeare before the eyes of the whole world, and so proclaim her faith in me, and give me my due, I can never, never marry her! I thought I had found in *you* the one woman who could do it. I see I was mistaken. This disappointment crushes me.'

He spoke with such earnestness, such dignity, such real feeling, that Evelyn couldn't choose but love and respect him. There was so much to love and to admire in him, after all, in spite of his monomania. For a second she paused, counting the cost with herself. It was a terrible thing wittingly to marry a madman. Yet she loved him, she pitied him, she admired him so much, that even in the first full flush of that terrible disillusion she was prepared for the sacrifice. She felt the whole hopelessness of it; yet she was prepared to face it. With a womanly impulse she stretched out her arms to him. 'Willie! Willie!' she cried, melting, 'take me! take me! I am yours. Under what name you will, I am ready now to marry you!'

Her poet stood forward again half a pace at her words. 'No, no,' he said, waving one hand with a deprecatory snap, 'that won't do. That's not enough. That's not at all what I want. I want you to marry me under my own true name as William Shakespeare, and to tell me from your heart you know I am he—the author of *Macbeth*, of the *Tempest*, of *Hamlet*!'

There was no way out of it. Evelyn drew back in alarm, and burst suddenly into a hopeless storm of sobs and tears. 'I can't,' she cried inarticulately. 'I know it isn't true. But I'll marry you for yourself, for the man I know you are, and try to win you back from this dreadful delusion.'

The poet caught at the word, and strange fire flashed in his eyes. 'Delusion!' he exclaimed, with mingled scorn and despair. 'You call it a delusion! And *you*, the one woman I believed in on earth, the one woman I thought capable of understanding me and sympathising with me.' He leapt to the mouldering parapet of the little red tower. 'This is the end of all,' he cried aloud, waving one hand above his head in frantic emotion. 'Farewell to life; farewell to Rome, to Venice! Farewell, a long farewell, to all my greatness! The jaws of darkness do devour me up. I will take arms against a sea of troubles, and, by opposing, end them.' He waved his hand wildly once more. Then he kissed it, to Evelyn. 'Now for my best tragedy!' he said with bitter emphasis, 'by William Shakespeare!'

Evelyn hid her face in her palms, and dared not look at him as he stood there. The custodian of the church, alarmed at the loud noise, had rushed out from his siesta. He saw the Signore Inglese standing aloft on the parapet of the old red tower, very tall and erect, kissing his hand to somebody. But before the old man had time to raise his arms and cry aloud in deprecation, 'Take care! take care! this wall is so treacherous,' the Signore Inglese had plunged—and all was silence. A splash in the lagoon, a black eddy on the surface, great bubbles that rose from the dense mud at the bottom, and no more was seen on earth of Evelyn Moore's Poet.

---

[1] **Grundyite.** GA's invention: a person raised according to puritanical religious and social principles, as exemplified by the fictional Mrs Grundy.

[2] **'You've read about him in Gibbon, no doubt, I suppose.'** In Volume 2 of *The Decline and Fall of the Roman Empire* Edward Gibbon claimed the legend of St George (the hero and patron saint of England) and his Dragon derived from a dubious real-life bishop of Alexandria. His theory is discounted now.

[3] **Clermont-Ganneau's abstruse affiliation.** Charles Clermont-Ganneau (*d.*1923) was an Orientalist who wrote a monograph on 'Horus [the Egyptian god] et Saint Georges', drawing connections between the two, in 1874.

[4] **Doge Dandolo's cap.** The characteristic symbol of the Doges of Venice was their stiff cap with a horned top.

[5] **Queen Catherine of Cyprus.** The Queen consort to the king of Cyprus: after his death she was forced to abdicate in 1489 and sell the island to the Venetians.

[6] **Runic inscriptions on the lions.** The lion statues outside the Arsenal are from Greece, and at some date around the 11th century one or more Vikings carved graffiti of variously-translated Runic characters on one.

[7] **in the Tauchnitz.** Well-known German publishers of thousands of English books of all kinds. Unlike many publishers in the 19th

century, Tauchnitz paid royalties to authors, limiting their editions to continental Europe only.

[8] **how curt and lifeless good Herr Baedeker seemed.** No earnest Victorian ventured abroad without his red Baedeker travel guide. The guidebooks covered much of the world and supplied minutely detailed, if rather arid, information about places and buildings of interest. The pre-1914 editions are notable for their cultural stereotyping. GA's own highbrow guidebooks to European cities provided serious competition in the 1890s.

[9] **'conveyed, the wise call it,' he said, with a queer smile, 'from the demolished church of St Saba at Ptolemais.'.** The pillars from this church in Libya were actually looted by Crusaders in 1156, thus the ironical 'conveyed'.

[10] *Galignani.* An English-language newspaper published in Paris.

[11] **felze ... barca.** The canopy or enclosed structure on a gondola, and (in this context) probably a barge with music and refreshments.

[12] **'If music be the food of love...'** The opening lines of *Twelfth Night.*

[13] **'Swift as a shadow, short as any dream'.** Lysander's comment to Hermia on love, in *A Midsummer Night's Dream,* 1:1.

[14] **'Things base and vile...'** From Helena's speech in 1:1 of the same play.

[15] **'Nay, trust me, lady...'** Suitably adapted from Juliet's words to Romeo in 2:2 of *Romeo and Juliet.*

[16] **'What you do/Still betters what is done...'** From Florizel's lines to Perdita in 4:4 of *The Winter's Tale.*

[17] **'Stali!' 'Premè!'** Gondoliers' traditional cries as they rounded corners, meaning (roughly) 'Stay there!' and 'Press on!'

[18] **'Mid the mountains Euganean...'** From P.B. Shelley's long poem in rhyming couplets 'Lines Written Among the Euganean Hills' (1818).

# Luigi and the
# Salvationist

This story was published posthumously in the *Pall Mall Magazine* in December 1899, a month after Grant Allen's death. It is probably the last story he wrote.

From his earliest years Allen was an atheist. Not an agnostic—he once took pains to correct a newspaper story that he was such a one. The agnostic says he does not know what lies beyond the phenomenal world. Allen's position was simpler: There is nothing to be known. He was a pure nineteenth-century rationalist freethinker. As he once told a clergyman who had protested at his view of life:

> Many years of study, historical, anthropological, scientific,
> and philosophical, have convinced me that the system of
> the universe which you accept as true is baseless and unten-
> able. ... I don't think the theory of Christianity is histori-
> cally justifiable; and if it is not true, I cannot do other than
> endeavour to point out its untenability to others.

In fact he disputed that a historical Jesus had ever existed. He thought the figure had been slowly evolved over time to authenticate the prophecies of the Old Testament.

Although all Christian belief is false, Allen thought, there are nevertheless levels of inanity. Near the end of his life he acquired a certain interest in Roman Catholic doctrine. It was a by-product of the last of his enthusiasms, for Italy. 'Italy itself I love—every artist must,' he makes one of his characters say. 'I love the very dirt. I love the squalid towns. I love the crumbling walls; I love every stone of them.' He visited Florence and Rome for the first time in 1893, and fell in love with the country, its people and aspects of its religious life, particularly Italian art and architecture and its popular rituals. He was interested in folklore and wrote extensively about it, especially the idea, then becoming accepted, that even the most sacred Christian rituals and ceremonies are pagan in origin and were co-opted and so rendered harmless by the Church. He was intrigued by the unquestioning faith of the Italian peasantry that as long as they followed to the letter all the precepts and customs of the Church—as represented by the village priest—they would be absolved of their sins and their place in Heaven assured.

None of this had any personal reference, of course. His novel *Linnet* of the year before takes every opportunity to make mocking remarks about Roman Catholic hypocrisy with respect to divorce. However, like some other rationalists of his day, Allen was intrigued by the internal coherence of Catholic dogma and the way it handles human frailty more realistically than the reformed churches; but that was all. For him, the trusting faith of the peasant Luigi is no more sensible than that of the bigot Arthur Biddle; but it is a faith much more graceful and generous in spirit.

By contrast, Allen reserved a particular scorn for Dissenting sects, like the 'Gideonites' in the story *The Backslider* in this collection. He was the gifted, highly educated son of an intellectual, semi-aristocratic family. From his perspective, the Salvation Army was a vulgar organisation whose members were drawn from the ranks of the lower middle classes: stupid, narrow-minded and (to put it rather more elegantly, as his mouthpiece Miss Beauchamp puts it) consumed by 'spiritual pride'. This is rather unfair, since the Army has never been classed as

a proselytising faith as, say, the Mormons are, and it has always preferred to seek converts by putting its energies into good works. And,
on the other side, Luigi, one of nature's gentlemen with his 'simple
childlike faith' is both a sentimentalised and patronising portrait. Still,
the story does dramatise two irreconcilable world-views with insight
and humour.

# 1.

THE FIRST Luigi knew about it was that he heard the words 'Are you saved?'[1] fired off at him like a blank volley, in a lugubriously hollow voice, and in most doubtful Italian. Now this was odd, for it was late spring, and flood time was over; so what could there be to be saved from?

Luigi looked up from the top-artichokes[2] he was carefully hoeing—hoeing with the ceaseless, uncomplaining industry of the over-taxed, hard-working Italian peasant—and beheld his questioner. The foreigner was a tall, gaunt man, with eager eyes and a quick, earnest manner: in point of fact, the ideal of an apostle, an ascetic, an evangelist. He wore a curious black cap, very military in its air, and marked with the words 'salvation Army,' in Italian[3], embroidered in red upon it. His fiery eye burned bright with undirected zeal. He was made for martyrdom. All which things, however, Luigi just at first only dimly perceived, for he was slow of perception. 'Has the river risen?' he asked, glancing about him nervously.

'Are you saved?' the gaunt man volleyed again, unheeding his question.

Luigi felt uncomfortable. A weird, strange creature! 'There is no flood,' he answered; 'and if it were earthquake, should not I too feel it?'

'There *is* a flood,' the gaunt man answered; 'a flood of liquid fire! It is coming down the valley and breaking upon you this moment! Seek salvation!'

Luigi took his measure with a deliberate eye. 'The district of Siena is not volcanic,' he replied in his slow way. 'You have come from Naples?'

The stranger began to pour forth a fervent stream of somewhat turbid and mingled eloquence. He spoke Italian fluently, though ill— he had learnt how to bring out a few fiery sentences of warning and exhortation. Luigi listened, and the truth began to dawn upon him. This man, though mad, was some sort of missionary. It was religious talk he was trying to shower upon him.

'Pardon me, signore,' Luigi laid at last with a gentle smile, leaning upon his hoe. 'I understand your mistake. You are a newcomer in these regions. You suppose we are heathens, and you wish to convert us. That is in itself a laudable design. But we are Christians! Christians!' To give more point to his remark and make himself better understood, he crossed himself demonstratively as he spoke, and murmured, half to himself, the usual formula. The Salvationist shuddered.

'Look at our hills,' Luigi went on. 'Do you not see that we have churches everywhere? Furthermore, we grow in this district one of the most generous red wines in Italy—a delicious wine which is called Chianti,' (another shudder) 'and is exported, I am told, not to Florence alone, but even oversea to England, from which country I doubt not your serenity comes. Your people in London begin to drink it: they prefer it to the beer which alone they can raise on their bleak hillsides. A most illustrious wine, our good Chianti. *Si, si, if* we are Christians!'

The Salvationist stared at him, aghast. What on earth was the man talking about? 'But you need salvation,' he cried strenuously,—'salvation, and we offer it to you. Freely we offer it! By blood and fire we offer it to you!'

Luigi shrugged his shoulders, bowed politely, elevated his eyebrows, and went on hoeing his artichokes.

The Salvationist continued a long harangue of the stereotyped sort with which we of the north are so familiar. Luigi had never in his life heard anything like it. He went on with his work, but listened in a quietly interested way to this mad creature's raving. It was odd; it was piquant. At last, it began to strike him that the man was trying, in his grotesque way, to preach some strange heretical doctrine. Luigi was a great-souled, tolerant being. He leaned on his hoe once more, and made becoming answer.

'Signore,' he said in a bland voice, 'you are new to Italy; you have not been here long: you do not understand us. That which you describe is not the path to Paradise for us Italians. We are born: well and good; they baptise us instantly: and thereby we obtain baptismal regeneration. We grow up: we are catechised: we make our first communion. We become men and women: we consult our parish priest: we confess at least three times a year: we communicate at Easter: if we do anything wrong, we seek penance and absolution. By-and-bye we grow old: we feel death draw near: we send for our good father: we receive the viaticum: we obtain extreme unction: and we depart, forgiven. To make all sure, our children and friends after our demise see that masses are said for the repose of our souls.' He expanded his palms. 'What would you have?' he asked rhetorically. 'We do all that the Church demands. We fulfil every obligation. We leave no command unobeyed. Where is the need for this strange thing that you call *conversion*?'

'You speak of the scarlet woman[4],' the Salvationist cried, horrified.

'The scarlet woman?' Luigi exclaimed in a puzzled voice. He looked round, but saw no woman, scarlet or otherwise.

'I mean, Rome,' the gaunt man explained.

'Ah, Rome,' Luigi repeated, delighted to hit upon a word he could understand. 'Rome is the capital of the kingdom of Italy, and the seat of the Assembly!'

They spoke two alien tongues,—those two—the tongue of the north and the tongue of the south: neither could comprehend the other's standpoint. Nevertheless, the human eye of the Salvationist attracted Luigi, who was above all things human. 'Might I enquire of the signore his honoured name?' he asked at last with sugared Italian politeness.

The Salvationist gave it. 'Arthur Biddle, a brother, and an evangelist,' he answered.

'An evangelist!' Luigi echoed. How strange! He had understood those holy men were all dead long ago. Matthew, Mark, Luke, John, he knew; but Arthur Biddle—incredible. He was confirmed in his belief that the fellow was mad. Evangelist indeed! And yet—he liked him.

'Has your serenity rooms in Poggibonsi?' he asked after a pause.

'I have not where to lay my head,'[5] the Salvationist answered, with quiet confidence. 'I rely upon those who love the Signore to find me lodging.'

Luigi reflected. 'Might my humble roof be honoured?' he suggested at last as the outcome of his reflection.

Arthur Biddle was not unwilling that this poor blind Italian should acquire the opportunity of entertaining an angel unawares, and he answered at once, 'You are very good. In the Signore's name, I accept your proffered hospitality. ... But,' he added as an afterthought, 'tomorrow I expect a lady to join me.'

'Ha: the signora your wife?' Luigi interposed sagely.

'Not my wife, but a fellow worker—a Salvation lady.'

Luigi hesitated. Would it be right to Chiara—a mere girl of eighteen—to introduce this doubtful lady to her? 'Indeed?' he said, with an interrogative undertone. 'A lady! And not your wife, signore!'

'But she is a sister,' Arthur Biddle put in quickly.

Luigi nodded acquiescence. 'Ah, yes: I understand: the signore's sister. *Quite* another matter!'

'Not my own sister,' Arthur Biddle continued, trying to steer his way through the dangerous rocks and complexities of Italian. 'A sister in religion.'

'What! A nun! *Si, si.* … Still, it is odd for a religious. But there! you English, you do such droll things. Your ladies travel alone. Without a cavalier! Such droll, droll things! Almost as droll as those mad Americans.' And at thought of the American women, strolling unconcernedly without a male protector across the breadth of two continents, Luigi could no longer control his sense of humour, and burst out laughing.

'You fear to take her in?' the evangelist asked, amazed.

Luigi sobered himself. 'Fear?' he cried. 'No, no! But … I have a daughter, look you: a girl of eighteen. This lady—this religious—she is one with whom a young girl?—your serenity understands. A father must be particular.'

Arthur Biddle in turn was fairly taken aback. It was a shock of nationalities. His Italian, such as it was, forsook him utterly. 'The lady,' he stammered out, '—*is* a lady: a lady.'

Luigi took his hand. 'Come on,' he said, with a burst. 'It is the hour of the *pranso*. You are a strange specimen of these *forestieri*, I allow, signore, but, I know not why, I like you—I like you.'

## 2.

The breakfast was simple—black bread, such as peasants use, polenta, and red wine. Chiara served it—a pretty dark girl with the piquant coquettish Italian eyes and smile. Her eyes looked through you. Even Arthur Biddle, who heeded not the things of this world, observed for himself that the girl was pretty. A soul to save! He felt at once a fierce impulse to save it.

Luigi pushed him the red wine, in its wicker-covered flask, stopped with cotton-wool, and having a drop or two of olive oil floating on its surface to preserve it from corruption. 'Help yourself, signore,' he said, with the generosity of his race. ''Tis our renowned wine of Chianti.'

The evangelist pushed it away with a deprecatory gesture. 'Nay, nay,' Luigi urged, mistaking his meaning. 'It is yours, signore. All we have is at your service. You are wholly welcome.'

'I do not drink wine,' Arthur Biddle answered, with an austere face. 'We do not in my religion.'

'Ah, now I understand,' Luigi put in with a bland smile. 'Then you are *not* a Christian! My son was with the army in Eritrea, and he wrote to me that the heathens in those parts—Mohammedan heathens—would not drink wine, so as to distinguish themselves from Christians. And *you* will not drink wine! I see it all now. You are a Mohammedan missionary,'—he smiled a tolerant smile—'come to convert us to your own religion.'

Arthur Biddle stood aghast. How he longed for words to confute this well-meaning but ignorant person! 'I *am* a Christian,' he answered, '—and I have come to convert Italy. But true Christians do not look upon the wine when it is red. A snare, a snare! They know its deceptiveness.'

'Ah, you prefer white wine?' Luigi broke in, eager to do his best. 'Chiara, my child, a flask of that good white Montepulciano!'

'No, no,' the evangelist exclaimed with an impatient gesture. 'No wine! no wine! I tell you, I am a Christian.'

Luigi was all sweet reasonableness. 'Every Christian,' he answered, 'drinks wine. It is a part of our religion. Why, even the priests must drink it. How can you be a Christian and refuse to partake of our good Chianti?'

'But when the priests drink it,' Chiara put in, 'it is no longer wine: you forget that, Father.'

'True, true,' Luigi said, crossing himself. 'I had forgotten it, I admit—sinful man that I am. But still, our Chianti! Why, do you not know, serenity, that holy bishops and cardinals are growers and sellers of Chianti?'

'Then they are snarers of souls,' Arthur Biddle answered, warming up.

Luigi poured himself out a second glass, and held it up to the light, much wondering.

'Oh, no!' he exclaimed. 'Why, the best men do it! There is Cardinal Casale, for example, the Cardinal Camerlengo[6] to his Holiness himself,—he owns a vineyard near Siena, and grows very rich wine, most luscious wine, which he retails in Rome at special *osteri*, under the cardinal's hat and arms: you will not say a thing is wrong which is done by the Cardinal Camerlengo to the Holy Father!'

Arthur Biddle held his peace. He had no arguments with which to meet this wholly unexpected line of reasoning. In the north, he knew how to answer all objections and return all assaults; but this fixed faith of the south, this creed of authority, with its elaborate ceremonial, its etiquette of salvation, entirely silenced him. To him, the individual was sole judge of conduct: every man his own pope: Luigi nonplussed him.

After breakfast, Luigi went out for a minute, and the evangelist was left alone in the room with Chiara. He let his eye fall upon her. Chiara glanced back with her most coquettish glance. The signore foreigner was about to address her! He gazed at her long and earnestly. Chiara in her heart wondered what was coming. Then he turned with a fierce burst. 'Are you saved?' he asked fiercely.

Chiara was not more retiring than most other Italian peasant girls: but when a strange man leapt upon her with such a weird question, her terror knew no bounds. She rose, glared at him, flashed fire from her eyes, clenched her fists instinctively, and then rushed with burning cheeks and beating heart from the table. She darted into her own room, slamming the door behind her. Arthur Biddle heard the turn of a rusty key in a lock, and a great sigh of relief. Thank Our Lady and the saints, she had got away from him in safety!

Presently, Luigi returned, and found the evangelist sitting disconsolate, with his head on his hands and his elbows on the table, a picture of misery.

'Where is Chiara?' the Italian asked in a rising tone of indignation. Arthur Biddle pointed with one hand to the bed-chamber.

Luigi felt the door, found it locked, then turned angrily to the evangelist. 'What! you have abused my hospitality!' he cried, in an angry voice. 'You have taken advantage of my back being turned to insult my daughter!'

Arthur Biddle recoiled like one stung. 'I only asked her if she was saved,' he answered; 'and she rose from the table and fled at if I had struck her.'

Luigi's sense of humour sufficed to take it all in. He burst into a merry peal of laughter. 'We do not understand one another,' he cried, laying his hand on the evangelist's shoulder. 'We are all at cross purposes! Can you not give up this attempt to convert the converted? We are Christians, I tell you, Christians. We grow the best red wine that is grown in all Italy. You are not satisfied to be as Christian as the Pope: you want to be more orthodox than the Holy Father!'

Arthur Biddle hardly saw the point of the joke even then. As Christian as the Pope! Why, if he had met the Pope, he would have accosted the venerable Pontiff with 'Are you saved?' exactly as he had accosted Luigi and Chiara.

## 3.

The evangelist slept at Luigi's that night, the father having succeeded after a little wheedling in convincing his daughter that the foreigner meant no harm, and was merely interested in her spiritual condition. Next day, the 'sister' arrived—a tall sweet looking girl, with a wealth of fair hair, in a most unbecoming bonnet, Chiara thought: but there! what would you have? Our own Dominican nuns do not enquire too closely whether their dress suits them! The pair put the family to a severe strain: but things were managed. The evangelist had a bed in Luigi's room, while the 'sister' shared Chiara's. Luigi was a great-hearted honest-souled creature: and in spite of everything, the evangelist attracted him.

Arthur Biddle and Sister Polly went out into Poggibonsi that very morning to save souls; and Luigi, fearing mischief, gave up an hour to accompany them. On the way, he met the Englishwoman. Now the Englishwoman was well known and much respected at Poggibonsi: she had a house there. She was unmarried, an amateur painter, and a lover of Italy: she lived at Poggibonsi to be near San Gimignano[7], and yet in touch with the rail to Florence and Siena. Her name was Miss Beauchamp. At least, it was spelt Beauchamp, and pronounced Beecham, or as Luigi would have put it, Biciam.

Miss Beauchamp drew the rein of her little white pony to smile at Luigi and to stare at the Salvationists. Luigi spoke to her awhile: but he spoke rapidly in Italian, and the evangelist could not follow him. The Englishwoman listened. Luigi's palms were eloquent. His shoulders spoke. At last Miss Beauchamp turned to Biddle with a rather grave face. 'You belong,' she said, 'to the Salvation Army?'

'I do,' Biddle answered. 'Are you saved?'

Miss Beauchamp's white hand waved aside the question. 'My personal welfare is not now the point at issue,' she replied with quiet firmness. 'I want to warn you. Be careful here what you say or do. These people are kindly people, good honest people, very friendly people: but, tomorrow is the *festa* of Sant'Ilario[8], the great local patron. Beware how you run counter to their prejudices at such a time. They are excitable, and eager. If you hurt their feelings, if you insult their religion, which they dearly love, they may become ungovernable.'

'I ask no better,' Arthur Biddle answered, 'than to be counted worthy to suffer for the truth's sake.'

Miss Beauchamp smiled serenely. 'Truth is relative,' she said in a low voice. '*You* may not have it in greater measure than *I* have. But let me urge you at least to deal it out, if you possess it, to these good people with extreme caution. You are a newcomer here, and I can see from what Luigi tells me, you do not understand the Italian temperament. In the North, the theology you take for granted is immediately understood: all your hearers admit what you postulate—the need for salvation, for immediate conversion, for some sudden and definite change of heart, for a day of reconciliation. They may put it off, and put it off; but, in principle, they believe in it. Here, it is quite different. Not one of your hearers knows what you are talking about. They will think you mad—that it all. Their way of salvation and yours are alien. Baptism, first communion, confession, penance, absolution, extreme unction—it is all mapped out for them: they fulfil their prescribed round with simple childlike faith, and have no misgivings. If you *must* disturb their rest, disturb it gently. Remember that they believe, and that their belief it dear to them.'

The evangelist stood shocked at such lukewarm Protestantism. Why, this English lady, brought up in the light, was scarcely any better than poor blind Luigi. He longed to save *her* soul too: but the pony-carriage passed on and whirled it away from him. They walked in silence into the main street of Poggibonsi.

### 4.

Next day, the evangelist and Sister Polly went forth with Chiara to survey the situation.

It was easy to see that something unwonted was happening. The little town was *en fête*: everybody was dressed in his *festa* costume: Poggibonsi was uproarious. All the little boys were engaged in firing most religious squibs, in honour of Sant'Ilario: all the little girls wore white flowers in their hair, and waved red handkerchiefs. Grave men stood smiling at the doors of their shops with a patronising air, as if the town, the crowd, and the saint belonged to them. *Confetti* strewed the ground—the degenerate modern coloured-paper *confetti*[9]: vendors of gilt gingerbread extolled their wares at stalls in the street: a circus stood ready for action outside the village, as soon as the churches should have poured forth their throng of worshippers. It was a sad, sad sight: all these heedless people were busy enjoying themselves in their own wicked Italian way, and taking no note of the alien evangelists who stalked tall and gaunt with their northern gospel through the midst of so much happy Tuscan humanity.

Suddenly, as Arthur Biddle looked, a loud cry rent the air—a cry that drew nearer and nearer each minute, with shrill variations: a cry which even his unpractised ears soon discovered to be composed of myriad voices all shouting with their might, 'Il Santo! il Santo!'

Next moment, a motley crowd swept round the corner. At its head marched a man with a sort of monstrous tinsel-covered barrel, adorned with ribbons, and flashing in the full Italian sunlight. The barrel was raised high on a pole; assistants by the side helped to carry off the weight by sticks attached to it. Its approach was the signal for redoubled cheering. The thing swayed and rolled, and the crowd surged round it, shouting and laughing. As it swayed, they shouted aloud, 'Ceri, Ceri, Ceri!'[10] That was what struck the evangelist's eye first: next instant, he beheld behind it a colossal doll or stuffed effigy, some fifteen feet high, similarly borne by poles on four men's shoulders. The image had a great smiling face, most inanely beneficent; it was attired in gewgaws of the flimsiest material. Around it men and women pressed shouting, 'Il Santo! il Santo!' As it approached they bowed their heads, exactly as if the doll were some worshipful object.

Just at the first glance, Arthur Biddle took the whole cavalcade for a mere toy or pageant—a sort of Southern Guy Fawkes or City Giant or King Carnival. But even as he watched while the crowd pressed forward, a procession of priests with a great gilt cross issued from a church, and met the tumultuous popular orgy at a street corner. A bishop, gorgeous in his plum-coloured dalmatic, led the measured cortege of ecclesiastics. Where the two lines met and crossed, he stopped for a moment, held up a couple of fingers in solemn benediction, and blessed the procession. The image in turn bowed its head, nodded three times, and then went on its way, inanely smiling. Arthur Biddle realised with difficulty that this was intended for a religious event. The image was a saint, and the bishop had blessed it and been blessed in return by it!

As a matter of fact, the procession is one of those immemorial traditional popular ceremonies, so common in Italy, which are not of ecclesiastical origin at all, and may possibly even be pagan survivals, but which the Church has had the wisdom in part to recognise, and by recognition to mitigate and nullify.

'What is this Juggernaut[11]?' the Salvationist cried, turning fiercely to Chiara.

Chiara had not the slightest idea what manner of wild beast a Juggernaut might be, but the man's tone appalled her. 'Oh, hush!' she exclaimed, crossing herself. 'Don't speak so loud! This is our holiest *festa*, the Procession of the Ceri, and the image that you see is the effigy of our blessed patron, Sant'Ilario!'

A mad desire to testify broke over Arthur Biddle. This was sheer idolatry! 'stand forward!' he cried in a tone of command to Sister Polly.

Sister Polly had less zeal or more common sense than her leader. She did not think the moment propitious for testifying. However, as in duty bound, after a second's hesitation, she obeyed her superior officer. She stood forth, very white, as the procession approached them.

Arthur Biddle seized the leader of the Ceri by the arm. 'Are you saved?' he shouted aloud, in a voice that could be heard above the bang of the drums. 'If not, I offer you, here and now, salvation!'

It took a minute before the crowd understood the interruption. They paused and listened, horrified. Stop the Procession of the Ceri in its mid-career? Check the blessed Sant'Ilario! Incredible profanity! This man must be a heathen! But Arthur Biddle, in quick short sentences, proceeded to testify. He told them, in plain words, that the holy Sant'Ilario was no saint at all, but a vile idol, the work of man's hands, a clear violation of the second commandment. Eyes it had, but it saw not[12]: ears, but it heard not: a vain tinsel-covered thing, powerless to answer the prayers addressed to it. He exhorted them to turn from this their idolatry to the living light; he implored them to be saved: he argued, he wrestled with them.

As for the crowd, half-mad with religious fervour, half drunk with many cups of good Chianti, it knew not what to make of this amazing fanatic. At first, it was incredulous. Disbelieve in the Saint—in our own Sant'Ilario! Try to stop the procession on which depended the prosperity of the town and the success of the vintage! impossible! Inconceivable! Why, even the Freethinkers and Freemasons and Liberals never sank quite so low as that! Signor Mancini[13] himself, the atheistical doctor (as men called him), yet approved of the Ceri, and actually gave money once a year to keep up and gild the image of Sant'Ilario: nay, had he not written several pamphlets conclusively showing that Sant'Ilario himself went back to a remote and unknown antiquity, having once been a pagan god of great renown and power, before he was happily converted and Christianised—pamphlets which the curious may read to this day in the library of the Folklore Society[14] in London? The Inglese, then, were worse than Freemasons or Atheists! Inglese?—a Moor! He *must* be a heathen!

Burning with zeal for the glory of Sant'Ilario, they turned upon him, red with rage. Sister Polly slank back, tore off her bonnet, and refused to testify. But the crowd heeded her not; it seized Arthur Biddle, and there and then almost tore him to pieces. He endured with courage—courage is a quality rarely lacking in Salvationists. They buffeted him about till he was more than half-dead. He thought at times he was on the very point of earning the crown of martyrdom. But just at that moment, while they wrestled and beat, Luigi stepped forward.

Politic man, Luigi! He did not attempt to check their rage, but, smiling serenely, he called out, 'Do not kill him, fellow-citizens, before the very eyes of the blessed Sant'Ilario! It would surely bring bad luck to the harvest and the vintage if blood were to defile the Procession of the Ceri! Make him over to me instead—I will answer for him to you: and when you have replaced the blessed saint in his home in the chapel on the hill, and feasted the Ceri, come for him to my house, and then do as you please with him!' But this he said guilefully, with intent to deceive, that he might protect the evangelist.

The crowd shouted back, 'Luigi is right! Don't kill him here! It would bring the evil eye! Go on with the blessed saint, and tear him to pieces when the service is over!'

## 5.

After the Ceri had been feasted, and the great cask broached and drunk, a body of roisterers at the inn in the Piazza shouted aloud, 'Now, off to Luigi's,—and short work with the atheist!'

Luigi had bundled his man meanwhile into the old wooden chest in Chiara's room, and bade Chiara and Sister Polly sit upon it carelessly. Lest Biddle should choke, he had bored two holes for air with an augur at the back: the evangelist had just room to lie in the box with his long legs tucked up; but the position was uncomfortable.

Without one moment's notice, the roisterers burst into the house. 'Where is he?' they cried. 'Produce him!'

Luigi came forward, wringing his hands in mock despair. 'Dear friends,' he exclaimed, 'the man is in league with Satan! I got him home with difficulty: but on the very threshold, he gave me the slip and escaped. I fear by this time he is at Empoli or Florence!'

The crowd was furious. Baulked of their prey, they turned to cuff and maul Luigi. Luigi cried out the more, 'I know not where he is! He fled and left me!' The evangelist in the chest, hearing this plain falsehood, was minded once more to rise up and testify. But on second thoughts he refrained—leaving Luigi to suffer vicarious martyrdom.

'Search the house!' one of the mob cried. The others turned to obey him. The evangelist lay low, feeling far from happy. Meanwhile, half a dozen enthusiasts kept punching and pummelling poor Luigi, to extract a confession. But Luigi was true as steel. He grinned and bore it.

They searched everywhere in the house, except the chest. Chiara had thrown a coverlet and a couple of cushions on that, so that it looked for all the world like a piece of household furniture. She and Sister Polly sat upon it by turns. As to Polly, the marauders never recognised her for a moment. She had flung away her bonnet, and with her rich fair hair hanging loose about her face the resembled anything on earth much more than a female preacher. For choice, a Bacchanal[15].

At last, after pulling to pieces everything suspicious in the house, the revellers dropped off, one by one, sulkily, leaving Luigi bruised and trembling, and the evangelist much cramped with lying so long in the narrow space allotted him.

## 6.

He *must* be got rid of somehow: that was clear. Poggibonsi was now too hot to hold him. But how? If he walked or drove openly from the scandalised town, the injured votaries of Sant'Ilario would tear him to shreds. The railway was out of the question. Luigi perpended. At last, he clapped his hand to his forehead suddenly. 'Ha!' he cried. 'The English woman!' 'she is good,' Chiara echoed. 'And the man is a compatriot! Yes, yes: she will help us!'

They waited till dead of night, till long past one o'clock, for strayed revellers were still abroad, more or less exhilarated, shouting 'Viva Sant'Ilario!' in somewhat liquid and uncertain accents. About two in the morning, all was silent at last; not a voice broke the gloom; the *festa* had worn itself out, and the revellers were quietly sleeping, in bed or out of it. Luigi opened the door and peered cautiously into the road. Nobody there! All well! 'Come this way!' he cried to the subdued evangelist.

Arthur Biddle followed him out of the village in the dark towards a big pink villa, standing in its own formal Italian garden, half a mile outside the precincts. With a hesitating hand, Luigi knocked hard at the door. After several attempts, a white-capped head protruded from an upper window. 'Who is there?' a servant asked. 'What do you want at this hour, drunken one?'

Luigi explained in a few short words that he was not drunken, and had not been keeping Sant'Ilario. It was a matter of life and death. A head was in danger. Could the English signorina come down to speak at the door with him?

In a few minutes more, Miss Beauchamp came down, lightly clad in a soft artistic dressing-gown. Luigi trembled to ask her. It was much to ask a lady to receive a Man into her house in the small hours of the night: but to save life, you know! Might he dare to ask it? He explained the whole circumstances. Miss Beauchamp, motioning them both inside into the hall, and closing the door behind them, listened, smiling.

But what strange creatures, these English! As soon as he had finished, the signorina, smiling still, made answer at once without the lightest hesitation. 'Take him in? Why, of course! He is welcome to a bed: and tomorrow I will drive him in my pony-carriage to Empoli, where he can catch the early train for Florence.'

Luigi was thunderstruck. A lady, in a house alone with her woman-servants, make no more bones than that about receiving a Man under her roof! These English are shameless—or else, they are irreproachable! He groped his way back by himself to his own house, and slept till morning, in spite of his bruises.

When morning came, Miss Beauchamp got ready the pony-trap. She had heard the whole story, and knew how Poggibonsi was thirsting for the blood of the man who had openly insulted and denounced Sant'Ilario. So she insisted that the evangelist must double his long legs under the seat of the pony-trap. Biddle protested in vain: Miss Beauchamp was imperative. He obeyed in the end and lay still in his place, while Miss Beauchamp and Sister Polly took their seats on the cushions and covered him with their dresses. Sister Polly had borrowed a hat with roses in it, and looked as worldly and as pretty as a Salvationist can look in her weaker moments.

A mile or two out of Poggibonsi, they allowed Biddle to emerge, much bent, and stretch his legs in the dickey. He rode on silently, ejaculating once or twice, in fervid asides, that he desired to save the soul of his present benefactress. Miss Beauchamp only smiled. The subject was one she declined to discuss before him and Sister Polly.

At Empoli station, who should meet them but Luigi, very hot and eager, still black and blue in the face with the beating of yesterday! He had spent a hard-earned *lira* in paying his passage by train, in order to make sure that his evangelist was safe from Sant'Ilario's vindicators.

Miss Beauchamp waited to see what greeting the preacher would give his preserver. Arthur Biddle took two tickets for Florence, and jumped into the train. He leaned out of the window as soon as he was seated, and took Luigi's hand in his. 'Good-bye,' he said, with the same eager, impulsive voice as ever. 'I will pray for your salvation. I will pray for your soul earnestly.'

Miss Beauchamp smiled again. 'I do not think it is Luigi's soul you need trouble about,' she answered in English. '*His* soul is right enough. There are others to see to. May not spiritual pride be worse, after all, than some things you think much of?'

The Salvationist stared. What could the woman be talking of?

'Remember,' she went on slowly: 'you know those words, "Other sheep have I which are not of this fold: them also will I bring in."[16] Do not mistake your own little wattled enclosure for the whole church catholic. Luigi is a hero in his way; he has deserved more than prayers from you. Does it not occur to you that you ought to thank him?'

Luigi understood the tone, though not the words. 'Oh, as for that,' he said modestly, casting down his eyes, 'it is nothing, nothing. I saw a man's life in danger, through a misunderstanding, and I tried to save it. If I did less than that, how could I call myself a Christian?'

The train began to move. The Salvationist thrust his head out of the window. 'I will pray for both your souls! he cried. 'For both of you, for both of you!'

Miss Beauchamp turned to the Italian peasant. 'I ask *your* prayers for mine, Luigi,' she answered humbly.

---

[1] **'Are you saved?'** According to William Booth, founder of the Salvation Army, the prime requirement was 'getting saved and keeping saved, and then getting somebody else saved.' A popular belief was that the 'S' on their collars stood for 'Saved'.

[2] **top-artichokes.** Probably so called to distinguish this thistle-like plant from the Jerusalem artichoke, which is the root of a species of sunflower.

[3] **the words 'Salvation Army,' in Italian.** The flag of the *Escercito della Salvezza* was first raised by three English people in Rome in 1887, though, as

its history says discreetly, 'subsequent difficulties necessitated withdrawal'. In its early days, in fact, the Army was subjected to continual and sometimes violent oppression. The first converts came from a northern Italian village.

[4] **the scarlet woman.** An alternative name for the 'Great whore of Babylon' mentioned in Revelations. She was identified as the Pope, or else the Roman Catholic Church generally, by Luther, Calvin, Knox and later sects like Jehovah's Witnesses.

[5] **'I have not where to lay my head.'** The words of Jesus in Matthew 8 and Luke 9: 'Foxes have holes, and birds of the air have nests; but the Son of man hath not where to lay his head.'

[6] **the Cardinal Camerlengo.** The *camerlengo* (chamberlain) is a senior post in the Church: he is acting head of the Vatican state in the period between Popes. That the family of a Cardinal should own a vineyard is neither unusual nor surprising.

[7] **Poggibonsi ... San Gimignano.** Small towns in Tuscany; the second is famous for its numerous medieval towers and popular with artists.

[8] **the *festa* of Sant'Ilario.** The festival of St Hilary was and is celebrated in Parma (not Poggibonsi) on 13 January and is now designated a 'folklore event'.

[9] **coloured-paper *confetti*.** Originally *confetti* were various objects thrown at carnivals, including chalk or mud balls, sugared seeds, *etc.*

[10] **'Ceri, Ceri, Ceri!'** 'Candles!' The decorated barrel is supposedly a stylised candle. A procession of enormous such structures occurs yearly in Gubbio, and is of pagan origin.

[11] **Juggernaut.** A huge richly decorated Hindu chariot used in processions, under which initiates supposedly threw themselves and were crushed.

[12] **Eyes it had, but it saw not ...** A phrase occurring several times in the Bible with variant wording, especially Mark 8.

[13] **Signor Mancini.** Probably Riccardo Mancini, an archaeologist who excavated Etruscan tombs in 1872.

[14] **library of the Folklore Society.** The Society was founded in 1878 to study traditional culture; among other things, it explored the pagan origins of many religious celebrations. Allen's friend Edward Clodd was a prominent member.

[15] **For choice, a Bacchanal.** An ancient Roman festival, originally for women only, dedicated to Bacchus, god of wine and ecstasy, and infamous for its orgiastic practices. According to Livy, it was eventually savagely suppressed as a danger to the State.

[16] **"Other sheep have I ..."** Jesus' prophecy, at John 10, that 'there shall be one fold, and one shepherd'.

# ABOUT THE EDITOR

Peter Morton, educated at London and Sussex universities, is an Adjunct Professor at Flinders University in Adelaide. He has written several books on Australian social and technological history. His biography of Grant Allen, *The* Busiest *Man in England*, was co-winner of the Robert Colby Scholarly Book Prize in New York in 2006. His latest book is *Lusting for London*, a historical and critical study of Australian literary emigrants to England before the Second World War.